KT-233-537

SCARLET WOMEN

Jessie Keane's story is one of idyllic early years, and struggles against the odds from her teen years onwards. Family tragedy, bankruptcy and mixing with a bad crowd all filled her life. Her first novel, *Dirty Game*, was published by HarperCollins in 2008, her second, *Black Widow*, followed soon after.

WITHDRAWN

B000 000 019 7578

ABERDEEN LIBRARIES

Also by Jessie Keane

Dirty Game
Black Widow

JESSIE KEANE

Scarlet Women

HARPER

This novel is entirely a work of fiction.
The names, characters and incidents portrayed in it are
the work of the author's imagination. Any resemblance to
actual persons, living or dead, events or localities is
entirely coincidental.

Harper
An imprint of HarperCollins*Publishers*
77–85 Fulham Palace Road,
Hammersmith, London W6 8JB

www.harpercollins.co.uk

A Paperback Original 2009
7

Copyright © Jessie Keane 2009

Jessie Keane asserts the moral right to
be identified as the author of this work

A catalogue record for this book
is available from the British Library

ISBN: 978-0-00-727400-0

Set in Sabon by Palimpsest Book Production Ltd,
Grangemouth, Stirlingshire

All rights reserved. No part of this publication may be
reproduced, stored in a retrieval system, or transmitted,
in any form or by any means, electronic, mechanical,
photocopying, recording or otherwise, without the prior
permission of the publishers.

This book is sold subject to the condition that it shall not,
by way of trade or otherwise, be lent, re-sold, hired out or
otherwise circulated without the publisher's prior consent
in any form of binding or cover other than that in which it
is published and without a similar condition including this
condition being imposed on the subsequent purchaser.

Mixed Sources
Product group from well-managed
forests and other controlled sources
www.fsc.org Cert no. SW-COC-1806
© 1996 Forest Stewardship Council

FSC is a non-profit international organisation established
to promote the responsible management of the world's forests.
Products carrying the FSC label are independently certified
to assure consumers that they come from forests that are managed
to meet the social, economic and ecological needs
of present and future generations.

Find out more about HarperCollins and the environment at
www.harpercollins.co.uk/green

Cliff my darling – this one's for you.

Acknowledgements

To Mandasue Heller, Trisha Ashley, Louise Marley, Judith Murdoch, Jane Harvey, Sue Kemish, Lynne next door . . . what would I do without you girls? All great women . . . and none of them scarlet!

Prologue

Annie Carter opened her eyes slowly. Her first thought was *what the fuck?* Her head hurt; there was a sore spot behind her right ear. She saw semi-darkness and a dim, familiar interior.

She was in the car. Shit, they'd hit her *hard*. Her brain was spinning.

Her car, yeah that was it. Had to get a grip, think straight.

The black Mark X Jaguar.

She was lying across the back seat, which smelled of leather and cologne; familiar smells, comforting smells, but alarm bells were ringing in her addled mind. Her guts were clenched with unfocused anxiety.

Tony?

Where the fuck was Tony?

He was usually up there behind the wheel, weaving easily through the London traffic and asking where she wanted to go next, saying okay Boss, sure thing. But he wasn't there now, so where the hell was he? She was the big car's only occupant.

And now it came back to her in a rush. Now she remembered what had happened to Tony. They'd coshed him too. Put him somewhere. But where? Was he all right? Was he dead?

How long have I been out of it? she wondered, sitting up, wincing as her head thumped sickeningly in protest at the movement.

Then she remembered Charlie Foster, and Redmond and Orla Delaney. She remembered it *all*. She'd been knocked out cold, Tony was fuck-knew-where, and now they were going to drive her off in her own damned car to some remote spot, where they would blow her brains out, what little brains she *had,* because who but a fool would push their luck as far as she had done?

She thought of Layla. Her little girl, her little star. Had to get out of here because she was all that Layla had; she couldn't afford to get herself wasted.

She was reaching for the door when the noise started – a high mechanical whine, deafening in its intensity. Her heart rate picked up to a gallop.

What the . . . ?

Suddenly the car lurched, knocking her back against the right-hand door. Then her horrified eyes watched as the left-hand door started to buckle inward. There was a ferocious shriek of tortured metal. With a noise like a gunshot, the glass in the door shattered, showering her with fragments. She ducked down, covering her head momentarily with an upraised arm, then staring with terror as the door just kept coming, buckling inward, metal tearing, screaming, ripping.

And now the door behind her was coming in too. The noise was beyond bearing, beyond anything she had ever known before. The window imploded, and again she was covered in pieces of glass, felt her cheeks sting with the impact of it, felt warm blood start to ooze from cuts on her face.

'*Jesus!*' she screamed in panic, knowing where she was now, knowing what was going to happen to her.

Then the roof crashed in upon her, folding inward like cardboard. She felt the floor lift and she fell sideways, ending up in the well behind the front seats, nearly gibbering with fear. She was going to die, she knew that now.

Just make it fast, she thought desperately. *Please make it fast.*

She lay there, powerless, and watched the roof coming down towards her.

Closed her eyes, and waited to die.

1

SUMMER 1970

Whack!

The whip cracked down across the nude buttocks of the man tied to the bed. He moaned but was careful not to scream. He'd had his orders.

'This is a *nice* place,' the woman told him, looming over him. She was dressed in a white topless PVC mini-dress and matching high-heeled boots. A white nurse's cap was perched jauntily on her coal-black hair. Her ample and naked coffee-coloured breasts bounced as she drew back the whip to strike again. 'Remember that. I don't want you kickin' off and yelling the sodding place down, now do I?'

The client strained to look back at her over his shoulder from his prone position. He said nothing.

Whack!

'Answer Nursy when she speaks to you,' trilled the woman.

'No! I won't scream,' he panted.

'Good, that's good. You'll take your punishment, yes?'

'Yes!' he groaned as she raised the whip again.

'Right answer.' The girl grinned and trailed the whip's leather lightly down between his quivering white buttocks. 'Now that's good, now we're starting to understand one another. Because you've been a *very* bad boy, ain't that right?'

'That's right,' he muttered into the pillow. He was sweating and his eyes were closed.

The woman watched him, judging her victim. Sure he was sweating, it was a hot night. Damp and clammy and airless – welcome to a summer's night in England, folks! The windows were closed though. She'd opened them earlier and shut them pretty damned quick; the constant roar of the traffic was an annoying distraction.

So he was hot. She was pretty fucking *hot* herself. Rubber might light the man's candle, but it was a bitch to wear on a humid night. Just for the hell of it, she gave him another swipe with the whip. He gave a faint cry, flinched and strained against his bonds. Hell, anyone would think he wasn't *enjoying* this. She sure hoped he was – it was costing him enough, after all.

Actually it was costing her too, in terms of

energy and stamina. After an evening of wining, dining and shagging, she now had to get down to the add-ons, the not-so-little extras that the man tied to the bed required.

Most men, you did an escort job for them, they expected a bit of straightforward hanky-panky too, and that was cool. This client had more specific needs and he was one of her regulars. Her reputation as a dominatrix was legendary. Her speciality was what this client wanted, and the price had been fair, she had to admit that, and the price was all that mattered.

Take the money and run, she thought.

But now she was tired. She wanted to crawl into bed with her man, get some kip if it was possible in this heat. When he closed his eyes again she glanced at her watch. The extra hour he'd paid for was nearly up. Soon she'd be out of here; soon she'd be home.

Whack!

Oh, how he writhed. She sort of enjoyed that, to tell the truth, when they writhed. Just a bit. But she'd been doing this S & M gig for so long that it was beginning to bore her. Once the thrill had been in doing it, socking it to the punters. But she was a married lady now, and maybe this was not the sort of thing that a married lady ought to do – not even with her loving husband's consent, which she'd always had . . .

The woman frowned. And maybe, just maybe, this was a thing that a loving husband ought to have a bit of a problem with: how was that for a thought?

This was something that kept popping into her brain more and more often. Did he love her so much, if he could be so fucking *cool* about his wife dancing the horizontal tango with strange men and then whipping them into a frenzy, and *then* coming home to him?

But the money was good, and money was always tight, and oh how she loved the money. Money to buy Biba dresses and Bill Gibb blouses, boots by the Chelsea Cobbler, waistcoats by Kaffe Fassett, and going to shows and dinners up West: she loved all that shit. So she did things sometimes that didn't make her proud. Like whipping this punter's snowy-white arse and wishing she was gone.

Time to draw their little sesh to a close now. Thank God.

Tenderly she leaned over and released the leather cords that bound his wrists to the headboard.

'There you go honey, that's all for tonight,' she cooed in his ear.

And the bastard turned and whacked her right across the jaw.

Agony exploded in her head.

The girl went flying off the bed and fell to the floor. She sat up on the expensive carpet amid a tangle of shoes, trousers and shirt. Her eyes were filled with tears of pain. She could feel her heart beating hard against her ribs with the shock of it.

Fuck, where had that come from?

She clutched her jaw and staggered back to her feet, staring down at him in disbelief. He'd collapsed back on to the bed, face down. As if what he'd just done was *nothing*. As if hitting her, hurting her, was *nothing*.

As if *she* was nothing.

She'd dropped the whip but now she snatched it up again with a grunt of rage. Bastard punters! They were like tigers in a circus act: you were the trainer and you never let your guard down, you never turned your back, you *always* had to keep control – or they'd maul you as soon as look at you.

She waded in with the whip again. This time she put a lot of force behind it. This time she was *angry*. She was the sadist here, wasn't she? Or that was the act, anyway. And he was supposed to be the masochist. He didn't do the beating up, *she* did.

'Better,' he moaned happily, rolling over to display an erection the size of a baby's arm. 'That's better, sweetheart, oh yes . . .'

And then he grabbed the hem of her rubber dress, nearly pulling her off balance, and held it over his nose and mouth. Twisted *bastard*. He always did that with her. Always.

She was *so* tired of all this.

It wasn't that big a thrill any more.

Seconds later, he came all over the thousand-thread-count Egyptian cotton sheets.

She watched him, her jaw hurting, her face carefully blank to hide her fear and disgust.

Boy, she was *sick* of all this.

Ten minutes later, she was out of there. She left the room with a big bundle of notes and a bad taste in her mouth – oh, and a jaw swollen to the size of a watermelon.

All in a day's work.

It was raining by the time she left the snazzy hotel in Park Lane. The smartly uniformed concierge gave her a knowing look and a nod as she emerged from the lift in reception and went towards the revolving door. She'd been there before, she was no trouble, he wasn't about to make a fuss.

Whatever the guest wanted, the guest got – that was his motto. A Roller to take them to the theatre? Certainly, sir. Champagne at a hundred quid a pop and a whole tin of Beluga caviar on the side? *Mais oui, bien sûr.* A nice tart to share it with? No problem at all.

And she was a nice tart. Tall, slim and with skin dark as cocoa. A shock of dreadlocks framing her gorgeous face. She gave him a grin. You couldn't get churlish looking at that grin, although it faded quickly and she seemed to wince.

Flamboyant dresser, too. Trailing a purple boa, toting a big carpetbag and wearing skin-tight denim hot pants. One of those cool-looking but very smelly Afghan coats flapping loose around her and big hoops of gold clattering at her ears. Could dress a bit smarter, but then it was late: few guests about, only him and the boy on reception, so all was well and why rock the boat?

Really, who gave a shit?

'Get you a cab?' he offered.

The grin returned. 'What, you think I made o' money, boy?'

'Bet you're making more than me.'

'Ha! Don't I just wish that was true. Nah, it's okay, honey. My man's pickin' me up.'

He nodded and smiled at her. Yeah, she was a nice girl. No harm in her at all. Stressed-out businessmen, tired travellers, they needed the release of a bit of female company now and then. It wasn't for him to judge. It was for him to say yes, sir, of *course*, sir, anything you want, we can get. Discretion was his watchword. Can-do was his attitude. It made him one of the best concierges in London.

He watched her swing through the revolving door and vanish into the rainy night. And then he thought of his own grown-up daughters, girls around the same age as this one, his precious girls tucked up safe at home where they ought to be at this hour of the night, and he thought: *Fuck it. What a sodding way to make a living.*

She walked quickly, head down against the rain, heading for the usual corner, around which her man would be parked up in his ancient Zodiac, waiting for her. Asleep, probably, stretched out across the single front sofa seat.

They loved that sofa seat; they'd made out on it a time or two, but really he enjoyed that more than her. She preferred their bed: good old-fashioned bread-and-butter lovemaking; no risks, no thrills, just deep warmth and contentment and waking up together in the morning, which they could do now that he no longer worked permanent nights, thank you God.

She was going to have a nice hot bath first. Wash the day away. Then crawl into bed, snuggle down. Forget the whole evening. She was good at doing that; she'd had plenty of practice. Keep her chin turned away and he wouldn't see the redness, the swelling. Maybe while she was in the bath she'd hold a cold flannel against it. That'd soothe it. She'd be careful to take the flannel away when he came in, brought her a glass of wine as was his usual practice. He was a good husband. Even if a little too forgiving of her profession.

It wasn't the first time a punter had walloped her, she wasn't about to get all girly and hysterical about it. She wasn't about to tell her loving husband that it had happened, either – he'd want to rip the bastard's arms off.

No, what she was going to do was *forget* it.

All in a day's work, and that was a fact.

You took a knock, so what?

There were footsteps behind her. High heels. Another working girl, heading home after a long day, poor bitch. She glanced back, saw who it was, and stopped walking with an exasperated sigh.

'Fuck it, I can't talk *now* . . .' she started to say, and then she was hit for the second time that night. It was beyond a bloody *joke,* that's what it was. But when she fell this time she wasn't falling on to Axminster. This time her head hit the pavement with a crack and suddenly the darkness came.

2

Annie Carter was standing at the top of the stairs in the Palermo Lounge, looking down at the shell of the place that had once been her late husband Max's favourite club. The builders were in – and running late. They were taking the curtains on the small stage area down. Huge red velvet drapes, a bit faded now, a bit tired-looking, like the rest of the club.

As she watched, a man up a ladder took out a hammer and chisel. He chipped loose the big gold letters 'MC' at the apex where the curtains joined together. He threw them down to his mate. The M hit the floor, and shattered.

And how's that for an omen? she thought with a pang of the old sadness.

There was so much to be done, so much to think about. The brewery had been in and agreed – after some hum-ing and ha-ing – that they would continue to supply liquor to the club. The drinks licence was, after all, already in place. The dance floor – which was a total fucking mess at the moment, broken up and knocked all to hell – was going to be relaid, and there were going to be strobe lights, the works.

But first the red velvet curtains, the plaster cherubs, the flock wallpaper, all that old dated tat, had to go.

Sorry Max.

She'd hired a good accountant, set out her aims. She planned that this club – and eventually the two others, the Blue Parrot and the Shalimar, which were currently standing empty – were going to earn her a good living, support her and her small daughter in some style. That was the plan, anyway.

Of course, the first thing the accountant had done when he'd seen last year's books, peering at her over his pince-nez spectacles, was to suck in his breath.

She got this all the time. From the brewery bosses. From the builders. Now from her accountant. She was a woman in a man's world, and all the men in it thought she couldn't cope.

'It would appear the business has been running at quite a loss,' he said, giving her a pitying glance.

'Or could it just be that the profits haven't

been finding their way into the accounts?' she suggested.

He'd shrugged, nodded. 'Certainly, that could be the case.'

Ha! Certainly, that *was* the case. He'd departed, leaving her sunk in gloom. But then she had a stern word with herself. Okay, she'd been shafted – royally worked over. But now she had to pull it all back together, even if the going was tough. Hell, she was *used* to tough.

She had lost her husband. She had loved gang lord Max Carter almost beyond life itself, and losing him had cut her to the heart. But she still had her daughter. She still had Layla. And that was in no small part due to American mob boss Constantine Barolli.

Annie frowned.

When they'd last spoken, Constantine had said he'd be back from his home in New York soon to see her. But three whole months had passed. Three *months* without a word, without a telephone call, with *nothing*. She felt furious, rejected, and she knew she'd made a bloody fool of herself into the bargain by asking him to call her. Because, guess what? He *hadn't*.

'Fuck it,' she muttered, her hands clenching around the wrought-iron banister. She closed her eyes for a second and instantly she could picture him – a smooth, slickly suited Mafia don, with armour-piercing blue eyes and a commanding aura, a tan and startling silver hair.

The silver fox.

The rumour was that his hair had turned from black to silver overnight when he was in his twenties and had been told that his mother and brother were dead, victims of a deliberate hit by another Cosa Nostra family in his native Sicily. That's what they called him on the streets of New York, the silver fox. And like a fox he'd slipped away.

Hell, she'd probably panicked the bastard, been too keen too soon. And, of course, he'd run straight for the hills. She'd blown it. *Fuck* it.

She went up the second flight of stairs to her office and slammed the door closed behind her. She slumped into her chair behind the desk. Once it had been her late husband's chair; now it was hers. Now *she* was in charge of the East End manor that he had once ruled.

It was a very different manor now. A very different firm. Times had changed. Gone was the old respectful Kray and Carter style no-drugs-but-plenty-of-the-hard-game rule of the Sixties. Now there was an active – and often violent – drugs scene in London.

Annie had made it clear from the start that she wanted no part of that sort of trade – but she had been quick to see how the firm could profit from its impact. The Carter firm was all about legitimate security now; the firm controlled an army of enforcers working all over London and Essex, keeping order at venues.

And shit, how it paid. The money was *rolling* in.

Even better, it was all above board. She'd come close once to going down, and she was never going to risk it again, not with Layla to consider.

So now it was *her* who took payment from the halls and arcades and shops, *her* boys who gathered at Queenie's – Max's late mother's – house, to meet with her and receive their orders.

As it turned out, everything had worked out pretty much okay. The boys had accepted her, and they had also accepted that Jimmy Bond – who had been Max's number one back in the day – was history.

She thought about that.

Yeah, they had accepted her, but she was concerned that it wasn't a full acceptance. It was an acceptance of her role as Max's widow, that was all. She knew her position was tenuous. These were hard men, men who'd grown up on the wild side – out on the rob, out on the piss; they took no shit from anyone. *Legitimate* business had been a shock for them, but – so far – they'd swallowed it. Or had they? She was never sure.

She looked down at her thumb, where Max's ring glinted. A square slab of royal blue lapis lazuli set upon a solid band of gold embellished with

Egyptian cartouches. Yes, he was long gone, but it calmed her to look at the ring, the symbol of his power and authority.

Only now, more and more, it was reminding her of another ring, the diamond-studded one that Constantine Barolli always wore.

Ah, what's the use?, she thought. *It's done.*

He'd gone, and he wasn't coming back.

Now she had a job to do, and that was good. She had to lose herself in getting the clubs up and running again. She was lucky to have an interest, a business that demanded so much of her time, because, if you were busy, you couldn't think too much of how you had fucked up your chance of a great love affair by playing it all so disastrously wrong.

There was a tap at the door and Tony, her driver and her minder, poked his bald head around it. The crucifixes in his cauliflower ears glistened bright gold in the summer sunlight streaming in through the office window.

'First of the girls is here, Boss,' he said.

She was interviewing staff now. Bar staff, kitchen staff, cleaners, dancers. Not the dancers that had been here before, swinging their enormous naked tits about for all to see. No, these would be discreet go-go dancers, twirling and whirling in fringed white bikinis on tiny strobe-lit podiums around the new dance floor.

She didn't want the dirty-mac brigade coming back in here. She wanted a better class of clientele, and she was going to make sure she got it.

Annie sighed. Tucked all thoughts of Constantine away.

He's gone for good, she told herself. *So forget it, okay? Move on.*

She got her mirrored compact out of her handbag and dabbed away the shine from her nose. Then she applied a slick of scarlet lipstick and paused, staring at the image reflected in the mirror; the steady dark green eyes, the arched black brows and thick black lashes, the good olive-toned skin, the straight fall of thick, cocoa-brown hair, the wide, sensuous, painted mouth. It was a face that could, in fact, be called beautiful.

Then why didn't he call?

She let out an exasperated sigh and closed the compact with a snap. Dumped it back in the bag, gave Tony a brisk smile.

'Right. Send her up, Tone.' She had fifteen girls to see this afternoon and opening night was just three weeks away. Best to crack on. Distract herself. Get *on* with it.

Annie sat at the kitchen table at the Limehouse brothel later in the day, sipping hot strong tea and looking at her friend Dolly, who was madam there – Dolly with her blonde bubble perm, her immaculate make-up and nails, wearing a neat lightweight powder-blue suit. Incredible to think that Dolly had once been the roughest brass in the place; now she was in charge and she looked the part.

'Good trade today?' asked Annie.

It was Friday – party day at the Limehouse knocking-shop. Drinks, nibbles, and floor shows on offer – everyone was happy. Young Ross was on the door to keep order, but mostly he didn't need to – his sheer size and presence was all the deterrent to bad behaviour that was needed. There was music coming from the front parlour, and laughter coming from upstairs. The place was packed with eager punters getting massages, blow-jobs and other personal services. Annie thought this would be enough for anybody to contend with, but Dolly had started up an escort business too. It ran alongside her well-run brothel like a Swiss clock. Slotted in just nice.

'Yeah, really good. Takings are holding steady.'

'And the new girls?'

Dolly pulled a face. 'Dunno yet. Rosie's a good worker, when she can be arsed to bother. But Sharlene's a bit of a bloody nightmare, the attitude on her. And Aretha didn't show up.'

Annie looked at her. 'Hasn't she phoned?'

Dolly shook her head.

'Well she will,' said Annie.

Aretha was Dolly's S & M specialist, their resident dominatrix. Her room was kitted out with punishment chairs, whips, chains, any quirk or fetish the punter desired; she could cater to any individual's particular perversion. She was tall, black and beautiful, strong as an ox and the best friend Dolly and Annie had ever had.

'Probably got pissed last night,' sighed Dolly. 'She was working. Probably overdid it on the bubbly. Bet she's sleeping it off. If she hasn't called by eight, I'll call her. Punters have been asking for her, it aint good.'

Annie stood up. 'Well, I'm off to pick up Layla from Kath's.'

'And how *is* Kath?'

Annie couldn't stifle a smile. Dolly had already passed judgement on Kath – declaring that she was a dirty mare, and beyond hope. But Annie didn't think so. Kath was her cousin; they were *family*. She was prepared to give the poor cow a chance.

'Kath's fine. Starting to shape up,' she lied. 'Hasn't Ellie kept you up to speed?'

Ellie had once been one of Dolly's little band of sex workers. Now she was working as a cleaner here, and helping Kath out too. Kath had suffered depression after her mother's death, and her husband had knocked her black and blue; she'd needed help. Ellie was busy providing it.

Whether Kath liked it or not – which mostly she didn't.

'Ellie tells me Kath's place is getting tidy, but I think you'd have to explode a fucking bomb in there first to get anywhere near it,' sniffed Dolly. 'Hey – you heard from that hunky American yet?'

Annie stiffened. 'No. And I'm not likely to.'

'That's a damned shame,' said Dolly. 'What happened?'

I killed it, that's what happened, thought Annie.

She was mad at herself, mad as hell. Because hadn't she done something very similar with Max? She'd gone after him with no holds barred, full throttle, even though he belonged to someone else, even though the consequences had proved to be dire.

She had no subtlety, not an ounce in her entire body. Damn, why couldn't she just hold back a bit? *Why* couldn't she play those delicious, teasing cat-and-mouse games that other women played? No kissing on the first date. No groping above the waist until the third. No touching anywhere else until there was an engagement ring on her finger. No fucking under any circumstances until there was a wedding band right beside it. Was that so difficult?

But no. Not her.

She went at the damned thing like a bull at

a gate. She was either on or off. No half measures, no holding back. She was either totally committed, or utterly detached. There were no in-betweens – and she guessed that she scared men shitless.

'Nothing happened,' she told Dolly briskly. 'Nothing at all. And it don't matter. I've got the flat straight, the club's being refurbed, I've got enough to think about.'

The flat was the one above the Palermo where she had first slept with Max. It seemed sort of fitting that she should be living there with Layla now.

'You could have stayed here while the work's going on,' said Dolly. 'You know it's no trouble.'

'Doll, ain't we had this conversation? I can't keep a child in a knocking-shop, it just ain't right.'

'Well,' pouted Dolly.

'It's kind of you,' said Annie firmly. 'But no. And besides Layla, I've got to consider my position. This is Delaney turf, Doll. I can't stay here.'

The Irish Delaney mob, who ran the streets of Limehouse and Battersea, were the Carter gang's bitter enemies. And although Annie had once associated with them, and even formed a business relationship with the chilly and devious Delaney twins, Orla and Redmond, the things they had done had turned her against them.

However, Redmond still allowed her to visit Dolly here, turning a blind eye to the head of the Carter firm walking his streets, and that was good of him. But she knew that what Max had always told her about them was the truth. They were vipers, he'd said, and not to be trusted. She knew now that he was right.

'Well, whatever you think best,' said Dolly.

Annie stood up. 'I'll catch you later,' she said, and went off down the hall, nodding to Ross. As a Delaney boy, it pissed him off to see a Carter here; but he'd had his orders from the top. Her presence was to be tolerated.

For now, anyway, she thought.

Through the open front parlour door, she glimpsed half-naked tarts bouncing up and down on happy punters, and the sounds of sex drifted down the stairs.

Ross sat there, impassive.

She opened the front door and to her shock found Tony standing there. He pushed inside, closing the door behind him. She glimpsed two policemen coming up the path. There was a cop car parked just in front of the black Jag.

'Shit,' said Annie.

'Don't think it's a raid, they're not mob-handed,' said Tony. 'Still, better keep it down in here.'

Ross was already on it. He'd shot out of his

chair at the word 'raid' and was already in the front room passing the word. The music was turned off. The laughter died. As the front door-bell rang he grabbed the visitors' book from the hall table and ran off up the stairs to spread the word. Silence fell up there. Then he came back down and went into the kitchen, told Dolly. White-faced, she came out along the hall and looked at Annie and Tony standing there. She straightened her suit jacket, patted her hair and opened the front door.

'Miss Farrell?' asked one of the young coppers, politely removing his helmet.

Dolly nodded: yes.

'Sorry to disturb you, miss. Can we come in?'

Oh hell, thought Annie.

They went on into the kitchen. Ross was gone, out the back way. Dolly gave Annie a quick 'don't you dare fuck off' glance, so Annie followed her and the coppers into the kitchen and they all sat down. Tony went off into the front room, out of the way.

'What's this about?' asked Dolly.

The coppers exchanged a look, then the older one spoke.

'Miss Farrell, a body has been found. There was a card on the body that led us to believe that the person in question was working out of an escort agency run by you from this address.'

'A body?' Dolly looked whiter than ever.

'A young black female.'

Annie felt as sick as Dolly looked. She thought of Aretha, not calling in this morning. Aretha had been out on an escort job last night.

'*Jesus*,' Dolly whispered. 'Not Aretha?'

'We'd like you to accompany us to the station,' said the copper. 'If you're willing to identify the body?'

Ain't that Chris's job? thought Annie. She looked at Dolly.

'It's okay, Doll,' she said, standing up, 'I'll come with you. Wait up while I phone Kath and let her know I'll be delayed.'

Five minutes later they were in the back of the cop car being driven to the police station, both sitting silent and shocked, wondering what the hell was kicking off here, hoping against hope that the young black female was anyone, anyone at all, but not – please God – Aretha Brown.

When they reached the station they were led into the bowels of the place, into an antiseptic-scented room.

'Oh fuck,' said Dolly.

There was a body laid out under a sheet.

Annie grabbed Dolly's hand and held it tight.

An attendant pulled the sheet back while the same two coppers hovered in the background.

Annie stepped forward, but Dolly seemed rooted to the ground. But she was close enough to see who was there. Together they looked down on the dead face of their good friend Aretha.

'Oh no. Oh shit,' whimpered Dolly, putting a hand to her mouth.

Annie was silent, staring, her guts churning with shock and grief.

Aretha's face was not her own any more: it was a mask of death, wet and greyish, all the life gone. The eyes were closed, the mouth half open. There was redness along the jaw and around the neck there was a thin, bloody line.

'Do you positively identify this woman as Aretha Brown?' asked the older PC.

Dolly nodded, unable to speak, tears starting in her eyes.

'Yeah,' said Annie shakily. 'That's her. That's Aretha.'

When they were being led back through the station to the front desk they came across Chris – huge, bald, heavily muscled Chris: Aretha's husband. Two more cops were taking him into a room. Annie saw to her shock that he was handcuffed. And his hands were bloody.

'Hey!' she said, quickening her pace. 'Hey, Chris!'

All three men stopped and looked at her. One

of the cops was tall and dark haired, the other one was dumpy and balding. Chris towered over them both.

'I didn't do nothing!' Chris yelled out, tears streaming down his face.

Annie hurried over. The tall, dark-haired one had the air of being in charge, so she addressed her remarks to him. 'What's going on here? Wait up! You don't think Chris had anything to do with Aretha . . . ?'

The two plain-clothes cops exchanged a glance, then looked at her as if they'd stepped in something nasty.

'And who are you?' asked the tall one.

'Annie Carter. This is Dolly Farrell.'

'We're interviewing Mr Brown. The officers will show you out.' He turned away.

'I'm going nowhere until I've talked to Chris,' said Annie.

He turned back and stared at her with dark, unfriendly eyes. 'What?'

'You heard. Chris used to work for me. He's a close friend of mine, I want to talk to him.'

He looked at her. Assessing her. He was going to tell her to bugger off, she just knew it. But then he surprised her.

'All right. You can sit in on the interview for ten minutes, then you're out.'

Annie nodded and moved forward. Dolly started

to follow. The tall one blocked her way. 'These officers will show you out,' he said.

Dolly gave him a glare and turned to Annie. 'I'll wait,' she said.

Annie followed Chris and his captors into the interview room.

3

The room was small, bare and windowless. On the near side of an oblong table were two chairs, one of which was quickly occupied by the portly, bald and sweaty-looking cop. They seated Chris on the other side of the table. He slumped there, his slab-like forearms spread out on the table, his big ugly ex-boxer's head resting upon them. He looked fucked.

Annie watched him worriedly. She'd known Chris for years. He was a big, hard man who had once been the bouncer on the door at the Limehouse brothel. He was a Delaney man, but he was rock solid. Tough as nails. Took no crap from anybody. Now when he looked up at her his eyes were full of desperation; his face was wet with tears.

'Oh Christ,' he said, and put his head back down again, and sobbed like his heart was breaking.

*   *   *

'All right, what the fuck you been doing to him?' Annie demanded.

The tall dark-haired one gave her that 'stepped in something nasty' look again. She was already getting a bit tired of it. He moved a chair to the other side of the desk, beside Chris.

'Take a seat,' he said.

'I'll take a seat when you start telling me what's going on here,' said Annie.

He looked at her. His dark eyes were unfriendly. 'Take a seat. *Then* I'll tell you what's going on here.'

Annie sat down. She looked at Chris, hulking great Chris, sitting there crying like a baby. She had a very bad feeling about all this. She patted his arm. She noticed his hands were cut. She dug in her bag and pulled out a wad of tissues and handed them to him. He took them, nodded, wiped his face.

'What's going on, Chris?' Annie demanded. 'They been knocking you about?'

The fat bald cop let out a laugh. 'You kidding? Look at the fucking size of him.'

Which was a point. Chris looked as if he could *eat* both these cops; put them between two slices of bread – even the tall dark-haired one, who had the look of a man who could handle himself in a tight corner. But she had never seen him upset like this. Never seen him shed a single tear.

'I want to know what's going on here,' she said, looking directly at the one in charge, the dark-haired, sour-faced one, who was now standing there leaning against the wall. He loosened his tie and stared at her *again* like she was shit on his shoe. He said nothing.

She turned her attention back to Chris. 'How long you been in here?'

'Jesus, I dunno,' he groaned, running a huge, shovel-like hand over his face. He looked at her wearily. 'Hours. Fucking hours.'

'Shouldn't he have a brief here?' Annie asked the cops.

'Probably he should,' said Prune Face. 'I'm Detective Inspector Hunter, this is Detective Sergeant Lane.'

'Oh. Right. I'll get a brief organised.' She looked a question at Chris. Wondered why Redmond Delaney hadn't done this already.

'Good. The sooner the better.'

'What happened?' Annie looked at Chris, who shook his head. Tears were still seeping out of his eyes, running unchecked down his face. 'Chris, come on. What happened?'

He gulped.

'It's Aretha,' he mumbled. He closed his eyes. His face was a mask of anguish. 'She's *dead,* Annie,' he said, and buried his head in his arms again, and cried hard.

'I know.' She thought of her friend with the huge grin, the shock of dreadlocks, the wildly colourful clothes, wafting in to Dolly's parlour just a few days ago shouting, 'Hey girlfriend!' and giving her a high-five and a warm hug.

'She's dead,' sobbed Chris. He lifted his head and looked at her. Desperation and despair and deep, heart-wrenching grief were all written large across his face. 'She's fucking *dead*, and they think I killed her!'

'No,' said Annie. She looked at Chris, then at DI Hunter and DS Lane. She shook her head.

'I'm afraid it's true,' said Hunter.

'There has to be some mistake.'

'There's no mistake,' said Hunter.

He nodded to Lane. The fat one stood up, went to the closed door, opened it, snagged a passing uniform and told him to fetch in some water. He closed the door, sat down again. DI Hunter was leaning on the desk and looking at Annie and at Chris as if they were *both* guilty as hell.

Annie looked up at him, trying to take all this in. 'Does her family know yet?' she asked him.

'Not yet,' he said.

A PC came in with a tray, plastic cups and a jug of water. He placed it on the desk, then left the room.

Annie cleared her throat. 'Look – Chris wouldn't

harm a hair on Aretha's head. You've got it wrong. Whoever did this, it wasn't Chris.'

But what about the blood on his hands? she thought, unable to help herself. *What the fuck was that all about?*

Hunter's fixed expression of disapproval deepened. He raised his eyes to the ceiling, as if she had cracked a really good joke.

'The evidence indicates otherwise,' he said.

'What evidence?' demanded Annie.

'Look, luv,' chipped in DS Lane. 'Fact is, this tart had a bag-load of S & M gear with her. Whips and rubber coshes and nursy outfits and peephole bras, stuff like that. She wasn't exactly a *nun*. If you know her then you must know that's true.'

What, and you think that means she deserved this? thought Annie in fury.

She said nothing, just glared at the fat, repulsive Lane.

'We know she worked as an escort,' said DI Hunter.

'So where's your evidence against Chris?' asked Annie.

'Mr Brown was waiting for his wife in his car, according to him,' said Hunter. 'Perhaps I'd better let Mr Brown himself fill in the details.'

Annie looked at Chris. He gulped, gave a shuddering sigh and wiped at his eyes. He looked at her.

'Chris?' she prompted.

'I was waiting for her. Around the corner from the hotel. In the car. It was raining, raining hard. She'd told me she'd be finished by one o'clock in the morning, but by one thirty she still hadn't shown and I started to get worried.'

He took a shuddering breath.

'But I didn't want to make a fuss. Aretha hates . . . *hated* it when I made a fuss. She was a free spirit. A real free spirit.' He paused, gulped, gathered himself again. 'At a quarter to two, though, I was getting really steamed up. Really worried. I got out of the car. It was pissing down, hard to see two feet in front of your own face, real hard torrential rain, a pig of a night.'

They sat there listening to him and suddenly they were there, right there; Chris getting out of his Zodiac, shrugging his collar up against the rain, cursing the weather, angry and worried, where the *fuck* had she got to this time? The rain beating down, cold as Christmas on his bare, bald head as he hurried around the corner towards the hotel; not a soul about, this fucking weather. Pissing down. Summer in England, what else would it be doing?

His shoes were getting wet, water seeping into his socks, bouncing off the pavements, and now his bastard *trousers* were wet too, right up to the knee, he was going to catch his fucking *death* out here, rain coming down like knives, deafening, blinding, and thunder rolling now, oh-ho, a summer storm to add to the fun, lightning flashing and crackling in the distance; oh, he was having a *whale* of a time out here, getting wet right through to his skin.

Bloody Aretha! Couldn't she ever be on time, just once?

As they listened they could picture him shuffling along the rain-slicked pavements, traffic still on the roads, wheels hissing through the rain, wipers going full speed; poor bastards, didn't they have homes to go to? But no one walking the pavements, no one about in the dark and the rain except working girls, and the guys who were unfortunate enough to be their pimps or their boyfriends or – more rarely, like Chris – their husbands.

'Go on,' said DI Hunter when Chris paused.

Annie poured out water, tried to force it down: couldn't.

'That's when I found her,' said Chris, his voice breaking. 'I . . . I tripped over her. I thought . . . I thought some fucker had left a bag of rubbish on the pavement, I tripped, fell over her, I didn't know it was her . . .'

Annie reached out, squeezed his arm.

'Then I realized. Saw it was her. I thought . . .' He looked up wildly at the two men seated opposite. 'I thought she was just unconscious, you know?

Thought she'd drunk too much in the hotel. I just thought, silly bint, you could catch pneumonia like that, laid out pissed on a sopping wet pavement in the middle of the night; you could catch any damned thing, ain't that right?'

He was looking at Annie. She nodded.

'Then I saw that she had this . . . this *thing* around her neck.' His voice cracked again.

He stopped talking, shook his head.

Annie looked at Hunter. 'What thing?'

'A cheese wire,' said Hunter. 'Length of wire with a toggle at each end. What the French call a *garrotte*. They used them during the war, to knock out sentries without a sound. Swift and very effective. Five seconds at the outside and you're unconscious, five seconds more and you're dead. Mr Brown's prints are on the toggles. And his blood is on the wire.'

Blank-faced with horror, Annie looked at Chris.

'I saw it around her neck and I tried to get it off her,' said Chris in a rush. 'I thought – I thought, oh Christ, it's choking her, cutting off the air, I had to get it *off*.'

But she was already dead, thought Annie, feeling truly sick now. She looked down at Chris's huge, ham-like hands, looked again at the deep cuts there. Looked back at his face.

'But it was sort of . . . it was *stuck* into her throat, embedded there. I pulled, yanked at it, I had to get it off her. I was . . . Jesus, I don't know what I was doing, I was talking to her, telling her it was going to be all right, that I'd get it off, that everything was going to be fine . . .' His voice tailed away to a whisper . . . 'But it wasn't, was it? I tried to wake her, I talked to her, I tried . . . but she was dead. She was *dead*.'

4

When they got back to Limehouse they sat at the kitchen table in a state of shock. Dolly had gone for the medicinal brandy, thrown it back, grimaced. Annie didn't drink. Her mother Connie had been an alcoholic, the booze had killed her, so she had never developed a taste for it. She sipped her tea, and thought of Aretha with the big beaming grin, Aretha telling her funny stories about clients, Aretha breezing into this very kitchen and lighting the place up with her exuberance.

She'd never come here again.

'They said two others had been killed the same way,' said Annie numbly as they sat there listening to the ticking of the clock and wondering what the fuck had happened to their world.

Dolly shook her head. 'I never heard about that.'

Annie had. Newspapers had mentioned it, but it hadn't been on the front pages. Because these were

40

whores. Who really gave a stuff if whores were killed? Many people would think they'd got their just deserts. Few would care. Few would want to know who did it. All they would say now was, well, they've got the bloke anyway, case solved.

Only it wasn't. Not in Annie's eyes.

Because she *knew* that Chris could never be a killer. She knew his opinion of men who beat up on women. To physically harm a woman would be beyond him. Like most of the real hard men around the East End, Chris had been raised to respect women, not batter them. He would look down on any man who did that. And to do it himself? No. It was impossible.

'He *did* hate her going back on the game,' said Dolly, looking awkward.

Annie looked across at her friend. She nodded. This was true.

Chris's job as a security guard at Heathrow never paid much. They both knew that this had been a source of embarrassment for him. He wanted to keep his gorgeous wife in luxury, give her everything she wanted – and Aretha wanted plenty – but he couldn't. He made a decent, solid living, but it wasn't enough for Aretha, who loved the latest clothes, who loved to earn her own money, and the way she'd always done that and earned plenty was through tarting at Dolly's. When Dolly had extended her business to include a small escort agency, Aretha had been right up the front of the queue for more work.

Oh, Aretha had *loved* money.

Through all this, despite his own unhappiness with the situation, Chris had supported Aretha's choices. He'd known his woman since way before he'd ever married her. To him, Aretha had been exotic, exciting, beloved. Annie guessed he'd closed his mind to the rest of it. Made sure as far as he could that she kept herself safe. Waited for her in a parked car on rainy London nights. Didn't want her on the bus or the Tube that late. Waited for her. Supported her. *Loved* her in the best way he knew how.

And now they were supposed to believe that he'd *killed* her?

'They've got it wrong,' said Annie, laying a hand flat on the table in absolute denial of this shit they were trying to stick on to Chris. 'Chris did *not* kill Aretha.'

Dolly was silent.

'Doll?' asked Annie after a beat or two.

Dolly shrugged. 'Yeah, but from what you told me they've got real evidence. *Real* evidence. That thing, that . . .'

'The cheese wire,' said Annie with a shudder. The garrotte.

'Yeah, that. But . . . well, you said it had Chris's blood on it. And his hands were cut.'

'From where he tried to get it off her,' said Annie.

'Yeah, but is that how it really happened?' Dolly frowned at her. She looked awkward. 'Is that really it? Or . . .'

'Or what, Doll?' Annie looked at her.

'Or – God, I hate to say this – did he get the cuts when he did the deed, you know? Did he get those cuts on his hands, cut himself, when he . . . when he strangled her with that thing?'

Annie was silent for long moments. Then she said: 'You don't believe that.'

Dolly swigged back the last of her brandy, slapped the glass back on to the table between them as if laying down a challenge.

'Fact is, I don't know *what* to believe,' she said, shaking her head wearily. 'But if the evidence is there . . .'

'Well I do,' said Annie firmly. 'I *believe* that Chris loved Aretha. I *believe* that he injured himself trying to get the garrotte off her neck. And I *believe* that unless we help him out here, the plod are going to fit him up with this and with the murders of those other two poor bitches that were topped. He'll be sent down for Christ knows how long, Doll, and I can't let that happen.'

'Yeah, fine words,' sniffed Dolly. She poured herself another stiffener, held the bottle aloft to Annie. Annie shook her head. 'But what can you actually *do*? Supposing he didn't do it, and you know what? I think he probably *did*. Once the Bill think they've got the right man, do you really think you're going to change their minds?'

Annie stared at the table, thinking hard with shock and disgust. How could Dolly believe Chris had done the deed? But she was right, up to a point. Convincing the police – particularly that cynical bastard Hunter – of Chris's innocence would be an impossible task. She knew it. But didn't they at least have to *try*?

'The Bill must have informed Aretha's Aunt Louella by now,' said Annie.

Dolly nodded grimly. She'd given them Louella's full name and address, the poor cow. Louella was Aretha's only relative in England so far as they knew. Aretha had been sent to her Aunt's to stay, by her parents in Rhodesia. Louella was childless herself and poor – she was a cleaner at the local hospital – but Aretha's parents, who scratched a meagre living in a squalid township, were destitute. They had no doubt sent their precious daughter to foreign shores with a heavy heart, but with the sincere hope that she could make a better life than the one they had.

And now look.

Annie remembered sitting right here with Aretha, and Aretha telling her the tale of how she became a brass. The London of the Swinging Sixties had seemed like paradise to the teenage Aretha, and she had joined in a life where everything seemed possible: a golden future, no more hunger, plenty of money, free love – the Pill was a miracle! – and *fun*.

Her happy pursuit of *fun* had soon convinced her that all the fun she was having with boyfriends could be turned into a good living. So she started to charge for *fun*. She had no qualms about that. Her impoverished background had taught her that you got money wherever you could, by whatever *means* you could – who gave a damn how?

Soon Aretha was coining it. Aunt Louella, who was a fierce Christian, found out about it and was furious. They argued, Aretha left and moved in with Annie's aunt Celia, who ran a quiet and orderly establishment in Limehouse before Annie and then Dolly took over the reins. And the rest was history. Aretha had settled right in as the house's resident dominatrix, its biggest earner.

But now look, just *look*.

Aretha lay in the morgue. Her husband was being held and probably being charged right now for her murder. It was an unholy mess.

Dolly looked sick about all this. 'That poor woman's got a world of grief to get through. They were still quite close, you know. Even though she disapproved of what Aretha did, she made a point of never losing touch with her. Maybe thought one day she'd bring her back into the fold. Very religious lady, Louella.'

Annie nodded. She knew that Louella lived on the Carter patch, *her* patch. Max would have paid a call, sent flowers, helped out the bereaved in any way he could. When you ran an area, when you *owned* an area, there was a certain etiquette to be observed, certain dues that always had to be paid. Even Redmond Delaney, who owned these Limehouse streets and the streets of Battersea, even *he* would understand that. And now that Annie was in charge of the Carter manor in Bow, she was determined to fulfil her obligations too.

'Give me her address, Doll. I'll go and see her.'

'Yeah, okay,' said Dolly, and stood up and went to the drawer where she kept her books.

'And I want to know who Aretha was with last night. And where.'

Dolly's expression was irritable.

'You're like a dog with a fucking bone, Annie Carter,' she grumbled, coming back to the table with books, paper and pen. 'I wish you'd drop it. I don't like this. I don't like it at all. You ought to leave it to the brief. That's my advice.'

Ross, the young heavy on front of house, knocked at the kitchen door. He poked his head around it and looked disapprovingly at Annie.

'Tony says a guy just handed him this,' he said, holding out a scrap of paper.

Annie looked surprised and then suspicious. It was late. Who would want to contact her here, tonight? Who would even *know* she'd be here?

She stood up and took it. 'Thanks, Ross.'

She sat back down at the table and spread out the piece of paper. Looked at it. *Numbers*.

'Jesus H. Christ in a sidecar,' she murmured.

'What is it?' asked Dolly, craning forward.

Annie sat back, shaking her head, her mouth twisted in a bitter smile.

Dolly looked at her. 'Come on! What is it?' She peered interestedly at the note. 'Numbers? Haven't you had some of these before? There was a name for them, I remember. Pizza somethings.'

'*Pizzino*,' said Annie.

'*That's* the feller. Oh!' Dolly's eyes widened. 'It's from that Mafia bloke. Barolli. Well, come the fuck on, what's it say?'

'What's it *say*?' Annie stared back at her in outrage. 'Look, Doll, mind your bloody own will you? I can't think about him now, how the fuck could I? Poor Aretha's dead because of some psycho, and he thinks he can just waltz back into my life, after three months of *nothing,* with a *note*?'

'Well, when you put it like *that* . . .'

'There's no other way to put it, Doll.' Annie screwed up the note and lobbed it angrily into the sink. She took a calming breath and nodded to Dolly's notebooks. 'Right, Doll, let's get back to business.'

She stood up. 'I'm going to phone Jerry, get him down the station to speak to Chris.'

Jerry Peters was Annie's brief from way back: a tall, overweight man with a shock of fluffy ginger hair, a florid complexion and a brilliance in legal matters that belied his shambolic looks. 'While I do that, dig out Aunt Louella's address. And – yeah – everything you've got about Aretha's last client, and where she met him.'

'Ah,' said Dolly awkwardly.

'What do you mean, "ah"?'

'Fact is,' said Dolly, her eyes downcast, 'I don't actually *know* who her last client was. A woman phoned in the booking, said room two-oh-six at the Vista in Park Lane and the time, asked for Aretha, and the client *paid* Aretha, so . . .' Her voice tailed off.

'You didn't know this woman? You didn't even take a *name*?'

Dolly looked up, her expression unhappy. 'Sorry,' she said, 'no.'

'Shit,' said Annie.

5

Mira Cooper would forever remember the first time she set eyes on Redmond Delaney. She'd been sitting in the luxuriously ornate dining room at Cliveden with Sir William Farquharson, married ex-member of the House, when they'd shown Redmond and his party to a nearby table.

He was just the most exquisite man she'd ever seen: tall and lithe, with red hair, lime-green eyes, smooth skin and an air of command about him. He was with a group of five others, and a dark-haired stunner was paying him a lot of attention. Redmond's attention, much to the brunette's visible annoyance, was fixed upon Mira, whose beautiful blonde looks had always been her fortune.

Chatting to William as they ate, her eyes were constantly drawn back to Redmond – and she couldn't help but compare the two. William was

*short, pot-bellied, balding and plain. Redmond
Delaney, however, was a god.*

*Oh yes, she remembered it all: being in the pool
the following afternoon, wearing her best silver
bikini, hoping he'd be there. And he was. Sir William
was lounging on one of the chairs at the side of the
pool, talking to another old man and smoking a
Havana cigar. Mira's heart almost stopped when
Redmond appeared at the edge of the pool. He
slipped off his robe and dived in, swimming a couple
of powerful laps until he ended up leaning against
the side of the pool, right beside her.*

'Nice day,' he said.

*She flicked a flirtatious glance at him. She knew
how to use her looks to good effect. He saw her
stunning blue eyes widen slightly, saw her pupils
dilate, and that was good. She liked the look of
him and she was determined to let him know it.
He was a handsome man, a striking man. He
wasn't old or pot bellied – and he had to be rich
to stay here; she knew that.*

'Lovely,' she said, and smiled.

*'Staying long?' he asked, glancing over at Sir
William, who was deep into his conversation,
noticing nothing, certainly not the way her eyes
were playing with the younger man's, certainly not
the way her nubile body was half turning towards
this new kid on the block.*

'*Until the weekend,*' she said, smiling.

He smiled back at her. '*Good. I hope we'll meet up again.*'

'*We might,*' she said playfully.

'*I think we should.*'

'*That's very forward of you.*' Her eyes were dancing; she was enjoying this.

'*I am forward,*' he said, '*in most things. My name's Redmond, by the way.*'

'*Are you a businessman?*' she asked him, entranced by his soft southern Irish accent.

'*Yes.*' It was true, more or less. He owned the streets of Battersea and a little pocket of Limehouse. He did business. Not legitimate business, but it was business anyway.

'*I'm here with—*'

'*Sir William. I know.*'

Mira was silent for a moment, but her eyes spoke volumes. '*Billy has a sleep after dinner,*' she said at last.

'*Does he?*'

'*For an hour.*'

'*You know what? A person could do a lot. In an hour.*'

'*Yes. That's true.*'

'*What's your name?*'

'*Mira,*' she said. '*Mira Cooper.*'

She flicked her leonine blonde mane and was off, streaking across the pool, her blood fizzing *with excitement. Oh yes, she remembered everything. The good bits . . . and the bad.*

She'd told him all about herself, something she had never done before, not with any man. That she had once worked in a high-class brothel run by her friend Annie Carter – who'd been Annie Bailey then – in the West End of London. She told Redmond that, while they lay naked together in his sumptuous Cliveden suite.

'I don't want you seeing Billy again,' he said as they lay back against the pillows, him lazily playing with her splendid breasts, her lightly caressing his flat, well-toned stomach. 'Not after this week.'

She turned her head, looked at his face. 'He'll be upset,' she said.

'Fuck him,' he said.

She grinned at that. Knelt up on the bed and straddled him.

'I'd rather fuck you,' she said, and bit his nipple quite hard.

'Okay,' he said, smiling up at her. 'Do it.'

6

Annie was in church. She never went to church except for the usual stuff – funerals, christenings and weddings. Apart from those, she normally wouldn't have been seen dead in such a place. She hadn't been raised that way.

Her mum, Connie Bailey, had never even sent her or her sister Ruthie to Sunday school. Other kids had attended, collected those neat little stamps with pictures of Jesus to stick in books and get a gold star, got those little raffia crosses from the vicar on Palm Sunday. Annie and Ruthie had spent Sundays wondering whether this was going to be the day when their mother finally up and died on them. Choked on vomit, drank herself into oblivion, take your pick. Their mother had been a drunk, and Dad was nothing but a faint memory.

So, no church. No giving thanks to the Lord,

because excuse me but what had there ever been to give thanks *for,* really? Annie and Max had been married in a no-fuss, no-frills ceremony in Majorca, and Layla had been christened there too. The Church of England, into which Annie had been born, was foreign to her.

But now here she was.

In church.

And a choir was lifting the roof off, singing 'Praise the Lord, *hallelujah!*' Twenty purple-clad black women were standing in front of the high altar, shafts of multicoloured sunlight illuminating them through the stained-glass window. They were moving rapturously to the beat. A dumpy, pop-eyed little man was at the organ, flapping one arm at the choir and mouthing along, obviously doubling up as choirmaster. The vicar was standing silently beside the lectern, listening and watching. The organ was belting out the backbeat, the beaming women giving it their all, the very rafters of the beautiful old building were vibrating with the power of the combined sound.

Annie sat in a pew and listened, feeling all the hairs on the back of her neck stand up. Yeah, it was magic.

She'd called first at Louella's address, expecting that a whole bunch of family would be gathered around to support her. But a neighbour told her that Louella had gone to church. Said Louella *always* went to church this time every week for choir practice. So Tony had driven Annie over, and now here she was, listening to the choir pounding and clapping and swaying and singing to the rafters and wondering what good she could possibly do here. But she had to be here, had to say how sorry she was, had to ask if there was anything she could do to help, if only for Aretha's sake. She didn't even know what Aretha's aunt looked like – but, as it happened, that proved no problem, because there, on the left-hand side of the group, bellowing out the words of praise and swaying in time to the beat, grinning and clapping with all the rest, was a woman whose eyes were full of tragedy and whose cheeks were wet with tears.

It had to be Louella, singing and sobbing at the same time.

Annie gulped as it hit her again. Aretha was gone. Had Aretha ever come here, with her Aunt Louella? Had she ever sat right here and listened to the choir? Before Aretha and Louella had fallen out over Aretha's career choices, had they come here together to worship?

Annie didn't know. There was so little that she really knew about Aretha Brown. All she did know was that she'd been a friend. All she knew beyond that was that she couldn't let Chris get stitched up for something he didn't – *couldn't* – do.

The choir roared out one last, bell-like note, and it echoed all around the great vaulted ceiling before finally fading away. Their organist clapped madly. The vicar clapped politely too. Annie stood up and joined in. The choir started to disperse. Annie walked up the aisle. Some of the women were patting Louella's shoulder, murmuring to her. The vicar came forward and talked quietly to her. Annie waited until he moved away, then she stepped up and said: 'Louella?'

The woman looked at her blankly. Her eyes were swollen with all the tears she'd shed.

'Louella, I'm a friend of Aretha's. I'm Annie.'

Louella's face closed down. She looked at Annie with suspicion.

'You one of them Delaneys?' she asked.

Annie shook her head.

'Only she was workin' at a Delaney place,' said Louella.

'I know.'

'And you ain't one of them? You ain't one of them that preyed upon my little girl?'

My little girl.

But Aretha wasn't Aunt Louella's little girl: she was someone else's. Someone thousands of miles away, toiling under the baking Rhodesian sun, had lost a daughter. The Africans had extended families; they shared their children, their grandparents, their joys and their losses. The English did not.

'I'm not a Delaney, Louella. I'm Annie Carter.'

Louella looked no happier. She rubbed a hand over her face, drying her tears.

'She spoke about you,' she said.

'Did she?' asked Annie.

'Yeah, she said you was tight together. But you was involved with that place she worked, I know that. You and that Dolly woman, and there was a boy too who worked there . . .'

'Darren,' said Annie, swallowing hard. Darren was gone, and she still missed him.

'He was homosexual, that's against the word of the Lord,' said Aunt Louella huffily.

'He couldn't help what he was,' said Annie.

Louella looked at her. She shrugged. 'Maybe. Anyway, the Lord says hate the sin, but love the sinner.'

'Can we sit for a moment? Have a talk?'

'They told you she's gone, my baby?' asked Louella, tears spilling over again.

Annie nodded sadly. She indicated one of the front pews. Louella heaved a sigh and sat down. Annie sat beside her.

'I'm so sorry,' she said.

'Oh, I sorry too,' said Louella, choking on a sob. 'I'm sorrier than I can say. The police, they come to me and they tol' me what happened, they tol' me they got the one who did it. I said to her so many times, don't do that stuff, why you got to do that when you could get a nice job, be a good girl like I promised your mama you would be. How could I tell her that her little one was doin' things like that when she sent her here to me, put her in my care, expected her to get a good life for herself?'

They tol' me they got the one who did it. Annie's guts churned and her mind rebelled. They had Chris; they were convinced he was the murderer. Annie was equally convinced he wasn't.

So prove it, she thought. She had to, or Chris was fucked.

Louella was looking at her. 'Yeah, she spoke about you,' she said again. 'You're one of the bad people, the people my baby should never have got herself involved with. I know about the big gangs, the things they do. I *know.* You were with Max Carter.'

Annie took a breath. 'I'm in charge now,' she said.

'Yeah, you're bad people. I know that,' said Louella.

'I'm not a bad person, Louella. I was a good friend to Aretha. She was an even better one to me.'

'Yeah, you say.'

'Hate the sin, not the sinner?'

Louella looked at her sceptically.

'That's neat, turnin' my own words back on me,' she said.

'We both loved her. *That's* what matters. We both want to see who did this brought to justice.'

'They got him, her husband, he done it.'

'Did you know Chris?' *Because if you did, you'd know this is all bullshit.*

Louella shook her head. 'No, but I seen him at their wedding. He sure was frightening to look at.'

Being frightening to look at was going to prove a problem for Chris, and Annie knew it.

'I was at the wedding, of course,' Aunt Louella went on. 'Even though I was angry with her for what she did to make a livin'. We're talkin' family. She was my *baby*. But we sort of drifted away from each other. I wanted her to change her ways; she wouldn't. It made things . . . hard.'

Annie was silent. It was cool in the church, peaceful. Outside, traffic roared, people fought their corner in the heat and glare of the City. In here was tranquillity. Annie watched the vicar moving about at the altar, repositioning a highly polished candlestick, brushing a fleck of dust from the altar cloth. The dumpy little pop-eyed organist was gathering up his sheet music, fussily arranging the papers in order.

'Do you need help? With the arrangements?' she asked Louella.

Louella shook her head. She sighed.

'They won't release her body yet,' she said. 'I asked them. I said I wanted to lay my baby to rest, but they won't do it, not yet.'

'When they do, I can help.'

Louella shot her a scornful look.

'You think I'd bury my baby with gang money?'

Annie looked at her steadily. Louella's eyes dropped away.

'It's what we're here for,' said Annie. 'To help our own.'

Louella shook her head. 'I don't want nothing to do with any of that.'

'Well, think it over.' Annie stood up. 'Funerals are expensive. I know you can't earn much . . .'

'Whatever I earn, I earn by honest toil,' said Louella sharply. 'I'll manage. Thank you.'

Annie nodded. The vicar had gone into the vestry; the organist was gone too. The church was empty, but for Annie and Aunt Louella. Their voices echoed when they spoke.

'My door's always open,' said Annie. 'If you should change your mind . . .'

'I won't.' Louella's face was closed off and truculent as she stood up too. 'Goodbye, Mrs Carter.'

Annie sighed. She looked up at the altar,

and then above to the glorious stained-glass windows. She stared at them and wondered where God had been when Aretha was fighting to stay alive.

7

Tony drove her up West to the hotel where Aretha had met her last client. She was sure she was wasting her time, but if there was anything, *anything*, she could turn up by poking around, then she knew she had to try.

'You want me to come in with you, Boss?' asked Tony as they pulled up outside.

'No, Tone. I won't be long,' she said, and jumped out of the back and trotted up the steps to the plush hotel. The doorman, resplendent in purple with gold braiding, tipped his hat to her.

'Good morning, Madam,' he said.

She nodded and pushed through the swing doors. She looked around as she crossed to the reception desk. It was *some* place. There was a lot of pink marble, a fountain in the centre of the lobby, big, cream, velvet-covered buttoned chairs and reading lights on console tables. She could see a guest lounge through an open set of double doors to one side, two lifts on the other, beside a huge, gold-painted sweeping staircase.

At the reception desk, a purple-suited and smiling blonde whose name-badge said 'Claire' asked if she could help.

'I hope you can,' said Annie. 'Two nights ago a friend of mine died not far from here. This was the last place she was seen alive. With a guest of yours.'

The smile vanished.

'I'm not sure I can help you with that,' she said.

'I'm not sure you can either,' said Annie. 'That's why I need to speak to the concierge who was on duty that night.'

The phone started ringing. The girl turned to it with obvious relief. 'If you'll excuse me . . . ?' she said.

'Sure,' said Annie, and waited while the girl took a booking for the following weekend.

Claire replaced the receiver and turned back to Annie.

'As I said, I'm not sure we can help . . .'

And then the phone rang again, and Claire gave Annie an 'oh, sorry' smile as she picked it up. She took another booking. Annie waited.

'So sorry about that,' said Claire, and then the phone rang again. She picked up. Then her professional smile died on her lips as Annie snatched the phone from her hand and replaced it on the base, cutting the call dead. Annie leaned over and pulled the phone jack out of its socket. Claire's mouth dropped open. Annie gave her a tight smile.

'The fact is,' Annie said, pausing to glance at the girl's badge, 'Claire. The fact is that my friend is dead and I'm upset, so bear with me here and don't even think about plugging that phone back in unless you want to be wearing it as a necklace, you got me? I need to speak to your concierge, preferably this year and not next. Preferably within the next five minutes. Preferably *now*. So call him up or have someone fetch him or whatever it is you have to do, and stop it with the fucking phone, please, because this is very, very important, do you understand?'

Claire nodded slowly. She'd gone pale.

'That's good,' Annie congratulated her. 'That's very good, I can see we have an understanding here, Claire. Now, what's his name, this concierge who would have been on duty two nights ago, at gone midnight?'

Claire fiddled about with some papers on the big curving desk. She found a list, and checked down it. She looked up at Annie.

'That would be Ray Thompson,' she said. 'He's on twelve to eight all this week. He's not here right now.'

'He'll be here at twelve tonight?' asked Annie.

Claire nodded, swallowing, her eyes wary.

'Then I'll be back to see him then. If he don't come in for any reason, you call me, okay? I don't want a wasted journey – that would upset me, do you understand what I'm saying?' Annie took a notepad and pencil out of her pocket and jotted down her name and the Palermo's number. She handed it to Claire. 'My name's Annie Carter, I've put it down right here so that you know. Reach me on this number, okay?'

Claire nodded.

'I'll be back at twelve if I don't hear from you first. Oh, and can you tell me who was in room two-oh-six two nights ago?'

'I shouldn't . . .' Claire started.

Then she looked at Annie's face. She gulped and flicked back a page or two in the guest book, scanned down it. 'A Mr Smith.'

Not exactly original, thought Annie.

Dolly had told her that a woman had made the initial booking and that there was no contact number because Rosie – being Rosie – had taken the call, and hadn't asked for one. Aretha had to meet a man named Mr Smith in room 206 at nine, that was all.

'Were you on duty that night?' asked Annie.

Claire shook her head.

'Write down the name of whoever *was* on duty,' said Annie.

Claire wrote down a name and handed the headed compliment slip to Annie.

'Thanks for that,' said Annie, pocketing it. 'And is this person going to be back on duty tonight?'

Claire nodded. 'I think so.'

'That's good, I'll see him too. Have you heard anything about what happened?' she asked. 'Anything that might interest, for instance, the police . . . maybe help them with their inquiries?'

'I don't know anything about it,' said Claire, shaking her head nervously. 'I just saw the police out there when I came in next morning, and people were talking about it. They said it was the third murder in as many months. I'm just really glad I don't do nights.'

'Okay. If I don't hear from you first, I'll be back at twelve to see Ray and the receptionist.'

Claire nodded. 'That's Gareth . . . Gareth Fuller,' she said.

'Gareth Fuller. Thanks Claire.'

Annie turned away from the desk and started to walk back across the reception area to the door. It spooked her, that feeling that she was walking in Aretha's footsteps, tracing the path the dead woman had taken on her last night on earth.

For a heart-stopping moment she felt she could almost *see* Aretha up ahead, swinging through the doors into the night, her feather boa trailing behind her, the smell of that horrible hairy Afghan coat she always wore clinging to the air, mixed with the attar of rose scent she favoured, dreads bouncing as she went, flashing a broad grin back at Annie.

Bye girlfriend, catch ya later.

And then the vision was gone, and it was daylight, and Aretha was dead.

It was too late now to bring her back. But not too late to find out who had taken her from them.

There were voices coming from the lounge, male voices, people moving on the edge of her vision. She'd paused there in the middle of reception, but now she moved again, heading for the door just like Aretha had done two nights ago. And then one of the men emerging from the guest lounge called out her name, and she turned and to her shock saw Redmond Delaney standing there – with Constantine Barolli.

They fell silent and stared at her. Shocked, Annie stared right back. Yeah, it was him. She couldn't believe it. Smooth bloody American, standing there as bold as brass with Redmond Delaney, boss of the Delaney mob and – because she was a Carter – her enemy.

Antagonism between a Delaney and a Carter was not in any way new. This particular fight went *way* back to the Fifties, to when Davey Delaney had come over from Ireland and tried to muscle in on Max's father's patch. Some things were set in stone. All through the Sixties the Richardsons and the Frasers had the South, the Regans the West, the Nashes had The Angel, the Delaneys held Battersea – and a small pocket in Limehouse, down by the docks, often disputed over – the Krays had Bethnal Green and the Carters had Bow.

Now it was the Seventies, and *still* the Delaneys had to keep pushing their luck, and when they pushed, the Carter mob pushed back. There had been all sorts of disputes over the years between the two warring clans. Sometimes it had turned downright nasty. Major gang fights broke out; serious damage was inflicted. And earlier this year, Billy Black, Annie's gofer – who for years had walked the Limehouse streets unmolested – had been killed, dissolving any illusion that there might be peace like flesh in quicklime.

For Annie, it was war.

Once, she had done business with Redmond and his twin sister, Orla. Once, she had even pitied them for their miserable backgrounds. Now, she looked at Redmond – tall, effete, red hair swept back from his white skin, his pale green eyes watching her, dressed in his usual sober black – and felt only hatred.

And what the *hell* was Constantine Barolli, who had for years been tight in business with the Carters, doing – having a private meet in a plush West End hotel with their worst enemy?

'Annie?'

It was Constantine who called her name, not Redmond. Redmond had always called her Miss Bailey or Mrs Carter. Always very formal, that was Redmond. Cold as black ice and twice as deadly.

Constantine *bloody* Barolli.

Annie forced herself to look at him with cool dispassion. And that was hard. Because – damn it – he looked good.

In fact, he looked just the same as when she had last seen him – a stunning man in his early forties, tall and silver-haired, with vivid blue eyes and an all-American tan, wearing a beautifully cut grey suit. Exactly the same as when she had chased after him like an over-keen schoolgirl to Heathrow and told him to call her.

And – *oh yeah* – he hadn't. He had called the *Delaneys*.

She looked at him, looked at Redmond – and walked on. She was down the steps and out on the pavement when Constantine caught up with her.

'What, are you ignoring me now?' he asked, catching her arm, and his voice was pure New York, just like she remembered.

Annie stared at his hand on her arm. He was very close, very overwhelming – even more physically imposing than she remembered. She could smell his Acqua di Parma cologne, she was dazzled anew by those intensely probing blue eyes, and she knew that she could all too easily fall under his spell again. If she let herself.

'It looks like it,' she said, voice cool, face blank. 'Don't it?'

'You got my note?' he asked.

'Yeah. I got it.'

'You didn't come over,' he said.

'You're right, I didn't,' said Annie as Tony pulled up in the Jag. 'Will you excuse me? I've got a lot of business today.'

'Why the big chill?' asked Constantine. She could see a flicker of amusement playing around his mouth. Fuck it, she was angry and that amused him. As usual.

'What big chill?'

'All right, put it another way, why have you got that stick up your ass? What's up with you?'

'What's up with *me*?' Annie opened her eyes wide and stared at him. 'What's up with *you*, arsehole?'

Probably Constantine had done her a favour, leaving her out in the cold for three long months. It had brought her to her senses, made her rethink. Yeah, she was well out of this. *Well* out.

'Excuse me, but people don't generally talk to me like that,' said Constantine, grabbing her arm again.

Annie saw Tony's attention sharpen, and he started to get out from behind the driver's seat. She shook her head quickly. She didn't want him starting anything up with *this* one; he'd be placing himself in more danger than any of them could handle. She couldn't *see* Constantine's minders anywhere, but she knew damned well that they were there, watching. Tony stopped moving.

'Excuse *me*, but I think you'll find I just did,' said Annie, and got in the car. 'The Palermo, Tone,' she said.

But Constantine still had the door open. He hunkered down and looked at her. He still looked as though he was finding this whole thing the biggest joke in the world.

'Listen,' he said. 'I'm not going to let this go.'

'Well, good luck with that,' she said.

'You asked me to call you.'

'Yes I did. Stupid of me. Hey, you'd better get back to your meeting. Redmond Delaney's a big noise around here, you don't want to go pissing him off. And if he sees you running after a *Carter*, that'll do it every time.'

Constantine stood up. 'Look, it was a business lunch. We met, discussed things, ate a little, drank a little, now I'm going home.'

'Home to Holland Park? Or home to New York?'

Constantine pursed his lips and stared at her.

'Is that what all this is for: you're sore because I didn't call sooner?'

'I don't know *what* you're talking about.'

'Yes you do. And okay, guilty, and you called me on it. But you know what? If I can finally find the guts to face this thing, then so can you.'

'So you were just having lunch with Redmond Delaney?' she asked.

'Is there a law against that, two businessmen having lunch?'

'Who invited who?' asked Annie.

'He invited me,' said Constantine.

'I knew it. He wants the contracts on your clubs up West. The Carter firm – *my* firm – has always held those contracts.'

Constantine nodded. 'Yeah, well. Maybe he was making a better offer.'

'Was he?'

'I didn't say that. And anyway, a deal's a deal. I was happy to work with Max, and I am now happy to work with you.'

'Big of you.'

Constantine paused for a beat. 'You know, I'd forgotten what a complete pain in the ass you could be.'

'Well, I'm glad I've refreshed your memory,' said Annie, and pulled the door shut.

Tony put the car in gear and they moved off.

I'm not going to look back, thought Annie.

But she did. Constantine was standing there, gazing after the car, shaking his head and grinning. When he saw her looking back, he waved.

Damn, he *did* look good.

Her heart was beating fast and hard. Her face felt hot. She was having a lot of trouble stopping herself from smiling.

Fuck it, she thought.

8

Redmond Delaney bought Mira diamonds. She loved diamonds. He bought her furs. She loved those too, but she loved him more.

'This is just between us,' he said to her, meaning their love, their lust, whatever the hell it was that drew them together.

Mira nodded her acceptance, but deep down she felt uneasy and hurt. She knew he had parents in Ireland, but there was never any chance that she would meet them. He had a sister too – his twin, Orla. She had met Orla once; they'd been having lunch at a restaurant, and Orla had come in. Reluctantly, Redmond had introduced her to Mira. Orla had looked at Mira like she was contaminated.

So she had become his dirty little secret, one he kept well away from his family. She understood that, even though it pained her. She knew she *wasn't fit for polite society, fit for any society really. Sometimes she even shocked herself. That blackness in her heart sometimes made itself felt in dark moods, wild behaviour. She knew her own weaknesses. She knew that what had been done to her in her childhood had warped her somehow. There were lines that most other people, most normal people, would never cross. But she crossed them every day, with every breath she took, and only occasionally would she think: Jesus, did I really do that?*

Not long after their affair began, Redmond bought her a flat in Battersea, close to his family's breaker's yard. Not Mayfair – which was what she was used to – but a nice flat in a decent area, a large and sunlit flat which she'd decorated in the latest styles at his considerable expense.

She was happy. William was a distant memory. The brothel she had worked in, the brothel where she met William, had been closed down long ago by the police – so that was all over. But then he already knew that. He made it his business to know things, particularly about Annie Carter and the mob of thugs she controlled.

'I'm all yours, darling,' she said, flinging herself into his arms one sunny Sunday afternoon in the sitting room of the new flat.

He'd told her how much he loved her voice, so mellow, so Home Counties. By now Mira knew that he adored the upper classes in general, and they got a kick out of mixing with him, because he was a bad boy and everyone knew it. A bad boy, but a rich boy too – a boy with clout; so the London glitterati flocked around him. From humble beginnings, he had climbed the greasy pole and now he was at the top, with a high-class mistress in tow. She adored him. He adored her. It was love.

'I was all yours from the minute I first saw you,' she said against his cheek.

'Oh?' Redmond buried his head in her fragrant neck. She wore Shalimar. He loved that too: it was a classic like her, he'd told her.

'In the dining room at Cliveden.'

'You noticed me too?'

'I couldn't keep my eyes off you. But I had to. Because of William.'

'He's the past,' he said, pulling her in tighter so that she could feel his erection. 'We're all that matters now.'

They had christened the new bed in the new flat, and it had been dusk before they were sated, lying together in the warm afterglow.

'I'm so happy,' she murmured against his chest.

He was happy too. She was beautiful, polished, exotic – of course he was happy.

'Tell me about yourself,' he'd said. 'I want to know everything.'

He settled down for an erotic treat, and was not disappointed. She reeled out the background he had already imagined her to have. Old family money, pony clubs, private schools, a year at Egglestone being 'finished' followed by lavish country-house balls and wild, carefree summer parties at Henley. And then, of course, should have come marriage, babies . . .

Suddenly she fell silent.

Redmond looked at her face. She was crying, silent tears slipping down on to the pillow.

'Hey . . .' he murmured, and held her tighter.

Faltering, she went on talking.

There had been a pregnancy. Her parents had been ashamed. They had demanded to know who was the father of her child, but she hadn't told them, she couldn't tell them that her father's brother, the beloved uncle who had dandled her on his knee as a child, had impregnated her.

'What happened then?' he asked her, wiping away her tears.

'They sent me away to my cousin's for the abortion,' Mira told him, choking to get the words out through her tears.

'Shh,' he said, rocking her.

'And after that,' she said when she could speak again, 'I never went home again. Never saw my parents again. Couldn't stand to see the disappointment in their eyes when they looked at me.'

She sat up, hugging her knees to her chest. He stroked her back, feeling oddly relieved. She was like him after all. She too had gone to forbidden places, and lived to tell the tale.

'You could tell them the truth. It wasn't your fault. It's not too late,' he said.

She shook her head vehemently.

'Yes it is. My father loves his brother better than anyone in the world, including me. He didn't believe me then and he wouldn't believe me now. Neither would my mother. It's too late. It's over.'

'I'm sorry,' he said, understanding completely, utterly. 'So after that you became . . . ?'

She shot a glance back at him. A tight smile.

'A whore?' With a heavy sigh she threw herself back on to the pillows. 'It wasn't that difficult a transition. Men flocked around me, wined and dined me, bought me jewels. Men always have. My family was dead to me, I had to make my own way and what was I good for? I'd never had any training. Anything beyond arranging a few flowers and making a perfect Sacher torte was beyond me. Stupid, yes? What a way to raise a girl to face the world.'

He said nothing.

'These men coveted me, wanted to pay for my company on holidays in the Bahamas and dinners at the best restaurants, in exchange for sexual favours. So I drifted into that life. And you know

what's strange? I never felt anything for any of them, never felt a thing, until I met you.'

He nodded, pulled her in close against him. He knew that she had instinctively recognized that taint in his soul, the same taint that was in her. That was what had drawn them so swiftly together. It would never leave either of them.

'My poor darling,' he said against her hair, and pushed her hand down to his cock again, because the tale of what her uncle had done to her had aroused him.

9

Kath, Annie's cousin, was up in the flat with her three-year-old son, Jimmy Junior, her baby Mo – and Layla. Layla saw Annie coming up the stairs and threw herself at her mother's legs. She clung on like a small, dark-haired limpet.

Annie scooped Layla up into her arms and smiled into her daughter's face, although she felt annoyed with Kath because the door had been open, the stairs were a danger, the workmen had been down there with masonry and shit flying in all directions; the kids could get hurt here.

'You didn't have to come over, I'd have come to you,' she said to Kath, who was cuddling her grizzling baby against her vast bosom.

'Ah, they were getting bored and Layla kept asking for you and I needed some stuff from the shop, so I thought, why not?' said Kath.

'How's she been?' asked Annie.

Kath shrugged her plump shoulders. 'A pain in the arse,' she said, but her grin said otherwise.

Annie kissed Layla's silky dark hair – so like her own – and inhaled the sweet scent of her daughter.

'You been a good girl for your Auntie Kath?' she asked Layla.

'Yeah!' said Layla.

'Is that the truth?'

'Yeah!'

'What about you, little Jim?' asked Annie of Kath's little boy, who was at the table, his sandy head bent over his paper and crayons. 'Been good?'

Jimmy gave her a tired smile and rubbed his eyes.

'He's ready for his nap,' said Kath. 'They're all getting overtired.'

'Can Layla stay with you tonight, Kath? I've got to go out late on business.'

'Sure,' said Kath with a sigh.

She didn't ask what business. After years of being married to Jimmy Bond, who had once been Max Carter's number one man, she knew better. But Jimmy Bond was history now, and Kath didn't seem sorry. In fact, there was a new spring in her step. Jimmy had knocked seven kinds of shit out of her, and she didn't have to put up with *that* any more. She was still a train wreck, though; still messy, still untidy.

Annie noticed that Layla had started to cling on tighter to her. She drew back and smiled into the little girl's eyes – eyes that were the same colour as her own: a dark, dense green. 'I'll collect you after breakfast tomorrow, okay? That's a promise.'

'You promise, Mummy?'

'On my life,' said Annie, hating the anxiety in Layla's eyes. 'Uncle Tony's going to drive you over to Auntie Kath's with her right now, okay?'

This seemed to reassure Layla, and she nodded and allowed herself to be ushered out the door along with little Jim, baby Mo and a mountain of childcare products and colouring books, plus her overnight pyjamas and Bluey, her new fluffy toy bunny.

At last they were gone. Annie sat in the flat and turned on the TV to catch the news. The Manson trial was still going on in the States, the army had used rubber bullets for the first time in Belfast, and a plane had crashed in Peru, killing all ninety-nine people on board. Her attention sharpened as the guy started saying that another escort girl had been found dead, this time in London's West End, and that the girl's husband was now helping police with their enquires into this and two earlier killings.

So they still hadn't formally charged Chris yet. Maybe Jerry Peters had convinced them of Chris's innocence, and maybe not. They might not have charged him, but neither had they released him.

It was too soon to open the bubbly and start dancing on the frigging tables, that was for sure.

There was a different girl on reception when Annie got back to the Vista Hotel just after midnight. 'Pippa', the girl's badge announced. Pippa had a mountain of dark hair on her tiny bird-like head, pale clear skin and blue laughing eyes; her purple fitted jacket and skirt suited her colouring. The place looked deserted, apart from this little bright beacon sitting behind the reception desk.

'I need to speak to Ray Thompson, your concierge,' said Annie, surprised to see this dainty little thing here and not Gareth Fuller, as expected. 'Did Claire tell you about me? I'm Annie Carter.'

Pippa did a flickering downward sweep of the eyelashes. Annie guessed that this wowed the male punters. She waited, expecting that Claire would not have told her colleague about this. Expecting in fact that she was going to meet with more obstruction, more hassle, more of the 'oh I couldn't do that' routine.

Should have brought Tony in with me, she thought. Tony's appearance tended to galvanize people in a helpful direction. But Annie didn't want to come over all heavy here. She just wanted to know what had happened two nights ago; she didn't want to go busting heads if charm and negotiation could do the business just as well.

'That's Ray over there,' said Pippa helpfully, surprising her.

Annie turned. A man in a purple uniform with flashy gold epaulettes had just stepped out of the lift. He walked with authority, shooting his cuffs as he came. He looked at Annie, half smiled, nodded to Pippa.

'Can I help?' he said.

He was a short man in his early fifties, full of bouncy East End confidence. He had dark curly hair turning grey, an elfish face etched with laughter lines, and he took in everything about Annie at a glance. She could see him briskly categorizing her. Expensive-looking female punter in a black silk suit. She could see pound signs flicking up in his sharp, acquisitive eyes.

'Can you spare a few minutes? I'm Annie Carter. Did Claire tell you I'd be coming?' said Annie.

'Yes, she did. Of course,' he said in his Cockney twang.

'Can we talk in the lounge, get some privacy?' Annie continued, aware that Pippa was sitting behind the desk, looking bored as tits, with her ears flapping like Dumbo's.

He nodded and led the way in. The lounge was spacious and decked out in soothing greens, pinks and golds. No fire in the grate – too late in the day and too warm for that anyway; instead there was a display of tasteful dried flowers. Lots of big couches. Lots of table lamps casting a cosy glow, side tables stacked with newspapers. It was a proper little home from home for the weary guest.

Ray politely motioned that she should sit on one of the big couches, and he sat down opposite her, at a discreet distance.

Annie got straight to the point. 'You were on duty the night Aretha Brown was murdered,' she said.

This seemed to jolt him, but he must have been expecting it. There was a sudden wariness in his eyes. He looked down at the carpet, then up at her again. Nodded.

'She was here, visiting a friend,' said Annie carefully.

He nodded again, but he half smiled and his eyes said: *A friend? Is that what prossies are calling their clients now?*

'Did you see her arrive?'

'No, I didn't.'

'Did you see her leave?'

'Yes. I did. Look, I went through all this with the police. What's your interest here? You a reporter?'

'Do I look like a reporter?'

Ray gave her a quick once-over. 'No, you don't.'

'You're an East Ender, Ray. Which part?'

'Bethnal Green.'

'Then you'll know my husband's friends and

business acquaintances, the twins.' Annie watched as Ray's expression froze. 'You know the twins, Ray?'

Everyone from that area knew the twins. Reggie and Ronnie. The Krays.

Ray swallowed nervously and Annie could see that he'd made an important connection.

'You're Max Carter's wife,' said Ray.

Widow, thought Annie, but she let it go.

Ray looked at her. 'The Krays are a spent force now,' he said. 'They've been banged up for over a year for doing Jack the Hat and Cornell.'

'You think so?' Annie asked him.

Annie knew different. Even behind bars the Krays were making a fortune off their firm. They had legitimate sponsorship arrangements going with many businesses – debt collection agencies were a favourite – and these businesses set up deals from which the twins got a cut of the profit in return for use of the Kray name. She was doing something very similar with her own firm now, using Max's and Jonjo's considerable clout in the business world to make a legitimate living in security.

'Aretha – the girl who died – was a friend of mine,' she told him.

'I'm sorry,' he said.

'It was a horrible thing that happened to her. And her husband Chris is a friend too. He's in the frame for this. I don't like people doing bad things to my friends. And I don't believe Chris would harm Aretha. So I need to find out anything I can about what happened that night, so that I can do something about it, okay?'

Ray nodded.

'So,' said Annie. 'You saw her leave, but you didn't see her arrive?'

He looked down, nodded again.

'So, when she left. She left alone?'

'Yes, she was alone.'

'Did she seem all right?'

He shrugged. 'She seemed fine. Happy. It was tipping down with rain and I said she ought to take a taxi, and she said she wasn't made of money.'

Annie's heart clenched with pain. If Aretha had taken that taxi straight home, and not walked the short distance to the corner around which Chris was parked up, waiting for her, then she would probably be alive right now.

'Has she come here before?'

'No, she was a new one here.'

Annie looked at him. 'Room two hundred and six. Mr Smith. I'm assuming that's not his real name.'

Again the shrug. 'Lots of men sign in anonymously and pay cash when they check out. Wouldn't you, if you were going to use a brass? He might be a man of some importance – probably is; this is a classy place, the prices we charge, I'm telling you. He might have a reputation to consider. He might be married. He wouldn't want to draw attention to himself.'

'Did you see this "Mr Smith"?'

Ray shook his head.

'Did anyone?'

'The police asked that too. But we see hundreds of people in a day here. No one remembers him.'

Anonymous and invisible.

'He checked in and the time was recorded, yes? So someone spoke to him then, face to face,' Annie persisted. 'Who? Claire? Pippa? The other one, Gareth?'

'I'll find out,' said Ray.

Annie sat back, waiting.

'You want me to do it now?' asked Ray.

Annie gave him the look. 'You got anything else pressing?'

Ray got up and left the lounge. Through the half-open door Annie saw him in a huddle with Pippa at the reception desk. Watched him come back into the lounge, sit down again.

'Yeah, that would have been Gareth,' he said. 'Mr Smith checked in at eight thirty-three in the morning three days ago. He booked in – with Gareth – for the one day and overnight, but no one saw him leave the next morning.'

'Hold on,' Annie told him. 'No one saw him

leave? He paid his bill, yes? Spoke to whoever was on reception? But no one saw him?'

'No one *remembers* seeing him. As I say, we—'

'—see hundreds of people in a day. What about the doorman?'

Ray shook his head. 'People come in and out all day. Whoever's on the door don't know their names and barely even notices their faces unless they give a good tip, and you don't get too many of those. And if this guy wanted to remain incognito, he wouldn't be doing *that*, for sure.'

Annie stood up. 'Gareth Fuller, wasn't it?' she asked.

'Yes.'

'And he's here when?'

'Actually he's not,' said Ray. 'He left yesterday.'

'Left?'

'Manager fired him. Bit of a slacker.'

'His address then?'

Ray went to get Gareth's address.

Annie looked around the lounge and wondered what had really been going down between Redmond Delaney and Constantine that they had to meet here. Constantine slipped the Carters three grand a month to keep troublesome elements out of his clubs up West, save him the bother of importing his own muscle from across the pond. Maybe Redmond was undercutting the Carters, and Constantine's true intention was to work out a better deal with him, or start a lucrative bidding war between the two rival gangs.

Damn, she had thought he was on *her* side. It hurt to discover that he might not be. And now this. She *had* to help Chris. She couldn't just let him take the rap: she *knew* he was innocent. She wandered back out into reception.

Trouble, every way she looked. Nothing new there, though. She was used to digging deep, standing alone. If truth be told, she was getting tired of it, but it was what she usually had to do.

Ray came over and handed her a piece of paper with Gareth Fuller's address on it. She thanked him and slipped him a fiver.

'If anything else occurs to you, anything at all, you call me, okay?' she told him.

'Sure,' he said, and smiled.

He wouldn't call. She knew it. But she was more interested right now in Gareth Fuller, who had checked Mr Smith in, and checked him out – and who probably wouldn't even remember what he looked like.

10

Next morning at eight there was a knock at the Palermo's main door. Annie was up and dressed. She went down the stairs and opened up. The club was quiet for once, peaceful. Too early for the builders.

The bald, portly man standing there peered at her with watery blue eyes, squinting past a curl of cigarette smoke. He threw the stub on the pavement and ground it out with his heel.

'Detective Sergeant Lane,' said Annie, looking up and down the street. There was nobody about, but still . . .

'We've charged him,' said Lane.

Shit, thought Annie.

'Can I have a few words?' he asked.

'Sure,' said Annie, and ushered him in, up the stairs, into the flat. She closed the door, indicated that he should take a seat. He did. He looked an utter bloody mess, corpulent and red in the face, his stubby fingers stained with nicotine, his white nylon shirt yellowish and sweat-stained and straining over his belly. He didn't smell exactly fresh. Annie sat as far away as she could get and thought about Chris, charged now. Poor bastard.

'I thought the rule was that we were never seen together,' she said irritably.

He shrugged. 'You're helping the police with their inquiries,' he said.

'Fair enough. What's the new DI like?'

'Like a bear with a sore arse. Just got divorced and transferred in and now I'm stuck with the picky bastard. I'm telling you, that sod's suspicious by nature.'

'But he's got no reason to be suspicious of you, has he?'

'None at all. I'm squeaky clean.'

Which was ironic, since DS Lane always smelled like he hadn't bathed in a month. *If we have to have bent coppers on the firm, can't we at least have clean ones?* she thought. But the boys had assured her that Lane was a very useful contact. She'd have to open a window the minute he'd gone. Either that or fumigate the fucking place.

'What have you got?' she asked.

'She was at the Vista Hotel visiting a Mr Smith in room two-oh-six,' said Lane.

'I know that.'

'But it fits the MO of the other two that got done.'

'Not the same hotel?'

'No, different hotels every time. This is the poshest one yet; our boy's stepped up a notch on the social ladder. The other two got done outside three-star places in the East End. But same meat, different gravy. Prostitutes calling and getting killed for their trouble. Same pattern, same method. You *really* think Chris Brown didn't do these?'

Annie swallowed a sharp stab of revulsion at his casual tone, his relaxed manner. He didn't care that Aretha was dead. Or the other two. He didn't care that Chris was innocent. He just had a curiosity about the case, an interest in the puzzle it represented. And he thought they'd already solved it.

'Did you find any trace of him on the other women? Any reason to believe he did those two as well as Aretha?' asked Annie coolly.

'No. None.'

'But he's been charged for doing Aretha.'

'Yeah. Look, I got to admire your loyalty, but let's face it, the man's going down.'

'The wire could get lost,' said Annie.

'What?'

'The cheese wire. Could go missing.' Annie was staring at him.

'And what difference would that make? There're

still the cuts on his hands, there's still his blood on the vic. Hunter's on it and trust me he won't let it go. You could lose the fucking *suspect* on this one, and everyone would still be one hundred per cent convinced that Chris Brown did it.'

'He couldn't kill Aretha,' said Annie.

'No?' Lane gave an unpleasant smile. 'If *my* old lady was out tomming – hell, even *I* could do it. Think you'll find men don't like that sort of thing.'

'He knew Aretha was on the game before he married her.'

'Yeah? I find that hard to believe.'

'It's true.'

'Then he's a tolerant bloke and my hat is off to him, it really is. I'm just saying, *most* men would consider offing the old woman if she was out pork-swording the whole neighbourhood. Ew, think of the stuff you could catch off it. And it was fucking with knobs on, let's not forget. When I saw the stuff in that bag of hers, I damn near blushed.'

'He didn't do it,' said Annie. 'I want you working hard on this, finding out who did. I want to know about these other two girls. I need to see copies of the case files.'

He screwed up his face. 'Tricky.'

'I don't care how fucking tricky it is, you do it.' If there was any sort of link between the two other girls and Aretha, then maybe some sense could be made out of all this. Maybe they could find not only Aretha's killer but their killer too. Find the bastard who'd killed them, nail him good. *Or her.* Best not forget that. A woman could have done this too. By doing all that, maybe she could get Chris out of the frame.

'Look, I'll give it my best.' Lane stood up.

'Do that,' said Annie, standing up too. Christ, she was going to have to air this place with a vengeance. 'You'll be well rewarded.'

'That's always nice to hear,' he smirked, showing yellow tombstone teeth.

'So you don't rate the new DI?' she asked.

'Hunter?' He shrugged. 'He's a pain in the arse, the miserable bastard, but he's a good cop. And there ain't many of *them* about, as you know.' He gave her a lopsided smile.

God, he was repulsive. On balance Annie preferred hard-eyed and tight-lipped DI Hunter to this rancid tub of lard. The immaculate and sour-faced Hunter might look at her as if she was lowlife, but at least he was straightforward in his intentions and she felt he simply couldn't be bought. You had to admire that. If you cut DI Hunter open, the words HONEST COP would run right through him like BLACKPOOL runs through a stick of rock. Slice DS Lane open and all you'd find would be the stench of corruption.

'Hey,' she said sharply. 'Don't take this lightly. And *don't* let me down.'

The smirk vanished. 'I said I'll do my utmost. But I can't part the fucking Red Sea or nothing. My name ain't Moses.'

Annie stared at him. Then she crossed the room and opened the door. Tony was standing silently outside it, at the top of the stairs, waiting to usher the copper out. Neither of them had heard him come up. Tony could move like a ghost, and he could move fast too, for a big man. Lane looked at Tony's huge bulk and swallowed hard.

'Do your best, okay?' Annie reminded him. 'Let me down and you'll be sorry.'

Annie cleared up, ushered in the builders for another day of hammering and banging, and gladly took her leave of the club. Tony drove her in the Jag over to where Gareth Fuller, the Vista's former employee, lived. It was a dump in a block of flats. Washing flapped on badly strung clothes-lines. Rubbish swirled in the summer breeze on each of the outside landings as Annie and Tony walked up five flights of stairs.

The graffiti-strewn lift was working, but judging from the stink emanating from it, someone had been using it to piss in. So it was the stairs, or being lowered down off the roof with a fucking *rope*, Tony complained – could you believe people had to live this way?

'Pardon my French, Boss,' he added politely as

they hit the top landing. Then, 'Oh fuck,' he blurted as he looked ahead.

Annie looked ahead. DI Hunter was standing outside a battered-looking door halfway along the grimy landing, his arm raised to knock on it. His head turned in their direction. Distinctly, they saw him mutter something under his breath and then return his attention to the door.

'Wait here, Tone,' said Annie, and she left Tony by the top of the stairs and strolled off along the landing to where Hunter, the warm updraught riffling through his dark hair, was still tapping at the door. 'Hello, Detective Inspector,' she said when she got to the door. She looked at the peeling paint-work. 'How's tricks?'

He looked at her, his face pinched tight with disapproval. He looked away. Knocked again at the door.

He wouldn't be half bad looking if only he didn't scowl so much, she thought.

A dog was barking in there. A high-pitched *yap yap yap*. It could drive you mad, a dog like that – pity the neighbours.

'No one in?' she asked. 'Apart from Fido?'

'What are you doing here?'

'Same as you,' said Annie. 'Trying to find out what the hell's been going on.'

He half turned towards her. Gave her the old beady brown eye again. 'Don't get smart with me,

Mrs Carter. I know what you are, I know about you.'

'Oh?' Annie looked at him.

'You know, I once worked for DCI Fielding, and do you know what his big ambition was? To nail Max Carter.'

'Really,' said Annie. 'Well, he left that too late. Max is dead.' She glanced at his left hand. He was wearing a gold wedding ring, but Lane had said he was divorced. 'Hey, how's *your* wife, DI Hunter?' she asked him with deliberate cruelty.

His lips tightened. 'In Manchester,' he said. 'The last I heard.'

'Trouble on the domestic front?'

His eyes flared. 'Just what the hell *are* you doing here?'

'I told you, same as you. But in the meantime, we're here outside this damned door. Which needs opening, by the way.'

'Mrs Carter. This is police business, and best left to us.' And he turned and knocked on the door again.

'That lock don't look up to much,' said Annie. There was a pause. The dog barked on, *yap, yap, yap.* 'A good kick could probably sort that door out,' she suggested helpfully.

'That's breaking and entering, Mrs Carter,' he said, giving her the look again.

'Well,' said Annie, 'I understand your reservations,

you being an officer of the law and all that stuff. But if you were to walk along to the end there, busy yourself in some way, my colleague there,' she nodded to Tony, 'could have it open in no time. And then we could move this along, because no one is going to answer this damned door. And that dog's doing my head in.'

DI Hunter gave her an appraising stare. Looked at Tony, standing there all polite and besuited, big as a barn door with his bald head polished to the colour of oak from the summer sun, the gold crucifixes glittering in his ears. Looking as if he could demolish the building, never mind the door.

'Don't think I approve of this, because I don't,' said Hunter.

Annie nodded. Hunter walked off. Tony approached.

'Open it, will you, Tone?' she asked.

Tony pulled back and gave the door a kick just below the lock. It bounced open and the dog's volume shot up by a few decibels. A Yorkshire terrier appeared in the doorway, yapping frantically but wagging his little stump of a tail. Tony observed the animal with disfavour.

'God, I hate dogs.'

'You a cat person, Tone?' asked Annie. She could see DI Hunter coming back now, not hurrying.

'Can't stand them either. You know if you drop

down dead, they'll eat you? How's that for loyalty? Shows their true nature.'

'Thanks, Tone,' said Annie, and Tony went back along the landing to stand at the top of the stairs again.

'Hiya,' she said to the dog, whose tail went into overdrive.

She nudged the door further open with her foot, and wrinkled her nose as a waft of something unpleasant hit her from inside the flat. DI Hunter was back. There was a brief tussle over who should go through the door first, so they pushed into the flat's lounge together, the dog backing up on its haunches and still doing that irritating high-pitched *yap-yap-yap* business.

The smell of shit was suddenly overwhelmingly strong. Urine was slowly dripping on to a faded, threadbare carpet in the centre of the room. Above it, there was a young man hanging from the light fitting, flex twisted tight around his neck, dead eyes bulging, his tongue lolling swollen and black from his mouth.

11

Annie was sitting with her head in her hands at Dolly's kitchen table. She still felt as though she was going to throw up. It was nearly lunchtime of the same day, the day on which she and Hunter had discovered that Gareth wouldn't be providing any evidence this side of eternity.

Dolly was busy ferrying covered plates of sausage rolls, tuna vol-au-vents and sandwiches through from the kitchen to the front parlour, in readiness for the rush. This only ever used to happen on Fridays – party day – but now it was something she tended to do most days of the week. Along with the bar, it kept the punters happy and kept them coming back for more. Plus, it added a bit to the takings. Everyone was a winner. All except Annie, who took one look at the tuna vol-au-vents and had to take a hasty trip to the loo.

Mungo Jerry was belting out 'In the Summertime'

from the little trannie over the sink. Dolly was hurrying about the place, absorbed in her various tasks. Annie sat down again, flinching at the smell of warm sausage rolls. She envied Dolly that facility, to be content in your own four walls and to shut out the chaos. She had seen Dolly perform this act of denial before; it seemed to come naturally to her.

Lucky cow, thought Annie, wishing she could do the same.

Annie knew that this capacity for turning a blind eye to trouble came from Dolly having been kicked out of the family home in disgrace and left to suffer alone through a really bad backstreet abortion. Under circumstances like that, you'd have to build stout barricades in your brain to stop yourself from going mad, and this was obviously exactly what Dolly had done.

Ellie was mopping the floor and giving Dolly dirty looks because she'd just *done* that bit, for Chrissakes, and here was Dolly trotting around on her clean floor like a ruddy racehorse.

'Someone certainly got out of bed the wrong side this morning,' observed Dolly as Ellie irritably redid her work on the floor.

Annie looked up at Ellie. Ellie had been at Dolly's place a long time, since before it had been Dolly's place at all. She'd been there when it had been Annie's, and there before that, when Aunt

Celia had been running the show. It was no secret among them that the knocking-shop paid protection to the Delaneys, because the Delaneys ran Limehouse. It was no secret either that Ellie was the Delaney insider, which had caused them all a problem or two over the years, but Ellie had come to know which side she was batting for.

Annie knew Ellie was loyal to the house now before all else. She'd been on the game for years, the chubby-chasers had loved her ample curves, but she had not long since started displaying all the worrying signs of someone who couldn't hack fucking for a living after all. Scrubbing herself, trying to get the scent of sex off her. So now she cleaned houses. She cleaned here, and she cleaned at Kath's place. Made a really good job of it too. Liked to see a place all spick and span.

'Jesus, you look just about ready to hurl,' said Dolly to Annie as she passed by. She stopped and stared at Ellie too. '*And* you. What a face on you. You miserable mares.'

'Doll, I *have* hurled,' said Annie. 'And if you'd seen what I've seen this morning, so would you.'

Rosie, one of Dolly's new working girls, wandered into the kitchen in a transparent powder-blue peignoir and fluffy slippers. She was a small, pretty blonde with dynamite curves and a relaxed attitude. Yawning, she filled the kettle and switched it on, jigging sleepily away to the beat. She sent Annie a vague smile.

'Oh for fuck's *sake*,' said Ellie loudly, slapping the mop back into the bucket. Rosie stifled another smile.

Annie could understand Ellie's bad mood. Ellie had carried a torch for Chris for years. To see him banged up and about to be sent down for a long stretch was upsetting her badly. And now Annie had to tell her even more bad news.

'They've charged him,' she told her bluntly.

'Oh no.' Ellie looked devastated.

'Sorry, Ellie, I really am.'

Dolly came hurrying down the hall and into the kitchen to butter more bread on the worktop.

'Rosie, for fuck's sake will you get tidied up?' said Dolly.

'I *am* tidied up,' protested Rosie. 'All I want's a cup of tea, for God's sake.'

'Well take it up to your room; we're up to our arses down here. Poor Ellie's trying to get the floor done. Stop winding her up.'

Grumbling good-naturedly, Rosie made her mug of tea and departed.

Dolly paused. Her face clouded as she looked at Annie. 'Did I hear you right? They've charged him?'

Annie nodded and glanced at Ellie, seeing the pain on her plump, pretty face. She'd scraped her long dark hair back into a ponytail and she was wearing a pale blue overall that gave the effect of an overstuffed sausage. She looked hot, irritable, and above all, worried. But then she would be. She'd always adored Chris.

'Oh no, it looks bloody marvellous,' said Annie tiredly, ticking off facts on her fingers. 'His wife's dead. And if that ain't bad enough, his blood's on her body and on the murder weapon. Our only possible lead's her last client, who nobody knows a damned thing about except that he's calling himself "Smith", and the only person who might have actually noticed this Smith bloke has decided to top himself. Or at least, that's the story.'

'What do you mean, that's the story? It was suicide.'

'It *looked* like suicide. There was a chair kicked over, and the flex was tied up just right . . . poor bastard. The cop in charge told me that he'd heard things in the hotel about the boy. That he was a loser. Always stoned out of his head on pot. Couldn't hold down a job for ten minutes before he started screwing up.'

'Well then,' said Dolly.

'Yeah, but ain't that bloody convenient? We're all after this "Smith" person like longdogs – and there's no saying he's the one who did this to Aretha anyway. In fact *anyone* could have rushed up behind her in the street and done this; any sly bastard with a length of wire in his – or her – pocket.'

'Fuck me, you think a *woman* could have done this?' demanded Dolly. She was looking at Annie in exasperation. 'You're crazy.'

'Who the hell knows? But still, we're after Smith,' she went on. 'It's all we've got. And our only link to him or her has just killed himself.'

'Wait up,' Dolly objected. 'How'd this person who killed him – supposing that's what happened – get into the flat?'

Annie shrugged. 'Easy. Knock on the door, he opens it, they barge in, shut the door behind them, exit through the same door, no problems at all. No need to break in.'

'What about the doormen at the hotel?' asked Dolly.

Annie shook her head. 'I had Jackie Tulliver talk to the doormen. They've got no recollection of the man, none at all.'

Jackie was an ugly, cigar-smoking little goblin who had been with the Carter firm forever. If Jackie said there was nothing, then there was nothing. End of.

'So that's that then,' said Dolly firmly. 'Now, will you just let it go, for the love of God? Chris did the deed. It's bloody sad, but he did. I suppose she goaded him about how little he earned, she went back on the game, they argued – and he just snapped. So just let it go.'

There was a loud silence from Annie and Ellie.

'Oh come *on*,' protested Dolly.

They both ignored her.

'What will you do now?' asked Ellie, sitting down at the table across from Annie.

'No idea.' Annie stared at the table. Her brief Jerry Peters had phoned her early this morning saying that it looked very bad for Chris.

'I fear for your friend, Annie,' he had said gravely. 'I really do.'

So do I, thought Annie.

'This must have hit Aretha's Aunt Louella like a sack of shit,' said Ellie. She looked at Annie. 'I hope the firm's going to take care of her.'

Dolly looked up. 'That's the first sensible thing either of you has said.'

'Yeah, but she don't want our help, Doll,' said Annie.

'Look, make her take it. She can't afford funerals and such: she's poor but she's proud. She'd probably like to accept an offer of help but it's beneath her dignity.'

'I'll try,' said Annie with a sigh, standing up.

'So what now?' asked Dolly. 'You seen that Barolli bloke yet?'

Oh yeah, thought Annie. *And instead of calling me, he's been calling Redmond Delaney. The bastard.*

'No,' she said. She really didn't want to get started on all that.

'Well, you ought to catch up with him. Have

some fun, forget all this business.' Dolly looked at her sharply. 'You know what I've got to look forward to this afternoon? An assortment of fat naked arses and the frigging washing-up. Oh, *and* I've got to find a replacement dominatrix now that we've lost poor bloody Aretha. The silver fox, eh? Damn, that sure beats doing the dishes. Oh, and I forgot to say, your cousin Kath phoned. She was moaning about when were you coming over to get Layla, you said just overnight and she's been there all morning. Kath says she don't *mind*, but she's got her hands full with her own two and you did promise Layla after breakfast at the latest, and Kath said where the fuck were you, in that charming way she has.'

Annie sighed again. Damn, it was true. She couldn't keep dumping Layla on Kath like this while she addressed all sorts of business crap. She was going to have to sort out something more permanent, more settled, for Kath's sake and for Layla's. Within a few months she was going to have to think about schooling for Layla, too. But for now, she was going to sort out something else. Something she had already put off for too long.

The Holland Park mansion was just the same – it was a large and imposing William and Mary house with beautiful proportions, standing full square in an elegantly shaded plot. Lollipop bay trees adorned either side of the vast pillared doorway. It was the very picture of prosperous English gentility, probably owned by a banker who was something big in the City – which just went to show how far you could rely on appearances.

The mansion was in fact owned by the don of an Italian-American mob *'famiglia'*, greatly to be feared, who loaned money at ridiculous rates then had people apply baseball bats to clients who were slow to pay. Who practised the ancient arts of loan-sharking and extortion. Who ran all-night poker games for high stakes. Who paid off bent cops – just like the Carters did, Annie reminded herself.

Annie walked up the steps with the strangest feeling that someone was watching her. She paused midway, looked around. She'd sent Tony home; said she'd get a cab back to the club. She looked up and down the quiet, sedate street. There was a brief flare from a doorway about a hundred yards up the road, as someone lit a cigarette.

Hey, is that all it takes to spook you now? she wondered. *Someone standing in a doorway taking a smoke?*

Exasperated with herself, Annie went on up the steps. She was getting jumpy and she didn't even know why – except maybe she did. Her friend had been killed. Another friend had been arrested. And then the horror in the flat today. Trouble, every way she looked, and it was putting her on edge.

And now she was remembering the last time she'd come here, distraught, almost senseless with grief and worry, her daughter missing, her husband gone, money to find and nowhere to find it. This time was different, but still she felt her stomach churn with nerves.

She knocked at the glossy navy-blue painted door. The door opened. A large mound of muscle stood there, looking at her expectantly.

Annie moistened her dry mouth. 'Is he in?' she asked. 'I'm—'

'You're Mrs Carter. Yes, he's in. Come in please.'

And now it was too late to do a runner like she wanted to. She looked around the hall, marble everywhere, discreet and tasteful flower arrangements set up on pale stone plinths. Long mirrors: those were new. She saw herself in them, dark clothes, dark hair, blank face. That was good, the blank face. At least if she felt terrified, she didn't actually *look* it.

The heavy was knocking at the study door. Faintly she heard the familiar American voice call out, 'Come,' and then the door was opened.

'Mrs Carter for you, Boss,' said the heavy, and ushered Annie inside and shut the door behind her.

Annie told herself firmly that it was childish to want to wrench it open and bolt straight back out.

She thought of Max, and fuck it, this wasn't the time at all to be thinking about him, but there he was in her mind: Max, all piratical charm and black hair and steely blue eyes. Her late husband, Max.

And now here she was. Picking up where she had left off with Constantine Barolli. Another powerful, ruthless man. She never could resist the allure of bad boys. And she feared that this could only end the same way, in death and disaster – perhaps it was stupid, but she *did* fear the consequences: the whole thing was fraught with danger, littered with hurdles.

His damned children, for instance. His son Lucco had hated her on sight. His other son Alberto she didn't yet know about, but she felt sure he was going to hate her too. Cara, Constantine's daughter, who was newly married, was sure to see her as a rival for Daddy's affection, and *already* Constantine's sister Gina had looked at her like she was a turd on the pavement.

'Well, are you going to come in, or go out again?' asked Constantine from behind the desk.

The study was the same as she remembered. Big tan-coloured Chesterfields, rows of books, a big desk with a buttoned leather chair behind it and a yellow banker's light casting a warm glow upon its tooled-leather top. There was a marble fireplace with a decorated screen in front of it. This was a clubby, masculine room, and she felt out of place in it, just as she had last time she was here.

'I'm not sure,' she said.

He stood up and came around the desk and over to where Annie stood against the door. He held out his hand, palm down. *Expecting her to kiss his hand,* she thought. Annie looked at it, then at his face, then shook his hand briefly. Constantine gave a slight smile.

The silver fox. After his mother and brother had been hit in Sicily, his grandfather had promptly shipped him off to join the family in New York where it was safer. He'd grown up running numbers around Queens and in the Bronx, learning the business, finally taking control.

Annie looked up at his face. It was a strong face, commanding. Tanned, with bright blue eyes. Deep laughter lines in the corners. He put his hands in his pockets and looked at her from just inches away.

'So what now, Mrs Carter?' he asked in that assured, deep American voice. 'You gonna bolt for the door, or give this a shot?'

'I don't know what you're talking about,' said Annie, although she did. She brushed past him, went to the desk, sat down. 'I'm here to discuss your clubs.'

Constantine went back around the desk and sat down too.

'There's nothing to discuss,' he said. 'I'm perfectly happy with the service I'm getting.' He looked at her. 'Which isn't to say it couldn't be improved upon, of course.'

The West End clubs that Constantine owned were gold mines. Annie knew that. Famous people were in and out of there all the time, the Beatles, Howard Keel, George Segal, anyone who was anyone, all the big names. If you weren't rich, famous or glamorous – and preferably you would be all three – you wouldn't get through the door.

Constantine knew many film stars and singers, just as Max had done. They were pleased to appear in his clubs and to bestow extra kudos upon them. Those he didn't know – the up-and-coming talents, the great emerging beauties flaunting their fabulous bodies and eager to press the flesh of producers and directors – people like that, he paid. For a couple of grand and a few freebies they'd be there, spotting and being spotted, adding new-face charisma and a sprinkle of stardust to the already heady mix.

His clubs – like the other top London nightspots, Tramp and Annabel's – were always packed out with wealthy punters, and wealthy punters liked tight security, locally provided, right there on the spot. While Constantine did business here, his main base was New York. Rather than spread his own resources too thinly, he preferred to hire in native muscle – and, up until this point, that muscle had always been the Carters.

'Look,' she said quickly, 'have the Delaneys made you an offer?'

Constantine gave her a look. 'The Delaneys are always making me offers.'

'*Have* they? What did Redmond have to say to you when I met you at the hotel?'

'Okay. He said that whatever the Carter cut was, he'd halve it.'

Annie let out a breath. 'I bloody knew it,' she fumed. She looked at him. 'And you didn't buy that?'

Constantine shrugged. 'Max was always a good friend to our family, he honoured his business dealings with us and I'm returning the favour.'

'Although it's costing you.'

'Yeah. But that goes with the territory.' He looked at her shrewdly. 'The Delaney thing's still ongoing then? I know they've spent years trying to muscle in on Carter territory, and now Max and Jonjo are not on the scene, I guess they're thinking the coast is clear.'

'It's not clear,' she said. 'I've told them that.'

'Well, that's good. Because it's tough, being a boss. And doubly tough being a lady boss. People looking to shake you down. Thinking it's gonna be easy, you know?'

'It's not clear, okay?'

'Okay, so that's the business talk wrapped up. How is Layla?'

'She's fine,' said Annie.

'Good. That's good news.'

He stood up and came around the desk and leaned back against it, then hauled Annie to her feet with one hand. Startled, she found herself standing between his legs, pressed up tight against him, his arms around her waist. 'Can we now get on to what's really on our minds?' he asked.

'Like what?' asked Annie, although she knew.

Her blood was fizzing with desire; she'd wanted this for far too long. But her desire was tainted with unease now. What if he was lying, what if he'd already got into bed – in the business sense – with the Delaneys? What if he was her enemy, even while he *appeared* to be her friend?

'Like this,' said Constantine, and bent his head and kissed her. Her head reeled and pulse accelerated. After a couple of seconds, Annie pulled back, bunching her fists against his chest.

'Wait,' she said.

'*Wait?*' Constantine's expression was amused disbelief.

'You said something and I want to know what you meant.'

'When did I say something?'

'Outside the hotel. You said if you could find

the guts to face this thing, then so could I. What did you mean?'

'Right.' His eyes lost their spark of humour. He looked at her, smoothed his hands over her back. 'Listen to me. Five years ago I lost my wife Maria in a hit organized by a rogue soldier from one of the other New York families. He was aiming for me. He got her.'

'I know that,' said Annie.

'Yeah, but maybe you *don't* know what it's like to have that sort of guilt on your shoulders, uh? Anyway, what I'm telling you is, bad things can happen to people who come close to me.' His eyes were intense as they stared into hers. 'You know what I am. You know I'm telling you the truth.'

Maybe I don't even want to get close to you, she thought. *Maybe I don't dare.*

'I'm not afraid,' said Annie.

'There have been bad things done between the families. Terrible things. Thirty members of one family, wiped out in a vendetta. A boy of twelve killed, his body dissolved in acid. Getting scared yet?'

She was scared all right – scared of loving him, and discovering too late that he was a treacherous bastard.

'You're quiet,' he said when she didn't answer.

'I think you're on my side.' Annie was staring at him. 'So I've nothing to fear, have I?'

'You *think*?' He was looking at her curiously.

He was warning her of the dangers of involvement – but she wasn't even sure she wanted to get in any deeper. 'And I've got the boys. Max's boys,' she said. It was safer, better, to rely on them.

'I'm glad you said Max's,' said Constantine. 'Because they're still his, you know, not yours.'

Annie shook her head. 'No, that's—'

'Don't tell me it's not true, because it is. It's a tough world out there: men run it and you're a woman. Max's people will think you should remain loyal to him. To his memory, anyway. So if you're not – if you start something with me, for instance – although *you* know you're free to do so, they won't ever accept it. And trust me, they'll be annoyed. They'll see it as a betrayal.'

Annie said nothing. She knew he was right. She'd been thinking much the same herself.

'I'm going to be honest with you,' said Constantine. 'After we parted last time, I thought . . . no. I didn't want to go there. I'd already lost people I loved. I didn't want to risk that sort of pain again.'

Annie opened her mouth to speak.

'No, let me finish. But I kept thinking about you. And I realized that it was already too late, I was already involved. So I knew I had to go for it. And I hoped it wasn't too late, that I hadn't kept you waiting too long, that you had the balls to go ahead with this even though there could be dangers involved, there could be risks. You know what I really *didn't* want to happen?'

Annie shook her head.

'That you should feel grateful to me for anything I've done in the past. I didn't want your gratitude, and I didn't want you on the fucking rebound from Max either.'

He pulled her in and kissed her again, harder.

Annie melted. But again she pushed him away.

'And the problem this time is . . . ?' asked Constantine.

'Is Lucco going to walk in on us?' Annie remembered Constantine's oily dark-haired son sneering at her, warning her off, bursting in on them at every opportunity.

'Lucco's in New York,' said Constantine, pushing her back a step. He took her hand, looked at the ring on her thumb. Max's ring, with the Egyptian cartouches carved into the gold, the solid slab of lapis lazuli a gleaming pure blue. Looked at his own ring, gold with small diamonds scattered like stars. 'Listen, if I kiss your hand, will you kiss mine?'

Annie started to smile. He could always charm her. His charm was her weakness. 'Did you *seriously* think I'd kiss it?'

'Wanted to see how you'd react.'

'That's cruel.'

He shrugged, his eyes playing with hers. 'Hey, I can do cruel. If it turns you on.'

Annie was aware of her heart beating fast. Her cheeks felt hot, her nipples hard. They looked at each other and there was a hot crackle of sheer sexual need between them.

'Let's take this upstairs,' he said.

'No,' said Annie, digging her heels in. She wasn't sure about him. No *way* was she going to be rushed. She was determined to take things at her own speed.

He gazed steadily at her face. 'Okay. I'll wait. I'll do the whole courtship thing, if you want. Why not come to lunch on Tuesday, meet the family properly?'

'Oh shit, Constantine . . .'

'They don't bite.'

'Are you *sure*?'

He laughed. 'I'm not going to let this go,' he warned her. 'And this courtship thing? I won't be patient for too long.'

She knew it. He knew it.

'You need me,' he murmured, trailing his lips lightly over her mouth. 'You need me like a drug. And one day soon you're going to admit it to me – and to yourself.'

'You know what? You're an arrogant swine,' said Annie, but he was right, damn it.

'Yeah, and you like that,' he said with a smile. 'So let's get this thing rolling. Come to lunch.'

'Okay,' she said at last, and wondered what the hell she was getting herself into.

12

They'd been so happy together, so very happy – two survivors clinging on to the wreckage of life; but to the outside world they were winners – a glossy, polished couple so wrapped up in each other, so much in love. Or so Mira had thought.

They were voracious in their appetites. Redmond had a taste for the high life and he also had a taste for excess, and she matched him in that. They ate at the finest places, mixed with TV stars and peers of the realm . . . and then there was the sex: they gorged themselves on stupendous sex.

And then suddenly one day she realized she was late. She was overjoyed. She knew he would be, too.

'What do you mean, late?' Redmond asked her when she told him, smiling happily.

'Late.' Mira threw her arms wide, let out a laugh. 'As in, I could be pregnant.'

'Pregnant?' He stared at her. 'But you're on the Pill.'

'It's not one hundred per cent reliable,' she said. 'You know that.'

He did know it. She'd told him, but he'd said they'd chance it anyway. He hated to use condoms, he liked to be naked inside her: wearing a condom was like trying to scratch your toes with your boots on; he hated the things. He'd known this could happen. So why was he standing there, saying nothing, looking at her as if she was a stranger?

'It . . . doesn't have to be a disaster though, does it?' Mira said hesitantly, the smile dying on her face.

Redmond ran a hand through his hair. He was still looking at her in that peculiar way, like he was wondering what the fuck she was talking about.

'I mean,' she went on hopefully, 'we love each other. We could . . . have a family.'

He walked over to where she stood. Sunlight poured through the big picture window on to her golden, tousled hair. She was a vision of beauty. But . . . pregnant.

Redmond heaved a shaky sigh and ran a hand lightly down her cheek.

'Get rid of it,' he said. 'I'll pay.'

*   *   *

She couldn't believe that he had said that. Get rid of it. Just like that. Her child. Hers, and his. She was in love with this man. She had never been in love before but she was now. It had been instant-aneous, like a lightning strike. The minute she had seen Redmond across that dining room, she had felt her heart seize up in her chest. Kept on chatting, kept on flirting with that sweet doting old fool William, but all she could think, all she could feel – and oh God, how wonderful, how completely stupendous, to actually feel something at last – was that he was watching her from that nearby table, and all she wanted was to go to him, throw herself at his feet, say I'm yours, take me, do anything, I don't care.

It was love. Total, absorbing – and now despairing – love. Because he didn't want their child.

'I can't believe you said that,' she said, half smiling, nervous, disbelieving. 'You don't mean it?'

But he was nodding his head. His eyes were cold. Chillingly cold as he stared at her face.

'Of course I fucking well mean it.'

He actually shuddered. He looked . . . revolted. Disgusted by the very idea. Mira drew back, shrank into herself. He really meant it.

'I don't want children,' he said flatly. 'Not now. Not ever. I thought you understood that.'

But she hadn't. Cringing with pain at his rejec-tion of the child she carried, she backed away from him. Now he looked deeply irritated. Like an impatient stranger.

'*Look, I said I'll pay and I will. Book yourself into the best clinic. Don't worry about the expense. Let's get this over with.*'

Mira couldn't believe he had said that, either. She was a Catholic. All right, she hadn't attended church in years; she wouldn't dare. They'd have to sluice the church steps down with Holy Water if she walked up them. She knew she was a dirty bitch, a whore. Her family had made that clear. But at heart she was still the Catholic girl she'd been raised as. She still believed human life was sacrosanct.

The first time she'd had an abortion had been bad enough – a crime against God – and she knew she would burn in hell for it. But she had wanted to get rid of the thing, couldn't even think of it as a child; it was a thing her uncle had forced upon her, not a child. So she'd got rid of it and had tried never to think of it again.

But this was the child of the man she loved. The child of a man she had believed had loved her. How could he, if he could say that?

'*Get rid of it,*' *Redmond said again, as she stood there, open-mouthed.* '*I mean it.*'

And so, numb at heart, pierced through with pain, Mira had waited until he'd gone and then she'd found the number, picked up the phone, and dialled.

They were quite kind at the clinic, although the receptionist was frosty and looked at her as if she was scum. But then, she was used to that. It had long since ceased to offend her. She knew she deserved it. They asked her questions, then gave her the tablets, and told her to come back tomorrow. She went back to the flat and felt nauseous. Overnight, she spewed her guts up.

She got up next morning – he was away, on business – and dressed and went back to the clinic. Then came the part where she was laid out on a table with her feet in stirrups while they inserted things inside her. It was brief, uncomfortable – not painful. Then she went back to the flat.

Within two hours she was bleeding heavily, her womb cramping hard. Shuddering, sobbing with grief, she sat on the toilet as blood poured out of her along with the baby she was carrying.

When the worst of it was over, she flushed the loo. She didn't look. She didn't dare. What she had done was wicked, unforgivable. Just another sin in the long line of sins she had been performing all her adult life.

She took a bath, lay there in a state of shock and horror, watching the blood still seeping out from between her legs. Then she dried herself, inserted a tampon, and took the painkillers they'd given her. She crawled into bed and stayed there all through that day and into the next.

For Redmond, it was as if nothing had happened. He came back within a week, bearing gifts of perfume and a pearl necklace. She wondered if he had really been away on business at all. No, she thought he had just been lying low, keeping away from her. Getting all the unpleasantness out of the way before he came back and picked up precisely where they left off.

Only Mira found she couldn't do that.

Something had changed in her when she had killed their baby. The wild highs were not so pronounced for her now; the depths were deeper, bleaker than ever before. She sensed he was irritated by her low moods, but he made no comment and she was glad of that. He took her to bed again three weeks after the abortion, and they made love, but she couldn't reach orgasm and that annoyed him all over again.

'Concentrate,' he urged her, touching her, caressing her, but she felt frighteningly blank.

This was the man she loved. But he had told her to kill their child.

Finally Mira gave Redmond what he wanted. She faked her orgasm. He was satisfied. That night she turned her face into the pillow for the first time and, when she knew he was asleep, she wept for the child that they had killed, and for their love, which had also died that very same night.

13

At the Palermo, the builders got back from lunch at their usual time of one, ready to start work after a brew and a glance at the day's papers. They had left the place as a work in progress, had started white-washing the cellar, stripping the old flock paper off the walls upstairs, knocked down the old plaster, repainted the ceiling, refurbished the bar, dumped all those tired old velvet drapes and soft furnishings. The job was coming along pretty well and they were pleased.

Now it wasn't. And they weren't.

'Fuck it,' said the foreman as he went down the cellar steps and found himself standing in several inches of icy wetness. One of the pipes on the wall by his head was spurting water out on to the floor. It was soaking down here; the water level was rising even as he watched; it was a mess and a half.

'What happened?' asked his mate, clattering down the stairs behind him and peering down.

'Damned pipe's fucked,' said the foreman.

He looked at the pipe. It was old. These buildings were Victorian, beautifully built – he appreciated that because he was a craftsman, a master builder; he had an eye for a lovely old place like this, wished he could own such a place; no sodding chance.

An old lead pipe like that could easily weaken over many years and eventually spring a leak. A miracle it hadn't happened before, really. He frowned at the pipe. Touched a finger to the edge where the breach was. His frown deepened.

'These old pipes, they can go at any time,' said Gordy, his mate. 'Jeez, we're going to have to get a pump down here now.'

'Yeah,' said the foreman, and made a mental note that he was going to speak to the Carter boys right now. He didn't want to carry the can for this. This wasn't his doing and he *hoped* it wasn't his mate Gordy's doing either. He'd known Gordy a lot of years and he didn't think he was a fool. Not fool enough to start arsing about for a wedge of cash-in-hand, because the Carter firm were very strong on loyalty, and the lack of it would upset them. You didn't want to upset the Carter boys, ever.

'You locked up behind us, didn't you?' he asked Gordy. Gordy had been last out, after all. Tel had strolled ahead to the pub, leaving his old trusted working mate to lock the door. But *had* he locked the door? That was the question.

'Course I did. I always do, don't I?'

And the lock hadn't been breached. It had opened sweet as a nut when they'd come back from their pie and pint. Someone had a key, then – unless Gordy was lying through his yellow buck teeth. Either way, they were in the shit, and if this was Gordy's doing, then he was going to beat the crap out of the stupid little git for landing him in it.

'This pipe ain't worn,' he told Gordy, and he turned and grabbed Gordy by the front of his paint-stained boiler suit and shook him, hard. Gordy's beery eyes were suddenly wild with alarm. He lost his footing, slipped down a step or two. Tel leaned over him, bigger and stronger than he was – his old mate, he'd always thought, his *friend*, but now he looked mad as a cut snake. 'Did you do this, you silly bastard? Come on, own up.'

'I didn't do nothing, Tel,' bleated Gordy, shocked at the change in his old pal and drinking mate. Fuck, what had got into the old fart? One minute he was normal, the next he'd gone berserk.

Tel shook him again. Gordy's balding head clunked painfully against the cellar's dank wall and he let out a holler of protest.

'What happened, did the other lot slip you the

cash to cause trouble? That what happened?' demanded Tel furiously. 'You stupid sod, you don't arse around with people like this. We're responsible. We left this place and now we've got trouble and it's down to us.'

'I didn't do nothing,' said Gordy breathlessly. 'Honest, Tel. I locked the cunting door, I swear it. I didn't do nothing.'

Tel looked into Gordy's eyes. If he was lying, he was a good liar.

'I 'spect the pipe just gave way, age and that,' said Gordy hopefully.

'It didn't give way, you stupid fuck,' said Tel morosely. He looked at the water gushing out, shook his head. He released Gordy. No good taking it out on him, whatever had happened here. It was his responsibility, *he* was the foreman, *his* arse was going to be chewed off, not Gordy's.

Tel looked morosely at Gordy. 'This pipe's been cut through,' he said. 'And if *you* didn't do it, then who the fuck did?'

14

'Somebody,' said Gary Tooley, 'is taking the piss.'

That evening, Annie sat at the head of the table in the upstairs room in Queenie's house. Queenie had been Max's mother. She'd been dead some years now, but Max had never got around to selling the place, so the Carter mob still met there, just as they had always done. It was mostly empty, full of ghosts rather than furniture. Only a spare bed in the back room and the large table and chairs in this one remained.

Ghosts.

Annie listened to what Gary was saying, feeling like she had the weight of the world on her shoulders. Didn't she have enough going on, without this? For *instance*, there was Chris banged up and Aretha dead. For *instance,* there was Kath who'd given her a verbal arse-kicking over her tardiness in collecting Layla. And Kath was right, absolutely right, but still the rebuke had stung her to the marrow. She'd left Layla now with Dolly and Ellie, left her in a fucking *whorehouse,* but what else could she do?

Was she a bad mother? Was she putting her business concerns, her friends, her own needs before Layla's? And the thought of her *needs* led her mind straight to Constantine. She thought of her visit to see him, and his invite to lunch with the family. She'd wanted to refuse, but she'd accepted. Now she was having doubts. A lunch with him, fine. With his sons, though, and with Cara and maybe even snooty Gina too – total bloody *nightmare.*

She ought to be putting Layla first and she knew it. Layla had been traumatized enough by all that had happened to her: didn't she owe it to her daughter to be there for her as much as she possibly could be? There for her, as Constantine was for *his* kids, ready to drop everything at a moment's notice and pitch in to help?

But Annie had all this other shit to get through, things that she couldn't delegate, things that were taking up so much of her time, and how could she help that? There was, for instance, this latest thing, which was all she fucking well needed.

All the boys were in. Steve Taylor on her left hand, Gary Tooley on her right. Jackie Tulliver down at the bottom of the table like a sulky elf, puffing on a large Cuban cigar. Deaf Derek was in. Tony was in. The gang was all here. All except Jonjo and Max.

Annie pushed all thoughts of that aside. Max and his brother Jonjo were gone. Now, she was in charge. *Yeah, right,* she thought.

Constantine was right, being a lady boss was hard. Because even when she felt like her head was coming off from all the stress, she had to hold it together, to be *seen* to be rock solid, or the boys would say, see, didn't we say this would happen? You can't expect a woman to be strong enough to run a firm, it just ain't *natural.*

And what would they think if she cosied up to Constantine? She knew he was right about that too. The boys were loyal to the Carters, but mostly to Max's memory, not to the living, breathing Carter in front of them – because she was female. If they got wind of a sexual liaison between her and Constantine, they'd take a dim view of it, of course they would. What would they say about her then? That she liked the old pork sword too much, that she was a slag, that there was no way they could take orders from a tart like that.

So she had to keep her secrets.

Hold it together. *Dig deep and stand alone.* As per fucking usual. And now, this thing.

'You say the pipe was *cut?*' she asked Steve.

He nodded. Steve was just five feet eight inches

tall, and all muscle. He had a round, high-coloured face, hard mud-coloured eyes, dark hair and a permanent five-o'clock shadow. He could shave three times a day and still look like he could use another.

Steve had many talents, though. He could chop the air out of your lungs with a squeeze. He could clamp his fingers around your ankle and fell you in agony, like a cut oak. Get into a wrestling situation with him and he could get you in his infamous 'grapevine', wrapping his legs around yours with such force that he could snap your femurs like twigs. He was squat, powerful, and much feared on the manor. He was also fiercely loyal to the firm.

'Cut right through. Nothing to do with Tel, though, I'd stake my life on that,' Steve went on. 'I asked him about it. Kicked his arse all around his kitchen. His old lady went wild, chucked a frying pan at me, grease and rashers and all sorts of shit all over the place, but Tel was sound. Apologized, said he'd get it repaired on him, give us a discount on the job even though it's going to cost him more, you know, pumps and all that stuff – that's dear shit we're talking about.'

'What about the one who was supposed to have locked up?'

'Gordy? Not stupid enough to fuck us around.

I had a word. He swore he locked the door, wouldn't budge on the story. Think it's the truth.'

'Then who got in? Who did it? The lock wasn't breached,' said Annie.

'Ways and means to do that,' said Gary, pushing back his chair and stretching out his stick-thin legs. If Steve was squat, Gary was long, like a crane. Blond and pallid and skinny, with eyes as vicious as a shit-house rat's. 'Place is wide open. Builders in and out all day like they are.'

There was a silence. The club refurb was another bone of contention. It wasn't going to be the Palermo Lounge any more, it was being renamed 'Annie's'. Nothing had been said, but she felt the boys were resistant to the change. They had resisted the dropping of the dodgy stuff and the expansion of the security business, too. They resisted, in fact, any fucking thing she cared to suggest and she was getting sick of it.

Security! What a laugh. They were in the security business, and someone had easily breached the club, cut the pipe and flooded the cellars.

Fuck it.

'Can we spare some muscle to keep an eye on things?' she asked.

'What, just the Palermo?' asked Jackie.

'All three clubs.' Better to be safe than sorry.

'Yeah, just.'

'Okay, do that. You all know about what's

happened with Chris Brown and his wife Aretha?' asked Annie.

'Yeah, Boss, we know,' said Deaf Derek. He shrugged. 'You marry that sort of trouble, you're going to get *more* trouble, am I right?'

He looked around the table. They all looked back at him blankly.

'I'm just sayin',' he said, reddening.

'Well *don't* just say, cunt,' advised Jackie, puffing vigorously.

Annie shot a freezing glance at Derek. If it wasn't for his usefulness in keeping contact with all the grubby little lowlife bastards that crawled around this area, milking them for information about anything that was going down, Annie would have gladly seen him out the door.

'I want someone keeping an eye on Aretha's Aunt Louella,' she said. 'Make sure she's okay for money, but take it easy. She's a proud woman.'

All the boys nodded. This was the way the firm was run, since way back before Max was in charge, since the days when his dad had held pole position. The boys looked after their own. Widows were cared for, and orphans. Guys who came out of nick and were known to them were looked after, set back up on their feet. Pensioners were helped out all around the East End. Kids' hospitals and even boxing charities profited from the firm's business – Max and his brother Jonjo had been keen sportsmen in their youth, and Annie saw no reason to stop any of that. It kept youngsters in the East End on the right path to get a bit of boxing in.

There was still, despite the growing influx of drugs on to the streets, a strong code of ethics among the various firms who did business around the City – despite any villainy they might perpetrate. The rules were still clear-cut. You didn't steal off your own, you *never* interfered with other men's wives, ponces and dealers were treated with contempt, sex offenders were the lowest of the low and to be seen off with a good kicking.

'That's all for tonight, then,' said Annie.

Jackie took a folder out from under his coat and pushed it towards her. 'Laney gave me this for you. Said it was a bitch to get hold of,' he said.

Annie nodded. DS Lane had done a blinding job, and that was good. 'Okay then. I'll see you all later.'

One by one they filed out.

'Want me to wait in the car, Boss?' asked Tony.

'No, Tone.' She stood up, picked up the file. It wasn't going to make very pleasant reading, but it had to be done. 'Come on Tone. Let's go home.'

Annie sat up late into the night at the kitchen table in the flat over the club, reading about the other two murdered girls from the case notes that

DS Lane had filched from the police collating department, photocopied, and delivered to her through Jackie Tulliver.

Layla slept peacefully in the next room. The building was silent, empty of all life but them. Because of the sabotage on the building work, there was a guard outside the main door of the club now, sitting in his car, watching. Knowing he was out there made Annie feel just a bit more secure.

Just a bit.

Because here she was, reading about these two women who had once lived, laughed, loved, *breathed*. And then looking at photos of them, dead. Teresa Walker and Val Delacourt.

It was enough to make the hardest person on the planet shiver. Both white, whereas Aretha was black. Both based in the East End, like Aretha. Both garrotted. Like Aretha.

She read on, looking for anything that could link the three killings – anything other than the same method; knowing the police would already have done this, and done it far better too. But still, she had to look, she had to *try,* tired as she was, or Chris was stuffed.

They were prostitutes, all three of them. Working girls. *Tarts*. And maybe plod didn't care too much if three tarts got the chop. She, however, did. So she had to keep looking, even though the pictures made her gag and made her heart wrench with pity; even though she felt she was probably wasting her time.

A tiny part of her knew there was no hope, that Chris was finished. She ought to admit it. But she couldn't. It was as simple as that.

15

Goods were moving around London and up and down the country all the time. It was money on the hoof and, usually, if you had your fences lined up ready, those goods were easy to dispose of. If security was the Carter speciality, then lorry hijacking was the Delaneys'. It was lucrative and easy.

A load of brand-new car parts had vanished overnight on the road to Basingstoke, and were already being taken to where a price had been agreed for them. *Money for nothing,* thought Redmond Delaney.

He and his twin Orla were in the static office of the family's scrap-metal yard, having a celebratory whisky after a profitable day's business. The fact that the car-parts depot that their boys had robbed was on Carter soil just made the heist that much sweeter. The Carter firm would get hassle from their clients over security fees paid out for fuck all. So it was business and pleasure, all rolled into one.

It pissed Redmond off that the Barolli family were still proving resistant to his offers on the clubs, but it was a minor annoyance. He had been interested to see the interaction between Constantine Barolli and Annie Carter when they had chanced to meet at the Vista Hotel. Maybe there was more than a business interest going on there. He would look into that. Knowledge was power: that had always been Redmond's motto. He'd discussed his suspicions with Orla.

'You really think there could be something going on?'

Orla was sceptical. If Annie Carter was risking an affair with the Mafia boss, she was risking a great deal. Her own standing as Max Carter's widow, for a start. The Carter boys would take it badly if she betrayed Max's memory. She'd be tossed out into oblivion at the very least.

At that moment, Charlie Foster knocked on the door of the static and poked his head in. He had crew-cut pale brown hair, a blob of a nose and very light blue eyes that always seemed to be having a private joke – at someone else's expense.

'That fucking Carter cow's here, says she wants a word,' he said.

Both Redmond and Orla tensed.

Speak of the devil, and she appears, thought Orla.

'She's alone?' asked Redmond. 'You checked her over?'

Charlie had reason enough to be careful around Annie Carter. He'd just patted her down with his own stunted hand. He had only seven fingers to everyone else's eight, and that was down to Annie Carter. He'd love to get that high-toned bitch alone down a dark alley. In fact, he was determined to do just that, one of these days.

'She's got her boy with her. And she's not packing anything but a good set of knockers.'

Orla stifled a grimace of disgust. Charlie Foster was like a wild thing, partially tamed but never completely stable. She hated his leering, ever-smiling face and his pale predatory eyes that seemed to strip every woman he encountered – even her. He might be Redmond's right-hand man, but he was also a vicious thug without any conscience. He was dangerous. Redmond valued that, and used it. It made Orla nervous. She had a mental picture of him frisking Annie Carter down in the yard, and had to suppress a shudder.

'Show her in,' said Redmond.

Charlie opened the door wide. Not quite wide enough to let Annie Carter enter easily. She had to squeeze past him, and Charlie's smile told them all how much he enjoyed that. Tony the driver came in after, nudging Charlie out of the way. Charlie's cocky grin widened. He stayed there, the door wide open, listening and watching.

'Mrs Carter,' said Redmond, not standing up.

They hadn't changed, Annie thought. They were still beautiful, the twins, with their red hair and pale, clear skin – and still chilly as the Arctic tundra. Dangerous people. But you didn't ever show fear when you faced down a foe – Max had taught her that. Be cool, be confident, be in control. Never let them see you wobble; never let them see you bleed.

'What can we do for you?' asked Redmond, his voice just the same as she remembered, a cool Irish lilt, almost soothing, almost lulling you into a false sense of security. But you had to be on your guard with Redmond. Redmond was smart, and he didn't care who or what he flattened to get his way.

It had been a risk, coming here again. Tony hadn't been happy about it. But things had to be said, and she had to show them that she was not afraid to say them.

'You can back off from the Barolli club contracts,' said Annie flatly. She could feel nervous sweat trickling down her back but she spoke steadily, clearly. 'Constantine Barolli told me you offered to halve our charges.'

'Did he also tell you that he hasn't yet decided whether or not to accept our very generous offer, or to stay with the Carters?' asked Orla.

Annie looked at her. Once, she had thought Max was all wrong about these two. *Vipers*, he'd told her. *Never trust a Delaney.* Once, she had tried to convince Max that this feud was madness. But not now.

Now, she saw things as they really were. Now she could not forget that Billy Black had died in her arms, dragged through the streets behind a Delaney car, on *Redmond*'s orders, the skin flaying from his body, every bone getting broken and every muscle mangled.

She looked squarely at Orla. Gorgeous pale green eyes, a long patrician face. Oh yes, they were beautiful, the Delaney twins. Beautiful, Machiavellian, and deadly.

'He won't accept your offer,' she said flatly, although in her heart she wasn't sure of that. 'He's loyal to the Carter firm.'

'Is he?' Redmond asked her curiously. 'Or just to you?'

Annie sent Redmond a freezing glance, but her stomach was suddenly in a knot. *What* had made Redmond say that?

'Barolli's content to deal with the Carter firm because we've always given a good, solid, reliable service. And I'd appreciate it if you'd *back off*.'

They looked at her blankly. Orla sipped her whisky.

'I mean it,' said Annie, her heart thumping madly in her chest.

'We're really scared,' said Charlie Foster from behind her.

Annie turned her head and looked at his sneering face. 'You ought to be,' she said, and Tony lunged at him and had him by the throat in a split second.

Charlie let out a half-strangled yell. Tony hoisted him off his feet and glared into his eyes.

'You be careful what you say to Mrs Carter, you cocksucker,' he growled.

Annie turned and looked at the twins, sitting there at the desk.

'Back off from Barolli,' she said, and turned on her heel and walked out the door and down the steps and off across the yard to the gate.

Tony gave Charlie a last shake and dropped him. He sagged, clutching at the wall, gasping in breaths. Then Tony followed Annie out the door.

'*Fuckers*,' hissed Charlie, his perennial smile gone for once. His eyes following the pair of them with hate. He had unfinished business with Annie Carter. He watched her go out of the gate, and promised himself that, soon, he was going to *get* her. Get her *good*.

16

'Try this,' said Redmond, and he had given her a small brown bottle with white pills in it.

Mira took it listlessly.

She saw him looking at her, and knew what he was thinking – that she looked like shit, not like his bright, vibrant beauty at all, and he was annoyed at this; he liked things right. He'd told her that what she needed was pepping up, and he knew where to get things that would help. He'd got these from one of the suppliers his people knew on the street.

'What are they?' she had asked him, awkwardly aware of the big shadows under her eyes. Shit, she hadn't even thought to apply her make-up. It wasn't like her to let herself go this way.

'Just some uppers to give you a lift.'

'I'm not sure . . .'

Redmond had drawn her in close and kissed her.

Mira turned her head away, just a fraction, but she knew he noted it. Noted it, and was angered by it. She could see the anger in his eyes, could read his thoughts again. For fuck's sake, he was thinking, she'd had an abortion. Millions of women had abortions. There was no need to go to bloody pieces over it.

'What, don't you trust me?' he asked her. 'I'd only ever do what's best for you. You know that, don't you?'

Mira nodded warily.

'That's good,' said Redmond. 'You love me, yes?'

She had nodded again. She didn't, not any more. But he was holding her, his strong hands encasing her jaw, his fingers brushing her neck. He smiled his angelic smile and gazed into her eyes.

'That's good,' he said. 'You know that if you ever tried to leave me, I'd kill you, don't you?'

Oh Jesus, thought Mira. But again she nodded.

He let her go, satisfied. He fetched water from the kitchen. Sun had been streaming into the flat and Mira stood there in shit order, unwashed – she knew she smelled stale, she knew he wondered where his glitzy girl had gone, the one who was scrupulously clean and drenched in Shalimar. She looked down at herself and found, almost to her surprise, that she was wearing a tea-stained dressing gown, at four o'clock in the afternoon. What was happening to her?

'Here, take a couple now, you'll soon start to feel better,' he said, and took the bottle and shook some out onto his palm. He held them out to her. She put out her tongue, as helpless and trusting as a child. He placed them there, and she took the glass of water from his hand and washed them down.

'Good girl,' he said, and kissed her brow. 'Now go and get cleaned up, we're going out tonight.'

Mira was surprised, but by the evening she did feel slightly better. Less gloomy. More energized. Redmond was right, the pills were just what she needed to lift her out of this maudlin state she was in. Next morning she took two more, and then at lunchtime two more, and then at dinner she took another two. By that evening she felt so wide awake, so up that she couldn't sleep. At two o'clock in the morning she was pacing around the apartment, playing records and singing and drinking wine. When he told her to shut up and come back to bed, they had great sex, just like in the old days.

She no longer thought of it as making love. And she couldn't forget what he'd said about killing her if she left him. She knew he meant it.

* * *

The uppers were great. They made Mira forget all her woes, but they also made her frenetic, jittery. The lack of sleep was the worst bit; she'd twitch and turn over, disturbing him, making him impatient with her. So Redmond brought her some downers, and she took them in the evening and was at last able to sleep properly again.

The problem was, she slept so heavily that she awoke feeling as if she'd been hit with a brick until she got the first uppers down her at break-fast – not that she ate much, her appetite seemed to have more or less gone – and then she was okay. Mira started to look forward to her first fix of the day, when her spirits would lift, when she would start to feel more like her old self again.

Redmond had changed too after the abortion. Sometimes he lost his erection, and then he got angry with her, blaming her, and then one particular Sunday night – she would never forget it – when it happened again, he rounded on her in fury.

'It's your fucking fault,' he roared. 'What's the matter with you?'

And then he hit her.

Struck her full across the face, then when she screamed and recoiled he rolled over on top of her and his hands locked around her throat.

'Bitch,' he said, and she froze, not daring to move in case he squeezed the life out of her. 'Whore,' he hissed against her mouth, and she felt his cock rising against her thigh. He nudged her legs roughly open and this time he stayed erect. He pushed into her furiously, rode her, finished in record time. Then he rolled off her and she gulped in a breath and lay there staring at the ceiling, thinking: He called me a whore.

He had never, ever called her that before.

There was a silence.

Then he said: 'I'm sorry,' and moved and was leaning over her. She kept very still. She could see his eyes glinting in the semi-darkness; see his teeth flashing in a smile. 'Sorry, darling. But I like to do that sometimes, don't be too shocked by it. I seem to enjoy it.'

He enjoyed calling her a whore and hitting her and putting his hands around her throat? She was shocked.

But now Redmond was cuddling her close, saying he was sorry, that she was wonderful, that she was his and that he would never, ever let her go, and she could see that she ought to object, ought to maybe call this off, stop it dead.

It was dead already.

She didn't love him any more: how could she when he had made her kill their baby?

But she'd taken her pills before bedtime, and she felt so listless, so exhausted, that she said nothing, and soon she dropped off to sleep, still wrapped in her rapist's arms.

17

Annie had learned from the stolen case notes that Teresa Walker, one of the murdered girls, had worked part time as an escort; but her *real* job had been as a stripper, doing lunchtimes and evenings – and some private dancing in between – with the punters at the Alley Cat strip club in Soho.

Teresa had been an enterprising sort of girl. She hadn't worked for an agency; she had merely touted her own business in the club, which hadn't gone down too well with management.

The following evening, when Annie got into the car, Tony folded his paper away with unusual swiftness, almost as if he didn't want her to see it.

'Something in the paper I should know about, Tone?' she asked with a sigh.

God, please don't give me any more trouble, she thought.

Short of the sky falling on her head, she didn't know what else could go wrong. She had a gutful to contend with, and now Steve and Gary had told her that a lorry working out of a car-parts depot that the firm protected had been robbed on the Basingstoke road, making the Carter security boys look like a bunch of useless tossers and costing them a lot in compo.

Delaneys, she thought. Truck heists were their thing. *Yeah – but try proving it.*

Tony handed the paper back to her and she looked at the front page. The headline shrieked at her: '"SCARLET WOMEN" KILLER STRIKES AGAIN.'

'Shit,' she said.

'I know,' agreed Tony.

Annie threw the paper down in angry disgust. It was so easy to point the finger, to disdain the girls who got into the game, to sneer and come over all superior and judgemental.

Yeah, she thought bitterly. *And to use their tragedies to make juicy headlines.*

But maybe these women were just more desperate and more alone in the world than other, luckier girls. Maybe they didn't have the softening, civilizing cushion of a caring family or ready money to keep them from the game.

Tony drove Annie over to Dolly's to drop off Layla for the evening – Kath was rebelling, saying *no way* – and then took her on over to Soho and went with her into the subterranean depths of the club. What they found there reminded Annie of what had been happening to the Carter clubs in the absence of Max.

Topless girls were everywhere, serving overpriced drinks to semi-drunk and furtive-looking punters who skulked at tables in the half-dark. There was a small, semicircular stage on which two tired-looking girls gyrated in a simulation of lesbian sex, to the strains of Jane Birkin and Serge Gainsbourg murmuring their way through '*Je t'aime . . . moi non plus*.'

The two girls wore silver thongs and nipple tassels, nothing else. They looked as though they'd done the rounds and then some, and were bored to tears. Annie felt the same, just watching them. But she glanced around the room and saw that the punters seemed fascinated.

Men. *So* easy to please.

She exchanged a look with the manager, who sat at the small round table with her. The manager was Bobby Jo, a six-and-a-half-feet-tall drag act, tricked out right now in a tight-fitting gold lamé dress and a huge red wig. Bobby's heavily made-up face and spidery false eyelashes would give you a hell of a fright if you came across him in a dark alley.

Bobby Jo didn't own the club, he just managed it. Gave the punters what they wanted.

'Which is very often lesbian action, as you see,' he told Annie with a light shrug. 'I know, it's a mystery.'

Annie nodded. Several tables away, Tony was reading his paper. He glanced up occasionally, checked out Annie and Bobby Jo, checked out the lesbian action, shook his head gently, got back to the paper. One of the girls, a hard-eyed brunette, was glaring at him.

'Can you tell your man not to read the paper? It looks bad. It upsets the girls, and that don't take a lot, believe me. Plus, we don't want to give the punters the impression that the acts are boring, now do we? Not at the prices we charge.'

Annie caught Tony's eye, nodded at the paper, shook her head. With a sigh, Tony folded the paper and slipped it inside his jacket.

'Thanks,' said Bobby Jo.

'So tell me about Teresa.'

'I've done all this with the Bill,' said Bobby Jo.

'Yeah, but you've heard about the latest case?'

'The black girl done up West? Yeah, I heard. Fucking shame.'

'Friend of mine.'

'Oh?' The ferocious painted mouth turned down in an expression of sympathy. 'Sorry.'

'Thanks. So tell me.'

Bobby Jo told Annie about Teresa's enterprising spirit, that she had been caught on several occasions handing out business cards ('Fucking *business* cards, I ask you, that girl') in the club, advertising her services as an escort.

'I mean you don't do that, do you? Work for one business and set yourself up in another, in the business's time? Ain't that unethical or some fucking thing?'

'Yeah.' Annie wondered how much these girls got paid for parading up there on the stage pretending they were batting for the other side. Not much, she guessed. A little more wedge would come in dead handy. A little sideline – keep the wolf from the door. Sadly, Teresa's little sideline had got her killed.

Annie looked at Bobby Jo. A big, lean man in women's clothing. Bobby Jo was narked with Teresa because she'd been promoting her own business on his firm's time. Maybe his boss had leaned on him to come down hard on her, and somehow it had got out of hand? But again, why go so far as to kill her? A sharp warning, maybe. Even the sack. But a terminal solution? No. And there were two other girls who'd gone the same way. Val Delacourt and Aretha. Which suggested someone who was developing a distinct pattern, not a one-off. Didn't it?

'She get on with everybody, did she?' asked Annie. 'Any cat-fights? I know what these girls can be like.'

Bobby Jo gave a low rumble of smoker's laughter. 'I've had the filth crawling all over the place asking me all this. Big tall bloke, dark hair, face like an undertaker.'

'Hunter,' said Annie.

'That's the one. I'll tell you what I told him. These girls always have enemies. They scrap like wild dogs over the best-paying punters. They worry over who's got the best tits, the flattest stomach. There's no sisterhood in *here,* my dear. Far from it.'

A weary-looking hostess came wobbling over on ridiculous heels and put their drinks on the table. Orange juice for Annie, a bottle of Krug in a bucket of ice for Bobby Jo.

'Perks of management,' he said, pouring the champagne and giving the girl a wink as she departed. He held the bottle up. 'Sure I can't tempt you?'

Annie shook her head.

'Your loss.'

'What about her friends?'

'Teresa? She didn't do friends. She was a chippy little cow, rubbed everyone up the wrong way.'

'She must have. After all, someone went and killed her.'

Bobby Jo was looking at Tony, sitting there peacefully watching the act.

'I like the muscle,' he said to Annie. 'Thinking of getting myself a minder.'

'What, you think you need one?' Annie sipped her juice.

Bobby Jo turned back to her. His perfect teeth flashed in a shark-like grin. His eyes were like little black stones behind the dense false eyelashes.

'These are dangerous times,' he said. 'People getting themselves killed, what's the world coming to? It makes a person nervous. You want to watch yourself, Mrs Carter, poking around in this sort of thing.'

'I'll bear that in mind.' Annie finished her juice and stood up, thinking that she really didn't like Bobby Jo at all – in fact he gave her the creeps.

Tony rose too.

'Thanks for the refreshments, Bobby Jo. If you hear anything of interest, let me know. You've got my number,' she said.

'Sure,' said Bobby Jo, and sank some more Krug.

Half an hour later, Annie was sitting in Teresa Walker's mother's front room. It was shabby, dated, but very clean. Teresa's mother was obviously poor, but proud. Like Aretha's Aunt Louella. Also, like Louella, this woman looked totally crushed by what had happened.

Teresa's mother had long, faded and brittle-looking red hair, a skull-like, careworn face, and pale denim-blue eyes that looked washed to grey by all the tears she'd shed. Tatty old slippers on her feet. Shapeless clothes hanging off her tall, thin frame. A woman who'd had the shit well and truly kicked out of her.

There were pictures up on the mantelpiece above the bare hearth – pictures of a big laughing girl with a shock of red hair. Teresa certainly wouldn't have looked like that now. Not after some lunatic had got hold of her.

Annie introduced herself and sat down opposite Mrs Walker. Tony was waiting outside in the car. The woman picked up a Bible from the arm of the chair and clutched it tightly, constantly stroking her bony fingers over it.

'Mrs Walker, I need to know everything you can tell me about Teresa,' said Annie.

'I went through all this with the police.' Mrs Walker sat opposite Annie and looked at her in confusion. 'Are you connected to the police?'

'I'm not connected to the police, Mrs Walker. There have been three . . .' Annie suddenly found she couldn't bring herself to say *murders*, not in front of this poor broken woman who looked as if insanity was only a moment away. '. . . *incidents* like the one involving Teresa. The last one involved a friend of mine. I want to find out who did this horrible thing. I don't want to hear about anyone else having to go through the same thing that me and you are going through right now. I'm in a position to look into these things, let's just say that.'

'You said your name was Carter?' Her expression was suddenly agitated. 'Oh my God. You're one of *those* Carters,' said Mrs Walker. 'You're to do with them gangsters.'

'The Carter family look after their friends, Mrs Walker. Always.'

Mrs Walker jumped to her feet. The Bible hit the floor. She looked frantically down at it, then at Annie. In that moment, she looked truly demented; the grief was eating her soul like a cancer.

'No! No, it was by associating with people like you that Teresa ended up as she did.'

'That's not true, Mrs Walker,' said Annie.

'I want you out of my house! You and your kind never do anything for nothing. I know how it all works,' said Mrs Walker.

Annie stood up.

'Mrs Walker, if I can find out who killed your daughter, and Val Delacourt, then—'

'*That* little tramp.'

'You know Val Delacourt?' Annie's attention sharpened. 'She didn't work with Teresa, did she?'

'No, she didn't. Not at that disgusting place run by that *weirdo*. Oh, I knew all about that place, don't you worry. Teresa thought she'd get into glamour modelling by working there. I told her it was beneath her, but she wouldn't listen.'

'Then where do you know Val from?'

'She's one of the Delacourt tribe.' Now Mrs Walker's bony little face was full of contempt. '*Everyone* around here knows the Delacourt family, and it's no surprise one of *theirs* came to grief, believe you me.'

But one of yours did too, thought Annie. She didn't say it.

'They live in the next street,' said Mrs Walker, sniffing and folding her arms. She told Annie which number. 'Rough lot. Bringing the whole area into disrepute. *Horrible* people.'

Annie said the address. She remembered it from the case notes that Lane had supplied her with.

'That's the place,' said Mrs Walker. 'Although I wouldn't go round there, if I were you.'

'Can you tell me anything else about Val?'

'Only that she's a whore,' said Mrs Walker.

Annie cocked her head questioningly. 'You mean that she worked the streets?'

Mrs Walker nodded emphatically. 'With her own brother as her pimp. That family's no good. Robert. Peter. Val. They're all bad.'

On the way back to Dolly's, Annie asked Tony to cruise past the Delacourt house. It was a pebble-dashed estate house almost identical to Mrs Walker's, but there the similarity ended; this house was grimy and the windows were dressed with filthy nets. A threadbare settee had been dumped out on what passed for the front lawn. A dog barked constantly from inside. A big one, by the sound of it. All the lights were on. There was a heavy, constant thump of a boom box from within.

'Nice place, Boss,' sniffed Tony.

'You know the Delacourts?' asked Annie.

'No.'

'We'll call tomorrow,' said Annie, and Tony drove on, back to Dolly's.

Layla was at the kitchen table, filling in her colouring book. Dolly was there with her. The kitchen door was closed, but Annie could faintly hear sexual activity from upstairs, grunts and gasps of pleasure. Ross was on the door. It wasn't right, leaving Layla here, and Annie knew it, but Kath would have burst a blood vessel if she had asked her to baby-sit again so soon.

Layla grinned up at Annie in delight when she came in. Guilt crushed Annie's guts in a vice.

Her darling little daughter. Max Carter's child. And all the more precious for that, because she had loved him so very much. The merest touch from Max had raced through her veins like a drug. And then she thought of Constantine – glossy, polished, alluring Constantine. She felt the same high, the same delicious giddiness she had known with Max, whenever she was near to him, and it worried her. She *couldn't* afford distractions like that, not right now.

'Mummy?' said Layla, as Annie and Dolly exchanged glances over her innocent head.

'Yeah, darling?' said Annie, ruffling Layla's silky hair.

'What's a whore?'

'Well, you can't wonder at her picking up things,' Dolly said when Annie turned up at her place next morning, having spent a lousy night churning everything around, unable to rest.

'Not things like *that*, for Christ's sake,' said Annie. She pulled out a chair and slumped down at the kitchen table, bumping against Ellie's bucket. Ellie gave her an exasperated look.

Annie gave her a look right back.

'Do you *really* have to do that right now?' she demanded.

'Listen, don't get all stroppy with me, *I'm* not the one who leaves her child in a knocking-shop and then bawls the place down when the poor kid picks up a fruity phrase or two.'

'Shut the fuck up, Ellie.'

'Well pardon *me*. And what nice language to hear from a *mother*.'

Ellie was right. She couldn't keep dumping Layla on Dolly, and she couldn't keep on dumping her on Kath either. Layla came skipping in from the hall, trotting around in Ellie's wake as she mopped the floor.

'Layla, honey, don't get in Ellie's way,' Annie sighed.

'It's all right. I don't mind her,' said Ellie, chucking Layla under the chin indulgently. 'You're a little sweetie, ain't you petal?'

Rosie came hurrying through in a leather mini and see-through white chiffon blouse with no discernible bra underneath it. She clocked Dolly standing there drinking tea, Ellie mopping, Annie at the kitchen table and Layla skating around the room, slipping and sliding, having a great time.

'It's like Clapham Junction in here,' she said with a lazy grin, throwing a flirtatious smile over her shoulder at Ross, who was sitting in the hall beside the front door, waiting for punters.

Ross winked at her and grinned right back.

Jesus, this was *no* place for a child.

'I've gotta go,' she said, and scooped up Layla and hustled her out of the door, passing a semi-dressed, dark-haired and sharp-faced Sharlene in the hall, giggling with an older man who was just coming downstairs doing his shirt up.

Back at the club, she found chubby, vile-smelling DS Lane waiting for her, his white nylon shirt stained yellow under the armpits, smoking a fag and chatting to the workmen who were trying to hoist the new sign into place.

Annie glared at him. He stank of stale sweat. Jeez, didn't the noxious bastard *ever* take a bath?

'What the hell do you want?' Annie asked, glancing sideways to where Layla was still sitting in the car, chatting excitedly to Tony.

'Phewee, who bit *you* up the arse this morning?' he enquired.

Christ, she thought. Bent coppers with body odour, prostitutes in see-through blouses and now workmen who stormed past her and vanished into the club, saying they couldn't get on because 'the effing plaster' hadn't arrived on time.

They brushed past her and Lane, gaily calling each other cunts and stomping around inside in their hobnail boots. This wa*sn't* the right atmosphere to bring a child up in either, and she was going to have to do something about it pronto.

'Well?' she prompted Lane in agitation.

'I gotta take those files back. Someone's noticed they're gone.'

Annie swallowed her pride and her reluctance to be parted from Layla. She phoned her sister Ruthie, who was living over in Richmond, to ask if she would look after Layla for a while.

'How long's a while?' asked Ruthie.

'Two, three weeks?' guessed Annie, and explained what was going on.

There was a pause. Annie could picture Ruthie there at the other end of the phone, her neat blonde hair, her kind and unremarkable face. A lovely woman, Ruthie. A *good* woman, and Annie needed her now.

'I know I shouldn't ask, I know I've no right to,' she hurried on.

'Oh, don't come over all humble, it don't suit you.' Annie could hear the laughter in her voice. 'Course I'll look after her.'

And so it was arranged, as easy as that: Tony drove her and Layla and all Layla's things over to Ruthie's. All Annie's anxieties were resolved when Ruthie opened the door. Ruthie had two kittens, and Layla was instantly entranced, but she still cried and clung to Annie when she had to leave. There were tears in Annie's eyes too, as Ruthie hugged Layla and told her that Mummy had business to see to, it would be fine, it wouldn't be for long, and could Layla help her name the kittens?

Annie kissed her daughter goodbye, and walked away with tears streaming down her face. Things had to be sorted out, and that couldn't happen until she knew Layla was safe. But Jesus, it hurt to be parted from her. It hurt like hell.

18

Next day Tony drove her over to Dolly's place.
Ross was already at his station by the door. Tall
dark Sharlene and cute blonde Rosie were in the
kitchen helping Dolly get the buffet organized.
Ellie was in there too, polishing the top of the
stove and wearing her pale blue overall that
bulged open over her curvy torso in all the wrong
places.

'Hi, all,' said Annie.

There were muttered greetings from all around.
Ellie was slumped at the kitchen table, looking
unhappy and doing what she always did in times
of crisis – digging into the biscuit tin.

Dolly, who had been leafing through her note-
book and having an increasingly heated conversation
about who was going out tomorrow night and
who was not with Sharlene and Rosie, paused and
looked across at Annie. Then she went on: 'Look,

nobody's taking the fucking booking, don't go getting all antsy about it, either of you. After what just happened to poor bloody Aretha? No escort jobs, not now. I mean it.'

'But Rosie's already taken the damned booking,' whined Sharlene, who was always up for an argument about anything.

'Well, she shouldn't have,' said Dolly. 'Even if she *did*, she should have got a contact number. Don't I always tell her to get a contact number so that we can call the client if we need to? Did you in fact *do* that small thing, Rosie?'

Rosie looked petulant. 'No,' she admitted.

'Oh for God's sake. Then we're going to have to let the punter down. And that's an end to it, okay?'

They both nodded.

'And Ellie,' said Dolly, 'put your bloody face straight, will you? And will you stop eating those fucking things? I know you're upset about Chris, but you're just going to have to accept it. I know you like Chris, but it looks as if he did it.'

Dolly's easy acceptance of the situation irritated the hell out of Annie. She would never understand it. She frowned as she thought of the mess Chris was in. He was banged up right now, awaiting trial. And her conversations with Jerry hadn't filled her with optimism for Chris's chances of escaping a substantial stretch.

And Dolly's ready to just accept all this shit? she thought angrily.

'Look, his brief's on it,' Annie told Ellie, trying to give the poor mare some comfort. She didn't look at Dolly; she was bewildered and offended by Dolly's attitude towards the shit-load of trouble that was hitting poor Chris right between the eyes. 'And he's a bloody good man, Jerry Peters – the best.'

Sharlene and Rosie were still bitching cheerfully over who would have taken the booking up West tomorrow night.

'I told you,' said Dolly sharply. 'Neither of you's going to take it, so pipe down the pair of you.'

And then a black tornado came bursting in the front door, barging through into the hall, nearly knocking Ross clean off his feet before he recovered and got to grips with this spitting mad apparition.

It was a stocky black woman of middle years, all heaving chest and huge arms and mad-crazy eyes. Ross grabbed hold of her, and she kicked and lunged, and then she spotted Annie watching slack-jawed with surprise from the open kitchen doorway.

'*You!*' she yelled, and struggled afresh. Ross was half grinning now, tickled by this demented woman's mad efforts to break free of his grip. His amusement was making the woman even madder.

'Ross!' Annie called out.

Ross looked up, almost laughing.

'Let her go. It's okay.'

Ross released Louella. She straightened her clothes and put her hat back on from where it had been knocked askew. Like a bull approaching a matador, she charged on along the hall. All the women in the kitchen except Annie drew back a bit. Louella came thundering into the kitchen.

Aunt Louella was holding a wad of fivers in her hand. When she got up close to Annie, she threw the notes into her face. Annie flinched. Notes fluttered. Rosie and Sharlene restrained themselves admirably and didn't make a dive for them.

'Hey!' shrieked Louella. '*Here's* what I think of your dirty money, girl. I tol' you I wanted nothing from you people. You think I'm not serious; you think I don't mean what I say? You think I *frightened* by those boys of yours, comin' around my house tellin' me to be grateful, to take this, to do that, that I oughtta show respect, that I oughtta take it and shut up?'

Annie stood there and let Louella get it all out. One of the boys had obviously got over-zealous in his efforts to help her out and had forced money on her. Annie guessed at Deaf Derek, the silly fucker.

'Excuse me,' said Dolly, getting steamed up on

Annie's behalf. 'Don't go coming in here shouting the odds . . .'

'And *you*.' Louella turned, glaring, to Dolly. Her eyes swept with disdain over the neatly dressed madam, then over the thinly clad pair of girls standing there, open-mouthed, enjoying the fight. 'You think I don't know what happens here, what bad people you are? You should be *ashamed*.'

'All right, that's enough.' Now Dolly was good and mad too. 'I don't have to take this. Ross!'

Ross came along the hall to the kitchen. Annie held up a hand and he stopped in the doorway, giving her a look that was half sneer, half question.

'Hey, you and your trained *ape* don't frighten me,' said Louella. 'It's because of people like you that my little girl's gone from me. It's people like *you* caused all this, luring her with your filthy money into this bad life.'

Louella's eyes were suddenly full of tears. She stepped up close to Annie and yelled full in her face: 'You want to have your boys work me over 'cos I've refused to take your dirty stinking money? Well, go ahead! They can't hurt me any more than I hurt already.'

The tears spilled over and now she was sobbing.

'My little girl, she was all I had and I lost her early on. I know I should have tried harder to stop her going to the bad but I didn't and that guilt I just gotta live with,' she cried. 'You think I afraid of what you'll do to me? I ain't afraid. God's my only judge, Annie Carter, not *you*.'

Louella raised her meaty fist and waved it in Annie's face.

'I don't know what to *do*,' wailed Louella suddenly. 'Vengeance is for the Lord, not for me. Yet I feel this *anger*. I want to hurt someone, beat someone, and that ain't right.'

Annie thought back to how she had felt when someone had snatched her whole life out from under her nose. She had wanted to lash out, to hurt, to maim.

'I know,' she said quietly. 'I know, Louella.'

'I don't know what to *do*,' Louella repeated hopelessly, her shoulders shaking with great, grief-stricken sobs.

Annie took a breath. After a moment's hesitation she moved a step forward. Tentatively, she put her arms around Louella's shoulders. The big woman stiffened for a second, then all at once she relaxed and cried hard. Annie hugged her, rocked her like a mother with a sick baby.

'I know, Louella,' she murmured, holding the shaking woman tight. Her eyes met Dolly's over Louella's head.

Dolly was nearly crying too. She'd loved Aretha. They all had; they were all hurting.

'I'll put the kettle on,' said Dolly. 'Ellie, get Louella a seat.'

In the kitchen it was warm, cosy and safe. Out there, a killer lurked. Annie knew it. She and Ellie settled Aretha's Aunt Louella at the kitchen table, brought her tissues, biscuits, tea. Rosie and Sharlene made themselves scarce. Ellie and Dolly joined Annie and Louella at the table.

'At least they got him, they've charged him with my baby girl's murder,' Louella said when she'd calmed down a bit.

Annie looked at Dolly, who looked away. She knew Dolly's take on this; Chris was guilty. End of story.

Annie looked next at Ellie, whose mouth had opened to protest. She shook her head and Ellie's mouth shut like a clamp. The police might have charged Chris but, like Ellie, Annie was convinced they had the wrong man. But this was not the time to start in on *that* again, not with Louella here.

'They've released her body,' said Louella.

'Oh,' said Annie, and drank tea, trying to warm up the film of ice that seemed to have formed over her heart. She thought of her friend Aretha lying dead because some pervert had taken it into his head to kill her.

'She's in the Chapel of Rest.'

'Have you been to see her?' asked Dolly after a beat.

The big black woman shook her head.

'I wanted to. Couldn't face it alone. I just couldn't,' she moaned.

'We'll come with you,' said Annie. 'Pay our respects. If you want to go?'

Louella looked at Annie, then at Dolly. She'd cursed them both a few minutes ago, called them bad people. Her dark eyes were full of hurt and suspicion. But she nodded cautiously.

'Yeah,' she said. 'All right. I'd appreciate that.'

Annie made a mental note to kick Deaf Derek's stupid arse up between his shoulder blades next time she clapped eyes on him.

19

First it had been the uppers: they had made Mira
feel so much better, had blurred the edges of her
pain, lifted her, repaired her shattered spirit even
though they ruined her appetite. She'd lost weight.
She could feel her ribs sticking out. She felt self-
conscious about that.

Then the downers, the wonderful downers, had
made her sleep without dreaming; she hated to
dream, her dreams were nightmares, technicolour,
hideous: she was pleased to be free of them at
last. But for every plus there had to be a minus.
She awoke every morning feeling vile, hung over,
and when she looked in the bathroom mirror she
saw that her skin had lost all its youthful bloom
and that her hair was dull. No amount of pamper
treatments and visits to the salon seemed to make
it any different, either.

'Try some of this,' Redmond said one evening

when they were laid out on the couch watching television, and put a line of white powder on to the glass top of the coffee table. He rolled up a ten-pound note and handed it to her and said: 'Just sniff it in. It's amazing.'

She was in a happy mood. She'd taken her tablets and they'd drunk a full bottle of champagne between them; she felt good. She felt good because she refused to think about anything, and the pills made it so much easier not to think. The sex between them, for instance. It had become increasingly experimental, veering into sadomasochism, stuff she didn't like, stuff that frightened her, and she wouldn't think about that, she refused to think about it, how it turned Redmond on when he hurt her, she just took her pills and felt good.

She took the little rolled note from him, leaned forward, inhaled the powder.

Suddenly, Mira felt like God.

Nothing was beyond her. Everything was possible. She looked in wonderment around the room, and saw that every colour was brighter, crisper; that he was more beautiful than ever, his hair like flames, the sheen on his white skin like alabaster, his eyes the brilliant pale green of fresh limes.

'Oh . . . oh shit . . .' she murmured, staring around her with eyes new born.

He was smiling benevolently. 'You like that,

darling?' he said, and trailed a hand down her bare arm.

It was ecstasy; she shivered and half closed her eyes, it felt so good.

Redmond leaned forward and kissed her, his tongue playing with hers. She felt hotly aroused in an instant, as if she was going to come right then and there. She leaned into his kiss; he unzipped himself, and pushed her head down; he was so beautiful, she kissed his rigid cock rising from its nest of red pubic hair and then did what he so loved her to do, and then she paused and looked up at his face, his exquisite, wonderful face, as handsome as an angel's, and he was holding a square of what looked like soft rubber over his nose and mouth, the material flattening out on his face as he struggled to breathe against it.

'Keep doing it,' he said, his voice muffled, gasping. He closed his eyes. His erection was huge now. Feeling drunk, feeling ecstatic, feeling high, Mira turned her attention back to his straining cock and did what whores did best.

'It's just a dental dam,' he said later as they lay entwined in bed. 'It makes it . . . more enjoyable. It enhances my orgasm. You should try it.'

Redmond had already had his hands around Mira's neck during sex. He had already beaten her.

The thought of him holding a square of rubber over her nose and mouth while they copulated did not excite her. But that thrilling white powder was still coursing through her veins, making her reckless, invincible.

'Do it then,' she said, and he did.

It was frightening, and arousing. He was right. They did it often, after that.

He never touched the white powder, but she did. She began to look forward to it. She started to look for it, to ask for it. It made her feel so good. Her weight kept going down and her appetite vanished. Her hair grew lank and her skin was dull and erupted in sores and spots. But she kept asking for the powder, and he said if she did what he wanted, let him put the dental dam over her nose and mouth while they fucked, let him have his hands around her throat while they did it, let him call her Bitch and Whore and slap her a little, just a little, then he would keep the supply coming.

'Anything,' she said, and led him to the bedroom, and did it just as he wanted it, the dental dam over her nose and mouth, his cock pumping hard inside her – he never lost his erection when they did it this way – and his hands clasping her throat, harder and harder as he got close to orgasm, harder and harder until he came, and she passed out.

'Darling?' He was tapping her cheek when she came round, wondering where she was, what had happened to her. 'Jesus, that was fucking wonderful,' said Redmond, falling back on to the bed and putting the rubber over his nose and mouth to see how soon he could get erect again.

It was then that Mira knew she had to get out of this, no matter what he'd threatened to do if she ran out on him – because if she didn't then she knew that he was going to go too far, and kill her anyway.

And so one day Mira packed up everything she owned and left Redmond. She had no idea where she was going, but she knew she had to get away from him before it was too late. She had some uppers in her bag, and a few downers, and a little nose candy too, although that was giving her a few problems, a few little nosebleeds, but she had enough to keep her going for a few days.

Finally she booked into a little B & B in Soho – several took one look at her and turned her away – not giving her own name, because she knew he would try to find her. If he found her then she was dead, and although she was low, tired and confused, she did not want to die.

But then she ran out of uppers, and then the downers were all used up, and soon the nose candy too, because she seemed to need more and more *of it just to achieve the same effect. The owner of the B & B wasn't too fussy, but when he found her convulsing and throwing up in the hallway, he drew the line.*

'Get your stuff and get out,' he said, his face twisted with disgust. 'Filthy junkie.'

For that was what she had become – a filthy junkie. Almost longingly, Mira thought of the luxury flat, the endless supply that never dried up. Nothing ever dried up when Redmond was around. She knew he was into all sorts of dodgy deals, although he had never discussed his business with her. Instant gratification was the name of the game when he was there to look after her. An ordinary man, a normal man, would say wait when she asked for something – a fur, a car, anything she desired; but he would always get it for her, straight away – whatever it was.

He would get her the drugs if she went back right now.

She knew it. She was almost desperate enough to do it. Almost.

But worse than the desperation was the fear of what he would ultimately do to her. She thought back to those choking, awful moments with the rubber thing over her face, his hands around her throat, and knew that she had done the right thing.

No. She daren't go back. He'd be furious that she'd walked out on him. God knew what he would do to her. She shuddered with fear at the very thought.

But, somehow, she had to get some stuff.

She had no family to turn to and she had no friends from way back. If Redmond wasn't normal, it was true to say that Mira wasn't normal either. She had never been able to form friendships in school and college like other girls did; if she got close to it, she always blocked it off, turned away, grew cold, afraid that they would discover her dark and disgusting secret. She had the mark of Cain upon her, she was cursed, she was a whore.

She walked alone. Until she met Gareth.

Gareth was nice. He was so gentle, so nonjudgemental. She met him one night outside one of the Soho clubs and he didn't seem repulsed by her, as most people did. He gave Mira a smoke of his weed – that was nice, too. She said she was looking for some supplies, and he said he had some supplies, and took her home with him to his little bare flat in a horrible graffiti-strewn square concrete block. A place where she would never have been seen, before. Now, she barely noticed her surroundings, stark and horrible though they were.

Gareth had a little dog, a stupid yappy little ball of white fur; she disliked dogs, her uncle had kept dogs, but she petted the thing and made a

*fuss of it because she wanted him to like her and
let her stay the night.*

*If he wanted sex, then that was perfectly okay
with her, but Gareth didn't make any moves in
that direction. He just poured the drinks and they
sprawled out with Dinky the dog, and soon he
produced some LSD tabs. They took some and he
started telling her about his life.*

*'My stepdad threw me out. I got in the way of
his "relationship" with my mum,' said Gareth
dreamily.*

*'Poor darling,' she said, although she barely cared.
She was away with the fairies, looking at the wild
colours on the ceiling, the dancing, twirling shapes
– even Dinky looked pretty after she'd taken acid;
he became a ball of writhing kaleidoscopic worms
moving like oil across the threadbare carpet.*

*'Your voice is funny,' said Gareth. 'So posh.
Anyway, she had a bit of cash from when her dad
died and so she helped me set up this flat,' said
Gareth. 'Did I already tell you that?'*

*Mira shook her head. He was spaced out. Well,
so was she.*

*'She was afraid of the bastard, my . . . my mum.
But she saw me right. Once I got the flat, I got a
job in one of the hotels up West. I thought I'd get
a live-in job, that's what I wanted because believe
me this ain't the fucking Ritz, know what I mean?
But I couldn't, so I had to make do with this and*

go in on the Tube. It's not too bad, but I might move on soon.'

She nodded.

'What about you?' he asked.

'Nothing to tell,' she said. 'No family.'

'None at all?'

'None.'

He let Mira stay the night, and then the next, and the next, until she was a fixture. They were bound together in mutual failure, two hopeless losers sheltering here against the world outside. He got a spare key cut and gave it to her.

A few weeks went by, and Gareth went on working odd hours at the hotel up West, while she walked the dog and turned a few tricks on Gareth's unmade bed to get a little cash. Gareth got the drugs; they watched the telly together in the evenings and then shot up if he didn't have to go out to work. Everything was cool.

Then she came home one day and Dinky was barking his head off inside the flat, which was weird because Gareth was home; he only ever barked like that when they were both out. She put her key in the lock, annoyed with the stupid little mutt, the neighbours would complain, fuck it, they were always complaining anyway, they lived to complain, saying the telly was too loud, that they were laughing too much, playing records into the small hours.

Fuck them. And fuck that damned dog.

She opened the door and there Dinky was, yap, yap, yap, silly thing. Then she looked inside.

A hot spasm of shock sucked all the breath from her body.

Gareth was hanging dead from the light fitting in the middle of the ceiling. The flex was around his neck. Mira fell back against the half-open door. A noise like a wounded animal emerged from her mouth.

She thought of Redmond, with his hands around her throat, or that awful rubber thing over her nose and her mouth. Redmond, who always liked to play around with throttling people, choking them.

'Haven't you heard of autoerotic asphyxia?' he'd asked her once in that lovely soothing voice of his – she'd fallen in love with his voice, with that southern Irish lilt. She'd been nervous and started to object. 'It heightens the sex, that restriction around the throat, it adds to the pleasure. So long as you keep the airways open, it's perfectly safe.'

He'd told her to put something in the mouth – her mouth – a golf ball, an orange, keep the airways open, and she'd been lying there freaked out, terrified, naked, almost shitting herself with fear, with him choking her, and no, no, no, it didn't feel sexy; what it felt like was the most

185

frightening thing she had ever been subjected to, and she wanted out.

Gareth had been strangled with flex.

She knew who'd strangled him.

Gareth was dead because Redmond had come looking for her, and, thank God, oh thank Christ in heaven, she hadn't been here. But Gareth, poor bloody Gareth, had been here and he wouldn't have told on her, would he? No, Gareth wouldn't have told.

But now look; he was dead.

Bile surged into her throat. For long moments the room and the nightmare in it spun and blackened, but then her head cleared and she swallowed hard. She still felt as though she might vomit at the smell and the pitiful sight of Gareth dangling there. But she had to stay rational somehow; she had to think straight.

Because he was looking for her. He'd bloody nearly found her, too.

He would have asked Gareth where she was, maybe when would she be back?

Gareth wouldn't have told . . .

Would he . . . ?

He could be watching her right now.

She backed out of the flat, closing the door on Dinky and his frantic barking, on Gareth swinging gently there from the light fitting. She looked wildly all around her as she stood exposed and vulnerable on the dingy outside landing, but she couldn't see anybody watching. She hurried, stumbling, nearly falling, babbling for God to help her, someone, help, like an idiot, trembling, and somehow she got to the lift and was then too terrified to press the button.

What if the lift doors opened and he was standing there?

She braced herself and forced herself to do it. Pressed the button. The lift hummed into action.

'Oh shit,' she muttered, tears streaming down her face. She'd wet herself, she could feel piss running down her legs.

She heard the lift approaching, watched the numbers change above the door until it came to this floor, her floor, her and Gareth's. She stood there, panting, retching, eyes fixed open wide with awful, gut-wrenching fear.

She knew he was here, somewhere, waiting to get her. She knew he was going to spring out, grab her throat and clamp that horrible thing over her nose and mouth, shake the life out of her, telling her that nobody walked out on him, nobody.

The lift doors opened. It was empty of all but the strong, biting smell of old urine.

She got in and pressed the button with shaking fingers. The doors started to close.

Then a hand reached in between them, and they slid open again.

She screamed.

'*Shit, you gave me a turn!*' *An old lady stepped into the lift, holding her hand to her chest.*

The old woman looked with disgust at the girl cowering there in the corner, yet another bloody junkie, skinny and dirty, and, for God's sake, the stink in here, her legs were wet – she'd wet herself, the dirty mare. The woman's jaw was set in disapproval. She turned and stepped back out of the lift.

The doors closed again. The lift went down.

Mira knew he'd be waiting for her at the bottom, that she couldn't get away from him, that he was too clever and she was too weak.

But Redmond wasn't there. Unsteadily she crossed the lobby and went outside. No one jumped on her, no one grabbed her by the throat and squeezed until she died.

She started to walk across the car park, crying, moaning, nearly prostrate with terror. Any moment one of the car doors was going to open and he would be inside, waiting for her, waiting to murder her.

But he wasn't.

Mira got across the car park. She could still hear Dinky barking up there in the flat, very faintly. She broke into a shambling run, and didn't look back, not once.

She didn't dare.

*   *   *

Mira's money ran out, so finally she slept rough on the streets and turned a few tricks. Her looks were all but gone, she knew it, but some men weren't too bothered. Stick a paper bag over your head, it was all the same to them. You were a cunt, to be used. And some of them gave her drugs. She tried to get a job in one of the clubs, but they all turned her down. She went in the one called the Alley Cat – anything to get some money in to buy the stuff she needed – but the trannie manager looked at her as if he'd stepped in shit.

'Fuck off out of it,' he spat, and she was shown the door.

Out on the pavement, shivering, needing a fix so badly, she stood there looking into the window of the little tattoo parlour next door. She pushed open the door and went in. There was a freaky-looking bull of a man standing behind the counter there, adding up figures on a piece of paper. He wore a white T-shirt and jeans, and every inch of his bulging-muscled body that she could see was covered in tattoos. She wondered if she was really seeing this man, or was she just having a bad trip? He was a walking billboard for his trade. He looked scary, but she had seen scarier. Truly scary was her gently smiling, handsome, twisted lover. With him she had seen into the very heart of blackness; she knew that in kissing him she had kissed true evil.

'*I need help,*' she said, her voice cracking with strain. Tears slipped down her sunken face. '*Please help me.*'

And, much to her surprise, he did.

20

Mad Mick knew the rules as good as any fucker. The rule was, you played by the light. You put your money in the meter, and the light over the table was on. Twenty minutes of snooker, and the light was off. If you weren't finished then, if you had say a pink or a blue or a black still to pot, tough tit. You stood aside and let the next players on to the table.

That was the rule. *Everyone* knew the rule.

But there was Rizzo Delacourt, playing up to the crowd, drinking beer and saying it was like gnats, saying the boys around here couldn't play fucking snooker even though one of the same boys had just soundly beaten him on the table. Getting aggressive, getting drunk. Calling for a whisky chaser as he set up the balls again in the wooden triangular frame, poncing around in his big-collared shirt and flared trousers – talk about a dedicated follower of fashion, what was he, a fucking nancy?

All this, despite the fact the light was out, despite the rule. Despite the fact that Mad Mick was waiting for a table to come free, and this table technically *was* free, the light was off, wasn't it?

Mad Mick put this theory forward for Rizzo to think about.

Rizzo Delacourt stuck some more coins in the meter and looked at Mick. 'Well, now the effing light's *on*,' he said. 'See that? On.'

Mad Mick had a reputation to consider. He was built like an outside craphouse and all his mates were watching. He reached out, removed the triangle and scattered the balls to the four corners of the table.

'It was *off*,' he said quietly. 'That's the rules, see? When the light goes out, you make way for the next people who want to play. It's only *polite*, I'd say.'

There was a deep hush in the snooker hall as everyone listened in, ready for Mad Mick to start the slaughter in his usual fashion.

'You don't shut your fucking mouth,' the runty little Rizzo said softly, 'my bruv Pete's gonna use your cunting head as a ball, you got me?'

Drunk people. They either wanted to fight you or fuck you, and sometimes both. And *what* bruv? Mick looked to where Rizzo's eyes were indicating.

There was a large figure lurking back there in the gloom, cloaked in the half-darkness that surrounded the brightly lit table. Now, the figure stepped forward. A gasp went up.

'Shit,' said one of Mick's mates, a fag dropping from his half-open mouth to the floor.

Mad Mick stared.

The man standing there holding the cue like a weapon was not just tattooed, he was *covered* in tattoos, *blanketed* in the fucking things. There were swirls of blue and red all over his face and neck and his thick, beefy arms.

They all thought, *Ugly great bastard*. Little piggy blue eyes and a massive shaven head; tattoos all over *that* too; he looked downright fucking fierce. Confident that he now had Mick's attention, the tattooed freak gave him a bone-chilling smile. His tongue flicked out, and there was a further collective gasp from the watchers. His tongue was *forked*, like a snake's.

Mad Mick did something he had never done before. He stepped away from a fight. The runty little man called Rizzo played another frame, and then another. And no one disturbed him, light or no light.

Later that night, Mick left the club. He was pleasantly drunk, because drunk was good when you'd been humiliated in front of your friends. Yeah, that was it, he'd been *humiliated*. He thought about that and suppressed rage ate at him.

He cracked his knuckles as he walked across the club car park, the fog descending. Jesus, this fucking weather, and it was supposed to be summer. It was hot, and it was damp. And misty as a bastard; out on the road he could just see cars crawling through it like ghosts, drivers suddenly nervous.

'Hey mate, you got a light?'

The voice startled him. He heard a girlish squeak emit from his own mouth. Then he turned and it was *him*, the freak from the snooker hall, leering and tattooed, standing there still holding the damned snooker cue, but no cigarette, because Mick realized suddenly that what he was doing – and Mick thought, *oho clever bastard are we?* – was making a little play on words.

He didn't want a *light*. What he wanted to do was remind Mick about the *light* over the table. Mick was still smarting from that disagreement. And now here the weirdo was, taunting him with it.

'You know, you ought to learn to shut your fucking mouth,' said Mick, his blood singing with the urge to knock this fucker into the middle of next week, fury and booze overcoming all his earlier trepidation.

'Make me,' said the tattooed man, and Mick didn't need any more in the way of an invitation.

He charged at the freak but he'd had several

pints too many and he missed his target. The tattooed man jumped lithely aside, and as Mick passed he whacked him hard across the back of the neck with the cue.

Mick let out a wheezing gasp as the pain lanced through him, stinging, biting. He fell to his knees, but he was tough: he whipped around, ready to sweep the freak's legs from underneath him, but he was fast. He'd already come in close behind Mick and now he had the cue over Mick's windpipe and he was pulling back, arching Mick's whole body like a bow.

Mick gurgled, spots weaving in front of his eyes as the blood was cut off to his brain. He felt himself falling into blackness as the freak pressed harder, harder . . . and then the man let go.

Oh thank Christ, thought Mick.

A huge waft of breath blew out from Mick as he slumped forward on to the tarmac. Fuck, he'd thought he was dead then. Relief flooded him. The freak kicked him hard in the midriff and again there was pain, mighty pain, but at least he was fucking *alive*, and Mick had been sure he was dead.

Mick keeled over on to his side, rolling into a ball to stop the bastard doing even more damage to his innards. He'd done some already. Something was rasping in there, something was broken. Mick closed his eyes. All right, he'd done his bit, now the cunt would leave him, he would go.

With his eyes closed, Mick didn't see the freak put the cue to his ear. Mick felt the movement there, then his eyes opened. He tried to move, opened his mouth to scream. The freak rammed the cue down, puncturing Mick's eardrum and then his brain like meat on a skewer. Mick's legs went into wild convulsions. Froth bubbled at his lips. His eyes rolled up in his head. Then, suddenly, he was still.

The freak pulled out the cue and stared down at his fallen adversary. Mick had thought he was dead. Now, he was.

'Hey! Pete Delacourt, ain't it?' shouted a voice from the mist-shrouded shrubbery.

The tattooed man's head whipped round. He saw a cluster of men there, spot-lit like pale wraiths beneath the yellow sodium glare of the streetlight.

'We want a word, Pete,' said another.

The men moved. Came closer. Pete saw that one of them was Charlie Foster, the Delaney mob's main man. His brother Rizzo had already warned him that Charlie was looking for him, that Redmond Delaney was chewing the carpet over something, some bit of skirt or other, and that wasn't good news – in fact it might be *bad*.

Pete turned, still clutching the cue, and ran.

21

It was two o'clock on Sunday morning when the phone started to ring right beside Annie's bed. She shot up, startled, disorientated, with her heart in her mouth.

'*Shit*,' she said, and fumbled for the light.

She knocked over the small table lamp, righted it. Pressed the switch. Light flooded the room and still the damned thing was ringing; it would wake Layla soon. *Oh – but Layla was at Ruthie's.* She felt the pain anew. Shoved it aside. She snatched up the phone.

'Yeah?' she asked. 'Who is it?'

There was silence except for someone breathing.

This is all I need. Heavy breathers at two o'clock in the sodding morning.

'Hello?' she said loudly.

'It's me. Dolly. Can you come over?'

Dolly?

Annie looked at the phone and frowned. 'Doll, it's two o'clock.'

'Come over. I think we got trouble.'

Annie dragged a hand through her hair. 'I was asleep.'

'Come. I wouldn't ask . . . but just *come,* will you?'

'Fuck *me,* Doll.'

'For God's sake *come.*'

And then Dolly put the phone down.

'Oh for . . .' Annie said, and slapped the phone back on the cradle. What the hell could have happened? Whatever, it sounded serious; she had to go.

She got out of bed, still feeling groggy, and pulled on yesterday's clothes. She phoned for a taxi – no need to bother Tony, not at this late hour. *This had better be damned good, Doll,* she thought as the taxi tore through the abandoned streets toward Limehouse.

It was anything but good. She could see that the moment Dolly opened the door to her. Dolly was in her dressing gown; without make-up her face looked naked, vulnerable – and white with strain.

She ushered Annie in and led her through to the kitchen.

Sharlene was sitting there at the table. Under the harsh glare of the light, Dolly looked awful, worse than in the hall. No slap on, a couple of curlers in the front of her hair, denuded of her armour of neat suit and faultless make-up; she looked like a different person altogether. Not Dolly, bold as brass and twice as mouthy, but a scared and shrunken woman.

Sharlene didn't look any better. Her dark hair threw her stark white face into sharp relief.

'What's going on, Doll?' asked Annie, sitting down at the kitchen table.

'You want a brandy?'

'Not for me.' Dolly knew she hated the stuff; what was she offering it to her for?

Because something's got her shit-scared and she's not thinking straight, thought Annie.

Dolly topped up her own glass, and Sharlene's, and slumped down in a chair. Annie watched Dolly, feeling more fearful by the second.

'What's happened?' she asked her.

'It wasn't my fault,' said Sharlene.

'I know it wasn't,' Dolly told her.

'*What* wasn't?' demanded Annie.

'The booking. The escort booking,' said Sharlene, tears starting in her eyes.

'What escort booking?' asked Annie. 'Wait a minute. When I was here on Friday you were saying to Sharlene and Rosie that there'd be no more escort bookings, and they were arguing over one that had come in . . .' her voice tailed off.

'Yeah,' said Dolly, looking haggard.

'Oh fuck. Are you telling me Rosie took it? That Rosie's gone out to meet this client?'

'She's such a dopey mare. I *told* her it was no go.'

Annie felt herself getting more screwed up about all this by the second.

'But Doll – this could be dangerous. Serious.'

'Nah.' Dolly was shaking her head, forcing her mouth into a tight, positive little smile. 'Nah, it's okay. She'll be fine. Because look, here's the point: they've got Chris. They've *got* their man, so Rosie'll be fine.'

'Doll . . .' started Annie.

'She'll be *fine*,' snapped Dolly suddenly, banging the tabletop with the brandy glass. Liquid slopped over the brim.

Sharlene and Annie exchanged a look. Dolly was saying it, but she didn't believe it.

'Then why'd you want me to come over?' asked Annie after a beat.

'I . . . I just . . . oh shit, I don't know. She'll be all right. Won't she?' Dolly's eyes were wild with anxiety.

'What happened, Sharlene?' Annie asked. She wasn't going to get any sense out of Dolly, that was for sure.

Sharlene shrugged. Her gesture was casual, but her face was creased with concern.

'Look,' said Annie angrily, 'whatever's gone on here, you'd better tell me now.'

Sharlene shrugged again, but this time she started speaking. 'We were arguing the toss over who'd take the booking. Just arsing about really. She put the piece of paper with the details on her dressing table, sort of taunting me with it. We were just mucking about. Then I went in to Rosie's room tonight, and she'd sneaked off out. I checked the book in the kitchen drawer, but she didn't write the details in the book like you're supposed to – she didn't even take a number. She just had it on that scrap of paper, and when I looked in her room about nine she'd gone out and that piece of paper was gone too. So I reckoned she'd taken the booking, just to get one over on me for a laugh.'

Sharlene paused, her usually sharp and sassy face looking faintly sick.

'Silly little bint. I waited a bit. I hoped that maybe she'd just gone down the pub and would roll back home after eleven, but she didn't. When it got to one o'clock, I woke up Dolly.' Sharlene looked at Annie. 'She'll be okay though, won't she?'

Annie tried to think. 'Do either of you know *anything* about this booking?'

They both shook their heads. Dolly knocked back a bit more brandy.

'Not the location, nothing?'

201

Again the head-shaking. And more brandy for Dolly.

If she's so certain Chris did it, what's she so worried about? wondered Annie, watching her friend's pallid face. There was a sheen of sweat on Dolly's brow and her hands, as she fumbled about with the brandy glass, were shaking.

Fact was, they had no idea where Rosie was or who she was meeting up with.

Fact *was,* Annie knew in her heart that Chris couldn't have done these vile things. There was still a killer out there, trawling the streets for more victims. But London was a big place. And lightning didn't strike twice, right?

Wrong, she thought. *It's struck three times so far.*

She felt pretty sick herself now. She thought of Rosie with her lazy, charming ways and her tumble of pale blonde hair. She was a likable girl, harmless. If anything should happen to her – well, it just didn't bear thinking about.

'You called the Delaneys, Doll?' she asked.

Dolly shook her head. 'I panicked, I . . . I just thought of you.'

'I can get the word out, get people looking for her,' said Annie. *Although I really shouldn't go stepping on Redmond Delaney's toes,* she thought.

'Yeah, can you do that?' asked Dolly, suddenly hopeful.

'Sure. I'll do it right now.'

Annie left the two other women sitting at the kitchen table and went through to the hall. She picked up the telephone and dialled Tony's number. It rang for some time, then finally Tony picked up.

'H'lo,' he muttered.

'It's me, Tone.'

'What's up, Boss?'

'We've got a problem, Tone. One of Dolly's girls has gone on an escort job, it's getting late, we're worried.'

'Where's she gone?'

'No idea. But she should have been back over an hour ago.'

They were both silent for a moment, both thinking the same thing: *No, it couldn't happen again. Could it?*

'Can you get the boys to check out some of the clubs, the hotels . . .' Her voice trailed off. It was an impossible job, and they both knew it.

'Sure, Boss,' said Tony.

Annie paused. Thought again. 'And maybe . . . maybe ring round the hospitals,' she added as there was a thump against the front door.

She looked at it, heart in her mouth. Heard a key being inserted into the lock. Saw it swing inwards. Rosie stood there, looking at her in surprise. A shriek went up from the kitchen and Dolly and Sharlene came rushing through to the hall and grabbed Rosie.

'What the *hell*?' laughed Rosie. 'What's going on?'

Annie started breathing again. 'You still there, Tone?'

'Yeah, Boss.'

'Cancel that. She's here. She's okay.'

'No sweat, Boss.'

She put the phone down.

'Where the fuck have you *been*?' Dolly was demanding.

'I met up with a pal down the pub and we went clubbing . . . what the hell's wrong with everyone?' Rosie was saying in bewilderment.

Sharlene, Rosie and Dolly bustled into the kitchen, chattering and laughing. Annie stood there in the hall and felt limp with relief. She looked at Dolly, who had gone from extraordinary fear to hysterical happiness in a single bound. Dolly glanced up and their eyes met.

Dolly looked away first.

22

Robert 'Rizzo' Delacourt might have been a runty little man, but he had a big attitude. Like many runty little men with attitude, he liked to display his masculine superiority by beating up on women. So the two girls he still ran, who shivered in miniskirts and little jackets night after night on the towpath under the canal bridge over the Mile End Road, were justifiably nervous of him.

Hey – they were nervous, full stop.

Because they'd heard about the girls getting done. They'd heard about it and experienced it *first hand*. Poor bloody Val, Rizzo's sister, for instance. She'd been a cow at times but she hadn't deserved that. But they were working girls. They had to eat, and anyway Rizzo wouldn't let them bunk off. So they huddled against the damp wall under the bridge near the lock, and talked loudly and smoked cigarettes and joked about the clients, to stave off the jitters.

Their profession was the oldest in the world but it could certainly pay better. Rizzo took a big wedge out of what they earned, but Rizzo was The Man. If they didn't hustle, then Rizzo would be mad, and that wasn't good. So no matter what they heard, and no matter what they experienced – first hand or not – then here they were, working their little patch, *Rizzo's* little patch, which now sported just two girls instead of three.

Rizzo wasn't happy about that. He'd lost a valuable asset in Val. And, incidentally, he'd lost a sister too. He'd drafted his little sis into the business when she turned sixteen. He remembered it well.

Their mum had been at bingo and Val, mouthy little bitch, had been sitting in their front room with him and their little cousin Paulie, watching *The Avengers* on the telly, him saying what a tosser Steed looked with that bowler, like a toff, what good would a geezer like that be in a ruck?

Val had been droning on all through the programme, which Rizzo had found pretty bloody irritating. On and on about what would she do now? She'd left school, she didn't want to work in no effing shop, not even in a *clothes* shop, the pay was piss poor and life was too short, but signing on was a drag. All the while painting her nails orange – Jesus, that stuff stank.

'Will you shut the fuck up?' asked Rizzo, popping a can.

The programme was getting interesting, Emma Peel was looking tasty in a leather catsuit and was about to get done by a villain if Steed didn't get a fucking move on and show up, and all he could hear was Val going yackety-yackety-yack in his ear.

Now she was saying she didn't want to work in a grocery shop either, she'd die of boredom, but maybe she could get an apprenticeship at the local hairdresser, what did he think?

'I think you should shut the fuck *up*,' said Rizzo.

Paulie, crawling around on the carpet, getting in front of the TV screen, sticky fingers all over the damned thing – for God's sake, was there no peace to be had?

'Yeah?' Val snapped. 'Well *I* think you should take an interest in what your own sister's doing. Would it kill you to just have a proper conversation with your *own sister*?'

At which point Rizzo wopped her a hard one around the chops. Orange nail varnish splattered all over the arm of the sofa and on to the floor. He saw the surprise there on her face as the redness bloomed on her freckled cheek. He'd never done that before.

Paulie froze on the carpet, his eyes going between the two. Val's expression changed from surprise to fear. *Good,* thought Rizzo, and right then and there he devised a plan.

'Don't worry. I can get you a job,' he said.

And so it was that Val Delacourt entered her new profession. Took to it like a duck to water, too.

Rizzo was pleased; she pulled in a good living and so did he – half her earnings went straight into his pocket to feed his little habit.

The escort work had been something else, just a little extra. He'd been mad about it when he'd found out. He didn't want his girls subcontracting; *his* business was what mattered, not their own.

And the escort stuff had resulted – sadly, really sadly – in Val getting herself killed stone-dead. Their mum had wailed and screamed and cried when the cops came by to break the news, he'd never forget it. Felt a bit guilty too. After all, *he'd* started Val out along the path to her own destruction, setting her up as a brass. Even if he didn't like her escorting, he had to admit that she wouldn't have *been* escorting if she hadn't started tarting first.

Still, he didn't feel guilty for long.

So now Rizzo had just the two girls, and one of *them* wasn't all that, until he managed to source a third. Because good girls were hard to find. *This* girl, this one who was standing on the towpath chatting to his two remaining girls, was not a good girl.

He could see it clearly as he approached, Benj his bull terrier tugging his arm out of its socket as usual, straining to get forward as always.

Rizzo loved Benj. You knew where you were with a dog. Step on its paw and it would howl, but ten minutes later it'd be there licking your hand, kissing your arse and humping your leg. And Benj helped Rizzo's reputation.

Benj had pulled down a Dalmatian belonging to one of the other pimps in the park last month, chewed the mutt all to hell. They'd had to haul the thing off to a vet's and have it put down. Benj had been going for the pimp, too – the bastard had been trying to muscle in on Rizzo's patch – when Rizzo called Benj off. The pimp had been traumatized and he hadn't been seen in the area since.

Now he looked ahead and saw a girl, no, a *woman*, whose stance told him she would not take orders. This one would try to *give* them, and there was no fucking way Rizzo Delacourt was taking any orders off any skirt, no sir.

'What the fuck you doing?' he asked loudly, coming nearer, Benj pulling him ahead like a tugboat hauling a liner.

Rizzo was pissed off.

He'd expected both of the girls, Jackie and the other one, Misery he called her, to be off earning by now, pulling in the johns like they were supposed to. It was nearly eleven thirty and the pubs had emptied out, but no, here they were, standing about shooting the breeze.

Shit! Couldn't you leave these bitches unattended for a couple of hours, go about your business in the expectation that they would be about *theirs*? It was hard running a business these days. You had to have eyes in your arse, and that was a fact. Couldn't turn your back for a minute. Who'd want to be in management when it was so damned hard?

'Hey! You hear me? I said what the fuck you doing?' he yelled. Yelling worked well with women, he knew that. Shout at them, get in close, act like a threat and they folded. Started to cry, poor little dears. Benj let out a yap, excited because Rizzo was, in tune with his master just as he'd been right from a pup. Bit anyone and anything, but never Rizzo. All the family were scared shitless of the hound, even the tattooed hulk Pete wouldn't touch him – although Pete hadn't been around lately – but not Rizzo. Rizzo was The *Man*.

Only this girl didn't look the type to fold easy.

He came up close and she just stood there. In the dim yellow light cast by the streetlamps he could see dark hair and steadily staring dark eyes. Jackie and Misery were acting nervous and that was good. Shooting looks at each other, shifting from foot to foot, they didn't want no hassle with

Mr Rizzo Delacourt. Misery, a skinny blonde, drew deeply on her cigarette and eyed him nervously but said nothing.

'We ain't doing nothing, Rizzo,' said Jackie, short dark bobbed hair and a skirt hitched high enough to show what she'd had for breakfast.

Rizzo ignored Jackie's whining and addressed himself to the tall dark woman who stood there.

'What you doin' here, wastin' my girls' time?' he demanded.

'Just asking them a few questions, that's all,' said the woman, who was not reacting to Rizzo as he was used to being reacted to. In fact, she seemed more interested in eyeing up Misery. Perhaps she was a lezzer. Maybe here to strike a deal, who knew? He took it down a notch. Business was business, after all.

'About what?'

The woman's eyes pulled away from Misery and fastened on to Rizzo. 'Val Delacourt. You're Rizzo? Her brother?'

Rizzo shot his girls a glare. Loud-mouthed cows. They shrank back. 'What's that to you?'

The woman shrugged. 'Just asking. Sad business, her dying like she did.'

Now Rizzo was getting mad. He didn't care if she was a punter; all this delving into his private business was strictly out of bounds. 'Look, I don't want you coming down here putting the wind up my girls by goin' on about all that. We had all that out with the Bill. They got the man, it's done.'

'It's not done, Rizzo. They got the wrong man.'

Rizzo's mouth dropped open. Then he rallied himself.

'Look.' He came in closer to the uppity bitch and poked a finger at her shoulder, ramming his point home. 'I want you to *fuck off*, girly. You're botherin' my girls. Val's dead and gone. They got the man who done it. End of story.'

Annie recoiled from Rizzo's breath. She glanced down at the dog, slavering and pawing the ground just like its owner.

Big dog, small cock, she thought.

'You understand me?' he yelled in her face, spittle flying.

'Yeah. Think I got that.'

Annie drew back, walked a few paces away. Looked again at the blonde skinny one, shivering in the shadows despite the mugginess of the night, turning her face away. She felt strongly that she knew the girl, knew her well. It *is*, thought Annie. It's . . .

'Mira?' she said suddenly.

The skinny girl's head whipped round.

Out of the shadows along the towpath stepped a squat, muddy-eyed geezer and a bloke wearing a deaf aid. Both dressed in neat, sober clothes, like the woman. Rizzo stiffened. His hand slipped into his pocket, folded over the knife he always carried for his protection.

'Hey, what's going on?' he asked.

'Nothing's going on, Rizzo,' said Annie. 'Just me asking questions and you answering them.'

She pulled her attention away from the girl she was sure she knew. Although the girl was so changed, so . . . bedraggled. She couldn't believe her own eyes . . . and yet. It was. It was Mira.

'Yeah, and you'd better fucking well hurry up and cough up the answers,' said Deaf Derek.

Annie sent him an annoyed glance. No use showing the tosser up in front of his 'girls'; he'd only dig his heels in and act tougher to maintain face.

'Yeah, or what?' asked Rizzo.

'Or nothing,' said Annie. 'We just want some answers, that's all.'

'I ain't talking to you. I told you, it's done.'

'How's your mum taking it?' asked Annie.

'I told you, *no more questions*,' shrieked Rizzo.

'Hey, you wanna show some respect,' said Deaf Derek.

Annie threw him another look. *Why don't you shut up, arsehole?*

She returned her attention to Rizzo, feeling a surge of disgust for this horrible little specimen who had put his own sister on the game, who kept these poor pitiful skinny girls out here come rain or shine, while he bunked off to the cosy pub or to his mum's nice warm house to get bladdered, watch telly or shoot up.

She held up her hands in a peacekeeping gesture.

'Hey, Rizzo, we don't want trouble. That's the last thing we want. What we *do* want is to get whoever did this, and that's not the man the police are holding. Your sister's dead, Rizzo. Don't you want to get him too?'

'Last warning,' said Rizzo flatly, shaking with rage.

He's on something right now, thought Annie. *No good reasoning with him.*

She stepped back, shrugging; okay, no worries. But at the same instant Derek stepped forward and waved a finger in Rizzo's face.

'Hey, you know who you're talking to, cunt?' he yelled.

And that did it. Rizzo let out a curse. Jackie and Mira screamed and shrank back as he let Benj off the leash.

Annie knew about bull terriers. She knew the damage they could do. The instant it was released, the dog lunged forward, teeth bared, huge shoulders bunched, all muscle and evil intent. Steve, who had said nothing yet, knocked her to one side so that she fell against the streaming-wet wall under the bridge, smearing her black jacket with green algae. *That'll be a bugger to get clean* – what a stupid thought when a bull terrier was coming at you about to rip your fucking throat out.

There was pandemonium under the bridge. Deaf Derek shouting, the girls screaming their heads off, Rizzo yelling, *Go on, Benj. Kill!*

The damned thing was going to do it too.

Annie stumbled, nearly fell to her knees, thinking, *That idiot bastard Derek.*

She felt the dog's hot fetid breath as it launched itself at her. She shrank back, shut her eyes, thought *Christ!*

But the dog didn't strike.

When she got her eyes open she found that squat powerful Steve had surged forward and was clutching the snapping, snarling, writhing brute by the neck. The weight of the dog drove Steve back so that he crashed into the wall beside Annie, the dog driving at him, squirming, its black eyes glaring hate, its jaws flecked with spittle and its teeth bared in hideous threat.

'Do something!' Annie roared at Derek, who was staying well out of it.

He did nothing.

Steve struggled with the huge, powerful dog but he couldn't win, the thing was going to get loose from his grip and tear them all to fuck.

The struggle lasted for seconds but seemed

endless. Annie struck the thing around the head with her fists. It had no effect whatsoever. She didn't have the kiyoga, the steel-sprung rod she usually carried in her pocket. If she'd had Max's gun with her she'd have shot the damned thing.

Steve was grimacing with effort, trying to move his grip on the animal.

Then he got his hand down, grabbed the dog by one back leg. Shoved the thing away hard, he got the other back leg in the other hand. The dog dropped down, front legs scrabbling for purchase but finding nothing, still snarling, still trying to get his teeth into Steve, Annie, anybody except Rizzo.

Steve got a firmer hold on both back legs. He took a grunting breath, and yanked hard, like Charles Atlas pulling on a Bullworker. There was an audible *crunch* as the dog's spine snapped like a twig. There was a whimper. Then the dog stopped moving. Stopped snarling. Just hung there, in Steve's hands. Steve tossed the dead animal into the canal.

The girls stood there, open-mouthed. Rizzo, too, was frozen in shock.

Then he stepped forward, eyes wild. 'You've killed my fucking *dog*,' he howled.

Steve straightened. Took a breath. Grabbed Rizzo by the arms, turned him like a rag doll, slammed him face-first into the bridge wall.

'Jesus!' screamed Rizzo as Steve yanked both arms up behind his back to his shoulders.

'You know what, cunt? You're starting to get on my nerves,' said Steve in Rizzo's ear. 'Now. Listen up. This is Mrs Carter, and you are going to answer her questions, you got that? Nod yes, you stupid little bastard.'

Rizzo nodded.

Panting, Steve glanced at Annie. 'Ask him,' he said.

Annie straightened up, pushing herself away from the wall. Got a calming breath down her. *Shit,* her heart was hammering away like a bass drum. The dog's dead body was floating off down the dark waters of the canal. Derek was standing back, watching.

He caused that, she thought.

She looked around. Jackie was still standing there, quaking with fear, but Mira was gone. But now was not the time for recriminations. Now was the time to ask her questions. She stepped forward, and talked to Rizzo Delacourt while Steve held him tight.

Steve dropped her off at the club an hour later, and was about to drive off with Derek when Annie shook her head.

'Hold on Steve, wait out here will you? I want a word with Derek.'

Derek trailed after her into the club. The watcher

in the car was there; he nodded an acknowledgement as she went in.

'Jesus, could you believe the way Steve handled that dog?' Derek was marvelling loudly as they went into the office and she shut the door behind them. 'Broke his back with his bare hands. That'll teach that sorry little runt to give out with the mouth the way he does.'

Annie went around the desk, sat down, unbuttoning her jacket.

It had been a wasted evening. Rizzo had been able to tell them nothing helpful about his sister's death – except how scarily similar it had been to Teresa's and Aretha's.

'Take a seat,' she said, nodding to the chair on the other side of the desk.

Derek sat down, looking at her expectantly.

'You let me down tonight,' said Annie.

His head went back a little, his expression surprised. 'What do you mean, let you down?'

'We could have got the information without it turning into a ruck.'

'So it turned into a ruck. So what? Little bastard deserved all he got.'

'This ain't the first time you've screwed up. If you'd kept quiet tonight, everything would have been sweet.'

Derek looked at her. Then he shrugged. 'Sorry,' he said offhandedly.

'You've done this before. Blundered in and made things harder. Messed up. Made mistakes.'

Derek's expression was sullen now.

Annie took a breath. She was fuming with this idiot. What she was saying was the absolute truth: he'd fucked up, big time. Not only in minor things, swaggering about the place provoking people when there was no need for it; she'd checked with Jackie Tulliver, she knew it was Derek who'd ploughed in and upset Aretha's Aunt Louella by being too pushy with her.

He'd also created that scene last night, resulting in Mira running away – and Annie doubted that she'd see her again, not after that. She and Mira had once been close – but something about Mira always seemed to repel rather than attract real intimacy. Still, they'd been friends. They had worked together, and got on well at Annie's West End parlour, and she was sad to think that the once gloriously beautiful Mira had sunk so low. She'd been shocked at the state of her.

There were other things too, though – *huge* things. She remembered Max saying that Derek had been with Eddie, Max's brother, on the night he'd died, and he'd gone off and left him alone. If he'd stayed, if he'd done his fucking job and taken better care of Eddie, then there was every chance that Eddie would be alive right now instead of lying cold in his grave.

Max had been loyal to Derek, even in the face of that extreme provocation. She knew he'd despised Derek after that, but he had not kicked him off the payroll. But then – she wasn't Max. 'You're off the firm, Derek. You're out of it.'

Derek's features rearranged themselves into shocked outrage.

'You *what?*' he said.

'You've had chances, and tonight you blew the last one.'

'I've been a part of this firm since I was a fucking *boy*,' protested Derek.

'You're still a fucking boy, Derek. That's the problem.' Annie stood up. 'Goodnight, Derek.'

He was still sitting there. 'You can't do this,' he said hotly. 'I worked for *Max*.'

Annie felt the fire of anger ignite. He'd nearly got her mauled by that fucking hound tonight; he'd slipped up in so many ways, too many to count. He was a damned liability.

'Max ain't here,' she reminded him. 'I am. The decision's mine, and it's made. So fuck off out of it.'

Derek stood up, flinging the chair aside with a furious gesture.

'You'll regret this,' he said, his eyes spitting rage at her.

'I doubt that,' said Annie.

And he went off down the stairs, slamming out of the front doors.

Sighing, Annie followed him and locked the main door for the night. She paused, went down the stairs into the main body of the club. Flicked on the lights. The underlit dance floor was in place now, and the three little podiums around it where the go-go dancers would strut their stuff were finished too, the strobes set out above them.

Around the edges of the dance floor there were now a few cosy banquettes, little recessed and sunken bays in which the punters could relax, drink, smoke, listen to the music, watch the girls. Some of the banquettes and chairs were still to come. Annie had picked out a classy chocolate brown; she was looking forward to viewing the full effect.

She could almost see how it would be now, when it was open. Heaving with punters eager to spend their money. Not the Palermo Lounge, Max's favourite club any more. She pushed another switch, and the red neon above the refitted bar flickered into life. The sign said '*Annie's*'.

It was her club now. Hers alone. Oh, she knew the boys didn't rate her. She wasn't Max. She was a *skirt*, and men like Steve and Gary, men who were used to pissing highest up the wall and swaggering about the place like tin gods, they might tolerate her but that was all. But still – she had *this*. She had achieved *this*.

Suddenly, there was a noise. Annie stiffened. *Again.*

A sort of shuffling movement, coming from the direction of the bar. Her heart started thumping fast.

'Hello?' she called out.

Silence.

It was just the old building making the noises it always made in summer. Just the popping and cracking of the beams – sometimes the old place creaked like a ship at sea. It had freaked her out when she'd first moved in, but now she was used to it.

Yeah, but it don't shuffle, she thought.

She remembered her mother, Connie, telling her tales of spirits. Newly dead, they came back sometimes and crashed about the place, not meaning to scare, but trying to communicate and not sure how to do it.

Communicate what? shot into her brain.

Shit! Was she really entertaining the notion that this was *Aretha* down here, Aretha's unquiet spirit, trying to tell her something about her death, trying to tell her who'd killed her?

She moved forward cautiously between the banquettes, peering ahead, the red neon lighting her way. Looked at the rows of optics, the mirrored backing behind them.

Saw herself in there, white-faced, worried. Seriously spooked. Everything was still, silent. Then something shot out from the far end of the bar.

Annie fell back, nearly overbalancing against the

edge of one of the brown banquettes. And saw that the 'unquiet spirit' was in fact a cat. A black cat that had got in here during the day while the builders were in and out, doors open, a fucking *cat* had just given her the fright of her life. And now the damned thing was rubbing up against her leg, purring, arching its back.

She'd seen this particular cat around here before, begging titbits and milk off the builders; it was a regular visitor.

'You little bastard,' said Annie, and a laugh exploded out of her.

She scooped the intruder up in her arms, smoothed its silken fur and took it to the door, put the cat outside, then shut and locked the door.

Still half laughing to herself, she stood and looked at the neon over the bar again. '*Annie's*'. She stared at it for a while. Then she turned everything off, and went back up the stairs to her flat, locking the door behind her.

23

Next morning at nine the builders were back, and at ten an immaculately dressed DI Hunter was knocking at the door. One of the builders directed him up the stairs. He went up and found the office door open with Annie sitting inside working on some figures. She looked up, surprised to see him there. Bloody good job she'd given the police case notes back to Lane. If she'd had them out on the desk, that would have taken a bit of explaining away.

'Good morning, Detective Inspector,' said Annie cordially.

DI Hunter didn't look in a friendly mood; then again he never did. His mouth was set in a thin line. His dark eyes were frosty. She was about to have her arse chewed, she could see it coming.

'Mrs Carter.'

'Have a seat.'

He stared at the seat as if he might have to get it deep-cleaned first. He sat down. Looked at her. 'We've had a complaint. A Mrs Vera Delacourt has said that her son was assaulted last night.'

'Oh yes?'

'By one of your . . . associates,' he said.

Annie's face was blank.

'She claims that he was badly beaten and that his dog was killed. But even as she was lodging the complaint, her son was denying anything had happened. His face was bruised, scratched. I asked him where the dog was. We've had a few complaints from neighbours about the dog's barking. He said it had run off. Said his mum was imagining things.'

'Really.'

'Yes. Really.' His eyes held hers steadily.

Bloody Derek, thought Annie. She hadn't got rid of him a moment too soon.

'I don't know anything about that,' she said. 'But I'll certainly look into it.'

He sat back in the chair. He wasn't done yet.

'I don't like the way you people do business, Mrs Carter,' he said.

'Us people?' Annie looked at him.

'Intimidation. Taking the law upon yourselves.'

'I'll have a word about it,' said Annie.

'Only, I'm wondering what your connection is to this son of hers, this Mr Robert Delacourt.'

Rizzo, thought Annie. Trust a loser like that to give himself a snazzy name.

'I have no connection with her son,' said Annie.

'I'm only asking because Robert Delacourt had a sister, Valerie Delacourt, a known prostitute who died a couple of months ago – killed, we believe, by Christopher Brown, who has been charged with her murder and with the murder of Teresa Walker, and with that of his wife, Aretha Brown – a close friend of yours, as her husband still is. So there is a connection.'

'Not a very strong one,' said Annie.

'I just want to say this once, Mrs Carter – don't interfere in the law's business. Be very careful.'

'In what way?'

'I've checked you out. You have associated with known prostitutes. You were charged with running a disorderly house and selling liquor without a licence.'

'And cleared.'

'You weren't cleared. Your sentence was suspended, that's all.'

Annie's eyes held his. 'Do you think it's possible the law has made a mistake in this matter?'

'No,' he said flatly. 'I don't.'

'Well, I do.'

He stood up. 'Remember what I said, Mrs Carter. Please. Or we may fall out, and neither of us wants that, I'm sure.'

Annie stood up too.

'It's the very last thing I'd want,' she said. 'Did you find out what happened to Gareth?'

'What?'

'Gareth. The boy we found dead in the block of flats?'

'It appears to be suicide, but the postmortem will tell us more. And Mrs Carter, *whatever* it was, it does not concern you. I hope we understand each other.'

'We do.'

He nodded and went off down the stairs. Annie phoned Tony, went down to make sure the builders were hard at it, and was out the door, her face set in grim lines, to catch up on business before doing something she really, really didn't want to have to do.

By four o'clock that same day, Annie and Dolly were at the funeral director's, looking at catalogues of floral arrangements and a variety of coffins. You could have mahogany – expensive – or pine – cheap. You could have elaborate brass handles, or plain ones. Sumptuous silk or cheap cotton linings, in pink or blue or cream or white. You could spend out whatever the fuck you liked. Push the boat out. Blow the whole family fortune.

But really it's all bollocks, Annie thought.

None of it was going to bring anybody back or make the pain of loss any better.

Aunt Louella arrived, still dressed in sober black. And then came the part they were all dreading. The funeral director's assistant ushered them into another room, the Chapel of Rest. And there, lying in an open coffin, was Aretha.

Annie felt her throat close, felt clammy sweat break out over her entire body.

Jesus, don't let me faint! she thought.

She breathed deeply and held on to Louella. Annie couldn't tell who was holding who up. Dolly moved forward first – she had balls, that girl. Looked down at the corpse in the coffin.

The funeral director's assistant withdrew discreetly to one side of the room, close enough to help if anyone got too distressed, far enough away to allow the mourners some privacy.

'Don't she look peaceful?' said Dolly in wonder.

It was the right thing to say.

Louella moved forward too. Because Annie was holding on to the woman's arm, she was forced to move with her, and as Aunt Louella looked at the empty vessel that had been her beloved niece, Annie also forced herself to look.

Aretha did look peaceful. Her dark skin was glowing with an almost healthy sheen, all the scratches and bloodstains skilfully washed away, covered over. Her hair was neatly drawn back, exposing the strong, beautiful bones of her face. There was a trace of lipstick on her full lips, mascara on her lashes. She was wearing a white gown that was gathered high on the neck with a ruff like a choirboy's. *To hide the marks*, thought Annie, and suddenly she felt sick.

This wasn't Aretha. Aretha was gone.

She could feel Louella shaking, sobbing. Couldn't look at the woman, because then she might break down as well, and she never cried. She was always the tough one, the one who stood strong. On the other side of Louella, Dolly fished out a wad of tissues and handed them to the grief-stricken woman, putting a warm arm around her shuddering shoulders.

Annie took one long, last look at the remnants of her good friend, and left the room. She waited for them outside on the pavement.

Tony sat in the car, watching her with a trace of anxiety. *You all right, Boss?* he mouthed.

Annie nodded and walked away, taking deep breaths, trying to steady herself.

But something wrenched at her guts, some spasm of grief and rage, making her wonder if she was going to throw up right here on the pavement. She paced about, clutching her arms around herself, feeling chilled, even though it was a clear bright day.

Aretha was gone. Other friends too, *and* her husband. She had lost so much.

And now, for the first time, it truly crashed in upon her. The intensity, the brutality, the sheer relentlessness of the losses she had suffered. She couldn't lose anyone else. Couldn't bear it. She pulled a hand through her hair, drew in a shaky breath, tried to get a grip.

At last Dolly and Louella came out. Annie approached them.

'All right?' she asked stupidly. She looked at Louella, who had aged ten years in the last half an hour. Looked at Dolly. Ditto.

'We'll give you a lift home,' she said to Louella.

The woman shook her head, straightened her spine. 'No. That's all right. Thank you.'

And with that she slowly walked away.

Dolly and Annie looked at each other.

'Fuck it, that was bloody horrible,' said Dolly.

Annie stepped forward and hugged Dolly tight, surprising her.

'You all right?' asked Dolly, when Annie released her.

'Fine.'

'What's wrong?'

'Nothing, Doll. Really. Just you're a bloody diamond, that's all.'

'Oh.' Dolly was staring at her curiously. 'You sure you're all right?'

Annie wasn't sure at all, but she nodded. Tony opened the back door of the car, and they both piled in ready to drop Dolly home. Then, at Annie's request, Tony drove around while she sat in the back, silent, thinking about life and death, turning it all over in her mind. Tony was watching her in the rear-view mirror, thinking that *something was really wrong with the boss.*

Finally she told him to take her on over to Constantine's. Once parked up, she told Tony to go home; she wouldn't need him again tonight, she'd phone when she did.

She saw Tony give her an odd look as she turned away and walked up the steps of the Holland Park mansion. A few seconds later she heard him drive away as she knocked on the big navy-blue painted double doors.

The usual man, huge and muscle-bound, opened it. 'Mrs Carter,' he said politely.

'Is he in?'

'Yes, he's in.' And he held the door wide.

He led the way across the silent marble hall and knocked on the study door.

Annie heard the familiar voice call from inside.

'Mrs Carter for you, Boss,' said the man, opening the door.

Constantine was sitting behind the desk. The banker's light was casting its usual cosy glow. He was sorting through papers but now he looked up, blue eyes bright in his tanned, healthy face. She stared at him. Mafia. Dangerous. Maybe untrustworthy, who knew? But he was sexy as hell. And so *alive*.

'It's Monday,' he said.

'I know,' said Annie faintly, moving closer.

'Monday, not Tuesday,' he emphasized. 'Tuesday for lunch we said, didn't we say that?'

'We did. Yes.'

Annie was standing in front of the big desk now with its tooled-leather top. Expensive, like him. A Mont Blanc pen was lying among the papers; here was a thug with class. Like Max, and yet nothing like Max at all. Max had been the roughest of diamonds. Constantine was smooth as silk. He wore an aura of immense power like a cloak. Scared the shit out of most people he came into contact with. Hell, he scared the shit out of *her*.

He kicked back his chair and looked at her. 'Problem?' he said.

Annie shrugged off her jacket. Breathing hard, she reached back, unzipped her dress, let it fall to the floor. Saw the surprise in his eyes as she stood there in her bra and panties, suspender belt and stockings. She walked around the desk, leaned against it, looked him straight in the eye.

'Don't talk. Just fuck me,' she said. 'Now.'

Constantine stood up. She suddenly felt small and vulnerable, semi-naked and shivering as if with fever, while he was fully clothed and tall and strong. His eyes holding hers, he put his hands on her waist and lifted her up so that she was properly on the desk.

'What's wrong?' he asked, an exact echo of Dolly outside the funeral parlour.

It was mid-evening; dusk was beginning to close in. For an instant Constantine stepped away from her, pulled down the blind at the window behind the desk. The room was suddenly cosier, more intimate. He came back to her. Gave her a questioning look.

'There's nothing wrong,' said Annie, linking her arms around his neck as he nudged her legs apart and came in close.

He bent his head and kissed her. Annie kissed him back, her tongue teasing. Then he drew back.

'Liar,' he said.

'Fuck me,' she repeated, and pulled his head back down to hers, absorbing his strength, inhaling the Acqua di Parma cologne he wore, feeling his heat, the sudden hard answering urgency of his desire.

Constantine unclasped her bra and pulled it off, releasing her breasts into his hands. Annie gasped at the touch of his thumbs stroking over her nipples, urging them into hardness. She reached down, pulling off her pants.

'Why the rush?' murmured Constantine against her mouth.

'Just do it,' she moaned, her hands trembling

233

as they unbuckled him, unzipped him, moved inside, found him gratifyingly hard, fully erect. Pulling his cock out, touching its moist tip to her clitoris, massaging herself, fully absorbed in her own pleasure, in beating back this awful dead chill she had felt stealing over her today.

Heat flooded her as he swore and pushed her back on to the papers, scattering them, slipping fully inside her and using no finesse this time, no hesitation, no questions. Filled, replete, Annie lay back and let him have her, relishing every hot stroke, clutching at his hips, muttering *yes, yes, do it* until Constantine grew huge and harder, almost hurtful; and then he came and it was over, it was done, but he kept her there, working her clitoris with his fingers until she came too, the pleasure crashing over her, making her jerk and writhe and scream out his name.

Finally they were still, panting, coming back to themselves.

Constantine leaned over her, still lodged inside her. His face was still and watchful as he stared down at her.

'Wow,' he said.

'Mm,' said Annie.

Constantine withdrew, zipped himself back up, buckled his belt. Pulled her up so that she was sitting on the desk again. Annie felt warm, relaxed. Better. *Much* better.

Constantine sat down in the chair again, looked up at her that same way again. Shadowed. Watchful. Cool, all of a sudden.

'Now are you going to tell me what's wrong?' he asked.

'I don't know.' Annie shrugged. 'I just felt . . . down.'

And now Annie could see it clearly. Aretha's death had brought to the surface things that she had been busy suppressing for months. She had never really dealt with her feelings over the deaths of her friends or Max, and Aretha's horrible passing had brought it all sharply into focus.

Before this had happened, she had been wrapped up in day-to-day concerns, totally absorbed in the business of just *surviving* – worrying over Layla and all that Layla had been through. Worrying about the boys and winning them over – wondering if that would ever happen, and doubting it every day. Worrying about the expansion of the security business, worrying about the club, worrying about legitimately making a success of the firm, bringing in money to keep her daughter and herself clothed and fed . . . but all that had been *before* Aretha had been brutally murdered.

Now she had to face the fact that life could be shockingly short. People you love could be cut away from you in an instant, never to be seen again. So you had to live as full a life as you could, grab it with both hands and shake it by the throat, because yours could go just as quickly, just as unexpectedly. She knew that now.

'Anything I can do?' asked Constantine.

'Think you just did it,' said Annie.

'Right. Staying the night?'

'That was the plan,' said Annie.

'I didn't know there was a plan.'

'Well there was. There is. It's all up here.' She tapped her forehead.

Constantine sat back and shook his head. 'Mrs Carter, you're a very forceful woman. And you know what? I sort of like it. Sometimes.'

'Only sometimes?' Annie was smiling, teasing.

But still he was looking at her in that same way. Watchful, yes, that was it. Almost mistrustful. Shuttered.

There was a pause. Constantine's eyes slipped away from hers.

'What?' she asked, still teasing, but now there was a twinge of concern in her guts, and she thought, *What happened? What did I do that was so terrible? Did he hate me taking the lead?*

His eyes came back, stared straight into hers. Something was wrong.

'Come on, Constantine, what is it?' asked Annie, anxious now.

'You don't even know you did it, do you?' he asked, still shaking his head slightly.

'I don't know what you're talking about,' said Annie, confused.

Suddenly she felt foolish, embarrassed, sitting here semi-naked with this man fully clothed beside her, this man who seconds ago had been a passionate lover but was now a cold, withdrawn stranger. She stood up, started searching around for her discarded clothes.

'Look, I'll go. Maybe this wasn't a good idea anyway.'

'Maybe it wasn't. Maybe this is all too soon for you.'

That hurt. She looked at him, and the hurt showed plainly in her eyes.

'You really don't even know you did it, do you?' he marvelled.

'Did *what?*' Annie demanded. What the hell was he talking about?

'You called me Max,' he said.

Outside the house, hidden in the shadows, Charlie Foster drew back. Thinking about what he'd just seen: the glimpse of Annie Carter stripped down to her undies, gorgeous, nearly eating Constantine Barolli's face off before he pulled the blind down. Then, all Charlie could see was their outlines moving through the blind, obviously fucking each other senseless. Felt quite turned on himself, watching that.

What a woman. What a *bitch*. He promised himself that he was going to catch up with Annie Carter very soon.

There was no point in staying after that. Annie got dressed and asked if she could call a cab.

'Sure,' said Constantine, very cool.

As soon as was decently possible, in as dignified a manner as was feasible after being made to look like such a fool, such a complete fruitcake, she left. Constantine didn't ask if she was still coming to lunch tomorrow, and she didn't ask if she was still invited.

No point.

Jesus, she'd called him Max.

She sat in the back of the cab feeling choked, humiliated, bewildered, adrift. *I'm a train wreck*, she thought, and put her head in her hands. But then she thought of the boys – *Max*'s boys, who was she kidding? They weren't hers at all, Constantine was dead right about that – and thought that it was all for the best. She'd killed it, once and for all. And that was a good thing. She kept telling herself that, all the way home.

24

First thing next morning she phoned Ruthie and spoke to Layla, who told her about the kittens and seemed happy. Warm, caring Ruthie was more of a natural mother than she ever was, she knew that. Okay, she didn't *like* it, but it was a fact. Then she left the builders to it and called over at Dolly's in Limehouse.

'Cuppa, Mrs Carter?' asked Rosie, sauntering around the kitchen while Dolly badgered her to smarten herself up, which Rosie cheerfully ignored.

'No thanks, Rosie. Got a busy day ahead. How's tricks?' Annie liked the girl. A real daydreamer, that was Rosie, padding around in bare feet and smiling nonstop.

'Ticking over,' said Rosie with a lazy grin.

'Yeah, not ticking very bloody *fast* though,' said Dolly, bustling through. 'Go up and get dressed, for the love of God, Rosie. And tell Sharlene I want her to get down the shops – preferably before this Christmas, if she can spare the bloody time.'

Rosie strolled off upstairs.

'Jesus, that girl,' said Dolly with a reluctant smile.

Annie thought again of how panicked Dolly had been when she thought Rosie'd taken that escort job. Panicked beyond all reason, it seemed.

'You okay now?' Dolly was asking her. 'You seemed a bit shook up yesterday.'

'It was bloody horrible, seeing Aretha laid out.'

'I know, I know.' Dolly patted her arm. 'Poor old Louella. Ten times worse for her. What you up to, then?'

'Just work,' said Annie, 'what else?'

'Ain't it the truth,' agreed Dolly.

An hour later she was in church again. Not her natural surroundings by any means. There was no choir today either, lifting the roof off. But the organist/choirmaster was there, playing *Jesu Joy of Man's Desiring*. He glanced back at her as she came in, big pop-eyes with bags underneath, balding, wet-lipped. Funny little chap. *Not* pretty, that was for sure.

She went up the aisle and settled herself into a pew. It was cool in here, after the heat outside. Christ on his cross up there on the stained-glass window, light filtering through, spilling jewelled splashes of yellow, red and blue on to the stone floor in front of the altar.

In actual fact, she didn't know what she was doing here today. Knew only that she felt lost and lonely and afraid. She was losing her grip on things. Couldn't believe what a screw-up she had become. Calling Constantine by Max's name. But she reminded herself that it was just as well. If the boys suspected that Max's widow was screwing the American mob boss, where would that leave her? How would they take it? Badly, she felt sure. Retribution could follow. What form it would take, she had no idea. But it wouldn't be pleasant.

But then, we're over, she thought. *So that's that problem solved . . . right?*

She thought about Dolly. Maybe Aretha's death had shaken her up more than any of them had realized, but Annie had the strong feeling that something wasn't right there, that there was something more to it, something deeper. Rosie's little trip out on Saturday had rattled the Limehouse madam badly too – and what the fuck was *that* all about?

'Can I help?' said a voice nearby.

Annie looked up. The vicar was standing there in his long black cassock and white dog collar. He was a thin, narrow-shouldered man, probably in his forties. His grey hair was receding and he had a neatly trimmed beard that was also grey.

His face was tanned, his eyes grey, quick-moving and kind.

'I doubt it,' she said with a half-smile.

He smiled back. 'Well, if you want to talk . . .'

'No,' said Annie.

The vicar watched her for another beat or two, then turned and started to walk up towards the high altar.

'Um . . . vicar?' Annie called after him.

He stopped, turned. Waited expectantly.

'Did you know Aretha Brown?'

'Aretha Brown.' His face was blank.

'I don't know if she ever worshipped here, but you must have conducted her wedding ceremony. And her Aunt Louella sings in the choir.'

The vicar nodded once. 'I know Louella. A great lady. When was the wedding?'

'A couple of years ago,' said Annie. She hadn't been here for Aretha and Chris's wedding. She wished now that she had. On that one triumphant, happy day, when Aretha had been vital and alive; when Chris must have been so very happy.

'I'd have to check my records. It's likely I took the ceremony, although I have a lay preacher who stands in for me when I'm away. I do a lot for various charities, it keeps me pretty busy. I'm away quite often.'

'Aretha's dead,' said Annie.

The vicar paused. 'I know. I'm sorry. Is that why you came here today? To feel closer to her?'

'I suppose so.'

'Do you worship here? I don't think I recognize your face.'

'No. I don't.'

They fell silent. The music was beautiful, winding its way like a balm around Annie's pain, soothing it.

Such an ugly little man, she thought. *And he plays like an angel.*

'If it would help you, we could pray together . . . ?' suggested the vicar.

Annie's eyes shifted, settled on his face. 'No,' she said. 'But thank you.'

He nodded and moved on, walking up to the altar, crossing himself before it. He knelt to pray. Annie stood up and went down the aisle to the main door. She opened it and stepped out into sunlight, and walked straight into the dark-haired, dark-eyed and immaculately suited DI Hunter.

'What are you doing here?' he asked.

'I've no idea. How about you?' She looked up at the church's imposing façade, then back at his face. 'You come to your senses and released Chris yet?'

DI Hunter almost smiled at that. 'Hardly. We're taking the car apart, looking for links to the Delacourt and Walker murders.'

Annie thought of Chris's old two-tone Zephyr.

He loved that car, wouldn't trade it in for the world. And now the Bill was pulling it to bits. That car was part of who Chris was, part of his history, part of the time when he had been young and invincible. She felt a sharp stab of sorrow. They'd be taking his house apart too, she knew that. Trashing his memories, trashing the life he had built there with Aretha.

Poor bastard. Somehow, she had to get him out of this.

'If you've got it all taped, why are you here looking for answers, like me?' she asked Hunter. 'Aretha's aunt sings in the church choir, you know.'

'Yes. I do know that.'

'Only I think all you've got against Chris is – what do they call it? – circumstantial evidence.'

Hunter shook his head. *Arrogant prick*, thought Annie. Standing there, looking all neat and tidy when her friend was stuck in a cell. Looking down his aquiline nose at her. Not a clue, of course, that she had his DS firmly in her pocket. Not a fucking *notion* that she had told Jackie Tulliver she needed more info on Aretha's murder, and on Gareth Fuller's too, and to get in touch with Lane about both cases. Lane was bleating about it all like a fucking baby, getting edgy, saying he'd only just got away with it the first time. Jackie had told him to stop whining and get the fuck on with it, or else.

'Circumstantial? I don't think so, Mrs Carter. Motive – he was upset that his wife had recently gone back on the game. Money was an issue between them. Means – he was ferrying her around late at night to meet her "clients". He said that word with such crushing disdain that Annie wanted to hit him. 'He had both means and motive. You know what I think?'

'I don't know and I don't care.'

'Does the truth hurt, Mrs Carter?'

'I haven't heard any of that yet.'

'Oh but you have. You just won't accept it. I think they argued that night. She went off to see the client and he'd had enough, he just snapped. He met her afterwards, as he usually did, but this time he put an end to her lucrative little career in a rather final manner.'

'He wasn't married to the other two. Why do them?'

'We don't know yet. But we'll find out. The MO was the same. Perhaps his impulse to kill his wife was a copycat of the other two, maybe he didn't do them, maybe he knew the person that *did* and just thought, what a neat idea. We're still looking into that. But he does have a dodgy past. Working as a doorman in a "massage parlour" is hardly indicative of sterling character.'

'That don't make him a murderer,' said Annie. 'What about the boy, Gareth? The boy on reception?'

'We still believe he hanged himself.'

'Or was he hanged?' Annie looked at him sharply. 'And if he was, you couldn't pin *that* on Chris. He was banged up at the time. In your cells. Question is, was Gareth hoisted up there and physically *hanged* by someone else?'

'Nothing points to that. But, as I told you, the postmortem on Friday will tell us more.'

'But he signed in this "Smith" that Aretha was visiting that night. And he signed him out, too. Perhaps Smith got worried; thought Gareth could identify him. Perhaps he decided to eliminate the risk. Followed him home. Hanged him.'

'You're clutching at straws,' said Hunter.

'No, *you* are,' said Annie hotly. 'Chris Brown ain't a killer.'

He said nothing. He turned and walked away from her, into the church.

Feeling cold despite the heat of the day, Annie went down the steps and got into the car.

'Where to, Boss?'

Annie's anger was eating into her. That bastard Hunter was going to get Chris sent down, she just knew it. She *had* to stop that happening somehow.

'Just drive around, Tone. I need to think.'

25

The grinding of the saw was usually the thing that sent him heading for the chair by the sink. DI Paul Hunter sat down there now, not wishing to suffer the indignity of actually *collapsing* on to it. There were advantages to doing this while Dr Penyard and his assistant worked on the corpse on the table. You couldn't get a clear view of the proceedings, for a start. Which was a good thing. And, even better, you couldn't smell much, either. He *liked* the chair by the sink.

Over the years he'd attended his fair share of post-mortems, and nothing had yet hardened him to the procedure. He'd started off this one just as he did all the others – standing by the table. But that hadn't been the wisest thing. Because hangings were never pretty, and Gareth Fuller's was downright appalling.

Once the corpse had been an averagely good-looking young man. Now, in death, all pretence of that was gone. His face was drained to blood-less white. The tongue, which still protruded from between the chapped bluish lips, was dry, scaly black. And the open eyelids revealed the worst horror.

'That's scleral haemorrhage,' said the gowned, goggled, gloved and chubby Dr Penyard cheerfully when Hunter had commented upon it. 'Turns the whites of the eyes red.'

It was a hideous sight. The whole *body* was a hideous sight, and a pitiful one. The marks on the neck were brutal, horrible. The boy had puncture marks on his arms: he'd injected drugs. The lower legs looked bruised and were scattered with tiny red haemorrhages.

'Tardieu spots,' said Dr Penyard, as he briskly finished up on the thoraco-abdominal incision. 'Consistent with hanging.'

Penyard put the saw aside and lifted off the ribs and breastbone to expose the pleural cavity.

Enough, thought Hunter. He didn't know why he put himself through this.

Dedication, maybe. Insatiable curiosity . . . and, okay, he admitted it, just a little doubt. Just a little *worm* of doubt that gnawed away at him, made him think: *Could she be right?*

He couldn't shake the image of Annie Carter's face from his brain. A gangster's moll, by all accounts. Tough as nails and twice as nasty, with a murky past. But stunning, he had to admit that. And with such intense conviction in her dark green eyes, such *certainty* that Chris Brown was innocent, such determination to prove that Gareth Fuller had not killed himself, but had been murdered to cover a killer's tracks. Her passionate beliefs made him ask himself the question again: *could* she be right?

That was why he was here, even though he wanted to be somewhere, anywhere, else. To gain certainty. To *know*.

Now Penyard and his assistant were removing the heart and lungs, impersonal as butchers working on the carcass of a cow. They went on to remove the intestines, the brain. Hunter detached himself from what was going on here. Thought of other things. Like how he had to get this job done. Like his suspicions about DS Lane, too. The man was basically unlikable, but that didn't matter. What mattered was that he was untrustworthy. Hunter felt that strongly.

'Hey Paul?'

Hunter looked up. Penyard was beckoning him over.

Groaning inside, Hunter stood up and walked over to the table.

'Found something?' he asked, keeping his eyes away from the gaping cavity in the corpse's chest and the big skin flap on the head, where the skull was exposed. At least it covered up those bloody, staring eyes.

Penyard was looking at the neck.

'The flex left a deep bruise,' he pointed out. 'Extensive capillary damage. Broke the hyoid cartilage.'

'Meaning?'

'The flex wasn't placed around the neck after death.'

'So?'

Penyard shrugged. 'Could be suicide, but could be murder too. There's no sign of struggle though.'

'What if he was drugged?' asked Hunter.

Gareth had a clear reputation as a drug user. What if his killer had come across him in a drugged state?

He could imagine that. The knock on the door. Gareth, half out of it on dope, opening it, letting his killer in. Too weak and spaced out by the drugs to fight, or even to protest. Hoisted up on the light fitting, killed.

Easy.

And all because he checked in Smith, and checked him out, on the night Aretha Brown was killed? wondered Hunter. *All because he might have been able to identify him?*

Hunter thought about that. Something about the Aretha Brown case was looking subtly different to the first two. Something was niggling at him.

'You tested for drugs yet?' he persisted.

'Not yet. We will.'

'Okay,' said Hunter, and left the autopsy suite with a huge sense of relief, but also a profound feeling of frustration. He wanted to *know*. That was his driving force, his reason to be a cop, a detective. He needed to *know*. It was what had wrecked his six-year marriage, his dedication to the job. He'd got home one night and there was a note on the table, *Goodbye*. Simple as that. It was his own fault, and he knew it. He loved the job too much. And maybe . . . yeah, maybe he'd loved his wife too little.

When he got back to his desk, Collating were on the phone and they weren't happy. DS Lane had been found down there taking out a couple of files.

'So?' he asked.

'Well, not so much "taking" them out as *sneaking* them out without permission, you know the procedure. He was heading for the photocopier room with them,' said the agitated voice on the other end of the phone.

'Which files?'

'The Aretha Brown murder. And the Gareth Fuller case too.'

Annie fucking Carter, he thought.

26

Dolly met Annie at the front door when she called in again at the Limehouse brothel.

'Someone here to see you,' she said in a whisper, her mouth pursed in a cat's-bum curve of disapproval. 'She's been here *ages*.'

'Oh? Who?' Annie took off her jacket, shook the rain off, hung it on the peg.

'She wouldn't give her name. Scruffy-looking little mare, looks sort of familiar but I can't place her.'

Annie's heart gave a leap. 'In the kitchen?'

The cat's-bum curve got deeper. The kitchen was sacrosanct to Dolly. It was the one place in the house where punters were never granted entry, where only favoured visitors were admitted.

'Fuck me, no. Tart like that, you're kidding. The girl said she wanted to have a word with you, and I said you might not call in, and she said well she'd wait until you did, and she whiffs a bit so I almost thought of letting her wait out in the street. But anyway, call me a soft touch, but it's peeing down out there, I couldn't do it. She's in the front parlour, which by the way I am probably going to have to get fumigated after this, and the bill's coming to you, Annie Carter, is that clear?'

'It's clear,' said Annie, trying not to crack a grin at Dolly's gruff but kind ways.

She went into the front parlour and found Mira sitting huddled on the sofa, clutching her thin bare legs with clenched hands. She looked up sharply when Annie came in, and shot to her feet.

'Mira?' Annie stood there at the door and shook her head. 'Fuck, it *is* you.'

But this wasn't the Mira Cooper she had known. The Mira who had once worked for her up West, as a high-class call girl, had been the most luscious creature, with a huge mane of shining blonde hair, a film-star gloss to her perfectly tanned skin. She'd had couture dresses to wear, and jewels and furs, all bought for her by doting admirers.

Annie found herself remembering that picture of Mira in the papers when the scandal hit and Annie's knocking-shop ambitions had come crashing to the ground – Mira striding along Bond Street in dark glasses, wearing a priceless mink coat.

And now, here she was.

253

The deliciously polished and beautiful Mira who had stayed at Cliveden and dined at the Ritz with the country's good and great. Mira, with the cut-glass accent of the Home Counties. Mira, who had made a fortune on her back.

She wouldn't make any fortunes *now*, that was for damned sure.

This girl looked so different to the Mira Annie had known. Skinny, unwashed. Her complexion leaden and marred with sores. Her once magnificent hair was short, lying lank and greasy around her gaunt face. Only her eyes were the same – clear, lamp-like, vividly blue.

Annie's heart clenched at the sight of her.

And Jeez, Dolly was right. Mira didn't smell too good. Hadn't washed her hair or had a bath in a month, Annie guessed. Out in the fresh air it hadn't been so noticeable. In here, it was horrible. She couldn't stop staring at the sores on Mira's cheeks; sores that hadn't been visible in the shadows under the bridge. *Junkie sores*, thought Annie.

When Mira opened her mouth, Annie noticed how yellow her teeth were, where once they had been pristine white. Dirty teeth, dirty hair, dirty body. There was a smear of what looked suspiciously like shit on Mira's skinny white thigh. *Pity the punters*, she thought. But then, if you were going to have a quick shag under the Mile End

Road, you probably weren't going to be all that choosy.

Mira looked nervous, like she might bolt.

'How did you know where to find me?' asked Annie, wanting to embrace this stick-thin object that had once been her old friend Mira. Mira with the beautiful speaking voice and huge blue eyes. But she kept her distance. If she got too close, she feared Mira would run again. And she didn't even *want* to get too close. Mira stank to high heaven.

'Rizzo was talking about you to one of the girls in the pub. Telling her about how you had one of your boys kill his dog.' The mouth twisted. 'God, I hated that horrible mutt. I'm glad that boy of yours killed it. Rizzo was sobbing into his pint after that, looking for a sympathy hand-job,' she added with a faint smile. 'I remembered you mentioning this place, back in the day. I thought I'd find you here.'

'Well, here I am.' Annie sat down well away from Mira. Then she finally said it. Couldn't hold it in a moment longer. 'Fuck's sake Mira, what went wrong? What's happened to you?'

But Mira didn't answer. She was looking around the room, taking in the soft furnishings, the spotless look of the place.

'It's nice here,' she said wistfully.

Annie felt her heart wrench again, hard and

painful. She saw why Dolly hadn't made Mira wait out there in the rain. Any one of the girls who worked here could have gone this way, tramping the cold and dangerous night streets with a rotten, uncaring male pimp in charge of them. This humble home-cum-brothel, so warm, so safe, must seem like heaven to poor Mira.

'We didn't really have time to talk much, did we?' Mira smiled nervously. Her hands were constantly moving, tugging her short denim skirt down, fiddling with her grubby off-white top, scratching at her forearms.

'No,' said Annie, 'we didn't. You ran off before I could get over the shock of seeing you there.'

'I knew Val really well,' said Mira.

'Did you? Rizzo's sister. Can you believe that grotty pathetic little worm would put his own sister on the game? What was she like?'

'She had a lot of attitude, just like Rizzo. Acted like the boss bitch in town because her brother was in charge.'

'Mira . . .' Annie looked at her intensely.

'No!' Mira said firmly, harshly. 'Just let me talk about Val, okay? I came here to talk about Val. Not about me.'

Annie sighed and gave up. Instead, she held out her wrist, where the Rolex glinted. She slipped it off, and held it out to Mira. 'Look. I've still got it. You and Jen and Thelma gave it to me on my birthday, on the day we got raided up West, you remember?'

Mira didn't touch the watch, but she nodded. 'I remember.'

Annie put the watch back on. Mira wasn't biting. She almost longed to say to this wrecked creature: *Come on, Mira, drop this peculiar disguise. I know you're in there somewhere.* But maybe *her* Mira, the confident and stunning Mira of old, maybe that Mira no longer existed. Maybe this sad, shabby shell was all that was left. And if that was so, then digging around looking for the old Mira was only going to cause her more pain.

Annie took a breath, and got back to the here and now.

'Okay. Rizzo gave us nothing, nothing at all. So he knows nothing, he can't do, or Steve would have got it out of him.' She paused, staring at Mira. 'Do *you* know something about all this? Something that can help get Val, Teresa and Aretha's killer?'

Mira nodded cautiously. Her eyes slipped away from Annie's.

Annie found herself holding her breath. 'You've heard they've arrested Chris Brown, who used to be bouncer here, and that the Bill have charged him with his wife Aretha's murder. They're trying to stick him with the killings of Val Delacourt and Teresa Walker too.'

'And you don't think he did it?' asked Mira, her face curious.

Annie shook her head. 'I know Chris Brown. He couldn't do any of this.' She looked at Mira. 'It's good to see you again, Mira. Really good.'

Mira ignored that. She hunched forward suddenly, clutched her bare mottled legs as if they were cold. The intense blue eyes fixed on Annie's face.

'Look, I shouldn't even have come round here. But you were always good to me. I heard that you were doing something, trying to get to the bottom of this and I . . . no, I shouldn't be here. But I don't like all this going on. Working girls getting killed. We have to stick together. Be loyal. That's all we have.'

Annie was nearly exploding with frustration. She kept quiet. It was pretty obvious that Mira had nothing much to tell, anyway.

'There's a parlour,' said Mira after a pause.

'A parlour?' Annie echoed, thinking of *this* parlour, the front parlour. 'Do you mean another massage parlour? Another knocking-shop? Did Val have connections to a madam, is that what you're saying? Rizzo wouldn't have stood for that, would he? He'd be spitting blood.'

Mira was shaking her head. 'Not a brothel. Not that sort of parlour. I mean a *tattoo* parlour.'

'Go on.'

Mira shrugged. 'A lot of the girls go there. It's

a sort of meeting place, you know? In Soho. Right next door to the Alley Cat club.' She shuddered slightly. 'Really freaky guy runs it, he's Rizzo's brother, Pete. Covered in tattoos. But he's nice to the girls, makes them coffee, they sit down and have a chat between themselves there while they get their tattoos done. Pete runs it, but there's another guy comes in and does a couple of days a week – or at least there used to be. Val had a tattoo done there a couple of days before she died; the other guy did it, not Pete.'

'And?'

'Val tried to talk me into getting one done at the same time, but I wouldn't do it. I sat with her while she was having hers done. She said there was money in it, she was *paid* to have it.'

Annie stifled a sigh. *Paid?* What the hell did that mean? So Val had been tattooed, so what? What could that possibly prove, what use could that conceivably be? Precisely none. Mira was shot away, hyped up on something.

'What's the tattoo?' asked Annie.

'It's a red flame, high up on the inner thigh.'

Annie was silent. This was crap, just total hogwash.

'Only you didn't hear this from me, okay?' Mira added nervously. 'I was never here. Okay? Annie?'

'Yeah, sure. Okay.'

Mira nodded, bit her lip. It was chewed all to hell, Annie noticed. 'I've been thinking it over, you know. All this. And I remember your friend, Aretha Brown. I *do* remember her. I know everyone thinks I'm just a stupid junkie, that my brains are fried, but I *do*. I met her at your party, the same day we gave you that watch, the same day as the police raid. She was great. Gorgeous.' Mira's ravaged mouth twisted into a grim smile. 'Fuck it, we *all* were back then. Val Delacourt wasn't great, and she wasn't gorgeous either, but she didn't deserve this. She was up against it, with rotten Rizzo and Pete Delacourt for brothers, that was for sure. And that's why I'm telling you about it, even though I shouldn't be doing this. Even though he'd kill me if he knew. I've worked it out. The flame tattoo's like a marker, do you see? You have the tattoo, then you die.'

'You really think that? Then why don't you tell the bloody police?' Annie asked, curiously.

Mira blew out her lips in exasperation.

'Come on. Look at me. Do you think the police are going to take notice of anything I say?'

Both Annie and Mira jumped as the phone rang loudly out in the hall. Annie swore under her breath. She was letting herself be spooked by a junkie's tall tales, and that was lunacy.

But then, this was still *Mira*. And Mira had never been anyone's idea of a fool.

They heard Dolly pick up and speak. Her voice was muffled. Suddenly the door opened. Dolly poked her head around it, looked with disapproval at Mira, then at Annie.

'Phone for you,' she said.

Annie stood up, went out into the hall. Dolly went off into the kitchen and started noisily clattering plates into the sink to convey her mood.

'Hello,' said Annie into the phone.

'So where are you, Mrs Carter?' asked Constantine Barolli.

'What?' Annie said stupidly, caught off-guard at hearing his voice.

'It's one o'clock. Didn't we say one o'clock for drinks, and lunch at two? We're just leaving.'

'Leaving?'

'For lunch at the hotel. With the family.'

Annie drew a breath. 'But I thought . . .'

'What? That one pretty understandable little slip was going to stop this?'

He sounded very calm about it now, very confident.

'You were pretty angry at the time.'

'At the *time*, I was. But you were in an emotional state and I was being unfair. So hurry up and get your glad rags on. Want me to send the car?'

Annie's head was spinning. Mira was in there perfuming the front parlour like a skunk, frightening her with fairy tales of flame tattoos, and now she was supposed to go to lunch, lunch with the man she had called by her dead husband's name in the heat of passion, and meet up with his ghastly family, and – oh God, she didn't need this.

But . . . he was giving her a second chance. The question was – should she take it? She thought of the boys again. She knew she was skating on thin ice here. Did she want to carry on, despite the difficulties, despite any possible dangers? She took a deep, steadying breath.

'Don't bother with the car, I'll meet you there. I've got some business to sort out first.'

'Okay, honey. I'll see you there.'

She put the phone down.

Honey.

It was the first time he'd used any sort of endearment with her, and it touched her. Made her feel . . . safe. Sort of protected. The way she used to feel with Max. But she hadn't been safe at all, or protected. All that had been an illusion, shattered in an instant. Shattered forever.

The phone shrilled again. She picked up.

'Hello?'

'Who is that?' said a male voice, deep and deadly cold, with a soft Irish lilt.

'Who is *that*?' asked Annie, but she knew. Way back when she'd been in charge here, she had received his calls every week. He liked to keep his finger on the pulse, to know that everything was running as it should.

'This is Redmond Delaney. May I speak to Miss Farrell please?'

Annie put the phone down on the little table. She went to the kitchen door and looked in at Dolly.

'Redmond Delaney for you, Doll,' she said, and turned back to the phone, back towards the front parlour. Suddenly the door on to the street was being thrown open and she saw Mira dashing out, slamming it hard behind her.

Annie ran to the door. But by the time she got to the gate, Mira was already haring off into the distance. Annie stood there, looking after her ruined friend.

'Fuck it, Mira, don't go,' she said to empty air.

But Mira was gone.

And that's that, thought Annie. *I'll never see her again.*

27

She made a couple of calls from a nearby telephone box and then summoned Tony. Within half
an hour she was standing at Mrs Walker's front
door. She knew she didn't have time for this, not
really, but then she didn't truly have time for lunch
at a swanky Park Lane hotel with the Barollis –
if she was a bit late, sod it.

Mrs Walker looked exactly the same. Her red
hair was scraped back and her face was lined with
exhaustion. She was as washed out as a faded
watercolour painting, clutching a pale lavender
woollen cardigan around her tall bony frame as if
it was a cold day. It wasn't. It was hot, bright, a
beautiful English summer day. She looked at Annie
for a moment without recognition. Then the pallid
eyes flared briefly. 'Oh!'

'Yes, Mrs Walker. It's me, Annie Carter. Can I
come in?'

Mrs Walker stood back. Annie went past her into the same scrupulously clean but very threadbare front room, looked again at the photos of Teresa lined up along the mantelpiece.

Mrs Walker followed her into the room and sat down. She picked up the Bible from the arm of the chair, sat there stroking it nervously. Annie sat down too.

'Mrs Walker, I need to ask you something.'

'Yes?'

'Did Teresa have any tattoos?'

'What?'

'Tattoos. Did she have any, that you know of?'

Mrs Walker's face contorted briefly. 'No. Of course not. I always hated tattoos – so common. Only sailors and sluts have tattoos.'

Like Teresa was a Sunday school teacher, thought Annie. But she kept quiet about that.

'You sure?'

'Yes, I'm sure,' said the woman emphatically. 'Teresa didn't have any tattoos.'

And that neatly knocked Mira's theory into a cocked hat. Unless . . . unless Teresa *did* have tattoos and simply kept them hidden or didn't tell her mother about them. The flame tattoo had been applied high up on the inner thigh, Mira had told her. Maybe, just maybe, Teresa had been tattooed but, knowing her mother's disapproval of them, she had not confided in her mother about it.

And a couple of days later, you're dead, that's what Mira had said.

Val had a tattoo. *It's a marker*, Mira had told her.

She wondered whether Teresa had been buried, or cremated. Couldn't bring herself to ask this poor little woman such a question. But there was an urn on the mantelpiece, among the photos.

'That your husband, Mrs Walker?' she asked her.

Mrs Walker shook her head. 'No, that's my little girl. That's Teresa.'

And there went the only way of ever checking out Teresa's tattoos.

She hadn't noticed any reference to tattoos in the police files and it was too late to take a second look. Lane had already put the damned things back. *Sod* it.

She didn't even want to *think* about what her next move was. It was too fucking horrible to contemplate. But she knew she was going to have to do it.

She went back to the club – and yes, now she was very late – and got changed while the hammering and drilling of the workmen downstairs went on in the background. The place was in chaos, as usual, but it was finally coming together, she could see it clearly now. It was going to be great. She didn't want a dingy club with prossies dancing round in their knickers; she wanted the place to radiate class. She wanted to get the big players in, make it *special* – and now she could see it happening, right in front of her eyes. There had been no more incidents, no more attempts at apparent sabotage. Everything was looking fine.

All she had to do now was block from her mind what she was going to have to do very, very soon and go and enjoy a lunch with a colleague, who just happened to have a family who'd give the Borgias a run for their money, and who also just happened to be a powerful Mafia don. Who *also* happened to be her secret lover. But then, it was just casual sex. And business, she told herself.

Oh sure.

She knew she was lying to herself. Trying to keep it cool even though, more and more, she was coming to crave Constantine Barolli like a boozer craves alcohol.

She put on a black silk shift dress and matching jacket, pinning a red silk rose into the dress's plunging décolletage, a red silk rose in a screaming hot red to match her lipstick. Slipped on high-heeled black courts, brushed her dark hair until it lay on her shoulders in a thick gleaming curtain.

When she was finished she looked at herself in the mirror and thought, *Not bad, girl.* And then of course she was reminded of Aretha, Aretha and her ebullient high-fives and huge grin, Aretha who was dead and gone. And then of Chris, banged up in Wandsworth on remand, awaiting trial for her murder, and possibly the murders of two more.

Dig deep, she thought. Hadn't she always done that? With a drunk for a mother and an absentee father and more shit than you could shake a stick at being thrown at her from all directions ever since she could crawl, there was nothing else she could do.

She went out of the flat, locked it. Went down the stairs.

'Mrs Carter?' One of the builders stopped her just inside the main door. He was a youngster, just learning his trade, spotty and bashful. She'd seen him around a lot. He approached her, carrying something wrapped in rustling cellophane. 'Someone left these out on the step.'

He handed the gift to her. She gasped. It was a bouquet, a bouquet of *dead roses*. All neatly put together, beautifully wrapped. But the flowers were dead, the petals curled and blackened, the leaves wilted and yellow. Annie stared at them and a spasm of unease gripped her. Who the hell . . . ?

There was a card, tucked in there. She tore at the cellophane, pulled it out. Read it.

Annie Carter, it said. Nothing else.

She looked at the youngster. He blushed. 'They were on the front step?' she asked.

'Yeah,' he said, and tried a smile. 'Practical joke, huh?'

Not much of a bloody joke, thought Annie. She slapped the dead flowers and the card back into his arms. 'Chuck 'em out,' she said, and went on outside into the sunshine. What sicko would send a thing like that?

Tony was there, holding the back door of the car open for her. She sank back into butter-soft leather, still seeing those dead flowers, that carefully printed card.

'Where to, Boss?' asked Tony, getting behind the wheel. The gold crosses were glinting in his ears as his eyes met hers in the mirror.

She told him the five-star hotel in Park Lane. Aretha had died in Park Lane. Annie pushed the thought aside. And the thought of the flowers too. She was in a position of influence, running the manor – of course she had enemies. But, just for today, she was going to forget all that bollocks. Tomorrow, she'd have to face up to it all, and she'd have to do *it,* that thing she was dreading. Today, she was going to drink a little champagne – even she could manage that – and *forget*.

28

A doorman in dark green livery and a gleaming top hat greeted her at the door. She told reception that she was with Mr Barolli's party and was quickly shown to the penthouse's private dining room. It was so exquisitely beautiful that she felt as though she was dreaming when she stepped into the room.

A big circular dining table was covered with white linen and set ready for lunch with silver cutlery, costly crystal glassware and low bowls of fragrant pink roses.

Living ones, not dead sprang into her brain and she threw it straight back out again.

All around the walls of the room were huge mirrors, edged with ornate and exquisitely delicate gold filigree. Vast windows, draped with ivory sheers, led out on to a terrace overlooking Mayfair. There was even a semicircular fountain out there and, as she took a glass of champagne from the tray offered by one of the staff, she saw Constantine standing out there beside it, glass in hand, talking to his son, Lucco.

Constantine's head turned and his eyes met hers.

She felt it again, that same hard physical jolt of sexual attraction that hit her every time their paths crossed. He was so gorgeous, so striking. His silver-grey suit exactly matched the tone of his hair and was clearly bespoke and straight from Savile Row. The blue shirt and striped grey and blue tie complemented his eyes. He was confident of his own attraction, an Alpha male to his bones. He was watching her with drink in hand, casually eating something, some little appetizer, and his eyes clearly said *first this – then you.*

Lucco had looked round too, alerted by Constantine's sudden distraction.

Well, there's one person who don't look pleased to see me, she thought.

Lucco had always made his feelings about her very clear. He didn't want her anywhere near his father, and he had always taken pains to make that obvious. It must be creasing him, having her show up here, invited by his father as an honoured guest.

'Mrs Carter?'

A young replica of Constantine came forward to greet her. She smiled.

'I remember you. Alberto.'

'That's right. And this is my Aunt Gina.'

Gina, an imposing-looking woman of middle years was standing by the dining table. She glanced at her watch.

'Mrs Carter,' she acknowledged frostily. 'You're a little late.'

'I know, I'm sorry.'

'I don't believe you've met Cara? And her husband, Rocco?' Alberto indicated Constantine's daughter and her new husband. The couple moved forward to be introduced. Cara, prettily blonde and with an unappealing spoilt pout to her lovely face, gave a sour half-smile. Skinny, dark-haired Rocco shook Annie's hand.

'My father's expecting you, come on out here,' said Alberto. 'It's beautiful, you can see the whole of Mayfair . . .'

Alberto had all the charm of Constantine without his dangerous edge. Instinctively she liked him. Out on the terrace, with the fountain tinkling prettily in the background, Constantine came forward and kissed her on both cheeks. For a moment, as Alberto moved off to talk to Lucco, they stood alone.

'You look ravishing, Mrs Carter,' said Constantine in a whisper against her cheek. 'I'd like to fuck you right now.'

Annie felt her body respond to that, to his nearness, his power, his strength. He smelled delicious, and she caught herself inhaling the scent of him, identifying the cologne he always wore, Acqua di Parma – and, under that, a muskier, darker scent of pure animal maleness. No kissing of the hand this time. She looked into his eyes, knew he was thinking about that too. Constantine put a hand on her back and turned her toward Lucco.

'Mrs Carter, you remember my son – Lucco?' he said.

Lucco gave an exaggeratedly formal half-bow and kissed her hand.

Oily little creep, she thought, and stifled the impulse to wipe her hand afterwards. He was still the same smoothly attractive package, all dark hair, black eyes and slimy poise.

'Shall we eat then?' asked Constantine, and led the way back inside.

They ate very well – seared scallops, rack of lamb with accompanying vegetables, lemon cake and lime sorbet, all washed down with exquisitely well-chosen wines – but Annie had known this was going to be a tricky occasion, and it was. Cara and Rocco were quiet, both obviously fulminating from some private row, Gina had a nasty smell under her nose the whole time and *yes,* Annie knew it was because she was there. Only Alberto set out to charm her, but then after a little while Annie realized that Alberto would charm anyone; he was a very likeable young man.

'It's Goodwood soon, the races. Papa has a box there. Perhaps you could join us, Mrs Carter?' asked Alberto with genuine warmth in his clear blue eyes. They didn't snap with authority, those eyes, like his father's did. Alberto was a much easier character to contend with.

'I expect Mrs Carter has business to attend to,' said his Aunt Gina coolly, mopping her lips with a napkin as if she had just tasted something bitter.

For fuck's sake, thought Annie, half amused and half appalled at the idea of this New York Mafia clan arriving in the English countryside among the unsuspecting natives.

'You're right, she does have business to attend to,' said Annie.

But Alberto was still smiling. 'Can't we persuade you?' he asked.

Annie looked at Constantine, who was watching her with a slight smile. His eyes said *having fun?* And she knew that this was a test, this lunch, this close-up and personal brush against his family. Constantine was assessing her, seeing if she'd sink or swim in this tankful of piranhas. No, he certainly wasn't anything like gentle young Alberto. But she liked that. She liked a man with an edge to him.

'Come on,' said Constantine. The meal was at an end. He stood up, saving her from the necessity of answering yes or no to Alberto's question. 'Let's take our drinks out on to the terrace.'

Annie escaped outside with relief. She found his family hard to take. He had a huge amount of personal baggage, and while Constantine had had plenty of time to confront his demons over losing his wife, it was all still new and raw for Annie. They both knew it. She'd blurted Max's name at the most disastrous time. And yet . . . he still wanted to pursue this.

After a little while she found herself standing alone at the edge of the terrace, close by the fountain; she glanced down and felt a swaying flicker of vertigo, the result of a little too much drink, when she usually didn't drink at all. A strong hand grasped her upper arm. She turned her head and smiled, expecting Constantine.

'Careful,' said Lucco in her ear, shocking her.

His face was inches from hers.

Her throat closed.

He glanced down and then his cold dark eyes rose again, very slowly, glinting with malicious amusement as they met and held hers. 'It's a long way down, Mrs Carter.'

She hadn't even heard him approach.

How long had he been standing there, right behind her? One good hard shove and she would have been over the edge, gone. Out of his hair, out of his father's life. She didn't doubt that was what he wanted. So why hadn't he taken the opportunity to get rid of her?

Or – and this was a scary thought, really scary – did he want to toy with her, drag out the pleasure, make her suffer?

Annie took a breath, gulped hard. He saw the movement, and his smile grew deeper, the sadist in him satisfied by the flash of fear he had seen in her eyes, by that convulsive movement in her throat.

'I'm not afraid of heights,' said Annie, having to force the words out. He really had given her a fright, even though she'd rather die than admit it.

Lucco's hand released her arm. 'No?' He looked at her curiously, then looked over the side of the huge building again. His eyes rose, played with hers. 'Good. I hope you enjoyed the lunch, Mrs Carter?'

Annie nodded. For a moment she couldn't speak. He'd scared her. She hated that. The little fucker had really scared her.

'And are you enjoying your visit to England?' Annie forced out, taking a gulp of her wine, trying to get her hammering pulse back under control.

'Absolutely.' His eyes were intent on hers. 'I only arrived last night, you know.'

'Did you?' Meaning . . . what? She stared into his eyes, refused to look away.

'In fact,' said Lucco, 'I believe you were in a

meeting with my father when I arrived. It was quite late . . . for a meeting.'

Annie stared into his eyes. Christ, he was a rotten little turd. And he was making her uneasy. She thought of her desperation last night, of the black, horrible place she had found herself inhabiting, of how she had flown into Constantine's arms, seeking solace, seeking comfort. Not thinking of anything except her need to get past this feeling of being frozen and alone. She thought of Constantine's surprise at her sudden seduction of him, how the cars had still been moving outside, how she had been semi-nude before he pulled the blind down . . .

Oh shit.

Had Lucco seen?

Had Lucco been out there, at the front of the house, arriving, and had he seen into Constantine's study, seen her undressed and in his father's arms?

Oh God. Was that what his eyes were telling her? She steeled herself to blank out the thought. It made her feel sick to her stomach. 'Nice flight?' she asked instead.

He paused. Letting her dangle, just for a moment. 'Yes, very pleasant. In the Gulfstream.'

'Oh yes, Daddy's jet,' said Annie, hating this whole conversation, hating being anywhere near Lucco, and intending to goad.

She saw a flicker of appreciation in Lucco's eyes.

Touché, Mrs Carter. 'He has two,' said Lucco.

'That's nice. For all of you,' smiled Annie cattily.

'We're his family, Mrs Carter. Everything my father has, he shares with us.'

And this time his meaning was clear. Annie's smile dropped in an instant.

'Not quite everything,' she said, and pushed roughly past him to rejoin Constantine.

After that, the lunch party was swiftly concluded and Annie was grateful for that. She made her excuses, said she had a business meeting to get to, it had been wonderful to meet them all again (like Lucco, she could lie politely when it was called for) and she looked forward to seeing them all again soon.

Yeah, shortly after hell's frozen over, she thought.

'I'll walk you down to the lobby,' said Constantine, getting in the lift with her.

'Christ,' sighed Annie, shutting her eyes and leaning against the back wall of the lift.

She opened them and saw that Constantine was grinning.

'It ain't funny. Your family are a nightmare. Cara hates me. Gina hates me. Lucco *especially* hates me.'

'They're having trouble with you because they'd have trouble with anyone after Maria,' said Constantine.

'They've had five years to get used to the idea.'

'Yeah, but I've never actually dated anyone since then.'

Annie folded her arms over her body and stared at him in surprise. 'What, nobody?'

'Just sexual encounters. Nothing more.'

Annie bit her lip and looked at him. 'What was she like? Maria?'

Constantine hesitated a moment.

Then he said: 'Gentle. Maternal. Nothing like you.'

That hurt. Dug straight into all Annie's insecurities. She thought of Layla, having to stay with Ruthie across town because it could be too dangerous for her to stay with her mother.

'But she *looked* like me. Lucco told me so.'

'She did. A little. But not that much.'

The lift glided on down. 'So this is more? You and me? Not just sex?'

'Don't you think it is?'

The possibility frightened her. Made her feel treacherous, as if she was betraying Max, which was ridiculous, she wasn't: but it was all so soon, *too* soon.

'This is dangerous,' she said.

'Yeah, it is,' he said, and closed the distance between them and kissed her, hard.

'I know you're prepared to gamble on this,' said Annie, wrenching her mouth free. 'Listen to me, will you? This could cause trouble. All Max's boys . . . they won't like it. This is . . . inappropriate.'

And I'm still not sure I can fully trust you, she thought.

But his mouth was on hers again, stopping the argument. Once again Annie pulled free.

'I've got a legitimate business up and running,' she said quickly, before he could kiss her again. 'It's legit, do you know how hard that's been, to get that working? The opposition I've faced to make that come about? I've got the new club to launch. I've got Layla to think about. This . . . on top of all that . . . I just don't know.' She looked at him. Her expression was deadly serious. 'If the boys found out, they wouldn't like it.'

Constantine took a breath. Leaned back against the lift wall. 'I could settle them down,' he said.

Annie felt a flare of temper at that. These were *her* concerns. Not his.

'Now what?' he asked, watching her face.

'Yeah, you could settle them down. You could take right *over*, how about that?'

'For fuck's sake, what are we arguing about this for?' asked Constantine, exasperated.

'I don't know. You tell me.' Men! When it came right down to it, they always had to be in charge. He could move right in here, steamroller the whole manor flat; they both knew it. It would be *his* manor then, not hers. Part of his empire. Not the whole of hers.

Ah, but is it mine at all? she wondered bitterly. *I think I know the answer to that. It ain't mine. It's Max's. Dead or alive, it's his – not mine.*

But maybe she could *make* it hers, if she tried hard enough.

Constantine was staring at her as if he was trying to read her mind. 'Come here and kiss me,' he ordered.

Annie shook her head. 'Constantine . . .' she started sadly.

Constantine stopped the lift. He stared at her. 'Don't,' he said.

'I've got to end this,' she said.

'Come here and kiss me and *then* say you've got to end it.'

'I've got to,' said Annie, and she reached past him and restarted the lift.

There was silence between them. The lift descended smoothly, and the doors opened; they were in reception.

Annie stepped out.

Constantine caught her arm. 'You can't be serious,' he said. 'After what happened the other day? After you came into my house and practically *raped* me?'

'Look,' said Annie desperately, 'that was a moment of weakness. I regret it now.'

'The fuck you do.'

'I *do*. I called you Max, for God's sake. I'm . . . I'm still in love with Max.'

She blurted it out; she had to stop this. Had to hurt him to stop it if necessary, and she did see a flicker of pain in his eyes.

'You're lying,' he said.

She looked him straight in the eye. 'I'm not lying. I'm serious,' she said flatly. 'This is too risky. It's finished.'

'No,' he said.

'*Yes*.'

'Look . . . think it over. And if you need me, call.'

'I won't.' She pulled her arm free and started to walk away. Tears pricked her eyes, but she knew what she was doing was the right thing, the *safe* thing.

'You will. Remember – you only have to say you need me,' he called after her. 'I'll be there.'

But I won't say it, she thought.

She knew it was over. She knew it *had* to be.

29

It was Wednesday morning, ten o'clock, sun bright in the sky, traffic honking and nudging along the roads, girls out in short skirts, the parks green and beautiful. And there was Annie, feeling depressed and queasy and sitting alone in the waiting room of the funeral parlour, alone this time and wishing she was out there in the noise and the heat and the fumes, *anywhere* in fact but in here.

She felt sick, thinking about what she had to do.

She snatched up a paper from one of the chairs, trying to distract herself and failing. Read about troops firing CS gas at rioters in the Bogside area of Londonderry, and scuffles between blacks and police in Notting Hill. Everywhere, it seemed, there was fighting, destruction, death.

Then the same thin woman she had seen last time came in, smiling and efficient as always. Black

Vidal Sassoon-type bob, black suit, neat white shirt and black buckled shoes. Clipboard clutched briskly to her nonexistent breasts.

Annie put the paper aside.

'Mrs Carter,' said the woman.

'Yes,' said Annie, and stood up.

'You'd like to spend some more time with Aretha, I understand,' said the woman in the same sugar-sweet and soothing tone she'd used last time.

'That's right,' said Annie, her tongue sticking to the roof of her mouth, it felt so dry.

'That's no problem at all. Were you very close?'

Oh God, she wants me to make polite conversation, thought Annie. I'm here to do the unthinkable, and now she wants a fucking *chat.*

'Yes,' she said. 'Very.'

That was, if you counted being madam and whore together. If you counted laughing together until your sides ached, and sharing breakfasts and dinners and sometimes tears and gripes about period pains and men and this face cream or that nail varnish and the state of the whole damned world. Silly little things, but all shared. She couldn't tell this woman how funny Aretha had been, or how courageous; how more than once Aretha had come through for her and for others, putting herself at risk to help her friends.

Now, all that was gone.

'Follow me then,' said the woman, her professional smile growing more fixed as she took Annie's tone for what it clearly was – a rebuff.

Annie followed her into the same room as before, the Chapel of Rest, where last time she had stood with Dolly and Louella. The coffin was still there, the coffin containing all that was left of Aretha. Annie felt her stomach constrict. She didn't want to do this.

'If you'd like me to stay with you . . . ?' the woman offered.

Yes please, thought Annie.

But this was something she had to do alone, without an audience. And once again she wondered why she was taking Mira's words so seriously. Mira the wreck, the junkie. But still, Mira. Mira who had once, long ago, strode through Mayfair in furs, adored, applauded, cosseted, her favours highly prized. Mira, who had known her own value to the nth degree. Who was nobody's fool.

'I want to see her alone.'

'If you need me, I'll be . . .' She indicated the next room.

Annie nodded. The woman withdrew, closing the door behind her. Annie took a breath and walked forward. Stopped, heart thumping sickly. Moved forward again, *forced* herself to move one foot in front of the other. Until she was right there, looking down at Aretha's slumbering face. No, not slumbering. The face was dead. The face was just a shell that would soon dissolve, disintegrate, fade back into the earth.

'Christ,' muttered Annie under her breath. She could feel cold sweat breaking out all over her body. She felt as if she was going to chuck up, right now.

But it wasn't really Aretha, lying there. She told herself that, very firmly. And when she half closed her eyes, she imagined she could see the real Aretha, the Aretha of the high-fives and wide watermelon grin, standing there in her hot pants and her Afghan coat by the dummy altar – watching her old friend, and amused by her trepidation.

Jeez, girlfriend, you so soft, said the real Aretha. *Get on with it, for fuck's sake. What, you think that poor empty thing's gonna leap out an' bite you or somethin'? Dream on.*

Annie gulped.

'Oh fuck this,' she muttered miserably, and reached out.

She had to do this. If only to be certain beyond a shadow of a doubt that it was all nonsense, all the product of a junkie's tormented mind. She stepped forward, leaned over the coffin. Reached down with a shaking hand and touched the frilled gown at Aretha's throat, pushed the fabric back. Saw the red contusions that the gown had concealed. Felt her heart squeeze tight with grief and pity. Then felt the rage come hot on its heels. That someone could do this to Aretha. The rage helped her, steadied her a little. Her hand drifted down, gently lifting the gown at Aretha's feet. She hesitated.

'I'm sorry as hell about this, Aretha,' she said into the still, cold air of the place.

Annie lifted the cool linen, pulled it slowly up. As she did so a faint fragrance wafted up. She wrinkled her nose and gagged. What she could smell was the sweet, almost sickly whiff of corruption. The ghastly smell brought it all home to her with vicious force. Aretha was *dead*. And although it was cool in here, slowing the natural processes, postponing the inevitable, outside it was high summer and it was hot. Soon, Aretha's remains would begin to rot.

Bile rose, hot and sour, in her throat. She swallowed and moaned. She had to force herself to stay there, force herself not to run away from this.

Got to dig deep and do this.

For Chris, she had to do this. Otherwise he was going down, for sure.

Again she had that strong feeling of Aretha standing nearby, laughing her head off.

Damn, girl, get the fuck on with it, what you waitin' for now?

'Okay,' said Annie, straightening up, gathering herself. 'Okay.'

She lifted the white fabric higher, up over the

dead Aretha's sheeny chocolate-brown skin, over her long calves, over her shapely knees, up over her long, strong thighs. The smell was stronger now. Annie was breathing through her mouth, trying very hard not to throw up all over the damned corpse.

'Oh Jesus, Aretha, help me out here, throw me a fucking *bone,* will you?' she groaned aloud, sweating, nearly crying aloud with revulsion and loss. She leaned in and lifted Aretha's leg. It was a dead weight, dead in every sense. A bubble of hysterical laughter almost escaped her then.

Who could have thought a dead person's leg would be so heavy?

Annie found that she was sweating heavily now, despite the coolness of the room. She felt disgusted with herself because she was doing this, disgusted with Aretha for being dead, disgusted with the sick bastard who had destroyed this living, breathing woman and inflicted a thing like this on them both.

'What in the name of God you doin', girl?' said Aretha's furious voice loudly from right behind her.

Annie's heart leapt into her throat. She dropped the leg and spun round, clutching her chest. But it wasn't Aretha at all, it was Louella, standing there with hands on huge hips, staring at her with horrified eyes.

'I'm . . .' Annie's mouth was so dry she could hardly speak.

'Well, what?' demanded Aretha's aunt, shaking her head. 'You *sick*,' she spat, turning on her heel and making for the door. 'I'm gonna get that woman in here and she goin' to kick your sorry arse right out on the street, you hear me?'

Annie heard her. And she knew she had to get this done quick. She turned back to Aretha's corpse, lifted the left leg again, put all her weight behind it this time, grunting with the effort. Looked high up on the inner thigh. There was nothing there. Nothing at all. Just pure, un-blemished skin. She could hear Louella screaming and bawling to the woman in the next room, could hear a chair scraping back, hurried foot-falls coming closer.

So little time.

Yeah, girlfriend, so get the fuck on *with it, why don't you . . . ?*

She dashed around the other side of the coffin and reached in and lifted the right leg this time. Hefted it up with a grunt of effort. *Right* up.

'What the hell do you think you're doing?' demanded the woman, dashing in with all pretence of charm gone, all guns blazing. She'd even forgotten her clipboard. She turned back towards the door. 'I'm calling the police . . .'

And there it was.

Annie stared at Aretha's inner thigh, and there it was.

Her mouth dropped open in surprise.

A flame tattoo. It's a marker, Mira had said. *There's money in it.* Aretha loved money.

But what the hell did that mean? And a marker for what – and for *who*?

Aunt Louella was babbling something, but Annie didn't hear her.

'Hey!' she shouted. The woman stopped, turned, her face a picture of total fury. 'Yeah, go on. Phone the police. Ask for DI Hunter. Tell him it's urgent.'

30

'Another complaint, Mrs Carter,' said Hunter coldly. 'This is getting to be a habit with you. First intimidation, now interfering – for God's sake – with a *corpse*. Anything to say about this?'

They were pacing about on the pavement outside the undertaker's. DS Lane was leaning against the cop car watching them, and Tony was leaning against the Jag watching too. Louella had thrown a few accusations about when Hunter had first arrived, and then she had stormed off, warning Annie not to go near 'her baby girl' again. The woman from the funeral parlour had filled him in with the unsavoury details of the situation.

Annie had sat in the waiting room, watching his face while he absorbed what had gone on here. He didn't look happy about it, and that was a fact. Finally, he said they'd talk outside, and told the woman goodbye. She'd watched Annie go with a sneer of disgust.

'Yeah, I got something to say,' said Annie. 'I was looking for a flame tattoo, on her inner thigh.'

Hunter stopped pacing and turned to face her. 'And this is significant how?' he asked.

'God, I don't know. Someone told me these girls who have been killed were all marked with this particular tattoo – I know, it sounds sick – at a parlour beside the Alley Cat club in Soho, shortly before they were killed.'

Hunter looked at her. 'In France, prostitutes used to be marked with the fleur-de-lys,' he said.

'Well these were marked with a flame.'

'Who is this someone?' asked Hunter. His dark eyes were probing, searching her face for answers.

'Can't tell you that,' said Annie.

His gaze got harder. 'Withholding information from the police is a serious matter, Mrs Carter.'

Annie stuck her hands in her jacket pockets and looked at him.

'I'm not trying to be obstructive,' she said. 'I think we can help each other out here. I spoke to Teresa Walker's mother, but she had no knowledge of a tattoo and Teresa was cremated so there goes all hope of checking it out now. But you must have things like that on record, distinguishing marks, moles, stuff like that.'

He was still gazing at her. 'Of course.'

'Then check it.'

'What about Val Delacourt?' he asked.

'You know she worked in the Alley Cat, stripping?'

He drew breath. Seemed to count to ten. 'Of course I know that.'

'Right next to the tattoo parlour. We can check that too.'

'Mrs Carter.' He raised a finger and pointed it squarely at her. '*I* can check it. *You* can stay out of trouble.'

They locked eyes. He had nice eyes, she thought. Dark as bitter chocolate. They could even be warm, if he ever unbuttoned himself enough to relax and smile.

'What about Gareth?' she asked.

'What the f . . . what *about* him?'

'You said the post mortem was on Friday.'

Hunter gave a sigh. 'You're a very annoying woman, Mrs Carter.'

'Yeah, it's a bitch,' said Annie. 'I'm annoying and you're uptight, what can you do?'

He ignored that. 'The findings were inconclusive. Consistent with asphyxia, but—'

'But? But what?' demanded Annie.

'There was evidence of a lot of drugs in his system. It seems that with that level of toxicity, it's unlikely the victim would have the energy or the inclination to hang himself. Open the door, possibly. But hang himself? Almost certainly, no.'

Annie's attention sharpened. 'So you think I could be right – you think someone hanged him?'

'It's possible.' Hunter looked at her. 'Have you heard of autoerotic asphyxia, Mrs Carter?'

'Oh come on,' she gave a half-smile. 'You know my history. Of course I've heard of it. You think Gareth was into that?'

'We don't know yet. And whether he was or not is actually no concern of yours.'

'This was my husband's manor,' said Annie.

'I don't believe in "manors", Mrs Carter, you know what I'm saying?'

'Now it's mine,' said Annie, ignoring what he'd said.

He was back at the finger-wagging again. 'Keep your nose out,' said DI Hunter.

Annie looked at the finger, thinking that if he wagged it in her face just one more time, she was going to bite the fucker, hard. But she kept a lid on it. After all, she needed his cooperation. 'Sure,' she said. 'Can I see Chris Brown? Is that possible?'

'No,' said Hunter. 'It isn't.'

'He needs a friend to talk to. I'm his friend. Let me talk to him.'

Hunter looked at her as if she was some interesting alien species. 'Despite all that he's done?'

'If I thought he'd done it, I wouldn't be asking.'

'Obstinacy isn't a virtue, Mrs Carter,' said Hunter.

'Persistence is,' said Annie.

He paused. Looked at her. His hand dropped to his side. She had the distinct impression that he was almost stifling a smile. 'I'll see if there's anything I can do.'

Annie nodded, satisfied. She went to the Jag and got in.

He watched her being driven away. *Her* manor, for God's sake. He approached the malodorous DS Lane, who was leaning there smirking against the car. He hated Lane. He was sure that the creep had been passing info to Annie Carter. He had a cop's nose for who he could trust and who he couldn't. Lane was bent. He just *knew* it. And Annie Carter? Who the hell knew *what* went on in that woman's brain?

It was her day for getting grief. Grief off Louella and the woman at the Chapel of Rest, then grief off Hunter, and now even *more* grief, from a thunderous Dolly this time, when she joined her in Limehouse for lunch.

'Something up, Doll?' she asked, since they were alone.

'You want to know what's up?' Dolly crashed the teacup down into the saucer. 'I'll tell you what's up. I've had Aretha's Aunt Louella on the phone bending my ear over you. Saying how you should be ashamed of yourself, you are a monster, a pervert, possibly a lezzer, no *probably* a lezzer, shouting down my ear, she was for about half an hour, and all because of what you've been up to.'

'Ah,' said Annie.

'You might well say "ah". When she told me, for fuck's *sake*, Annie Carter, when she told me that, I didn't blame her.'

'Doll—'

'I don't *believe* you. I really don't. I cannot believe that you'd do a thing like this, fiddling with a fucking corpse.'

'Doll, look—'

'Shut up, I'm not done. You've really put the tin lid on it this time. You're off on some bloody wild-goose chase again looking for something you'll never find, looking to pin this whole horrible business on someone other than Chris – well, let me tell you, Annie, you won't. Because – face it – Chris did it. He did Aretha, and he did the other two as well. He's guilty as sin and they've got him for it and he's going to go down for a long, long stretch and that's good because *he did it*. Now.' Dolly stood up, placed both hands flat on the table and glared down at Annie. 'Aretha's funeral's on Thursday, and you'd better be there and you'd better apologize to Louella for all this upheaval. God knows if she'll ever forgive you, but it's the decent thing to do and so you're going to do it. Got that?'

Annie pursed her lips and looked up at Dolly.

Trust Dolly to tell it exactly how it was. And maybe she was right. Maybe she was right and Annie was wrong. But while they were flinging mud about, what about *Dolly?* What about her weird behaviour when Rosie went walkabout? She'd been shitting bricks, and Annie hadn't asked her to explain that yet, because if Dolly thought that Chris had killed them girls, then why was she so worried for Rosie? It didn't add up.

'Look,' said Annie. 'I had a good reason for acting like I did. Mira told me something . . .'

'That *junkie?*' snorted Dolly.

'Yeah, that one.' Annie's voice hardened. 'Doll, you're just going to have to trust me on this. I had reason, okay? But listen. I'll be at the damned funeral. And I *will* apologize.'

Dolly let out a breath. 'Good.'

'Now I've got to go,' said Annie.

'I had to say something,' said Dolly.

'I know, Doll.' Annie slipped on her jacket and went down the hall, past a boot-faced Ross in his seat by the front door. 'Where are the girls?' she asked him, pausing there. 'It's quiet.'

'Sharlene's got a client in. Rosie's out,' said Ross reluctantly. He hated her, she knew that. She was a Carter, he was a Delaney boy. They couldn't get past that.

Annie went on outside, closed the door behind her. She knew one thing for sure. She had to pursue this thing with Aretha, whatever else might get in the way. She had to *try*. And the first thing on her to-do list was finding Mira again.

Tony dropped her back to the club. As he pulled away, a florist drew in and threw open the back doors of his van. Annie stepped inside the club.

'Mrs Carter?'

She stopped. 'Yeah?'

'Flowers for you. Where do you want these?' asked the man, hurrying up behind her.

Annie felt suddenly apprehensive. *Dead flowers*, she thought. *It'll be dead flowers like the last time, some sick gift from some sick bastard.* She shuddered.

But the man was bustling forward and there was the familiar crackle of cellophane – but this time there was a huge bunch of fifty living, breath-takingly beautiful blood-red roses in his arms. She relaxed and started to smile.

Constantine, she thought, her pulse picking up speed.

'Is there a card?' she asked.

The florist nodded, handed it to her. She pulled the card out of the tiny red envelope and read it. Words this time, not numbers. No codes, no *pizzino*. This was plain speaking, straight from the heart. It said: *Just say you need me. Any time, day or night. I'll be there. C.*

'Bring them upstairs,' she said, pocketing the card.

When the florist was gone, she put the roses in the sink to keep them fresh and stood there looking at them. The flat was empty, quiet. She turned on the radio over the sink. James Brown started punching out 'This Is a Man's World'.

Annie smiled grimly. *Yeah, you got that right*, she thought.

She was a woman in a man's world, but she was going to make her own way in it, she was determined about that now. She wasn't going to call him. She didn't need a man, *any* man. Not even one as red-hot as Constantine Barolli. As soon as all this shit was over, it was going to be just her and Layla. She picked up the phone and dialled Ruthie's number, feeling a sudden overwhelming need to hear her baby's voice.

31

The Alley Cat club was busier in the evenings. In fact, the place was heaving, with bare-titted hostesses in little frilly skirts shimmying through the seated throng bearing trays of wildly overpriced drinks. 'Get Back' was pounding out of the huge sound system until Bobby Jo swaggered on to the stage in a long gold-sequinned gown and huge red bouffant wig to a wave of rapturous applause. He promptly started turning the air blue with his jokes.

Struggling to see through the rising smoke of a hundred cigarettes, Annie and Tony descended the stairs and took a table while Bobby Jo did the build-up to the next act. Annie was annoyed and worried. At her instruction, Steve had checked out the canal bridge under the Mile End Road last night, and Mira hadn't been there, only Jackie.

When asked, Jackie had shrugged and told Steve that she hadn't seen Mira and it looked like she was gone for good, and while he was there how about a blow-job for a fiver?

Steve had graciously declined. Asked how Rizzo was doing. Told her to go get a life, kick Rizzo to the kerb. Jackie graciously told Steve to fuck off.

'That one won't bail out,' he told Annie on the phone when he reported the news. 'Thinks the little runt loves her or something.'

'Don't worry about Jackie,' said Annie. 'It's Mira I'm concerned about. She's a friend from way back. I want her found.'

'I'll put the word out. And I'll check again tonight, okay, but don't hold your breath. She won't be there.'

Annie had said: yeah, do that. She looked at the Rolex on her wrist and hoped and prayed that Mira wasn't gone for good.

'Now the ONE, the ONLY, SASHA!' Bobby Jo roared at last, and stepped down from the stage. Spotting Annie there, he came across to her table. On the way, he snapped his fingers at one of the hostesses, pointed to the table. She instantly swerved around a punter's grasping fingers and made her way back to the bar.

Bobby Jo pulled up a chair as whoops and shouts erupted all around them.

'Nice to see you in again, Mrs Carter,' he said loudly in her ear. 'Welcome back to the jungle.'

'Thanks.' The hostess was back with Bobby Jo's ice bucket containing an opened bottle of Krug.

Expensive tastes, thought Annie again.

'Drink?' offered Bobby Jo.

Annie shook her head. Tony too. He looked as though he wished he'd brought his paper, like last time. Annie saw him glance at the act unfolding on the stage. Sasha was up there doing something obscene with a boa constrictor. She turned her attention back to Bobby Jo.

'Do you own this place, Bobby Jo?' she asked him.

The sharp black eyes met hers from beneath their concealing forest of fake lashes.

Talk about Halloween, thought Annie. She really didn't like this man at all. There was something sinister, something deeply hidden, about Bobby Jo.

'Nah,' he said shortly, turning his gaze back to Sasha and her pet. 'Wish I did,' he said, pouring himself a glass of champagne. 'I'd make a mint. This is a fucking Wednesday night, can you believe it?'

There was no accounting for taste, that was for sure. Annie refused to be sidetracked.

'So who owns it?' she asked.

The ferocious painted face of Bobby Jo was still for a moment. The black pebble eyes looked coldly into hers. Annie didn't look away.

'Consortium of businessmen,' said Bobby Jo. 'You know the sort of thing. Tax write-offs . . .'

'Money laundering?' suggested Annie. 'Clubs are good for that.'

She knew that all too well. Years back, this had been the main function of the Carter clubs. But now she made sure that any cash that passed through them was squeaky clean.

Bobby Jo gave a grin, shrugged.

'As I said, I'm only management.'

'And you don't know any of the owners?' Annie stared at him. 'That's hard to believe.'

Bobby Jo gave a tight, mirthless grin. 'I'm paid to know nothing,' he said. 'That's the deal.'

'How about the tattoo parlour next door?' She and Tony had paused outside the little parlour on the way in, looked in the dirty windows, seen the faded pictures of clients and their tattoos, the charts detailing all the many and various designs a person could have tattooed on to their body. The CLOSED sign was up. In the flat above the shop, a dim light burned behind closed curtains. 'They own that too, these businessmen? I heard Pete Delacourt runs it.'

Bobby Jo looked at the act. Annie looked at Bobby Jo.

'No, they don't,' he said.

'You know who does?'

Bobby Jo turned his head and his eyes met hers. 'No.'

Annie nodded and looked at what Sasha was doing with the python. 'Did Sasha know Teresa?' she asked.

'Yeah, I suppose. But I told you. All the girls in here hate each other. They compete. They don't do bosom buddies.'

'Did *you* know Teresa?'

Bobby Jo squinted at her. 'Sure I knew her. I told you, she pissed me off by passing around her business cards in here. *And* she was nicking stuff from behind the bar. I can't prove that – but I'm sure it was her because the minute she went AWOL, the thieving stopped.'

'I *mean*, were you intimate with her?'

'Intimate?' The grotesque face was a picture of shock, then suddenly Bobby Jo was laughing. 'What, me and that little slapper? Jeez, I wouldn't touch her with someone else's, let alone my own.'

'Then who was? Someone must have come close to her.'

'Nobody in this place,' said Bobby Jo. 'Not that I know of. I told you. She was a right little cow, good at making enemies, shit at making friends.'

'You don't know much,' said Annie. 'Considering you run the place.'

Bobby Jo turned his face to hers. No flicker of amusement there now.

'I keep my head down and do my job,' said Bobby Jo. 'Best that way. Safer.'

'You don't mind if I have a chat to the staff?'

Again the shrug. 'I've no objections.' But he didn't look happy.

'Good,' said Annie, and stood up. 'No time like the present.'

After about an hour it became clear to Annie that the bulk of the staff neither knew nor cared whether Teresa Walker was dead or alive. But the hard-eyed hostess who had waited on their table, Tamsin, visibly wobbled when questioned about Teresa's love life. Bobby Jo was watching Annie's progress around the room; she could feel those cold shark eyes boring into her back everywhere she went.

'Hey,' Tamsin said above the roar of the crowds, her eyes darting nervously around the smoke-filled room, 'I don't know nothing about that. I keep my head down and do my job.'

Echoing, with spooky accuracy, Bobby Jo's own words.

Annie told her thanks, and Tamsin hurried gratefully away.

When Tamsin emerged fully clothed at the end of the night into the alley at the back of the club, Annie and Tony were there, waiting for her. Tony moved in.

'What the fuck's this?' whined Tamsin, eyes anxious in the semi-dark as they moved between Annie and Tony.

'I'll tell you what the fuck this is,' said Annie. 'It's about you telling the truth for once in your shitty little life.'

'Oh Jesus, I *told* you . . .'

'You told me nothing, and that's not good enough because I think you know something more.'

'I told you, I don't know nothing.'

Annie nodded at Tony, and he moved in closer still. Tamsin shrank back.

'Hey, there's no need for this,' she yelped.

'Yeah there is,' said Annie.

'I don't know a thing. Not a *thing*.'

'That's a pity,' sighed Annie. 'Tone . . .' she said, and started to walk off.

All Tamsin could see was blackness as Tony loomed ever closer. He raised his hand.

'All right, all right! I'll tell you, okay? Shit, there's no need to go getting all *physical* about it.'

Annie walked back, and Tamsin started talking. She knew nothing about the flame tattoo, nothing at all, but Teresa's boyfriends? Well, maybe she knew *something*, but they didn't hear it from her, was that clear?

Annie said that it was.

'Teresa always thought she was a cut above,' said Tamsin breathlessly. She was still watching Tony with a worried look in her eye. He had drawn back, but he was still close enough to do damage. 'She liked the high rollers, the men with plenty of cash to splash.' Tamsin tried a shaky all-girls-together grin at Annie. 'Hey, don't we all?'

'Anyone in particular?' asked Annie coldly. Tamsin bit her lip.

Tony moved forward again, big as a barn door and with a face to frighten the kids.

'Okay, okay,' gabbled Tamsin. She swallowed nervously. 'Hold up. No need to get nasty. She said she was seeing one of the club owners sometimes, but none of us believed it. She was so full of crap.'

'Who?'

'She never said who,' said Tamsin, and Tony came forward. She winced but stood her ground. 'It's the truth! I only know because I heard Teresa bragging about it backstage on the phone. She liked to rub people's noses in it – "Look what I got," you know the type. It was all bullshit anyway. I've never seen any of the owners, they never come here, they run a con . . . cons . . .' She faltered.

'Consortium?' supplied Annie.

'That's it! Yeah. A consortium.'

'I need names. Or a name, at least.'

'I *told* you . . .'

Tony moved forward and grasped Tamsin very gently by the throat. She let out a startled cry.

'Something more,' said Annie, staring into Tamsin's widening eyes. 'Anything. Come on. A name. Give me a name.'

Tamsin did just that, and it was the last one Annie expected.

When Annie got back to the Palermo later that night, she was still thinking about the fruitless evening spent at the Alley Cat club, questioning people who neither knew nor cared whether Teresa Walker had lived or died. Teresa Walker was nothing to them. Teresa Walker might never have existed, for all they cared. But Tamsin's news, now that had been interesting.

In the lounge, she looked at the mountains of red roses. Looked at the phone. Hesitated. Then picked it up and dialled.

'Yeah?' Constantine was yawning.

'You still working? It's late,' she said. She could picture him there, at the big tooled-leather desk, the banker's light cosily aglow.

'Oh. It's you.'

'Thanks,' said Annie. 'For the flowers.'

'Pleasure. Was there something else? Something you wanted?' He paused. 'Or *needed*, maybe?'

I want you, thought Annie. And then wondered if she was right to want that. Wondered if she really was on the rebound; if this was just a physical thing, nothing more than that. Just sex, not love.

'I just want to ask you something,' she said, trying to shake her own brain clear of all this.

'Ask away.'

She told him.

'Why would you want to know that?' he asked. 'And why can't you get information like that yourself?'

'I want to know because when I asked the manager he was evasive. So maybe there was some link between Teresa Walker and one of these businessmen who own the Alley Cat? Maybe not. Whatever, I'd like to know.'

'Your boys could ask him,' said Constantine. 'Simple dark alley job.'

They both knew how persuasive the boys could be, down dark alleys.

'I'm trying to keep it down. Had two warnings off the police.'

'Okay. I'll see what I can do. Oh, Mrs Carter?'

Annie sighed. 'Annie. Call me Annie, for God's sake.'

'Something wrong?' He'd caught the sharpness in her tone.

Everything.

'Nothing. Just a long day.'

'I'm going back to the States at the weekend.'

'What?'

'Just over the weekend. Business.'

'Right.'

She sounded blasé, but anxiety was clamping down on her breathing. He'd said something similar last time. I'll be back soon, wasn't that what he'd said? And it had been three months. He didn't even *live* here, although he owned the Holland Park place and the clubs up West. He lived in New York. His *life* was there. Not here. Not with her. This whole thing was doomed, why couldn't she just face that?

'Remember. If you need me, I'll be right there. All you have to do is say it.'

She wanted to say it. Knew she mustn't.

'Goodnight, Constantine,' she said, and put the phone down.

She went to bed, and slept. Then she awoke with a start, her heart pounding madly in her chest because there was someone hammering at the main door. She groped for the light, switched it on and looked at the clock. It was three-fifteen in the morning.

Groaning, she slipped on her red robe and got out of bed. She went out of the flat and down the stairs to the main doors, which were securely bolted.

'Who is it?' she asked.

'Me, Boss. Barney.'

Barney was the man who was currently keeping an eye on the club from outside, doing nights because the word was he couldn't stick the sight of his rampant, plug-ugly old lady and he jumped at any chance to escape the marital bed.

'What's up?' She threw back the bolts and opened the door, flicking on the outside light. The door stuck a bit, felt – weirdly – heavier than normal.

Barney stood there, a thin balding bundle of aggression, his face tinted yellow by the light. He was blinking worriedly.

'What is it?' she asked again, and it was then that she followed the line of Barney's eyes and saw the small dark shape on the door. She reached out a hand and touched black fur, and dampness. Her hand came away bloody.

'Oh *God*,' she gasped.

It was the cat. Someone had killed the poor damned cat, and nailed it to the club door.

'I didn't see who did it,' said Barney. 'Honest.'

By a quarter to four, Steve Taylor and Gary Tooley had arrived on the scene. Barney was looking more nervous than ever, and Annie found that annoying. He hadn't been bothered about *her* reaction, but he was shit-scared of theirs.

Squat Steve and lanky blond Gary stood there with faces like the wrath of God, looking at the cat on the door.

'You didn't see who did it?' asked Steve in disbelief.

'I went for a piss,' whined Barney.

'You don't go for a piss, dickhead. You piss in a bottle. What are you, stupid?' asked Gary.

Barney looked as if he was about to expire with fright. He was small fry on the firm, but these two were number ones, mean machines, real hard men.

'Sorry,' said Barney.

'Sorry don't cut it,' said Steve. 'You cunt.'

Steve turned to Annie, who was still standing there in her robe, shivering and – until now – being ignored by the three of them. 'You got any ideas who done this?' he asked.

Annie shook her head and looked at the cat, feeling sick at the sight of the poor thing hanging there, *nailed* there. What twisted arsehole would do a thing like that?

'It's a warning,' said Gary.

Of what? she wondered.

She thought of Bobby Jo, warning her off poking around. And Charlie Foster, who hated her and was clearly keen to get even for all she'd inflicted on him in the past.

Steve, Gary and Barney were now arguing about the cat, and Steve was reiterating the fact that Barney should *not* be taking comfort breaks when he should be doing his effing job.

'Hey,' said Annie.

They just carried on talking. Steve swatted Barney upside the head.

'Ow! Fuck!' complained Barney.

'Hey!' Annie tried again, her temper stoking up fast. What the hell was she here, the little woman, to be ignored? '*Hey!*' she bellowed. 'Person in charge here trying to make herself heard!'

They fell silent. Breathing hard, she glared around at the three of them.

'Barney,' she snapped, 'get back on watch, and no more buggering off. Piss out the window if you got to. Steve, Gary – get rid of *that*. I'm going back to bed.'

She stepped back inside and bolted the door behind her.

Oh Christ. She still felt as though she was going to spew her guts up. She'd rattled *someone's* cage, that was for sure. She hurried back upstairs to wash the blood off her hands.

32

On Thursday, Annie got an unexpected call from
DI Hunter. By eleven that same morning she was
sitting in a chilly, blue-painted and comfortless
room in HM Prison, Wandsworth. The room
contained two hard chairs and an oblong table.
There was no window. The light was coming from
a forty-watt bare bulb hanging overhead. It glim-
mered weakly on Annie and on Chris Brown,
who was sitting opposite her wearing prison
fatigues.

Annie thought Chris looked sick. He'd lost
weight, his skin was developing a greyish pallor,
his eyes looked haunted. She knew that look. She'd
seen it in the mirror. But she was disturbed by
how quickly this had happened to him. Chris, the
strong ex-boxer, built like an armour-plated tank.
Chris the tough and uncompromising Delaney hard
man. Who also happened to be her friend.

She thought about that. Yeah, here she was again. Crossing over the invisible line that had been drawn long ago between the Delaney and the Carter firms. The Delaneys ought to have been fitting Chris up with a brief and pushing for a visit – but instead here she was, doing their work for them.

Over the years she had come to appreciate this man. He looked like a terrifying bruiser – but in fact she believed he was gentle to the core. She knew his appearance gave the lie to that. He had shoulders like slabs of beef, a huge neck, hands that could knock nails into wood. No doubt about it, Chris was a fearsome sight, even diminished as he was by suffering. Easy to see why Hunter was trying to pin this on him. He looked guilty as fuck, a perfect fit for a frame.

Annie frowned, watching Chris. Hunter still seemed convinced that Chris was their man.

And what if he's right and I'm wrong? What if I get to prove Chris is innocent because I'm too stubborn and I'm trying to prove a point as usual, and he gets off and then tops some other poor bitch?

But no. She looked into Chris's eyes. No. She couldn't be wrong. She had to carry on believing that.

'They treating you all right in here?' asked Annie into the leaden silence of the room.

'Yeah. Fine.' Chris passed a hand over his eyes, as if they were sore. He looked at Annie.

'They released her body yet?'

Annie gulped down a breath and nodded.

'When's the funeral?' he asked in a whisper.

'Friday.'

He nodded heavily. 'They won't let me go. Not a chance.'

'No. I don't think so.'

There was a pause. 'I didn't do it,' said Chris. 'And those others. I don't know them from a hole in the ground. Honest.'

'I believe you.'

'Can't prove it though, can I? Same MO.'

'We're all trying to help, Chris. Seriously.'

Chris nodded again, tried to smile. 'Friday,' he said, and his voice cracked. 'Christ. Friday. And I can't even be there.'

There was absolutely nothing Annie could say to that. Nothing at all.

She went straight from the prison back to the Alley Cat club. Tony followed her round the back, to where they had questioned Tamsin. The door there was unlocked, so they went in. It was just coming up to lunchtime, and the girls were getting ready. Tony started throwing open doors. Girls in various states of undress got all prim and started clutching pieces of clothing in front of their modesty.

'Hey!' complained Sasha the snake girl loudly as her door was flung wide to reveal a tangle of tits, python and sparkling g-string.

'Sorry,' said Annie, and Tony shut it. He went to the next. A pair of girls in this one, turning angry, stage-painted faces to the door.

'Do you *mind*?'

Tony shut the door. Went to the next and opened it. A very tall woman in a sparkling blue dress and red wig was sitting in front of a mirror, applying purple eye shadow above a thick outcrop of black lashes.

'What the cunting hell?' demanded Bobby Jo furiously.

'Hi,' said Annie with a smile. 'Time for a visit?'

They went in, and closed the door behind them.

'What do you want now?' asked Bobby Jo.

Tony stepped forward. 'Mrs Carter wants a word with you. Be nice,' he said.

Bobby Jo's mouth opened, then shut again. His temper level went down several notches.

'All right, but can it be quick? Lunchtime trade's waiting.'

'Is that what you said to Teresa?' asked Annie.

'What?'

'You know. Teresa.'

'*What*?' He was looking at her as if she'd gone mad.

'Is that what you said to her: we'll have to be quick before the lunchtime trade?' Annie elaborated.

Everything about Bobby Jo was suddenly very still.

'I don't know what you're talking about,' he said after a beat. 'You're crazy.'

Annie stepped forward. She hated the sight of this git. And she couldn't help wondering if *he* was the one who had put that grisly little present on her door. She wouldn't put it past him.

'No, Bobby Jo, I'm not crazy, but I'll tell you what, Tony here *is*. He has the shortest temper, you can't imagine. People start giving him shit, and whoosh! Off he goes. Flies straight off the handle. Haven't you got a terrible temper, Tone?' she asked him.

'Yeah,' said Tony. 'Uncontrollable.'

'Listen, I don't know what you've heard . . .'

'We've heard plenty. About how Teresa used to come in here about eleven in the morning, and the door would be closed – but these walls are thin, you know. Paper thin. And people hear things. Things like – I dunno, let's think – oh yeah. Like you fucking Teresa Walker's brains out up against the wall here.'

Bobby Jo was gulping, his eyes going from Tony to Annie.

'It was a one-off,' he said at last.

'Like hell,' said Annie sweetly. 'You and Teresa

were a regular thing, twice, sometimes three times a week. Up against the wall was favourite, ain't that right?' She tapped the wall beside her. 'Very thin, these walls. What, did you pay her?'

Bobby Jo was fidgeting like a caged animal now. Tony moved in closer.

'Okay!' Bobby Jo held his hands up. 'Yeah. All right. You got me. I gave Teresa a quick hump a couple of times a week, is that a crime? I tell you, that girl was *hot*. And she came on to me, not the other way round. What can I tell you? When Teresa started coming in here and offering it on a plate in exchange for a bonus or two, what was I supposed to do? Turn it down?'

Annie shrugged. 'Why should you?'

'Exactly!' He half smiled, but it quickly faded back to that edgy, uncomfortable look. 'But serious. Straight up. Can we keep this between ourselves, for God's sake? If you ever tell anyone I was getting my leg over with Teresa, I'll deny it flat out.'

Annie stared at him. 'Why the big secret?'

Bobby Jo's eyes slipped away from hers.

'No reason. Just wouldn't want it getting around, that's all.'

'Why, you got a boyfriend too?'

'No.' Again with the fidgeting. Annie could see that this was making Bobby Jo extremely uncomfortable.

'Steady girlfriend then?'

'No. Yeah. That is . . .' he faltered, half grinned. There was a faint sheen of sweat on his brow. 'Yeah, my girlfriend's the possessive type. She heard I'd been screwing around, I'd be toast.'

Annie was silent. So was Tony. Bobby Jo's eyes were darting between them, wondering what was coming next.

Finally Annie spoke. 'Did Teresa have a red flame tattooed on her inner thigh?'

Bobby Jo stiffened and his eyes met Annie's. 'Yeah, she did. Had it done a couple of days before she died. They did it next door. She said it was still sore, when we—'

'When you fucked her in exchange for a bonus.'

'Hey, it was a bit of business, that's all,' said Bobby Jo with a return to his former self. 'I gave her kickbacks; she gave me sex. Then she had to go and take advantage, start passing her cards round, I ask you. I found out about the cards just before she got herself done.'

'Really?'

'Oh, now hold *on*,' he said, half laughing. 'You think I had anything to do with that? Think again. Sure, I'm sorry for the girl, but she was always pushing her luck, and it couldn't be a surprise to anyone that she ended up the way she did.'

'You weren't so mad over the cards incident that you thought you'd stop her little games once and for all?' asked Annie. 'Maybe you got a taste for throttling working girls and you did Val Delacourt too, and Aretha Brown?'

'Hey, no.' Bobby Jo's eyes were desperate now. 'I didn't do a thing to Teresa, or those others. I *didn't.*'

'Really?'

'You have to believe me. I didn't do nothing.'

'I know he's lying about something,' said Annie to Tony. They'd left Bobby Jo and were now standing on the pavement outside the tattoo parlour.

It was closed again. It was early afternoon, music blaring out from the club next door, girls taking up their places in fetish-club and strip-joint doorways to hook in the punters, big guys enticing people into the smoky depths with offers of free booze and topless bar girls who'd let you lean over the bar and suck their delectable tits. They would also arrange for anything else you fancied sucking in one of the discreet little rooms they had out back, for a price.

Everything had a price.

Again her thoughts turned to Aretha, who had loved money so much. She wondered how that had really sat with Chris, who earned so little in security at the airport. Whether it caused rows between them. Rows that might possibly have tipped over into something worse ... But no. Surely not Chris. *Never.*

She looked around. Women of all descriptions: Asian, Chinese, whatever took your fancy; it was all here for the asking. And rent boys – posh ones for the East End villains who leaned that way, cheeky little Cockneys for the toffs. All human life was here, and it was all on sale.

But Pete Delacourt's tattoo parlour was still closed. The curtains were still pulled over in the flat upstairs; there was still a light shining dimly through the tatty drapes. They got back in the car and sat there, looking at the little shop. Not a soul moving in there.

'Did you think Bobby Jo was lying about something, Tone?' asked Annie.

'Through his teeth, was my feeling,' said Tony.

'Yeah, me too. Get one of the boys to watch him, okay? See where he goes, what he does. And why is that place never open?' She indicated the tattoo parlour with a nod of her head.

Tony shrugged. 'Where to?'

'Head back East, Tone.'

They were passing Victoria Park along Old Ford Road, Annie deep in thought, just gazing out at the people and the traffic rushing past the window, when she saw the huddled figure sitting on the park bench. Looked once. Did a double take. Leaned forward and tapped Tony sharply on the shoulder.

'Stop the car.'

There was a shit-load of traffic bringing up the

rear. Tony clapped on the anchors. Cabbies started doing their nuts, leaning out of their windows and saying was he considering ever learning to *drive* that bloody car, or was his sole ambition in life to just get it mangled to a pulp? Other drivers honked their horns, indicated, tried to get round the sudden obstruction the black Jaguar had become, as it pulled in to the kerb with a screech of wheels.

'Wait here,' said Annie, and shot out of the car and into the park.

She ran to the bench.

The hunched figure was gone. Had no doubt heard the commotion on the road, and legged it.

'Fuck it.' Annie looked frantically around.

Not a hundred yards away, a thin girl was walking fast, head down, hurrying away.

'Mira!' Annie bellowed.

The girl stopped. Turned. Then started walking again, away from Annie.

Annie sprinted after her. Caught hold of her arm. It *was* Mira.

Annie was elated, despite the state Mira was in, despite everything. She'd thought the silly mare was in some sort of danger – if not actually dead. Yet here she was. Mira, her old friend, still stinking like a polecat, still skinny and covered in sores – what a bloody mess she was; but it was *Mira*, thank God.

'What the hell do you want now?' asked Mira,

wild-eyed, twitching away from Annie when she reached out to touch her.

'Hey, is that any way to greet a friend?'

'What do you *want*?' asked Mira, shivering. *Shivering,* on a summer's day with male office workers out on the grass in shirtsleeves, secretaries with their cheesecloth tops rolled up to expose pale midriffs, all of them just lapping up the heat, and here was Mira – emaciated, filthy and shivering like she was in the teeth of an arctic gale.

'I want to help,' said Annie. 'For fuck's sake Mira, come on. Why'd you run off like that? I'm trying to help you.'

'You can't,' said Mira. 'No one can.'

'That's crap.'

'You can't make me do anything,' said Mira weakly.

'No? Look at yourself,' said Annie. 'You couldn't knock the skin off a fucking rice pudding. So you're coming with me.'

'I can't,' said Mira, and now there were tears trickling down from her eyes. 'I can't.'

'You can,' said Annie, still holding on firmly to Mira's arm. It felt like a skeleton's, all bone, hardly any muscle at all. 'Come on, Mira,' said Annie more gently.

Mira just lowered her head, all the fight going, draining from her in an instant. Annie led her over to the car, and got her seated in the back.

Tony looked at Annie in the mirror as if she'd finally taken leave of her senses. His boss had just put a female *tramp* in his nice clean car. Annie cranked open a window and gave Tony a winning smile.

'Dolly's place, Tone,' she said.

'Jesus, no!' snapped Mira, making panicky movements to throw open the door. 'I can't . . . don't make me go there.'

Annie stared at her in puzzlement.

'It's *his* patch. I shouldn't be there. It's *his*,' said Mira, wide-eyed with fear.

'Redmond Delaney?' Annie was still staring – and now she was remembering how Mira had run last time from Dolly's place, just as she'd told Dolly that Redmond was on the phone. 'You scared of Redmond?'

Mira nodded. More than scared: she looked terrified.

'It's okay,' she told Mira. 'He never goes there.'

Hardly ever, thought Annie. She wasn't about to add *that,* or Mira would freak again.

Mira didn't look convinced, but at least she stopped looking as if she was going to throw herself bodily from the car.

Now what the hell is that all about? wondered Annie as Tony drove them over to Limehouse.

33

'This is Mira. You remember Mira, she's been here before. She used to be one of my girls up West,' said Annie.

Dolly was staring at the apparition that had materialized in her spotless kitchen. So was dark-haired, sharp-faced Sharlene, who looked as if someone had just dropped a dead rat at her feet. Even easy-going, sleepy-eyed little Rosie was struck dumb. Ross was out. Just as well, really.

'I remember *Mira* from your place up West,' said Dolly, her eyes travelling up over the bag of bones standing there whiffing the place out. 'Jeez, I thought this one looked familiar when she came here last time, sort of. But you've got to be kidding me. This ain't Mira.'

'Yes it is, Doll. This is Mira.'

'Well, for fuck's sake. What happened, she get hit by a truck?'

'Don't talk about her as if she ain't here,' said Annie, getting miffed on Mira's behalf. She might be a wreck, but she still had feelings.

'I'd prefer it if she wasn't,' said Dolly smartly.

'I'll go,' said Mira listlessly, turning on her heel, heading for the hall. 'I should go, let me go, for God's sake . . .'

'No, you won't,' insisted Annie. She turned to Dolly, who was nearly quivering with disgust at this *thing* Annie had brought into her tidy, homely little place. 'Look, Doll. I can't take her to the flat over the club, I'm never there and she needs keeping an eye on.'

'She needs her next *fix* by the look of her,' said Dolly in disgust. 'Get her out of here. I don't want her here.'

Annie looked at Mira. Whatever Mira was on, she was clearly starting to feel withdrawal symptoms. The shivering had stepped up a gear. Dolly had a point. But it wasn't like her to be so bluntly uncharitable. 'Yeah, about that,' she started in.

'You can't be thinking she's going to *stop* here,' said Dolly, reading her mind.

'I'm not stopping here,' said Mira through chattering teeth.

'Yes you bloody are,' said Annie. She turned to Dolly. 'Yes she is, Doll.'

'No,' said Mira.

'See? She don't *want* to stop here,' said Dolly

triumphantly. 'So for fuck's sake get her *out,* okay?'

Sharlene and Rosie were watching from the sidelines like spectators at a tennis match, their heads moving back and forth, following the action.

'Will you both shut it?' snapped Annie. 'Mira – you're stopping. Dolly – she's stopping. I hate to ask, but—'

'Oh, here we go,' snorted Dolly.

'Come *on,* Doll. I wouldn't ask if it wasn't necessary. Please. I want someone I can trust to keep an eye on her. Just tuck her away nice and quiet. Keep her out of the Delaneys' way.'

Dolly's mouth dropped open. 'What the . . . now look, if she's crossed up the Delaneys in some way, I don't want to know. I don't get involved in their business, you know that.'

'I'm not stopping here,' bleated Mira.

'You're stopping,' said Annie, her eyes flinty with determination as she turned her gaze on Dolly. 'What is *up* with you?'

'Me?' spat back Dolly. 'Nothing wrong with me. *I* didn't bring this piece of shit in here.'

Annie turned away from Dolly. 'Rosie, take Mira up to the back room, settle her in. Oh yeah – and run her a bath.'

'Why me?' whined Rosie.

'Because you're a nice girl, Rosie. And you can see that Mira needs your help.'

'Oh fuck,' complained Rosie, and went past a grinning Sharlene to stand in front of Mira. 'Jesus – she *stinks*.'

'The bath will sort that out,' said Annie, and Rosie ushered the shambling Mira out of the kitchen and into the hall and up the stairs. Sharlene stood there leaning against the worktop, smirking. Dolly gave Annie an angry glare.

'I hope you know what you're bloody doing,' she said. 'Me, I don't think you do.'

'I'm helping a friend in need,' said Annie, following the two girls out into the hall. 'And for God's sake, Doll, I'd have thought you'd do the same. Seems I was wrong. Oh yeah – keep Ross away from her. And tell the girls not to throw her name around, okay? Call her – oh, I don't know – Susan or some fucking thing, but not Mira. And look – after she's had a bath, you'd better make sure there's a lock on her bedroom door. She tends to wander off.'

'Fuck *you*, Annie Carter,' said Dolly with feeling.

And now it was Friday, and they were burying Aretha. Leaving Rosie ambling cheerfully around the kitchen, boogying along to the radio, Sharlene in with a punter and Mira locked in her room upstairs, Dolly joined Annie in the Jag and Tony drove them to the church.

'Christ, she was married in this church,' said Dolly grimly.

'I'm sorry I missed that,' said Annie.

'It was a great day. Aretha was so happy. And Chris too. And now look. Fucking disaster. But what a day that was. I'll never forget it. Ellie got drunk, poor cow. Couldn't believe she had to give up on Chris. You know how she's always been about him. And the vicar came back to the house for the reception after he'd done the ceremony, had a bit of a skinful.'

'What, the *vicar*?'

Dolly nodded.

'Skinny chap, little grey beard, looks like butter wouldn't melt?'

'That's the one. Fell down and couldn't get up. Got a bit abusive, truth be told. Had to help him home.'

'In what way abusive?' asked Annie.

'Oh, the old fool was staggering about upstairs looking for the loo and got into the Punishment Room by mistake, saw all the gear in there and saw the light. Came downstairs shouting the odds about dens of iniquity and fallen women, then keeled over like a sack of spuds, right in the hall.'

'How's Mira doing?' asked Annie after a pause.

'Fucking wonderful,' sniffed Dolly. 'After we deloused her and scrubbed her hair and generally cleaned her up and *burned* all those filthy disgusting clothes she had on – Rosie gave her some of hers to wear, they're about the same size, even though Mira's about a foot taller than Rosie. There's no meat on her bones at all. And thank God you said about the lock on the door. She's been hollering to be let out, and throwing up, and frankly I think she's *seeing* stuff, hallucinating, that's what she's doing.'

Annie sat there, feeling chastened. Christ, and she had inflicted Mira on Dolly without a second thought. She looked at Dolly. 'I'm sorry, Doll.'

'What the hell's she been on?'

'I could tell she was on something, but I don't know what. I bet that's why she got tucked up with Rizzo Delacourt, he could feed her habit in exchange for her doing a bit on the game. Everyone a winner, right?'

'A couple more months out there on the streets and she'd be finished,' said Dolly. She looked out of the window, thoughtfully. 'How does that happen to a classy girl like Mira used to be? She was bloody gorgeous. Top-of-the-line tart. All the lords and stuff wanted a piece of her. And now . . . this.' She let out a heartfelt sigh. 'I've told Rosie and Sharlene to keep her under lock and key. Think she's so spaced out that she'd take off again at a moment's notice. And then she'd be fucked.'

'Thanks, Doll. You been careful about Ross?'

'Fucking sure. He thinks she's Susan, a druggie mate of Shar's.'

'You done good, Doll.'

'Well, I'm not happy about it. But if I was that far into the gutter I'd hope someone would try to hoist me out of it, too.'

It was a beautiful day. A peach of a day. And that seemed wrong, on such a sad occasion. There was a fair turnout, and Louella was there, crying copious tears for her baby girl. Annie remembered her promise to Dolly, that she would apologize to Aretha's aunt for her behaviour in the funeral parlour, and cringed inwardly at the very idea. Not that it would do much good. An explanation might be better.

People were wandering into the church as the hour approached, but Annie and Dolly lingered outside. Annie saw a familiar face among the crowds. He was keeping a watchful vigil on the mourners, his expression pinched as if in disapproval.

Looks like the bloody Grim Reaper, she thought, looking at his dark hair and eyes, his neat black suit, crisp white shirt and black tie.

Annie went over. 'DI Hunter,' she greeted him civilly.

'Mrs Carter,' he said in return.

'Checking out the villains?' asked Annie.

He looked at her, straight-faced. 'Something like that.'

'Nobody here very villainous.'

'Who knows? Murderers sometimes feel an overwhelming urge to revisit their crimes.'

Annie looked at him. 'Yeah, but you've *got* your murderer, ain't you? Chris is already banged up for this. Unless you've charged the wrong man.'

'We try always to keep an open mind, Mrs Carter, even if the evidence is pretty conclusive.' He gave her a tight smile. 'We've got our hands full, to say the least. Not only this nastiness, but also plenty more.'

'Like what?' snorted Annie.

'Oh, like drunks and fights and road accidents and domestics and all sorts of other things, Mrs Carter, including three dead escorts, prostitutes, call them what you will . . . but at least we've got the man who did it.'

Annie was watching the hearse bearing Aretha's coffin as it turned into the church driveway.

'Yeah,' she said to Hunter, 'but you're still here, ain't you? Still looking.' Her eyes were hard on his face for a moment. 'So you're not one hundred per cent sure. Not yet.' Then she straightened with a forced, brittle smile. 'Here's the hearse. Party time,' she said, and went into the church.

It was the same old shit. The pop-eyed little organist launched into the 'Dead March' from Handel's *Saul*. The vicar gave a lovely service, the choir – minus Louella – lifted the roof and brought a tear to many an eye. All through it Annie stood up or sat mouthing words; everything was muted by a huge sense of loss. Maybe it was easier for people like Louella – although not much, she suspected – because as Christians they had a firm belief that Aretha had gone to a better place. Annie wasn't sure about that. All she could see was the coffin, draped with multicoloured flowers; all she could think was: *Why did this have to happen to Aretha?*

She wanted to know why. It burned her like a branding iron, this need to know. And even more, she wanted to know *who?* What sort of bastard could do this? Did he feel sorry, once the deed was done? Did he actually enjoy that feeling of taking a life? Did it make him feel powerful?

She thought of Bobby Jo. A man dressed as a woman. Who had incidentally been shafting Teresa, who had *also* incidentally been the proud possessor of a flame tattoo until someone had decided it would be a good idea to kill her.

The flame was a marker, wasn't that what Mira had told her? Once they were marked, they were marked for death. A sort of ritual. A *sick* sort of ritual.

She thought of Gareth from the hotel, hanging dead in his shabby flat, his dog barking endlessly in distress . . .

And then it was over. The coffin was carried back down the aisle by the pallbearers, Louella following behind in floods of tears, being supported by another stout black lady. Her eyes met Annie's as she passed by, and she visibly flinched. Annie looked away. Christ knew what Louella thought of her. It wasn't a very comfortable feeling.

She followed on with Dolly, stepping out into the vivid sunshine. Annie looked around, but Hunter was gone. At the graveside there was the same old horrible, painful routine, and she stood through it stoically, endured it, as they all did.

Finally it was over. The vicar, the same slender man with the beard that Annie had talked to last time she'd come here, the same one who had apparently been falling-down drunk at Dolly's place, withdrew. The organist, who had played throughout the ceremony and conducted the choir was hurrying off along the path to the gate. The mourners began to disperse. Annie stepped forward, Dolly trailing a pace behind, and was suddenly face to face with Louella.

'I'm sorry if I upset you at the funeral parlour,' Annie said without preamble. 'That wasn't my intention.'

'Your *intention*?' Louella echoed tearfully, her eyes full of disgust. 'Girl, you one sick lady.'

'No, Louella. I was looking for something. Something that might explain why Aretha was killed.'

'You wonder why Aretha was killed? I'll tell you why, you just listen to me,' said Louella forcefully. 'She died because she did bad things, mixed with bad people. People like you. People who use others. People who have no morals, no beliefs, no *nothing*.'

'That ain't true,' said Annie.

'It is true. You want to apologize? Well, I don't accept your apology, and I don't accept your explanation either. You just keep out of my way, you evil creature: that's all I want from you,' said Louella, and barged past Annie.

Annie caught her arm. 'Louella . . .'

'No!' Louella whipped round, her face twisted in anguish, sobs making her voice come in fits and starts. 'Don't you dare say another word. You got nothing to say that I want to hear, you got that?'

Annie let go of Louella's arm. She stepped back. Louella turned away.

'Shit,' said Dolly wryly, 'that went well.'

Annie turned and glared at her. She was being buried in crap right now and Dolly was making fun.

'Sorry,' said Dolly, dropping her gaze.

'No.' Annie took a breath. '*I'm* sorry. I've caused trouble and I've messed up, and I'm sorry, Doll. Look, you go on to Louella's place for the wake if you like.'

'Shit, no. Don't think I could take all that today, not after this. Think I'd rather just go home.'

'Okay then. Take the car. Be sure and check on Mira, will you?'

'What are you going to do? I tell you, you'd better leave Louella the hell alone for now. She's had a gutful, and next time she'll swing for you, I swear.'

'I'm not going near Louella. You go on. Tell Tone I'll get a cab.'

The vicar was already in the vestry, taking off his white robe, his ceremonial black sash. Annie knocked on the half-open door. He looked up, gave a slight smile that didn't quite reach his eyes.

'Can I help you?' he asked.

'I hope so. You remember me? I came here before, talked to you about the . . . the deceased.'

Jesus – deceased. Aretha, the deceased.

'Oh yes.' He was hanging up the robes, his movements hurried. 'It's a bit of a bad time, actually. I've another service this afternoon, and things to do before then.'

'I won't take up much of your time,' said Annie.

'I'm afraid I can't spare any time at all, not today,' he said, turning back to her, his long-fingered hands busily folding the black sash, laying it neatly aside.

'I'm afraid you must,' said Annie.

The vicar was suddenly still, staring at her blankly. 'I beg your pardon?'

'You heard me. A few minutes, that's all. Oh.' Annie fished in her bag, pulled out a couple of tenners. 'And a donation. For the church roof. Or whatever. Don't the steeple need repointing or some damned thing?'

Now his face was distinctly unfriendly. He looked disdainfully at the money, then back at her face. 'Just say what you've come to say and go,' he said.

'Aretha. Girl you've just buried, you did her wedding ceremony.'

He shrugged. But his eyes were watchful.

'Only she was pretty memorable to look at. Gorgeous, tall, black. Very distinctive. And the man she married was huge – a bouncer, an ex-boxer. I think you would have remembered them, but when I spoke to you last time, you weren't sure. You thought maybe one of your lay preachers had done the job. But they didn't. It was you.'

'Oh. Well.' He shook his head, his eyes moving away from hers. 'I do a lot of weddings. Hundreds.'

'Bet you don't go to many receptions though,' said Annie. 'And get wasted.'

That touched a nerve.

'Look, what is all this about?' he demanded, an edge of aggression to his voice now. He stepped towards her, and now she could see the broken veins on his cheeks, the yellow cast to his eyes. Heavy drinker. Heavy *regular* drinker.

'Nothing much,' shrugged Annie. 'I'm just wondering how you could have forgotten doing that particular wedding – tall black girl, big bouncer; *very* memorable pair – and getting drunk afterwards at the reception and running off at the mouth about fallen women . . . Or maybe you just wanted to forget you'd done it. What's up, did your guard slip, did your secret come out, do you often end up lying blotto on someone's else's floor?'

'All right!' Now he was angry. 'I conducted the ceremony.'

'Then why not come straight out and say so?'

'I drank too much that evening, made a laughing stock of myself, I didn't *want* to remember it, and I didn't want any of my parishioners remembering it either. I felt ashamed of myself, I'd let myself down – is that good enough for you?'

Annie stared at him for a beat. 'Ain't there a line in the Bible, "Judge not lest ye be judged"?' she asked. 'Only, you were making judgements left, right and centre, by the sound of it. Which don't seem quite right, coming from a man of the cloth.'

'I'd had too much to drink. I may have said some unfortunate things . . .' he started, colour mounting in his mottled cheeks.

'Oh, you remember that much then, we're making progress here. Now you remember you did Aretha's wedding, and you remember you got abusive and drunk at her wedding reception, upset people all to hell. If we keep on going with this, do you think you'll remember anything else?'

He looked at her. 'I don't know what you mean.'

'I *mean* that three working girls are dead, and you denied all knowledge of one of them, which has incidentally turned out to be a lie. I *mean* that you got falling-down drunk and started showing your true colours at Aretha's wedding reception, and now I'm wondering if you had contact with the other two as well.'

'Get out,' he said suddenly, trembling with indignation. 'Go on, get out of here!'

Annie stared at him for a beat. 'For now,' she said at last, 'but this ain't the end of it.'

She tucked the tenners back into her purse. 'Thanks for your help, Reverend,' she said, and left.

34

'Thank God you're back,' said Dolly frantically, meeting her at the front door of the Limehouse parlour.

'Why? What's up?' Annie asked, freezing in alarm as she saw the expression on Dolly's face. And then the noise came. It sounded like a soul trapped in hell, wailing and moaning. Goose bumps sprang up on her arms, and all the hair on the back of her neck lifted. 'What the fuck . . . ?'

'Mira. It's bloody Mira,' said Dolly, and hurried away upstairs. 'I *told* you I didn't want her here.'

Annie followed, her heart in her mouth. Ross was nowhere to be seen. When they got up to the top landing, Rosie was standing with her face bleached white with alarm outside Mira's door. Along the landing, they could see Sharlene through the open bathroom door, running water into the sink, splashing her face, groaning. The water was running pink.

'What's happened?' Annie demanded.

'Sharlene took her in a cup of tea, that's all,' said Rosie shakily. 'No good taking her in food, she just chucks it at you, she never eats a thing. I was in my room, I saw Sharlene go past, and that girl in there – she's been shouting and screaming all morning, it's enough to drive you mad, she just went bloody crazy. Sharlene said she upped and cracked her one in the jaw, split her lip and everything, and Sharlene just got the hell out and locked the door on the mad bitch.'

Something hit the door, hard. They all stepped back. Annie went along to the bathroom and looked at Sharlene. The sink was a mess of blood, and Sharlene now had a white towel clamped to her mouth. The towel was slowly turning red.

'You all right?' she asked Sharlene.

Sharlene nodded, but she looked shaken all to hell. 'Just a cut lip,' she said, her voice muffled. She tried to smile. 'I've had worse off punters.'

'Rosie.' Annie beckoned the blonde girl along, and she gratefully moved away from the door and came to the bathroom. 'Stay with Shar and look after her, okay?'

Rosie nodded.

Annie went back to the door and looked at Dolly. Dolly returned her stare.

'You ever see anyone go cold turkey before?' asked Dolly.

Annie shook her head.

'Well I have. That's what's happening here. It ain't pretty. One of my cousins got into drugs and his dad shut him in the shed for three days to dry him out. I'm telling you, by the time it was done and he was clean again, the inside of that shed looked like a fucking nuclear fallout zone.'

A huge thump hit the door.

'Gotta get out! Out! Let me OUT,' shrieked Mira.

Annie and Dolly exchanged tense looks.

'I'd better go in there,' said Annie. 'She knows me, maybe I can talk to her, calm her down.'

'Rather you than me,' said Dolly, wincing as something smacked hard against the other side of the door again. The key in the lock fell out and hit the carpet. 'I *warned* you,' said Dolly in agitation. 'I told you not to bring her in here. But would you listen? No. As per fucking usual. You always have to fly around like a fart in a bottle, messing around in things you don't even understand.'

Annie turned to her with hands on hips. 'Okay, let's have this out in the open. What the fuck are you talking about?'

'Nothing.' Dolly's eyes slipped away from hers.

'I don't want a ruck with you, I just don't want this girl here, she's killing my business. I want her *out*.'

'You're coming in with me,' said Annie, snatching up the key.

'Thanks a *bunch*,' said Dolly.

Annie took a breath to steady herself. Christ knew what they were going to find in there. She put the key in. Suddenly the howling and screeching from the other side of the door stopped dead. She paused. Looked at Dolly. Dolly mouthed, *Get the fuck on with it then*.

Annie turned the key in the lock.

Nothing.

She turned the handle and pushed the door open wide with the flat of her hand.

Inside, it looked as though an army of chimps had been marauding around the room. There was blood and shattered crockery on the floor, tea seeping into the carpet. The bed was shit- and urine-stained. The mirror above the dressing table opposite the door was cracked right across, talcum powder dusted all over the top of the dressing table and on the floor too. Scent bottles were thrown to the four winds, some broken, their jagged bits of glass strewn all over the place.

But . . . silence. Sudden, unearthly silence. A sort of *waiting* silence.

But this was Mira. Skinny, weak, no threat

to anyone. So really there was no need – was there?
– to feel like just relocking the door, turning tail,
leaving whatever demons had been unleashed in
there to play on and do their worst.

Annie stepped forward, aware that Sharlene, her
chin still swathed in the reddening folds of the towel,
was watching with Rosie from the open bathroom
door. Annie walked cautiously into the room. China
and glass crunched underfoot.

'Mira?' she said quietly into the silence.

No answer. She took another step forward. Saw
a movement in the broken mirror across the room
and ducked instinctively back, out of the way of
the sliver of broken perfume bottle that Mira
brought crashing down, intending to strike her
head with.

'*Jesus!*' hollered Dolly, as Annie fell back against
her.

A flailing figure came at them, arms pin-wheeling,
slashing, trying to inflict harm. Wild hair flying,
face twisted in a rictus of hate, eyes glaring. Annie
was faintly aware of the two girls along the hall
erupting into hysterical screams, but the only
thought in her mind was: *Christ, she meant to kill
me with that. Mira was going to kill me stone dead.*

Trapped between this crazy whirling dervish and
the staggering too-slow body of her friend, Annie
pushed forward hard, grabbing hold of the wrist
of the hand holding the lethal glass shard.

Mira was snarling, spitting, her other fist raining blows down on Annie's head. Dolly recovered herself and charged in too, trying to get a hold on that arm. But Mira was out of it and – shockingly – she had the strength of ten men.

'Let me out, I've got to get out!' she was yelling and screaming, panting with the effort of trying to do damage.

'Mira!' Annie shouted, trying to get through to her. 'Mira, for God's sake. It's me, it's Annie!'

But Mira was shoving forward, both hands caught, the two women struggling against her single-minded fury. Even though they had hold of her, they were losing the fight. She was pushing frantically, edging them back out through the door, literally throwing herself against them. Dolly went down on to her knees but held on tight to the wrist whipping about above her head. Annie pulled back, not wanting to do it, *hating* to do it, but what choice did she have? She pulled back as far as she could and punched Mira hard on the jaw.

Mira toppled, the glass fragment flying out of her hand. Dolly let go of the girl's skeletal wrist and hauled herself back to her feet.

'Shit a *brick*, who'd believe she'd be that strong?' she panted in wonder.

Annie sagged against the door, nursing her aching knuckles. Gasping, shaken, she stared down at Mira, who was squirming weakly on the floor, her eyes closed, her face screwed up in pain. Sharlene and Rosie crowded into the open doorway behind them.

'What's she been on?' marvelled Rosie.

'Who gives a fuck?' muttered Sharlene, wincing behind the towel. 'She ought to be locked up. She's a sodding nut job, that one.'

'What the hell we going to do with her now?' Dolly asked, looking at Annie.

Rosie screamed.

They turned. Mira was scrambling back to her feet. *Damn,* thought Annie, bracing herself for the next onslaught. But Mira didn't run at her. Mira gave the women in the doorway one desperate, despairing look, and her eyes shifted sideways. All at once, she was running across the room, towards the *window.*

'Shit!' said Dolly loudly.

Oh God help us, thought Annie, and dashed after her.

Everything seemed to move in slow motion. Mira up ahead, arms pumping, ready to fling herself into a sheet of glass to get out, ready to run herself into a messy and final oblivion. Annie rushing after her, the screams coming from Rosie, Dolly yelling something that Annie neither fully heard nor understood. Had to be *quick*, and oh shit she was so slow, too slow, surely too slow . . .

She caught up with Mira when she was right on top of the closed window, caught her and held her, pulled both her arms back, uncaring of how badly she might hurt her, intent only on stopping her committing suicide.

'Let me go, I've got to get out, I can't stay here, he's after me, for fuck's sake *let me go!*' Mira was shrieking incoherently.

'Mira! Stop it! You're going to kill yourself!' shouted Annie, losing her grip, struggling, Mira kicking back, trying to get free, trying to throw herself right through a solid pane of glass that would surely kill her, cut an artery, make her bleed to death even if she survived the long drop on to the paving below.

Mira got a hand free, and to Annie's horror she started punching the glass, shouting, yelling, screaming, and the glass cracked, the crack running across the surface, and then another blow, and the cracks were deepening, spreading, and now there was blood on Mira's hands, splashing out scarlet on to the curtains, spurting on to Annie's face. And oh fuck Annie could feel her grip starting to go.

'Jesus . . .' she muttered, knowing that in an instant Mira would be through the glass, cutting herself, damaging herself irreparably.

'It's okay,' said a male voice by Annie's ear, 'I got her.'

Ross was there. At last. Grabbing Mira bodily around the waist, ignoring her kicks, her struggles, her screams; taking her over to the dirty, disgusting bed and dropping her down on to it.

'Restraints,' he said as Annie sagged to the floor beside the window and tried to get her breath back.

Dolly had her head in her hands. The two girls in the doorway were standing there bloodied and tearful.

'We need something to restrain her,' said Ross again, to his exhausted audience.

Dolly dropped her hands. 'The punishment chair,' she said, and left the room and came back with what looked like two huge leather belts. Ross took them from her, and secured Mira, who was sobbing uncontrollably now, to the bed.

'Well thank fuck,' said Sharlene from behind the towel.

'You can say *that* again,' said Dolly, and went and hauled Annie back to her feet.

Annie looked at Ross. Wondered if he'd heard her scream out Mira's name. Maybe not. She hoped not.

'She's written something,' said Rosie half an hour later.

'What?' asked Dolly.

They were down in the kitchen. Ross had gone

out to fetch bandages from the local chemist, leaving the four women down there drinking tea and recovering their scattered senses. After a little while, Dolly had sent Rosie back up to see that Mira was okay. Or as okay as she could be, tethered to a filthy bed and out of her head with the need for a fix.

But the operative word here was *tethered*. Mira couldn't harm anyone now, not even herself. Annie looked at Dolly and then up at the ceiling. Mira was still shouting and swearing up there, cursing them, telling them she had to get *out*.

'What do you mean, she's written something?' asked Annie as Rosie came and slumped in a chair. 'She's tied to the bed, she can't write something.'

Unless she'd got loose. Annie sprang to her feet in alarm.

'It's okay, she's still tied to the bed,' said Rosie. 'But she's written something on the sheet. In blood, I mean.'

Frowning, Annie left the kitchen and went along the hall and up the stairs. She hesitated at the open door into Mira's room. Mira fell silent and stared at her, wild-eyed, from the bed. She was still tied down, unable to move. Thinking of what Mira had almost succeeded in doing to her, Annie was thankful for that.

She moved forward cautiously until she was right by the bed. She looked down at Mira's bleeding right hand. It wasn't bad, not an arterial bleed, thank Christ, but it was seeping steadily, and with her index finger Mira had scrawled something in blood on the soiled sheet.

Annie looked at what Mira had written. Her heart seemed to stop in her chest. She stared at the letters and then looked at Mira's face, her eyes rolling in her head, still out of it but not quite, because she had started to write a name.

Holy fuck, thought Annie.

She heard the front door open with a key. Ross was back with the medical supplies. But then she heard other low voices – male, not female. She moved back to the door, crept out on to the landing. Peering over the banister, her heart froze in her chest. Ross was there, but so was Charlie Foster, the Delaneys' number one man. For a moment she stood there, immobilized with fear and horror. Then she quickly returned to the woman on the bed. Touching her fingers to Mira's wounded hand, she scrubbed more blood on to the word Mira had written on the sheet, obliterating it. They were deep in the shit already. Better to be safe than sorry. Mira squirmed, seemed almost to protest.

'It's okay,' said Annie. 'I know. I got it.'

But now what? she wondered, guts churning in panic as she stood looking down at Mira. Would she understand what Annie was about to say to her?

She leaned closer to the woman tied to the filthy bed and spoke in a whisper.

'Mira, listen. This is important. I don't know if you understand me or not, but you should be quiet now. Do you hear me? Don't make another sound. Gonna try and get you out of this, Mira, but help me out here will you? Be very, very quiet.'

Mira's eyes rolled, but she fell silent. She understood. Somewhere in there, Mira – *her* Mira – was still alive.

The voices downstairs mingled with Dolly's. She didn't blame Dolly. She couldn't. Not for this. And now heavy footsteps were coming back along the hall, and she heard the first tread on the bottom stair. With a last glance at Mira, she raised her finger to her lips and then quickly crossed to the door. She went out on to the landing, closed the door behind her, locked it, slipped the key into her jacket pocket and took a deep, calming breath as she waited for Charlie Foster to join her upstairs.

35

Charlie Foster got the shock of his life when he got up on to the landing and found Annie Carter standing there. She was pointing an old .38 Smith & Wesson revolver at his head. He froze on the top step. Ross, coming up right behind him, paused, looked ahead, saw her standing there.

'What the fuck?' he asked in annoyance.

'Hiya Charlie,' said Annie.

Charlie carefully put his hands up. He was staring at the gun, which was now pointing towards his chest.

'Hey,' he said with a nervous half-smile, a thin shadow of his usual predatory leer. 'Careful with that.'

'I'm always careful, Charlie.'

'We don't want no trouble, Mrs Carter,' he said, his pale eyes still on the gun in her hand.

'What *do* you want?' asked Annie.

'You've got something of Mr Delaney's here, Mrs Carter. That's all we want. Just that.'

'You're talking about a friend of mine,' said Annie, holding the gun steady although she could feel her heart stampeding inside her chest, could feel her stomach clenching with terror and loathing. Charlie Foster was a tough, mean bastard and she was scared shitless, but she wasn't going to hand Mira over to him, not in a million years.

But here was the thing. She was here, standing in a parlour that paid protection to the Delaneys. She was on Delaney soil. The Delaneys owned this patch and controlled everything in it; she was only *permitted* to be here because Redmond Delaney said she could be. When he said she couldn't, she was going to have to get the fuck out of it pretty damned fast – and it looked like that time had come.

She had something Redmond Delaney wanted, and that thing was *Mira*. She had no intention of handing her over. He wasn't going to be hanging the flags out about this; in fact he was going to be seriously pissed off with her.

Charlie smiled coldly, his eyes running over her. 'She's ours, Mrs Carter, and you are out of your depth here. Let's make this nice and easy. You put the gun down and stand aside, we take the girl, no harm done, no comebacks. How does that sound?'

Scarlet Women

'Like a bad idea,' said Annie. She was sweating with nerves. She could feel her hand growing slick with it on the burred walnut stock of the gun. 'I've got a better one.'

'Yeah?' His eyes were watchful.

'Yeah. Here it is. You turn around and go back out the door, and I don't shoot your balls off. How's that?'

Charlie's gaze didn't waver but his ever-present smile dimmed a bit.

'Like I said, we don't want no trouble,' he reiterated, taking a step forward. 'Just hand the gun over—'

Annie fired. The shot deafened them all. The bullet struck the ceiling above Charlie's head. A chorus of screams went up from the kitchen below, but not a peep out of Mira, locked inside the bedroom, tied to the bed, helpless. *Good girl*, thought Annie. Plaster plumed out in a thick cloud, dusting down over Charlie like snowfall. He staggered back a step, blinking, choking, and was steadied by Ross.

Annie stepped forward.

'I told you, Charlie. Back off. Just keep going. Because I'm telling you, the next one's going to blow your bollocks into mincemeat. You're a young man with lots of productive years in front of you, do you really want that to happen?'

Charlie started to back down the stairs. Ross backed up too. Someone was pounding at the

355

front door. *Tony*, thought Annie. He'd heard the shot.

Charlie held his hands up. The dust in his hair was white; he looked like he'd aged twenty years in the last few seconds. He wasn't smiling any more.

'Hey – okay. I'm going, see? I'm going.'

'Yeah. Keep going, that's the way,' said Annie, moving forward, following him down the stairs as he backed up.

'You ain't heard the last of this,' said Charlie when he was at the front door. Ross opened it, glaring back at her.

Tony was there, ready to break heads.

'Keep out the way, Tone,' said Annie, and Tony saw the gun, saw the situation, and moved swiftly to one side. To Charlie, she said: 'Keep going. You too, Ross.'

Annie was aware of Dolly and the two girls watching her from the open kitchen doorway.

'What the hell?' demanded Dolly, her eyes opening wide in horror as she stared at the gun in Annie's hand.

Nobody answered her.

Charlie backed up out to the front gate, Ross following behind him. Tony fell in behind Annie, who was out on the front step now and still pointing the gun at Charlie's undercarriage. In bright daylight, Charlie looked pale as milk.

'You're bang out of order, you,' said Ross angrily to Annie.

'I'm doing what I have to do,' said Annie. 'Go on now. Piss off, Charlie.'

With one last poisonous glare at her, Charlie went.

Ross stared at Annie and shook his head. 'You're fucking crazy.'

'You too. Go,' said Annie.

Ross went. When they were both out of sight, Annie handed the gun to Tony, who slipped on the safety and pocketed it. They went quickly back indoors, shut the door behind them. Tony threw the bolts over.

Dolly was staring at them both, aghast.

'What the fuck have you *done*?' she shouted at Annie.

Annie went to the phone. 'Don't worry, Doll, I'm going to make sure the Delaneys know you had no part in this.'

'Are you crazy?' asked Dolly, barging along the hall and glaring angrily at her. 'Of course they'll think I had a part in this. I run this place, what the hell do you think you're *doing*?'

Annie snatched up the phone. Then she paused and looked at Dolly.

'Doll – they were going to take Mira.'

'Why the hell would they want to do that? What possible interest could a wreck like that be to the Delaney boys?'

'They came to get her. Ross heard me say her name and they came for her. Redmond wants her, I don't know why. I couldn't let them take her, Doll, even you must see that.'

'All I *see* is that you've landed me in the crap right up to my neck, that's all. I told you she was trouble. How am I supposed to explain this away to Redmond Delaney?' Dolly's eyes were crazy with exasperation and growing fear. 'I don't question what he does or don't do. That ain't my place.'

'Yeah,' said Annie. 'You've made *that* clear enough.'

'And you didn't fucking well listen to me!'

'You mean you'd have let them take her? I don't believe you.'

'Don't be a silly cow, Annie. If the Delaneys want to snatch a junkie – even one who's a friend, or one who has been in the past, anyway, and let's face it, she was your friend, not mine – then I don't question it. What, do I look suicidal? And what am I supposed to do about Ross? You can't just order him out of here, he's my bloody doorman, he's a Delaney boy . . . what the fuck are you up to *now*?'

Annie was dialling a number.

It was ringing.

She was praying he was there. Oh shit – what if he wasn't?

Constantine picked up. 'Yeah?'

Thank you, God.

Annie gulped down a breath and pushed the words out. 'I need you. Right now.'

'What's happening?' His voice was suddenly sharper.

'And a safe house, you got a safe house for somebody? And a doctor?'

'You okay?'

'I'm fine.'

'Where are you?'

Annie told him.

'Don't move.' He put the phone down.

Annie glanced at Dolly, who looked mad enough to spit blood. At the two girls, cowering in the doorway. At Tony, whose expression said nothing. He just folded his arms and prepared to wait for backup to arrive.

Half an hour later, someone rapped at the front door. Dolly and the girls were sitting around the kitchen table. Annie was still standing in the hall, so was Tony. All was quiet. Even Mira had given up kicking off.

'Jesus, what now?' muttered Dolly.

Tony approached the door. 'Who is it?'

'The cavalry, who the fuck else?' said an impatient American voice from outside.

Tony drew out the gun, slipped off the safety, opened the door a crack. A youngish dark-haired man was standing there wearing a black biker jacket. He had a heavy nose and cleft chin and looked as if he had Mediterranean blood running through his veins. He was holding an automatic pistol. He looked at Tony standing there with the revolver, and gave a grin.

'Hey, pal, that's a proper museum piece you got there. You're Tony, right? Mrs Carter's driver?'

Tony nodded.

'Hey, how ya doin'?' The man stepped forward and patted Tony briskly on the shoulder. 'Mr Barolli's compliments.'

Tony pushed the door wide open. Outside were six handy-looking hard men, all grouped around Constantine Barolli. He looked up and saw Annie standing there in the hall.

'The gorgeous Annie,' he said with a grin. 'You at home to visitors?'

36

'I'll clear it with Redmond Delaney,' said Constantine, sitting in Dolly's kitchen with Dolly, Rosie, Sharlene and Annie. 'No worries.'

'No *worries*?' echoed Dolly angrily. She'd had a shock when Charlie Foster had come in and Annie had fired the gun, then an even bigger one when Constantine Barolli pitched up with half an army, but she was recovering fast. She always did. 'How can you say that? I pay protection to the Delaneys, and there's a Delaney man on the door – at least there was until this one,' she indicated Annie with a tetchy twitch of the head, 'took it into her head to throw him out in the street.'

'I'll sort it,' repeated Constantine. 'The Carter family and me, we got a mutual thing going; everyone knows that. The Delaneys won't want to cross me up. It'll be fine.'

Annie felt limp with the aftermath of fear. Even cocky Sharlene and laid-back little Rosie seemed shattered by the experience they'd just been through, too traumatized to even give a magnificent hunk like Constantine the glad eye.

Annie had half expected to die, or to see Mira perish in front of her. She couldn't believe that they were all sitting here in one piece. Now Tony and Constantine's men were bringing Mira down the stairs, and she was wailing and crying again.

Redmond wanted Mira, and I've thwarted him, she thought worriedly. *Is he really going to let this go?*

She thought of Layla, across town at Ruthie's, both of them unprotected. And her cousin Kath and the kids. She went out into the hall. 'Tone?'

Tony drew back from the crowd and looked at her.

'Send some of the boys over to Kath's, and to Ruthie's in Richmond, right now.'

'Sure, Boss,' he said, and went out the front door.

Mira, her face haggard and streaked with blood, was stretching out a bony hand to Annie as they manhandled her carefully, wrapped in a clean blanket, down to the bottom of the stairs. Annie took the girl's hand.

'It's okay, Mira,' she said, squeezing her hand tightly. 'These people are on our side. They're not going to hurt you. You're going to see a doctor, we're going to get you well again.'

'I don't want him to get me . . .' sobbed Mira.

'Jeez, is she out of it or what?' complained one of the men. 'That's all she keeps saying. I keep telling her, everything's cool. But she keeps on saying that.'

Because she's terrified for her life, thought Annie, her heart wrenching with pity.

'Be careful with her,' said Annie.

'Hey, no problem.' The young one who'd knocked at the door gave Annie a winning smile. 'A friend of yours is a friend of ours, Mrs C. Don't you worry about it.'

They took Mira out to the car. Annie went back along the hall and met Constantine coming towards her.

'I'm going to phone Redmond,' he said. 'But until I do that, I'm leaving one of mine on this door, okay? Just until I straighten him out. You want one of mine with Layla?'

'No, I've got that covered,' said Annie, feeling suddenly awkward.

Well, she'd said it. She needed him. Now she knew that if she was honest with herself, she wanted him too. Not out of gratitude, and not on the rebound from a dead man.

She looked at him. Constantine stared back at her.

'You got some time to spare?' he asked her, eyes sparkling with challenge.

She didn't waver. She nodded.

'Then let's go,' he said.

This time was better – slower, more sensual. This time *he* set the pace, not allowing her to rush towards climax, holding her back on the edge until she was gasping, sweating, panting out his name. *His* name. Not Max's.

'Oh God, here I go again,' said Annie out loud.

Constantine propped himself up on one arm and looked down at her. It was warm in his bedroom in the Holland Park mansion with the windows shut, and they'd certainly generated a fair bit of heat, rolling around naked in his huge bed.

'That sounds like regret,' he said, smoothing back a lock of dark hair from her shoulder, running his hand over her skin.

Annie shuddered deliciously. Oh fuck, she was in trouble here. He knew all the moves, this mobster. But she'd thought she was pretty safe. That no one could please her in bed the way Max had pleased her.

Welcome to the new world, she thought.

She felt high, like somebody had stuffed a fistful of amphetamines down her throat. She felt relaxed, and satisfied, and – oh shit – ready for more any

time *he* was ready, which please God would be some-
time soon.

Constantine understood the responses of the
female body and knew exactly how to make
those responses happen in spades. She shouldn't
be surprised by that: like Max, he was a man of
formidable intelligence and considerable experience.
Once in bed with him, any woman was putty in
his hands. And of course he'd been married.

Annie thought about that.

Had Constantine been happy with his late wife?
She couldn't bring herself to ask. This whole situation was fraught with danger and difficulties and
she didn't want to think too much, not yet. She
just wanted to sink into bliss and stay there.

But she knew she wouldn't be able to do that
for long. There was so much to consider, so much
trouble in store. Why could she never resist the
allure of bad, powerful men? First there had been
Max, someone else's property, and what a shit-storm
that had caused. Now there was Constantine. Mafia.
Enough baggage to sink a battleship. His family –
all except Alberto – had made it plain that they
were determined to set up barriers rather than
welcome a new woman into his life.

She knew why.

If Constantine got seriously involved, if he
remarried, then the pecking order would change.
Annie would come first to him. Well, she was *used*

to coming first. She didn't do second fiddle, and that was a fact. And if things progressed, if they – oh fuck – if they had a *baby* together, then the fur was bound to fly. Lucco would throw a fit. Gina would disapprove. Cara would feel usurped. The whole balance of the clan would be upset.

And the boys – *her* boys. They wouldn't swallow this. Not in a thousand years.

Oh shit, she thought, and sighed. But then – she had never yet, not once in her life, pulled back from a fight.

'So do you regret this?' he asked her.

Annie shook her head, cuddled in close. 'No,' she murmured against his chest, thinking that she really was up the creek this time, but that it was wonderful, that her veins were fizzing with happiness and desire, but that it was awful too because she had never faced such difficult choices. When they had made love, she had stifled the urge to say it, unwilling to give too much of herself away. But now she thought it, and knew that it was true: *I'm in love with you.*

She loved him. She knew it. All her fine intentions to cut this dead had come to nothing because that *wasn't* what she wanted in her heart of hearts. Damn. She really was in trouble.

She sat up, ran her hands through her hair, clutched her arms around her knees. 'I've never been so glad to see anyone in my entire life as I was to see you, when you pitched up at Dolly's place. Do you think you can really square it with Redmond?'

'It's done, that's who I was speaking to on the phone when we got in,' said Constantine, smoothing a hand down her back.

He'd taken her up to the bedroom, then gone back downstairs to his study. Ten minutes, and he'd been back. Redmond sorted. Or was he?

'Hey, he wants to kiss my ass, or have you forgotten?' Constantine went on when she sent him a dubious glance. 'He still thinks I might cut him in on some business.'

Annie looked back at him. 'And will you?'

He shook his head slowly. 'If he goes against you, he goes against me.'

Annie nodded, but she wasn't completely re-assured. She knew that Redmond was no normal man. She knew that he and his twin had been abused as children, and that the trauma of it had made them both cold and controlling. What lengths might Redmond go to, to get hold of Mira? And *why* was he so intent on doing that?

'Dolly's really pissed off with me. Did you explain to him that it wasn't down to her? That it was nothing to do with her?'

'Yep, I did. Say, what's the deal with this Mira?'

'Let's just say that a lot of things that didn't make any sense before are starting to add up now,' said Annie. She stared at Constantine. 'And you're really not intending to cut him in on the clubs up West?'

She was keeping it businesslike, even though she was here in this intimate situation with this extraordinarily gorgeous man, even though something softer would be in order, some warm words of love or adoration; anything rather than chewing on and on about a business matter that he had *already* reassured her over.

'For fuck's sake,' said Constantine, 'didn't I already say it was cool? What do you want, that I should try to hammer the deal down with you? That I should ask for extras? Actually,' he smiled, 'I think I've just *had* those.'

'I don't want the Delaneys stepping in, that's all,' said Annie, now feeling as flustered as a teenager on a first date.

'They are not stepping in,' said Constantine. 'They are not anywhere *near* stepping in, okay? Three thousand sterling a month's not a bad deal, and the Carters have done a good job over . . . I guess it's six, seven years . . . so that's sorted and there's no need for concern. Or are you just trying to keep this business when it so obviously is pleasure?'

Yeah, he was clever. Like Max had been clever. Good at reading signs. Perceptive. It was fucking irritating how clever he was.

Because he'd hit the nail square on the head. She felt uneasy with all this. Happy about it, yes – but worried too. Of course, if she hadn't enjoyed this little interlude (and here she glanced at her Rolex and discovered that in fact it had not been so little. In fact, they had been indulging themselves shamelessly for nearly three *hours*), she wouldn't feel quite so bad about it all. But enjoy it she had. She owned up to that. To be touched, caressed, overwhelmed by passion, she had forgotten how good all that could feel.

But now what? Where did it go from here?

'You know your trouble?' Constantine said, sitting up and dropping a kiss on to her forehead.

'No, what?' asked Annie distractedly.

'You think too much. Analyse too much. *Agonize* too much.'

'You think so?'

'I do.' His mouth moved to her lips. His tongue ran warmly over them, parted them. After a moment, Annie kissed him back. Jesus, this man was seriously *hot*. She could feel his erection stirring again against her hip, feel her own insides melting like cheese on a hotplate.

Then Annie could hear the sound of the front door opening, and then voices, male and female. She became aware that the female voice was young-sounding, and distinctly American, and she stiffened.

'Who's that?' she asked, sitting up.

Constantine sprawled back on the bed and groaned. 'It sounds like . . .' he started, and then the female American with the young-sounding voice yelled, 'Papa! Papa, where are you?'

Annie looked at Constantine.

He looked at her. Sighed. 'Sounds like Cara,' he said.

'Where is he . . . ?' they heard Cara ask impatiently, and again the male voice, maybe telling her not to do what she was about to do, but then they heard light footsteps coming quickly up the stairs.

Annie tucked the sheet up around her and shot her lover a furious look.

'*Constantine*,' she said warningly, but he was springing off the bed already, slipping on his robe, belting it. Before Cara could come bursting in – couldn't these people ever knock on doors? – he opened the bedroom door and went out on to the landing, closing the door firmly behind him.

Annie sat there, royally annoyed, feeling like a stupid kid caught necking in the back of a car. She slumped back on the bed, hearing their murmuring voices right outside the door. Any moment she expected the spoiled brat to come bursting in, demanding to know what her father was doing in bed with a woman in the middle of the afternoon.

Eventually, she heard Cara walking off along

the landing, and Constantine came back into the bedroom and closed the door behind him.

'Can you stick a chair under that handle?' asked Annie in annoyance.

She grabbed her undies and started to get dressed.

'You don't have to go yet,' he said, coming over to the bed and sitting down.

'Yeah, I do. I've got business to see to. Can I use this phone?'

He nodded. Annie called Tony's place, and he said he'd be there in ten minutes.

She put the phone down and got dressed.

Annie held up her hair so that Constantine could zip up her dress.

Maybe Cara had done her a favour, interrupting them. Did she really need any more complications in her life? Did she really want the boys turning against her? Did she really want to embark on a full-blown affair with someone whose family clearly disliked her and saw her as an unwelcome interloper, someone who was based on the other side of the *Atlantic,* for God's sake?

Annie fiddled for her bag, got out her brush, applied it with hard strokes to her hair. Avoided his eyes. 'I'm not sure about any of this,' she said, keeping her gaze averted.

'Hey.' He caught her shoulders, forced her to look at him. '*Hey.* Mrs Carter.'

'What?' demanded Annie tensely, her eyes meeting his. Oh God, she loved his eyes.

'No pressure,' he said. 'And . . .'

'And what?'

'I love you,' he said, and kissed her.

No pressure, my arse, thought Annie.

37

Annie told Tony where she wanted to go next, and Tony drove in silence. It wasn't his usual relaxed, amiable silence, however. This silence had a voice, and that voice was *disapproving*. Annie read the paper in the back seat and waited for him to tell her what was wrong. He kept glancing at her in the rear-view mirror then, when she glanced at him in return, his eyes flicked away.

She sighed and looked at the paper. Ulster was still in turmoil, Coronation Street had been running for a thousand episodes now. She put the paper aside.

'All right,' she said at last. 'Come on. Say it.'

'Say what?' Tony shrugged, smoothly changing gear.

'Whatever's on your damned mind, Tone. Either that or stop with the face, will you? I got troubles enough, without you throwing a strop on me.'

Tony was still silent.

Fuck it, thought Annie, and sat back.

'Okay,' he said suddenly. 'You shouldn't have done that, Mrs Carter. Called in the Barolli mob when we've got people of our own at hand. It gives a bad impression. Makes it look like the boys can't soak up a bit of trouble, and you know they can. They'll hear about it, and they won't like it. You're belittling them. That's all I got to say.'

Annie let out an exasperated breath.

'Is that what you're brooding about? For fuck's sake.' Annie stared at him wrathfully. 'Look, Tone. Here it is. I was in a mess and I had to act fast, I didn't have time to think about hurt *feelings*, for the love of God. But what I did think was this: I couldn't call the boys into a dispute with the Delaneys on Delaney turf. It would have looked like an aggressive act – hell, it *would* have been an aggressive act. And they would have had to retaliate or look like weaklings, like fucking pussies. Redmond Delaney could have moved against Dolly in reprisal, and then it would have been outright war.'

Annie paused. In the past, she knew she had acted on instinct, recklessly, without thought, causing things to happen that could have been avoided. She regretted those things every day, with all her heart. Now, she had learned. She was more careful. The tragedies of the past still haunted her, and her own culpability had made her more

circumspect in her actions. She didn't want Dolly
or anyone else hurt if she could avoid it.

'You ever play any chess, Tone?' she asked him.

'A bit,' said Tony.

'Max taught me when we were abroad. It's an
interesting game, you know. Moving pawns and
knights and stuff around the board. What I did by
calling on Constantine was checkmate. It ended
the game, cut all repercussions dead. Redmond
Delaney wants to get in good with Constantine.
He respects him. But more important than that, he
fears his power. I knew that only someone with
Constantine's clout could smooth this over without
unnecessary bloodshed. *Now* do you see why I
didn't just call up the boys?'

Tony's eyes met hers in the mirror. His expression was slightly warmer.

'Yeah, Boss,' he said.

'Happier?'

'Yeah.'

'And you'll explain it to the boys, pass the word?
I wouldn't want to make *them* unhappy.'

'I'll tell them, Boss. Count on it. Where to now?
Back to the Alley Cat?'

'No, I've had another thought. We're overdue
a visit to the Delacourts.'

'Holy fuck, not you again,' said Rizzo Delacourt,
standing in the doorway wearing pyjama bottoms

and nothing else. He was yawning, stretching, running a hand through his thin, messy hair, scratching his navel. His skin was white; he was scrawny with a sunken chest and a small pot belly. *Not* a pretty sight. The heavy reggae backbeat of 'Israelites' was thumping off the dingy damp-stained walls of the hall; Desmond Dekker was giving it his all.

Out in the front garden, Annie and Tone had picked their way past a threadbare sofa, a pile of pallets and a mound of dog shit. Now, Annie stepped into the house without waiting for an invitation, and Tony followed.

'Hey, I'm busy you know,' said Rizzo, following them into the front room.

Tony looked around in disgust. It was filthy; he could smell dirt and piss in the air. A woman who could have been anywhere between forty and sixty looked up dully at them as they came in. Her hair was scraped back from her skinny face, her eyes looked sunken and red and without hope. She was smoking a fag, drawing the stuff deep back into her lungs and sitting huddled in a scruffy armchair beside an empty fireplace. There were photos on the mantelpiece above it, all thick with dust.

Inside, the row was deafening.

'Turn the music off,' said Annie to Rizzo, but she couldn't make herself heard above the din.

She looked at Tony. He picked up the boom box and searched for the off switch. When he didn't find it, he smashed the box against the wall. Desmond Dekker fell abruptly silent.

'Hey! There's no call for that,' shouted Rizzo into the sudden peace.

'I want a word with Mrs Delacourt, Val's mother. Are you Mrs Delacourt?' Annie asked the seated woman.

'Well, maybe she don't want a word with you,' said Rizzo furiously.

'Hey, my friend, keep it down,' said Tony.

'This is the one, Ma,' said Rizzo, hopping from foot to foot in rage. 'This is the one who had her bastard yobs kill Benj. Can you believe anyone would do that, kill a helpless animal?'

Annie looked at Rizzo.

'That dog was a fucking menace,' said Mrs Delacourt.

Annie looked at her in surprise.

'Used to scare the shit out of me, that bloody thing. You had grandkids, you couldn't let them anywhere near a dog like that.'

'But you don't *have* grandkids,' said Rizzo.

'The neighbours got kids. They complained to the council.'

'Well fuck them.'

'I know I ain't got grandkids, you don't want to go rubbing it in,' said Mrs Delacourt, almost talking to herself. 'Not gonna have any now either, am I? Val's gone. Fuck knows what's happened to Peter, he never even shows his face these days. All I got left is you, Robbie, my little Robbie, and look how *you* turned out.'

'Well, that's just fucking charming,' said Rizzo.

Litle Robbie, thought Annie.

She stared at this *object* standing there and thought of what he had done to his own sister, luring her into a life on the streets; and to Mira, feeding her drugs until she was clean off her head. Both of them, sinking into a pit of despair and dependency. Mira might yet be pulled back from the edge, but Val was beyond hope, beyond anything at all. Cold anger flooded Annie at the thought of what this pathetic little man had inflicted on them.

She held it down to a dull roar. Looked at the mother sitting there, also without hope. Poor cow. Annie looked at the photos on the mantel. A pretty blonde there, could be Val. Two dark-haired boys, seven or eight years old, arm in arm, laughing on a beach. A tattooed man, flexing a huge bicep for the camera.

'Is that Peter?' Annie asked Mrs Delacourt, pointing to the photo.

Mrs Delacourt looked up at the print, nodded. 'I don't like all them tattoos,' she said with a scowl. 'Ugly things. He's a handsome man, my Pete, why does he want to go covering himself in all that stuff?'

'Is he here?'

'Nah, he never comes over, never bothers with his old Ma. He's got his own shop,' Mrs Delacourt said.

'I know,' said Annie. 'The one next to the Alley Cat nightclub in Soho. You see him much? Only the place seems to be shut up most of the time.'

Mrs Delacourt opened her mouth to speak.

'Hey!' Rizzo cut in. 'Who d'you think you are, coming round here asking all these damned questions? We don't have to answer to you, bitch,' said Rizzo.

Annie turned her gaze on Rizzo. 'What did you say?'

'Hey, you heard. You got something else you want to say to me, sister? Like, sorry for barging in like this, you being not even dressed yet, something like that?' asked Rizzo, returning her stare.

Annie looked over at the huddled woman in the armchair.

'Not in front of your mother,' said Annie. She turned and walked out the door. 'Bring him, Tone,' she said over her shoulder.

Rizzo Delacourt wasn't pleased to be hauled off God-knew-where while still wearing his night attire, and he said so loudly on the way out to the car, causing a few net curtains to twitch in the neighbouring houses. Tony gave him a backhander across the cheek, which quickly quietened him down. He then forcefully shoved him in the front of the car, where he could keep an eye on him.

'Where to?' he asked Annie when he was back behind the wheel.

'Soho. The tattoo parlour. To see Rizzo's brother Peter.'

'Hey, you don't want to go upsetting Pete,' advised Rizzo, swivelling round in his seat to give Annie a challenging grin. 'Get him in the wrong mood and he'll chew you up and spit you out. He's mean, that one.'

'Yeah?'

'Oh yeah.'

'Well, Tony's pretty mean too. So I'm not too worried.'

Rizzo was still grinning. He delved into his pyjama jacket pocket and pulled out a dog-eared rollup, then stuck it in his mouth. 'You got a match, girl?' he asked her.

'Yeah, I got a match. Your face and my arse.' Annie leaned forward and snatched the cigarette out of his mouth and flung it out the window.

'Hey!'

'*Shut* it, Rizzo,' advised Annie. 'You know that girl you had on the game – Mira?'

'Mira? I don't know no Mira.' He frowned in mock concentration. 'Oh, you mean *Misery*.'

'Why'd you call her that?'

'Because that's what she is, the miserable cunt. Thank Christ she's wandered off somewhere, because I'm telling you, seriously, I was going to have to let her go.'

'Shit, I bet she'd have been sorry about *that*,' said Annie.

'Hey, is that sarcasm? That's the lowest form of wit, you know that?'

'Yeah, I do know that. And you're the lowest form of *life*, Rizzo.'

'You think that? That ain't true. I took her under my wing. Gave her work when she was on her uppers. And Pete ain't exactly the antichrist either; he passed her on to me.'

'What?'

Rizzo nodded. 'See, now that's surprised you, ain't it? He did the girl a big favour. Word was she had to lose herself for a while, some hard faces were on her tail, she was in a panic about it, and Pete did the good thing, he put her on to me.'

Annie stared at him. 'And you put her on the game by the canal under the Mile End Road.'

'Yeah, sure. She did a little business for me, got paid, got a little nose candy to keep her going, but was the girl grateful? I don't think so.'

They'd arrived in Soho. Tony eased the car into the kerb. Annie got out.

'Hey, I'm in my fucking jimjams here, I ain't getting out,' protested Rizzo.

Tony hauled Rizzo out on to the pavement. Passers-by looked at him, stifled smiles.

'What *you* staring at?' shouted Rizzo.

Business was obviously brisk in the Alley Cat. Punters were going in, music was pulsing out, heavies were handing out flyers. But in the parlour, nothing. The tattoo parlour was empty of customers again, the closed sign up on the door. Upstairs, the curtains were still pulled closed, and there was the same dim light shining behind them.

'Let's go round there,' said Annie, and Tony grabbed Rizzo by the arm and walked him down the road and into the alley.

They walked around the back, passing a Chinese chef in dirty whites, loitering at the back of his open kitchen door, smoking a fag during a lull in business, then on past the chemical waft and hum of a dry cleaner's. They came to the back door of the tattoo parlour. Rizzo surged ahead and swore, loudly, when he saw the door was hanging open. He swore even more loudly when he saw that the lock was shattered.

'Look at this!' he said to Annie and Tony. 'Someone broke in here.'

Annie and Tony exchanged a look.

'Maybe he got locked out and busted it to get in,' suggested Annie.

Rizzo was shaking his head.

'He wouldn't do that. He's careful, Pete is. He don't mix much. Lives for his work. Well, he *is* his work. He's tattooed all over. Started doing them to up his self-esteem, and it did, but it made people scared of him, the way he looked, so he got sort of stay-at-home in his habits, you know what I mean? He's sort of what you might call *reclusive*.'

'That's a big word for an idiot,' said Annie.

'That's a big *mouth* for a bitch,' retorted Rizzo.

'And you got a death wish, my friend,' said Tony, shoving Rizzo through the mangled door and along a short dingy corridor, bypassing a flight of stairs to their right. 'So shut your trap before that wish gets granted.'

They arrived in the front of the tattoo parlour. It was full of charts displaying various tattoo designs, a few chairs, a little counter with a till. The CLOSED sign was up at the door, and the windows hadn't been clean in a long while.

There was a dirty little kitchen, a small cloak-room, a little room with a massage bed in it, draped with a white sheet. There was a table beside the bed with tissues, disposable rubber gloves and a large silver box, bigger than a toaster.

'What's that?' asked Annie as Rizzo wandered in behind her.

'That's an Autoclave, like dentists use, for sterilizing the needles,' he said. 'Pete's very hot on cleanliness.'

Judging from front-of-house, Pete didn't look *that* keen on cleanliness. Tony pushed Rizzo ahead of them again and they went upstairs to Pete's flat. They could hear a faint buzz of conversation. No lock here to bust, and the door at the top was open.

'It ain't like him, leaving these doors open like this.' Rizzo was still babbling on. 'Pete's a big door-shutter, you know the type? Always closing doors into this room, closing doors into that room, drives you nuts after a while, I'm telling you, and he always says to me, what's the matter with you, were you born in a fucking *barn* or something, shut the damned door.' He went through the door and bawled: 'Hey, Pete, you here?'

There was no answer.

Annie and Tony exchanged another look and followed Rizzo in. The noise of conversation was just the TV. They looked around the little bedsit, which was lit by a single bare low-wattage bulb in the middle of the room, with the curtains still pulled closed. The bed was unmade and the sheets stale, an empty beer bottle and half a plate of congealed shepherd's pie was on the floor by the couch.

The TV in the corner was roaring away to the

empty room. Everything was dusty and the carpet was peppered with tea stains. They looked in the loo, and found it empty. Stared at a large cupboard. Annie and Tony glanced at each other. *Big* cupboard, and what did they expect to find in it? None other than Pete Delacourt hanging up by his neck. Annie thought about finding Gareth strung up. Thought that if *Pete* was strung up too, she really was going to hurl. But they couldn't smell anything. Not *yet*, anyway.

Tony moved forward and threw open the big cupboard's doors.

Annie was holding her breath. But they looked inside and there was nothing. Nothing in there but outsize jeans, and T-shirts so big that boy scouts could have camped out in them. No Pete.

'Looks like he left in a hurry,' said Tony to Annie. *And not of his own free will*, his eyes added. He crossed to the TV, grabbed the edge of the curtain beside it. With his hand covered by the fabric, he turned the TV off. Silence descended.

'Now where the fuck's the fat cunt got to?' Rizzo wondered aloud.

Annie and Tony stood there and looked at each other. They said nothing.

38

They left Rizzo at the flat and then Tony dropped Annie off at Dolly's. She was scarcely through the door when Ross looked up with a scowl from his chair beside it and said: 'Mr Delaney wants a word with you.'

'Does he?'

Ross nodded towards the closed front room door. 'Yeah. He's in there, with Dolly.'

Shit, thought Annie. But what else had she expected? Had she really thought that Redmond Delaney would take the Mira incident lying down, even if Constantine was involved? She braced herself and went in, closing the door behind her.

Dolly looked up quickly as Annie came in. She was sitting on one of the couches, her hands clenched white in her lap. Redmond Delaney, tall and imposing, with his red hair slicked back and his green eyes cool as ice, was standing a small distance away from Dolly.

'Mrs Carter,' he said when she came in.

'Mr Delaney,' said Annie.

'Certain things have come to my attention,' he said. 'Things I'm not happy with.'

'Oh?' Annie could be cool too. Even if her heart was threatening to burst right out of her chest, it was thumping so hard. 'Things like what?'

'Annie . . .' Dolly started, her eyes desperate.

'This is between Mrs Carter and myself, Miss Farrell,' said Redmond, his voice as cutting as a whip.

Dolly flinched and fell silent.

'Things like what?' asked Annie again.

'The girl,' said Redmond unblinkingly.

'You mean Mira? My friend, Mira?' prompted Annie.

'The *girl*,' he repeated coldly. 'She's mine. And you refused to hand her over.'

'She's a friend,' said Annie, her mouth as dry as dust. 'She was in a bad way. I didn't want her moved.'

Constantine was supposed to have sorted all this with Redmond. She couldn't believe that Redmond would go against Constantine's wishes. This whole thing must mean a huge amount to him, if he was prepared to risk confrontation with the Mafia.

Redmond let out a mirthless laugh.

'Mrs Carter,' he said smoothly, 'the decision was not yours to make. The girl is *mine*. She was to be collected from here. And *you* had the audacity to try to prevent it.'

Annie gulped. 'I think you'll find I didn't just try. I *did* prevent it.'

Dolly made a small suppressing movement with her hand, and her eyes said to Annie, *For fuck's sake button it. Can't you see how mad he is?*

But Annie couldn't stop herself now. She had to get it out, or choke on it.

'And while we're on the subject of what's "yours" and what's "mine",' she went on, 'what about *your* girl Aretha Brown? She worked out of this place, out of your manor. How come you're not doing something to hunt her killer down?'

Redmond gave Annie a baleful look. 'They have the killer, or has that escaped your attention?'

'That ain't true,' flung back Annie. 'You and I both know that Chris Brown is no woman killer. He'd spit on any man that was. He's a friend of mine, but for God's sake he's one of *your* boys, so how is it that I had to get him a proper brief sorted; why is it that you ain't been moving heaven and earth to get him out of the shit, like I have?'

Redmond's jaw was flexing with tension. His eyes were flat, murderous, but Annie wasn't about to show any fear. Not this time.

'I *said* they've got the killer,' he repeated with deathly slowness. 'It's beside the point whether Chris Brown is one of mine or not. Now, Mrs Carter. Take heed of what I'm telling you or you're going to be extremely sorry. I'm telling you for the last time – back off.'

Redmond walked forward and stood directly in front of Annie, very close. Dolly got up quickly and touched Redmond's arm. Redmond turned suddenly, like a cobra striking, and grabbed Dolly's wrist.

'*Get your dirty hands off me,*' he hissed furiously.

Dolly winced. He was hurting her. 'I only meant to say, Mr Delaney, please – can't we talk about this?' she said in a rush.

Redmond released Dolly with a disdainful flick of the hand. Dolly tottered sideways and fell back down on to the couch. She crouched there, her face screwed up in pain, rubbing her wrist.

'I think the time for talking's past,' said Redmond, his eyes glinting with icy fury as he turned his attention back to Annie. 'Mrs Carter, we have new terms now. Our previous arrangement is revoked. You're not welcome here. I don't want to see you in this house or on my streets again.'

Annie could feel sweat trickling down her back. She had never seen Redmond in a fury before, never seen him lose control by one single iota, but she was seeing it now, and it was a frightening thing. But you couldn't afford to show fear in a situation like this; she knew that. She put her hands on her hips and faced him full on. 'And what if Constantine Barolli says I can go anywhere I damn well please?'

'Annie!' said Dolly in anguish.

'You know,' said Redmond, coming even closer to Annie as she shrank back against the door, 'you ought to listen to Miss Farrell, Mrs Carter. You have a tendency to push onward when you *really* ought to draw back.'

His hand lifted.

Fuck, he's going to hit me, thought Annie. *Or wring my neck, one of the two.*

His hand was quivering, and in his eyes was something that Annie had never seen before. Real, undiluted rage. His hand was inches from her neck. And he really, really looked as though he would like to choke the life out of her.

All right, you bastard, just do it, she thought. *Do it, and Constantine will wipe you off the face of the earth once and for all.*

Then suddenly he was back in control again. His hand dropped to his side. His eyes cleared. He gave a tight smile.

'Our deal is revoked,' he said again. 'No more hiding behind the big boys. If I see you around here again, Mrs Carter, with or without Constantine

Barolli's backing, I'll snap you in half. Depend upon it.'

And he pushed past her and left the room, slamming the door behind him. An instant later, the front door closed. She looked at Dolly, sitting there white-faced on the couch.

'You okay?' Annie asked her shakily.

Dolly gave her a look that should have dropped her on the spot. 'Oh, I'm fucking marvellous,' she said.

Annie collapsed on to the couch beside Dolly before her legs collapsed from under her.

'You know what, Doll?' she said. 'That day when Mira ran out of here, she heard me telling you that Redmond Delaney was on the phone. And you know Rosie told us Mira wrote something in blood on the sheets? I looked at it. She'd written *DEL*. For a minute I thought, yeah, that's it, she's writing *DELACOURT* . . .'

Dolly shook her head, her eyes wide with disbelief as she gazed at her friend.

'Annie, for the love of God let it go. Whatever the fuck she was writing, forget it. That's my advice. Jesus! I don't know what the fuck's got into you, facing down Redmond Delaney like that. Are you mad? He'll fucking lynch you, you daft mare.'

But Annie knew she couldn't let this go. Not when she'd come this far. Not when she could almost *smell* the answer to all this.

'I'm not scared of him, Doll. Not any more. Mira wasn't writing Delacourt, was she?' Annie said, almost to herself. 'She was writing *DELANEY*. This is all about Redmond Delaney. And I'm not going to let it go. Not as long as I've got breath in my body.'

Dolly looked at her. 'Yeah? And how long's *that* going to be?'

39

So that was that. Annie sat alone over breakfast at the club next morning and knew that she could never again visit with Dolly and the girls over in Limehouse. The painters were in, starting early, putting the finishing touches to the walls; the stink of the paint and the rising heat of the day made her feel nauseous.

A night's fitful sleep had done nothing to ease her turmoil. Her brain kept throwing up an image of Redmond Delaney's face, white with fury, glaring at her as if murder was intended. She had never once seen Redmond lose it before. It had shaken her, although she would never admit that to a living soul.

He'd cut part of her life, part of her history, away with one fell swoop. She couldn't go back to Dolly's. Didn't dare. But her visits there had become such an integral part of her life that she knew she would miss them like crazy.

Bastard.

She was drinking tea and forcing down a bit of toast when there was a knock at the flat door.

She went and answered it. It was skinny Gary Tooley with his blond hair flopping over his forehead, his blue eyes hard as they looked at her; he was leaning his lanky frame against the wall.

'What?' she asked.

He fished a flick knife out of his pocket and shot the blade out. Annie flinched back. He looked at her, his expression almost amused. Then he started to clean his nails with it. 'Tony told me you wanted the dirt on that trannie Bobby Jo Hopkirk,' he said casually.

'You got some?' She swallowed.

Gary nodded. 'Some. Bobby Jo's fucking one of the club owners,' he said.

'Who?' asked Annie, her eyes on the knife. She thought of the last time she and Tony had cornered the transsexual club manager, the way he had sweated and looked evasive and asked them not to spill the beans over him and Teresa.

'A Mrs Selma Callow. Jewish princess. Husband's loaded and busy making the next million and she's bored. Sunk some of the old man's money into the club along with a few other investors, and spotted the manager, who looks okay without the skirt and the wig . . . it's a story as old as time.

Enter Bobby Jo for a walk on the wild side, spice up her dull little days. We've seen them together; she treats him to nice things, plush hotels, the works. Hubby ain't got a clue but he's old school. Okay for him to boff the secretary over the desk, but I'm not sure he'd take to wifey doing the same, know what I mean?'

Annie nodded. Which would explain why Bobby Jo had been so nervous when questioned; he didn't want to rock the boat and end up losing a cushy number.

'You know any of the other club owners?' she asked.

'Not yet. We'll dig around,' said Gary, excavating dirt from beneath a nail.

'Constantine Barolli's doing that too,' said Annie, feeling the need to say it, have it out in the open.

Gary's eyes clouded. He paused in his manicure. 'Yeah. About that.'

'What?'

'Barolli.'

'Yeah, what?'

'What's the deal there? You and him?'

Annie stiffened. 'It's none of your fucking business.'

Gary let out a laugh and closed the knife, pocketed it. 'Yeah, but you see it *is*. Max and Jonjo out of the picture. You ruling the roost.

That's fine. But now, this. Word on the street is you and him are tight together. Word is that you ain't in charge any more, *he* is.'

'That ain't true.'

'No?' Gary's eyes were acute on hers.

'No.'

'Only the boys like to know who they're taking orders from, that's all.'

'They're taking orders from me. Tell them that. Not Constantine. *Me.*'

'So long as we understand each other,' said Gary.

'Oh, I think we do.'

'None of the boys would like that,' he went on. 'Taking orders off the Yanks. Could cause a *lot* of trouble.'

'Such as?' asked Annie, straight-faced, but she felt sick to her stomach.

'Such as, well, Steve and me could take over the show and Constantine Barolli could go fuck himself.'

Leaving me nowhere, thought Annie.

'You want that?' she asked.

Gary's eyes locked on her for a long moment. Then he looked away.

'We're Carter boys,' he said finally. 'Always have been, always will be. You're a Carter. We're loyal to the Carters. But if *Carter* became *Barolli* . . .'

He shrugged and left the sentence hanging. Didn't need to finish it.

She was walking a tightrope here with her connection to Constantine – but then, she had always known that.

'Okay, Gary, I've got the message,' she said, and the phone started to ring.

'Glad to hear it. Right. See you.' And he loped off down the stairs.

Annie closed the door and let out a shaky sigh before dashing over and snatching up the phone from the side table beside the couch. 'Yep?' she snapped.

'Bad day?' said Constantine.

'Worse than bad.'

'Your friend,' he said.

'Mira? How's she doing?'

'She's asking for you. Making a bit more sense now, they say. You could visit tomorrow.'

'Okay. Give me the address.' She scrabbled around for pen and paper. 'Should I phone ahead, let them know what time?'

'That would be good,' he said, and he gave her the address and telephone number of the safe house.

'Thanks. Constantine?'

'Yeah?'

'I've been getting grief off Gary Tooley about hooking up with you.'

'Well, that was sure to happen. He's loyal to Max. Assert your authority, stamp it out.'

'Yeah, only he seems to think it's *your* authority.'

'A woman in a man's world,' said Constantine.

'Thank you Sigmund Freud.' Annie felt a flare of anger at the injustice of it. 'The fucking cheek. They see me as Max's wife or your girlfriend. Not as *me*. Annie Carter. The boss.'

'Well, *be* the boss.'

'Easy for you to say.' She sighed. She wanted to tell him she'd had grief off Redmond, but fuck it, she was too proud. She didn't want to show herself up as the little woman begging for protection. *Fuck* that. 'What about the investors in the Alley Cat? You got any names? I've got one, Selma Callow.'

'I've got three besides that one. Hold on, here it is. Colin Stringer, City financier. Evan Davies, banker. And Redmond Delaney, who I think you know?'

Annie nearly dropped the phone. 'Holy shit. Redmond's got a share of the club?'

'Is that significant?'

'I don't know. I've got to think about it. He was mad as hell at me crossing him over Mira.'

'He giving you any trouble?'

She ought to tell him now. She knew it. But she couldn't.

'He just told me not to go to Dolly's again. Like, ever,' she said, watering it down, conveying none of the viciousness, none of the fury that Redmond had displayed in Dolly's front parlour.

'Then don't. He's been pushed far enough. Pull back.'

'But for God's sake! I've spent half my life going in and out of Dolly's place. Why's this got him so hot and bothered? I've never seen him like this before.'

'That's something you're going to have to ask Mira about. They were there to get her, after all.'

'I know. I will.'

'Anything else I can help with?' he asked.

Yeah, thought Annie. *Come over here and give me a hug, tell me this is all going to be okay even though I just know it never will be.*

'No. Nothing,' she said instead.

'I want to see you.'

She felt herself weaken when he said that. 'Yeah,' she said. 'Okay.'

A pause. 'I'm going home soon,' he said.

Don't, she thought, clutching the phone tighter.

He paused. 'I have a penthouse in Manhattan. It overlooks Central Park.' He paused again. 'The family never go there. Just me.'

Annie was silent.

'Are you still there?' he asked.

'Yeah,' she said, dry-mouthed.

'You could go there too. Anything you want. A charge account. A life of luxury. Ten nannies for Layla. Anything.'

Max had offered her the same thing. History was

repeating itself. Back in the day, she'd been Max Carter's mistress. Now she would be Constantine's. He'd found a way to have her in his life without upsetting the family order. She felt deflated.

'We'll talk,' he said. 'Okay?'

'Yeah. Okay.' She put the phone down. Thought about it. Tried to see it as a good thing, that he wanted her close, that his intentions towards her were serious.

But she *still* felt like a kid whose balloon had burst.

40

First thing next morning she phoned Ruthie to speak to Layla. But Ruthie had a question for her first.

'I've seen a man hanging around, watching the place,' said Ruthie worriedly. 'What's going on, Annie?'

Annie took a breath. 'He's there for your protection. There's been a little trouble. Nothing to concern you, it's just insurance.'

'Right. I see.'

'You okay?'

'Fine. Just . . . I'd forgotten what it was like. All the gang stuff. This reminded me.'

'I'm sorry,' said Annie. 'It's necessary, just for now.'

'You want to speak to Layla now?'

'Yeah. Please.'

'You're all right?'

Annie had to smile. Ruthie was still her big sis, still looking out for her.

'Yeah. I'm great,' she said, and then Layla came on the line, chattering at her, blowing her kisses down the phone, and for a few blissful minutes she was just a mother again, *Layla's* mother, and it was bliss, it was wonderful.

At eleven Tony drove Annie over to a large mock Tudor villa in Harrow-on-the-Hill to see Mira. She was admitted by a grey-haired woman in a white coat, obviously a private nurse. The interior of the house was clean and quiet, with chequered black and white tiles in the hall, and glossy aspidistras as big as Triffids placed around it.

Annie was led into a big conservatory where the tiles were the same as the hall, and the greenery even more pronounced. It was like taking a trip up the Orinoco in there. A huge grapevine, clusters of black grapes dangling from its lush foliage, was twining around the top of the conservatory, casting welcome shade from the midday sun.

The door was open into the garden; somewhere a blackbird was singing. There was a wicker table with a tea tray on it, and several comfy-looking chairs. In one of them was Mira, still looking scrawny but at least clean, with her hair washed and her face scrubbed. She wore a clean set of oversized pyjamas. Her hands were bandaged. Her eyes looked lucid, as they hadn't done before.

'Hi, how are you doing?' asked Annie, as the white-coated woman quietly vanished back inside the main body of the house.

'I'm fine,' said Mira, although she clearly wasn't. She tried to smile, but it faltered.

Annie sat down. 'You wanted to see me,' she said.

'Yes,' said Mira. 'I did.'

Silence.

Then Mira said in a small voice: 'I think . . . I can't really remember too well what I did, but I think I tried to hurt you. I'm sorry.'

'It's okay,' said Annie hastily. It hadn't been Mira anyway; it had been the drugs. 'You want to tell me what's been going on?'

And, haltingly, slowly, Mira started to tell her about her descent into hell.

Falling in love with Redmond Delaney. Then, the abortion. The despair quickly smothered by the drugs, and then the drugs taking over her life. His love – if he had ever loved her at all, if he was *capable* of love – then turning to irritation, to violence, to twisted cruelty, so that she had to get out because she was in fear for her life.

'Christ, Mira,' said Annie when she paused for breath.

'He was abused as a child,' said Mira. 'He told me about it. Him and Orla. God, that can really fuck a person up. I should know, Annie.'

Annie knew about this; she had talked to Orla about it, years ago. A normal life was beyond Orla. What little affection she had, she lavished upon Redmond.

'With Orla, she's distant, can't let anyone near her,' Mira went on, 'but Redmond is different. Once he has you, he can't bear to let you go. He hit me, throttled me, suffocated me because he loved me. He said I was his, that if I ever left him he would kill me, and I believed him. He'd learned that controlling whoever he loved was the only way to be certain they didn't hurt him. But now I have. I've hurt him. I've left him. And he'll get me for it, I know he will.'

'He won't get you,' said Annie. 'You're safe here.'

Mira gave her a tired smile and leaned back in her chair.

'You know, it wasn't so bad on the streets,' she went on. 'At least I was free of him. I used to go down the Sally Army some nights and sleep there. Other times a doorway would have to do. There were always church types who wanted to help, volunteers coming round with chat and blankets, and there's a soup kitchen run by St Aubride's in the hall beside the church. I used to go there – a lot of us did.'

Annie paused in pouring the tea. Aretha's Aunt Louella sang in the choir at St Aubride's. She had questioned the vicar there. They had buried Aretha there.

'Did the vicar run the soup kitchen?' asked Annie.

She remembered what Dolly had said about him falling down drunk at Aretha's reception, and how he had vilified prostitutes.

'I suppose he had a hand in it, but the volunteers were working the coalface.'

Annie thought about the vicar. A little grey man who had simply blended into the background. One of those men who could walk into a room and out again, causing not so much as a ripple; afterwards, you would not remember what he looked like. No one would.

Annie took a breath and pushed a full cup towards Mira. 'Did Val go to the soup kitchen?'

'Yes.' Mira took a sip of the tea. 'And Jackie too. We used to go in there for the soup and bread, get warmed up, then back to the bridge under the Mile End Road. Rizzo didn't like it much.'

'Fuck Rizzo,' said Annie. 'Did you ever see Teresa Walker there?'

Mira looked blank.

'Big, loud-mouthed, red-haired girl.'

'Oh, *her*. Yes. Couldn't miss her, could you?'

'Mira, Teresa Walker's dead. So's Val Delacourt. They were both garrotted.'

Mira's gaunt face lost even more of its colour. 'I know,' she said weakly.

'My friend Aretha was garrotted too.'

But Aretha wouldn't have been on the streets, she wouldn't have been frequenting soup kitchens, so what am I proving with this? Annie wondered.

But there *was* a connection. The soup kitchen was attached to St Aubride's church. Louella sang in the church choir. The vicar had officiated at Aretha's wedding, showing himself up for a bigot in the process.

There was a connection. Someone hated prostitutes and wanted to kill them. *Had* killed three of them.

'You know what?' Mira's face was blank, hopeless. 'I've realized something about myself. I'm poison. Everyone around me gets hurt. I just attract shit. Gareth never did anything . . .'

Annie sat up straight. '*Who* did you just say?'

'Gareth,' said Mira. 'Gareth Fuller.'

Holy shit, thought Annie.

'He was a good friend to me. I moved in with him, he was so gentle, such a complete no-hoper, the poor thing, wouldn't hurt a fly . . . and someone hanged him.' Suddenly, Mira started to cry.

'Hush, it's all right,' Annie said soothingly, fishing out a tissue and pressing it into Mira's hand. She was thinking: *Jesus, it's all connected. It's all linked.*

406

'It's not bloody all right,' said Mira, her face twisted with woe. 'It's me, isn't it? Everything I touch, I ruin.'

'That's bollocks,' said Annie.

'Is everything all right? I hope you're not tiring her too much?' asked the white-coated nurse, appearing suddenly and hovering anxiously beside her patient while shooting hostile looks at Annie.

'No! I'm fine, I'm fine,' Mira sniffed, trying to compose herself again.

'You want me to go?' Annie asked Mira. 'I can come back later.'

'No, stay.' Mira looked bleary-eyed up at her nurse. 'She stays,' she said firmly.

'All right, but try not to upset her,' tutted the nurse, and departed briskly once again.

'You all right?' Annie was holding on tight to Mira's bony, bandaged hand.

'Yes.' Mira blew her nose, got herself back together again. Her hands were shaking. The drugs weren't out of her system yet, they couldn't be. Poor cow, how low she'd sunk.

Annie squeezed her hand.

'Tell me about Gareth,' she said.

'He was so nice. Completely useless, but nice. You know?' Mira rubbed at her eyes like an exhausted child. 'We were sort of friends. I moved in with him. I thought he'd be like all the other men, want sex in return for a roof over my head and a few fixes.'

Christ, she really hit rock bottom, thought Annie.

'If he had I wouldn't have minded,' Mira went on. 'I expected that. But he didn't. Well, he was so spaced out most of the time that I don't think he could have managed sex anyway. What he seemed to want from me was company. We sort of looked out for each other. He had a job at one of the hotels up West, working odd hours. Some early morning shifts, some late evening, just filling in, you know? He had a little dog, thought the world of it. Dinky the dog.'

Annie thought of the dog barking endlessly in distress, of Tony breaking the door of the flat down, of her piling in there with Hunter and finding the pitiful remains of Gareth dangling from the light fixture in the centre of the room.

Poor bastard.

'*He* was looking for me. But Gareth wouldn't have told Redmond where I was. And look what happened to him!' Mira was off again, crying softly now, the tears wrenching at her body, making her gasp and shudder. 'It's me! I'm just no good.'

'For fuck's sake, Mira!' Annie burst out angrily. 'You can't blame yourself for what other people do. And you *are* good.'

'I'm not!'

'Yeah, you are. You were always good to me. And you gave me this – you, Jen and Thelma.'

Annie indicated the Rolex on her wrist. 'You needn't have bothered but you did and that was kind of you. I was really touched.'

'That was just money,' sighed Mira through her tears. 'I had plenty of that then.'

'No, you took trouble. You got it engraved. You're a good kind person, Mira, whether you'll admit to it or not.'

Mira half smiled at that. Then she frowned again. 'I haven't told you about Pete, either.'

'Pete?'

'Pete Delacourt, who runs the tattoo parlour beside . . .'

'The Alley Cat club,' finished Annie for her, feeling a sick swaying in her stomach as all this unfolded.

Mira looked at her in surprise.

'You know Pete? Only he was good to me, took me in for a while, got me some work . . .' She wrinkled her nose. 'Well, he got me in with Rizzo, his brother. He ran the little patch under the canal bridge on the Mile End Road. Rizzo kept me supplied, got me punters.'

'Oh yeah, he's a fucking saint, that Rizzo,' said Annie grimly. She was totting up the score so far, and it wasn't looking good. Association with Mira was obviously a dangerous thing. Gareth was dead. And Pete was missing, forcibly removed from his little parlour and probably propping up a new motorway bridge by now.

But how could this tie in to Val, Teresa and Aretha? Right now, she just couldn't see it.

'I tried to write his name, didn't I? I wrote it in my own blood . . .' She looked down at her bandaged hands. 'I remember doing that . . . and trying to hurt you, I was just so desperate, I had to get out, had to get away. I knew he'd come for me, he always said that, that I was his and that no one else would ever have me, that he'd kill me if I tried to leave him . . .'

'Redmond can't get you now,' said Annie. 'You're safe here.'

Mira looked at Annie with tired, red-rimmed eyes.

'Oh, Annie. We both know I'm not safe anywhere. Not from him. And you shouldn't have crossed him, not for me, not for anything. Because now you're not safe either.'

41

On Monday Annie went to the cop shop and asked for DI Hunter at the front desk.

'He's busy,' said the desk sergeant.

'I'll wait,' said Annie, and sat there for nearly an hour.

Finally she was ushered through to an interview room. Hunter was there, alone. No DS Lane to fug up the place with his BO.

'So what can I do for you?' he asked, indicating the chair.

An honest, upright cop. She looked at him and thought once again that he was worth ten of Lane's sort – although scummy cops like Lane could be useful, she had to admit that. She wouldn't have known any more than the bare bones of the case against Chris without Lane's help, but she still despised him.

'Where's your friend?' she asked, indicating

411

the empty chair beside him on his side of the desk.

Hunter looked her straight in the eye. 'Suspended.'

'Oh?'

'Yeah, turns out he was taking bribes,' said Hunter. 'Passing information around in exchange for cash.'

'Really?' Annie kept her face expressionless with an effort.

'Really. And we can't have that, now can we?'

'No way.'

'So.' His eyes were still fixed on her. 'What can I do for you?'

Annie swallowed. 'I have a friend,' she said, 'who has told me things. Important things. About Teresa Walker and Val Delacourt.'

He eyed her sceptically. 'Like?' he prompted.

'Like where they used to hang out together. The tattoo parlour next door to the Alley Cat club. And the soup kitchen at St Aubride's.'

'Peter Delacourt, who owns the tattoo parlour, has gone missing,' he said. 'Do you know anything about that?'

'Only what you do. I went there with Rizzo his brother, but he was long gone.'

Hunter was quiet for a moment, digesting that.

'And what's this about the soup kitchen?'

'Val and Teresa used to go there on a regular basis.'

'So?'

'Can you check out the vicar? He ran it.'

'The *vicar*?' Hunter's mouth dropped open. 'So he runs a soup kitchen to try to help out these unfortunates. I'd call that a Christian act. So what?'

'So would it hurt to do that? Check his background? He's a creepy little guy who gets drunk and says inappropriate things to working girls and he's got easy access to them through the soup kitchen.'

'Well they can't shoot you for inappropriate language.'

Annie felt anger building in her gut. 'Look, I know you're an upright honest citizen and you think a cleric's got to be above suspicion, but excuse me, *I* have other ideas. These girls, these *women*, deserve the protection of the law as much as anyone else.'

He looked at her coolly. 'They have the protection of the law, Mrs Carter. That's the purpose of the law.'

'Well it's not doing a very good job of it, is it?' demanded Annie. 'Val and Teresa are dead. Aretha's dead too, and poor bloody Gareth. Not a very great effort on your part so far.'

'Can we stick to the point? The vicar. Do you have anything else on him? Anything concrete, I mean?'

'Concrete? No. All I know is that the vicar's a

bigot who hates working girls, and maybe we should be checking him out. What do you think?'

'Was there anything else?'

'You haven't found a thing to link Chris to Val and Teresa, have you?' she guessed.

'Same MO,' he said.

'He didn't do them. I know the man. I'd trust him with any woman.'

'Except possibly his wife?'

'He didn't kill Aretha. He *loved* Aretha.'

'So you say.' Hunter stood up, indicating that their interview was at an end. 'Thank you for the information, Mrs Carter. We'll follow it up.'

And she was dismissed, just like that. Annie went out of the station and down the steps to the Jag, feeling that she'd like to kick the crap out of something or somebody – preferably Hunter. Tony folded his paper and looked at her expectantly.

'Where to, Boss?' he asked.

'The Palermo,' said Annie.

It wasn't the Palermo any more, not really. It was no longer the place it had been: Max's favourite, the jewel in the Carter crown.

It was all coming together now.

Outside the club the new neon sign was up and it shouted '*ANNIE'S*'. The doors had been repainted bright pillar-box red. No trace of her hideous 'present' remained. Inside, they were laying the heavy-duty carpet in a non-dirt-showing shade of dark brown. Then, on down the newly painted staircase and into the club itself. She went down, looking around.

The bar refurbishments were complete. The see-through resin dance floor was installed, and there was an electrician beside it tinkering with the underfloor lighting so that it flashed green, blue, red. The strobes overhead were in darkness. The three small circular platforms for the dancers, enclosed in their gilded 'cages', were set up ready for the pro dancers to shake their stuff. The deep-chocolate-brown banquettes, still in their plastic coverings, were being positioned around low tables so that people could sit comfortably, chat, drink, and eat chicken and scampi in the basket.

Over the next few days the newly hired kitchen and bar staff would come in, set up the cellar and restock the freezers in readiness for opening night. The new bouncers – skilled security boys straight off the firm: good solid dependable men – would be looking around, familiarizing themselves with the layout of the place. New waiting staff and cloakroom people would be in, picking up their new uniforms, getting to grips with the job. The DJ would come and set his decks up and start checking sound levels.

And then . . . opening night.

She ought to have been looking forward to that,

but in the midst of all this other shit she didn't have the heart. She went up to the office and shut the door, blocking out the pungent smells of new furnishings and freshly dried paint.

She sat down behind the desk, thinking of Lane's suspension and thinking, *Damn it*. She'd never get more inside info on Gareth Fuller or Aretha or Chris's situation now. If Lane had been caught in the act, the Bill would have tightened up their systems, and that was bad news for her. Then the phone rang. She snatched it up.

'Yeah?'

'It's me. Dolly.'

'Oh. Hi, Doll. You okay?'

'Yeah, but it seems weird, you not popping in.'

'Can't, Doll. Redmond would blow for sure if I did. It wouldn't be pretty.'

'Yeah, I know that. Maybe I'll come over and see you then.'

'Yeah, why not? Any time. Will you come to the opening?'

'I'd come to the opening of a fucking envelope,' said Dolly.

'We'll have some celebs in,' said Annie.

'Even better. Can I bring the girls?'

'Course you can bring the girls.'

'How's that nutter friend of yours, then?'

'Mira? Doing better. She's not out of the woods yet by a long chalk, though.'

'Listen, I've got to go,' said Dolly.

'Yeah. Catch you later.'

She put the phone down, thinking about Hunter. Would he follow up on what she'd told him? Maybe. Maybe not. She wanted to tell him about Redmond Delaney, but she couldn't. She just *couldn't* bring herself to grass, no matter how much she wanted to do it. No, the pigs would have to find out about Redmond for themselves.

42

Annie gave Tony his orders and told him to be quick about it.

'Hey, you getting religion, Boss?' he joshed.

'Not at this late stage,' said Annie grimly.

The church was quiet today. No choir practice in progress. She got out of the car and put her umbrella up and stood there in the humidity of a summer downpour for a moment, wondering if Hunter had already trodden the same path, wondering too if the church would be locked up and if she was going to have to schlep over to the vicarage to see the little squirt.

Little was the operative word, but it took very little strength to garrotte someone, she knew that. Blackout in seconds, death shortly afterwards. For fuck's sake, even a woman could do it. Certainly the vicar could, maybe thinking in his twisted, crusading mind that he was liberating these girls from their life of vice.

Bastard.

'You want me to come in with you, Boss?' asked Tony from inside the car.

'No, Tone.' She didn't want the vicar spotting Tony and running for the hills before she could collar him. And she wasn't about to turn her back on the noxious little ferret, not for one second. She had a martial arts weapon, the lethal kiyoga, in her raincoat pocket. She was confident that she could handle this, was almost looking forward to it.

She went down the path to the church doors and tried one of the big circular iron handles. To her surprise, she found that the door opened. Inside, the lights were burning. Either the vicar or the verger had put them on, so she was in luck. Putting down her umbrella, she stepped into the silent church and stood at the bottom of the aisle looking up towards the altar. Rows of empty pews stretched away in front of her.

She couldn't hear a sound. Not a murmur.

'Hello?' she said, and stepped forward, putting the umbrella down on the nearest pew. She slipped her hand into her pocket and clutched the cold comforting steel of the kiyoga. She felt uneasy. All the hairs on the back of her neck were erect.

No answer came. Maybe there was no one here.

Or maybe they're just waiting for you to walk up the aisle so they can jump you, she thought.

The door crashed back on its hinges. Annie spun round like a cat.

'What the fuck are you doing here, Carter?' asked Hunter, coming in with his dark hair plastered flat from the rain, droplets catching the church lights on the sodden shoulders of his raincoat. He really was a good-looking bloke; it was just a pity he was such a pain in the rear. She got her racketing heart rate back under control.

'I'm doing your bloody job, by the looks of it,' she hissed, angry because she'd been getting spooked.

He came towards her, shaking himself like a dog. 'I'm *doing* my bloody job, for your information,' he returned. 'We've checked out the vicar. And on the surface, he looks spotless.'

'Bollocks!'

Hunter winced. 'We're in a place of worship,' he reminded her.

'*Double* bollocks,' said Annie. 'Look – if this little shit's been doing these girls, I want him nailed.'

'He's a boozer. And when he gets drunk, yes, he gets abusive, granted.' Hunter ran a hand through his soaking hair, leaving it stuck up all over the place. He looked at her. He was obviously itching to say something.

'Come on, spit it out,' said Annie.

'There are other people involved in running the church and its charitable concerns beside the vicar,' he whispered. It echoed. Everything echoed like crazy in here.

'Like who?'

'The verger, two lay preachers, the choirmaster, plus several female volunteers who make tea and clean the church and arrange the flowers for Sunday service.'

'And you've checked them all out?' Her voice echoed eerily: *out, out, out . . .*

'Yeah – and they're all clean except for one.'

'Like who?'

'Like *who*?' He stuck his hands on his hips and stared at her. '*Back off*, Mrs Carter. This is *police* business. I've told you before.'

'It's my business too,' said Annie.

'Is it fuck,' he snapped.

'We're in a place of worship,' Annie reminded him with a grim smile.

'Look.' He was back to the finger-pointing again, jabbing away at the air in front of her face. Christ, he was irritating. '*Look*, Carter . . .'

'No, *you* look,' Annie cut in. 'My friend's been done. Those other girls, too. I don't want to see any more of this. I want it cut dead *now*.'

'We're in agreement about that,' he said tersely.

'So bloody well *talk* to me. Tell me what the

fuck's going on. You say there are other people running the show? Tell me who.'

He let out a heavy sigh and walked away a couple of paces. He seemed to count to ten. Then he walked back. 'Okay. But this is a two-way thing, agreed? I tell you, you tell me. Clear?'

'Clear,' said Annie, thinking: *Dream on my friend. Become a fucking grass? I don't think so.*

'All right then. One of them's got previous. I've just had it confirmed.'

'Previous? What for?'

'Statutory rape.'

Oh fucking hell.

'Served four years, been out for two. And listen – I'm not telling you any of this.'

'Okay. Understood.'

He looked at her. 'And anything else you know, you tell me. Yes?'

'Yeah, right.' *Yeah, right.*

'He's a loner. The people who do this type of thing usually are. He was employed at his local parish church in Lincolnshire and was caught saying suggestive things to the ladies who cleaned the church. But they let it pass, thought it was just eccentricity. He befriended and finally raped the daughter of one of them. He'd encouraged her to get a flame tattoo done on her inner thigh beforehand. You know these teenage girls – susceptible to flattery, new to male attention and not sure how to handle it. She fell for it, anyway. Pretty nasty business. He got violent during the rape and nearly choked her with a scarf around her neck.'

Oh fuck me, thought Annie.

'Called the poor kid a whore. She was severely traumatized. When the case came to light, a couple of prostitutes in the area came forward and said that they'd been raped and nearly throttled by the man; that he'd paid them extra if they got a tattoo done on their upper inner thigh, a flame tattoo, so they had, but then he'd turned aggressive and raped them and called them whores and said the flame was a sign they were going to burn in hell. Nice man, uh? They hadn't bothered to report it because would the police think it possible for a prostitute to be raped? You can see they had a point.'

Annie nodded, feeling slightly sick.

'He got a prison sentence for the rape of the girl,' went on DI Hunter, 'then he came out and moved to London. That's always a problem with these people. They move, they fade into the background, and re-emerge somewhere else. Sometimes with a new name, a new identity. Hard to keep track.'

'Wait up,' said Annie. 'So . . . you're not talking about the vicar?'

'No. I'm talking about Cyrus Regan.'

'Who?'

'Cyrus Regan. He moved to London. His family had disowned him anyway. He signed up for a charitable ambulance association and started giving first aid at summer shows, so that he could grope women when they collapsed in the heat. All heart, that boy. He looked for work of a musical nature, pitched up at St Aubride's because church music was what he knew best. He then concentrated on making himself indispensable. Took over the vicar's charitable business with a home for single mothers, which will no doubt yield other tales of touch-ups or worse when we look more closely. The vicar took him on out of Christian kindness, no doubt. As choirmaster and organist.'

'Jesus,' whispered Annie, thinking of the fat, pop-eyed little man she'd seen in here several times – and hardly even noticed.

'And I haven't told you any of this.'

She nodded. *Okay.*

'Cyrus has been a busy boy. Fingers in a lot of pies. He even ran the church soup kitchen, catering for the homeless – and for the girls who work the streets.'

Now Annie felt really ready to throw up.

The choirmaster. An ugly little man of no great significance. Easy to overlook, just like the vicar himself. But the vicar wasn't a really bad man. He was prejudiced and he had a drink problem; he wasn't a seasoned abuser of women; he wasn't a rapist whose sick obsessions had now pitched over into murder.

'Can I help you?' asked a loud male voice.

They both spun around, looked up towards the high altar. The vicar was standing there; clearly he'd been in the vestry. He'd probably heard them whispering heatedly at the back of the church.

He was staring at them, waiting for a response. Hunter walked up the aisle. Annie followed.

'Reverend,' said Hunter, flashing his ID as he approached the vicar. 'I need to speak to your choirmaster, a Mr Cyrus Regan.'

The vicar looked blankly at Hunter. 'You mean on police business?' he asked, looking taken aback. He flicked a glance at Annie, and in that instant she could see that he recognized her. His expression changed to one of distaste.

'Yes, I mean police business. Is he here . . . ?'

'Yes, he . . .'

The vicar's head turned towards the organ back in the shadows near the chancel, the huge pipes rising majestically above it. Someone was there, in the semi-darkness.

'Cyrus,' said the vicar, but he wasn't given a chance to finish whatever he'd intended to say.

The bastard was *there*.

And for a dumpy little guy, he could move like lighting – as he now proved.

Cyrus Regan turned and bolted for a small door

near to where he'd been standing. Annie had a quick impression of the man: middle-aged, greying, with a chubby face and bulbous eyes. Then Cyrus was gone through the door, slamming it behind him.

'Well, I . . .' started the vicar, open-mouthed with surprise.

Hunter pushed past the vicar and was after the choirmaster in an instant, Annie hard on his heels. They tore through the low door and up worn stone spiral steps that wound upwards towards a faint chink of daylight. They could hear Cyrus wheezing and puffing up ahead as he fled. The ascent seemed endless.

'Stop! Police!' shouted Hunter, but Cyrus wasn't listening.

They raced on upwards. Annie could feel her heart pounding madly in her chest, Jesus, were they ever going to come to the end of this?

Hunter was gasping too, and Cyrus up in front sounded like a good candidate for a heart attack. She could hear the vicar coming up behind them, bleating about something or other, who the fuck cared what? They had to catch this arsehole before he did any more damage.

Then suddenly there was more daylight. They were near the top of the church tower. The chink of light became a flood as Cyrus flung open the door at the top. Seconds later, Hunter charged out on to the square crenellated roof of the tower. Annie followed.

Cyrus flung himself gasping across the roof and pitched up panting and wild-eyed against the low far wall. He turned and saw how close they were.

'Stop right there or I'll jump!' he screeched, and stepped up on to the wall.

They stopped.

'I just want to talk to you, Mr Regan,' said Hunter, trying to sound calm and reassuring when he could barely get his breath back.

'No, I'm not talking to *anyone*,' he shouted, glancing back at the drop.

Annie's heart was in her mouth. *Fuck, he really means it*, she thought.

'Cyrus,' said the vicar, coming full-pelt through the door behind them. 'Come on. DI Hunter only wants to talk.'

'They'll lock me up again,' babbled Cyrus, teetering on top of the narrow wall. 'That's all they ever want to do, lock me up.'

'We have to ask you some questions,' said Hunter, his voice soothing. 'That's all.'

As he spoke he was edging forward, carefully, slowly.

'Yes, that's how it starts,' yelled Cyrus. 'I'm not coming with you.'

And he turned and flung himself off the tower.

* * *

Cyrus let out an unearthly scream as he fell. Hunter moved fast, flinging himself at the edge. He caught the back of Cyrus's jacket and grunted as he suddenly took the man's full weight.

Cyrus dangled there, screaming and goggle-eyed with terror, swinging loose over a hundred-foot drop. Annie ran forward and grabbed at Cyrus's flailing arm, but couldn't catch it. She had a faint-inducing view of how huge the drop was, two uniformed cops standing down below and pointing upwards, beside a cop car straight from Toytown, tiny gravestones dotting the green lawns down there, and she thought: *Oh fuck.*

'Grab his arm, grab his arm,' Hunter was gasping through gritted teeth as the rain continued to fall, making his grip on the man even more precarious.

'Give me your hand!' Annie was shouting at the panic-stricken Cyrus. From being ready to throw himself off the tower, he was now hanging there yelling with terror at the prospect of the fall, unable to react sensibly to anything that was going on around him.

Annie glanced back at the vicar, who was standing stock-still just outside the door to the tower.

'Help us!' she screamed at him, and he stumbled forward and tried to get a grip on Cyrus too.

'I'm losing it,' said Hunter, and Annie could see that he was. One of Cyrus's arms was nearly out of the jacket; in a minute or two all that Hunter would be holding would be the jacket, and she couldn't get hold of Cyrus's arm. Once she almost reached his hand, but it was slick from the rain and her grip slipped almost immediately. She caught it again, and somehow held on.

The two uniformed cops were running into the church now, coming to help.

'Don't let me fall!' sobbed Cyrus.

Jesus, and just a minute ago that's exactly what he wanted, thought Annie, feeling like her arm was being wrenched out of its socket as she struggled to hold on to the little worm.

There was no way they were going to get him back in. The vicar was fucking useless. Hunter was trying valiantly but the jacket was folding back on itself and soon it was going to peel right off and drop Cyrus like a stone.

Cyrus's fingers were now clamped around her wrist in a frenzy of desperation. His weight was jerking her forward and for one crazy moment she thought she was going to join him in a one-way ticket to the bottom. Then the vicar had the sense to grab Cyrus's arm and heave.

Cyrus came up, a little.

He was babbling and crying about how he wasn't ready to die, and Annie thought bitterly that the girls he'd killed had probably said much the same thing.

Ought to just let the sick bastard go, she thought, and was tempted to do it.

But instead she pulled and struggled, and somehow the three of them dragged Cyrus blubbering and shouting back over the wall and on to the flat roof of the church tower, where he lay sobbing, his arms over his head. They stood around him, panting, choking, trying to breathe.

'Fuck *that*,' said Annie, watching Cyrus Regan with disgust.

The vicar gave her a pained look. So did Hunter. At last the two bobbies arrived on the scene, gasping for breath as they burst out of the door at the top of the stairs.

'Holy *shit*, I wouldn't want to do that again in a hurry,' said one. He looked down at Cyrus. 'Thought he was a goner,' he said to the assembled company.

Hunter looked at Annie, standing gasping against the wall.

'You okay?' he asked.

She nodded.

He turned to the two uniforms. 'Get him down the station. For questioning.'

43

'He's talking,' said the voice of DI Hunter when Annie picked up the phone three hours later.

She was in her robe, having soaked in the bath to recover from the trauma of going against her better judgement and actually *rescuing* a sick little parasite like Cyrus Regan instead of letting him top himself.

She'd have been perfectly happy to let him go. But there Hunter had been, hanging on like a dog with an oversized stick. And really, he had a point. They had suspicions, they had form, but what they didn't have until Cyrus talked to the police was a confession, and until they had *that*, the police had no real case against him and he couldn't be locked up where he couldn't hurt any more women.

Annie sat up on the couch, all attentive.

'And saying what?' she asked.

'Saying that he murdered Valerie Delacourt and Teresa Walker.'

Oh thank Christ.

'Uniformed division's been checking out his flat. They've already found a garrotte, and that's gone off to the lab boys. Also some pretty sick photos of girls with flame tattoos high up on their inner thighs.'

'*Another* garrotte,' she said, having a horrible sinking feeling about where this was going. 'You've already got the one that was used on Aretha.'

'He claims to know nothing about the murder of Aretha Brown. I believe him.'

'No,' said Annie.

'Nothing links Regan to your friend's murder. I'm sorry.'

'*No*,' said Annie again, shaking her head. This wasn't what she wanted to hear.

'Look. There were personal items and blood traces from the two girls at his flat and in his car. Nothing on Aretha Brown, though. But in Chris Brown's car—'

'Both you and I know that Aretha must be all over that car. Fuck me, she was in it often enough,' objected Annie hotly.

'On the night of her murder, he called the police from a phone box in a very agitated state,' said Hunter patiently. 'When uniformed got there, they found Aretha Brown's body still on the pavement where he'd apparently "found" it, and parked nearby was the Zephyr. They found Chris Brown sitting in the car, the garrotte on the front seat beside him with his wife's bloodstains – and his – on it. He's tied in tight to this killing, Mrs Carter, whether you like it or not. Cyrus Regan isn't.'

'You're saying it was a copycat? That Chris saw the stuff in the papers about the first two girls, and thought that would be a good way to polish off the wife he loved? Are you serious?'

'Crimes of passion happen, Mrs Carter. More often than you'd believe.'

'Wait up. That don't explain the tattoos. Aretha had a flame tattoo just like the other two.'

'She was a working girl, Mrs Carter. It's entirely possible that she met Cyrus Regan, if not in the soup kitchen then probably at the church where her aunt sang in the choir. She was actually *married* at that church, wasn't she? Maybe she met up with the choirmaster to arrange the music for the ceremony. Do you agree that's possible?'

'Okay, it's possible,' allowed Annie grudgingly.

'He paid these girls to have the tattoo done; isn't it possible he paid Aretha Brown and she had it done too?'

Annie was silent. Yeah, it was *possible*. The twisted little shit. But probable? She didn't know. She wasn't happy about any of this.

'We're thinking now that this was a premeditated

act of violence by a man who'd been pushed too far by his wife. Yes, a copy of the first two. He did this, thinking that when we nailed the killer of the two street workers, we would see this new case in the same light, and pin it on whoever *their* killer was,' said Hunter.

Annie sat back with a sigh. Her relief at Hunter finally catching up with Cyrus had been short-lived. They were still trying to fit Chris up with this. It was all wrong. To plan a copycat killing would take a level of deviousness she was sure Chris did not possess. But at least she *knew* who had killed the boy, Gareth, and that it hadn't been suicide; she knew who and she even knew why.

It creased her that she couldn't tell Hunter about it. She couldn't turn grass, not even if she was just itching to do so.

'Look – thanks for your help today,' said Hunter, surprising her.

'I wanted to let him fall,' said Annie.

'I know. But then, Mrs Carter, no confession.'

'I know. That's why I held on. Been divorced long?'

There was a silence. 'I'm guessing DS Lane told you about that.'

'Just heard it somewhere. As you do.'

'How about you? Been widowed a long time?'

He knew the answer to that. He had to. 'Not too long,' she said.

'I haven't been divorced long either. It's tough.'

'Yeah, but you're tough too. You'll cope.' Better than Chris was going to cope, having lost his wife and *still* about to be banged up for something he didn't do.

'I have to go,' said Hunter.

'Chris didn't do it,' said Annie.

'Prove it,' he said, and put the phone down.

That was what she intended to do. She dialled the number of the Limehouse knocking-shop with dread and determination in her heart. Spoke to Dolly, then hung up. She was going to rattle a few cages and see what emerged. Then she went and got dressed, and was brushing out her hair when someone started banging at the main door of the club.

She went down the stairs and paused at the door. 'Who is it?' she called out.

'Gentleman to see you, Boss,' said the voice of the boy who was on duty outside. Not Barney. This was the day-boy.

Annie opened the door. There was a small, portly man standing there. He had a goatee beard, calm grey eyes and the gloss of extreme wealth. Everything about him shouted *expensive* – his clothes, his smooth skin, his demeanour. Her heavy, standing behind him, made him look like a highly polished gnome.

'Hello my dear,' he said, smiling slightly. 'Do you remember me?'

Annie did. She smiled right back.

'Of course I do.' She stepped back and let him in. And wondered what the hell was going on for Sir William Farquharson to come knocking on her door.

'Mira Cooper,' said Sir William when she'd taken him upstairs and got him settled on the couch.

Annie sat down opposite. Sir William was a small man, his feet barely touching the ground in front of the couch, but he had a regal bearing about him. She waited for him to go on.

'You remember your wonderful establishment, Mira worked there. We had some stupendous times there, didn't we?' he asked.

Annie nodded and smiled, still wondering, *What is he doing here?*

Back in the day, Sir William had been one of her best clients: married, of course, but paying out a fortune at her knocking-shop up West for drinks, cigars and the best tarts in the business. He had always asked for Mira. Had taken her to Cliveden with him; Mira had been so happy, so excited, she remembered that. Thinking of Mira now, and Mira then, made her want to cry.

'What you probably don't know, Mrs Carter,' Sir William went on, 'is that Mira and I continued our association even after . . . well, after that little unpleasantness.'

He means after the Bill closed us down. 'I didn't know that.'

He shrugged. 'Well . . . we tried always to be discreet.'

Yeah, or Lady Fenella would have kicked your arse.

'Mira was a lovely girl,' he said wistfully. 'I set her up in a flat in Mayfair; we had such lovely times together. I enjoyed treating her to things, and she was such a happy soul, so amenable.'

He paused.

'Go on,' prompted Annie.

'When I travelled on business she often accompanied me. Mira was a complete delight. I took her back to Cliveden several times. *Three* times, I think it was. And on the third time, of course, she met *him* there. Redmond Delaney. They say three times a charm, don't they? Well, for poor Mira I'm afraid that it could have been a curse. And of course,' he gave a tight, sad little smile, 'then I lost her. I have few illusions about myself, Mrs Carter. I'm getting old. I'm short. I'm nearly completely bald. No oil painting.'

Redmond was tall, stunningly handsome, vigorous. Also, rich enough to show a girl a really good time. *No contest.*

'You're a lovely man, Sir William,' said Annie. 'And Mira was lucky to have you.'

'And *you* are very kind.' He paused, seemed to gather his thoughts. Then he went on: 'I was concerned for her. I'd heard things about the man. Bad things. I knew he was a villain. I tried to dissuade her from seeing him, but she wouldn't listen. I think she was actually in love with the man.'

'I'm sorry,' said Annie.

'I saw her in town sometimes . . . I could see that at first she was happy. Radiant. And then she seemed to wilt, like a crushed flower.' Sir William looked down at the carpet, then back up at Annie's face. 'I was worried about her. So I hired a private detective to watch them both, to try to see what was happening with my poor Mira.'

Annie waited.

He went on: 'I had a very bad feeling about that man,' he said firmly. 'An *extremely* bad feeling.'

Yeah, well, you wouldn't be the first, thought Annie.

'He saw other women, you know.' Sir William looked at Annie acutely. 'When Mira was with me, I saw no one else.'

Except your wife, she thought.

'Why would anyone want more than Mira?' Sir William was shaking his head as if in puzzlement. 'She was . . . exquisite. Perfect in every way.

Mrs Carter, I'm talking to you about this because you have an understanding of the situation, and you have connections. I can't talk to the police about it. I have my position to consider.'

'This private detective,' said Annie. 'Did he see something the police should know about?'

Sir William nodded slowly.

'What did he see?'

'He saw Redmond Delaney checking in early one morning at the Vista Hotel in Park Lane. Nothing much happened for the rest of the day. Then, in the early hours of the following morning, my man was in the park opposite the main entrance and he saw a black girl, obviously a prostitute – forgive me, my dear, but apparently her style of dress made it obvious – leaving the Vista.'

Annie's heart was in her mouth. *Aretha*. 'Go on,' she said urgently, leaning forward.

'It was a foul night. Hot, clammy, raining. But he clearly saw a tall woman with long red hair running up behind the black girl. Then the rain started coming down harder. It was a real summer storm, there was thunder and lightning. Visibility was obscured. By the time it was clearer and he could actually see what was going on, the red-haired woman was gone and the black woman too.'

'Oh fuck,' whispered Annie.

'If the papers are to be believed, the black woman . . .'

'Aretha,' said Annie.

'*Aretha*. She must have been lying on the pavement. My man couldn't see her down there, of course. As I said, visibility had turned bad. Look, Mrs Carter – Annie – I can't be involved with the police. It can't come out that I was trying to keep track of Mira, to see that she was well, because I was frightened for her. I knew of this man, the type of dealings he had a hand in. I know he's a wicked man.'

Annie was silent, taking it all in.

'My detective watched the hotel again the next day. Police everywhere, swarming over the place like flies. He went back there the following day too, and *you* were there, asking the receptionist questions. And Redmond Delaney was there, meeting up with another man.'

Constantine.

The perpetrator sometimes felt an overpowering urge to return to the scene of the crime, Hunter had told her. But the crime had been this red-haired woman's. Redmond had suggested the Vista as a meeting place, not Constantine. And Redmond and Orla were twins.

They moved as one, she thought.

'Would this detective stand up in court as a witness?' asked Annie.

'No,' said Sir William shortly. 'I am sorry, my dear, but that's out of the question. And I have to warn you – any mention of my involvement in this would have to be suppressed. Vigorously.' Sir William stood up. He handed her a business card with his number on it. 'And now I have to go. Contact me if you need to on this number, but give it out to no one else, is that clear? Do what you will with this information, but no mention of my name. You understand? Leave me out of it.'

44

Christie were giving 'Yellow River' their all from the club's brand-new sound system when Dolly arrived early that afternoon in a state of high excitement. It hurt Annie to see how happy Dolly looked, because she knew she was about to destroy her happiness.

'Fuck me, this is fantastic!' Dolly enthused at the top of her voice as they stood halfway down the stairs and watched the DJ at his deck, familiarizing himself with the levels in the club.

The dancers were rehearsing in T-shirts, hot pants and leg warmers inside their gilded cages around the dance floor. The bar staff were in, setting up, and when they swung through the door into the kitchens, Annie and Dolly could see a hive of activity in there. The whole place smelled of new beginnings and fresh hope. The electricians were testing the strobes, showing the dancers in a mad series of bright flickering images as they boogied along to the beat. Above the bar, the red neon '*Annie's*' sign glowed warmly.

'I hardly recognize the old place,' yelled Dolly in Annie's ear.

'Come on. Let's go up to the flat,' Annie shouted back.

They went back out of the double doors at the top of the stairs and Annie unclipped the rope barrier, ushering Dolly through and up the smaller set of steps that led to the office and to Annie's flat. Once inside, it was quieter. The deep jungle beat of the bass kept going, but at least up there they could hear themselves think.

'Drink?' offered Annie, as Dolly cast an interested eye around the flat.

'Yeah, thanks. Hey, this is nice.'

Annie shrugged as she went over to the drinks tray on the sideboard. 'I ain't done much to it yet. Been concentrating on the club itself.' *And other things.* She poured out a sherry for Dolly and orange juice for herself.

'Take a seat,' she said, and Dolly sat down on the couch, taking her drink from Annie.

'So,' said Annie, sitting opposite Dolly and putting her drink aside. 'How's the business?'

'More punters than we can handle.'

'That's good. Girls okay?'

'Oh, fine. Rosie's a nice girl. Too tired to shit,

but so likable that you can't take offence at it. That Sharlene's sharp as a tack, but she's pretty honest and she's a good worker, so I can't complain.'

'Gave you a bit of a scare though, didn't they?' said Annie with a faint smile.

'Hm?' Dolly was sipping the sherry.

'I mean, when we thought something might have happened to Rosie. And before that, when they were arguing the toss over who was going to take that escorting job, you remember?'

'Oh, that. Yeah. Sure.'

'Because you knew who one of them was booked to see,' said Annie. 'And you'd made it clear to them that you didn't want to take the booking.'

Dolly's face had gone very still. She took another sip of the sherry and looked at the carpet.

'Because,' Annie went on relentlessly, 'you were afraid for them. Because you knew what had happened last time you took a booking from that person, and you didn't want to risk that happening again. When Rosie took that booking and went out, you thought she was toast. You were white as a sheet, terrified.'

Dolly raised her eyes and looked straight at Annie. Annie stared back at her. Dolly. Her dearest friend, the one person she would always turn to in a crisis. Big-mouthed and immaculately dressed in her suits, her bubble-permed blonde hair always neatly coiffed, her manicure and make-up always perfect. Dolly wore the mantle of the successful madam with ease and authority.

But here was the crunch, the point at which Dolly would stop and turn away. Dolly still had to pay her dues. And she paid them to Redmond Delaney.

'I don't know what you're on about,' she said, and looked puzzled as she sipped the sherry again.

'Come off it, Doll. Shit, I've taught you all I know and you still know fuck-all. But you *do* know this. You know *exactly* what I'm talking about. I'm talking about taking an escort booking for Redmond.'

Dolly choked.

She went bright red, coughed, spilled sherry down her powder-blue skirt and on the couch. With an unsteady hand she put the glass on to the coffee table and rummaged around in her handbag for a hankie. She coughed into it, then looked at Annie with streaming eyes.

'*What* the hell?' she managed to wheeze.

'You heard.' Now Annie's eyes were hard. 'Sharlene wanted to take the booking, but she thought Rosie had beaten her to it. So did you. It scared the crap out of you. Just as well Rosie didn't. I can't see Rosie hacking the rough stuff. I think we both know by now what a night out with Redmond involves, and it ain't pretty.'

'Annie . . .' said Dolly desperately.

'Don't give me any bullshit, Doll,' she snapped, and Dolly recoiled. 'You went to a lot of trouble to lose any information about that last escort booking that Aretha took, didn't you? You said a woman placed the booking, was that true? Or was that just more smokescreen, more fucking *lies*?'

Dolly had gone very pale. She sat there looking very small on the couch, the hankie bunched in her fist, her bag clutched against her like a shield. Annie felt bad, having to do this to her.

'No,' she said at last. 'That wasn't a lie. A woman phoned through the booking. I told the police that, you know I did.'

'Yeah, and of course they couldn't trace the number. Because it was made from a phone booth in the arse end of nowhere. Who was the woman, Dolly? Did you know?'

Dolly was swallowing convulsively.

'No,' she said.

'I said no more *bullshit*.'

'I didn't know her,' yelled Dolly straight back.

'The fuck you didn't. You knew her then and you know her now. You just won't say it out loud.'

'I *can't*,' said Dolly, suddenly dissolving into tears. 'For the love of God, Annie, how can I? He'd *kill* me, you know he would; you *know* what they're capable of.'

Now it was Annie's turn to be still. What Dolly

had just said was as good as a confession in her book.

'Yeah,' said Annie. 'Okay. So say nothing, Doll. Keep yourself safe – even if some other poor bitches are put at risk because you're so concerned with covering your own arse. You saw what associating with them done to Mira, and that boy Gareth, just because he was a friend to her. And you believed that Redmond did for Aretha. If that poor little bitch Rosie had done that escort job, she could have come back in bits. She could have been *dead meat*. You knew how it was going to go, Doll. I only had to look at your face when you thought Rosie'd taken that booking. You were shitting yourself. If he'd done it before, you *knew* that one of these days he'd do it again.'

'I *couldn't tell you*,' sobbed Dolly, tears cascading down her face.

'Okay. Well, I'll tell *you* then. Redmond Delaney damn near did for Mira but didn't quite succeed. She was a messy loophole and he wanted her closed up neatly – that was why he was so hopping mad when he heard she was at your place; that was why he sent in the troops to get her. Gareth? I'm guessing *he* tracked her to the boy's flat, but Gareth knew what had happened to her with Redmond, how low he'd brought her down, and he wouldn't grass on her, wouldn't tell where she was. He paid with his life for that. How am I doing so far?'

Dolly said nothing.

'And then,' said Annie, 'Aretha. Our friend. Yours and mine. A specialist in S & M, and that's what he liked, that's what he wanted. I know the history of the Delaneys, Doll, and I guess what happened to them as children twisted them up good and proper. That's their only excuse for being like they are. It ain't much of one. But Redmond was happy to let the Bill fit up Chris for it.'

'What could I do?' demanded Dolly through her tears. 'You tell me! Go up against that lot? You must be fucking joking! I *had* to keep quiet. There was nothing else I could do – not if I wanted to get out of it without getting *my* neck stretched too.'

Annie understood Dolly's point of view. She knew how scared and how horrified, how *powerless* she must have felt, to find herself embroiled in something as messy as this. Dolly had backed away, buried her head in the sand. You couldn't blame her for that.

The rage burned in Annie again – rage against these monsters who thought they had the right to use women so badly. Monsters who thought it was perfectly okay to piss and shit on a girl, as long as they were paying for the privilege. Monsters who drew no line at the level of abuse – who beat them and terrified them and finally killed them, as if the girls were to blame and not their own sordid, twisted natures.

She had once believed that Redmond was not a sexual being. Later, she had suspected he might be queer. She had *never* expected him to be a woman-beating sadist.

'It was Orla Delaney, wasn't it?' said Annie. 'Orla made the call for Aretha's booking, and it was Orla who phoned again on the night you thought Rosie had taken a booking with Redmond.'

Dolly shot her one swift, ashamed glance. Then she bit her lip and nodded, and let the tears fall once again.

45

'She's having a bad day,' said the white-coated nurse, looking at Annie with disapproval as she stood on the doorstep of the safe house in Harrow-on-the-Hill.

'Hey, we're *all* having one of those,' said Annie, pushing past her and into the hall. 'Where is she?'

'Upstairs. In bed. I think she may be asleep and she really shouldn't be disturbed—'

'Which door?' asked Annie, already trotting on up there.

'The one on the left, but I don't think—'

'Thanks.'

Annie got up on to the landing and went to the door. She knocked softly, received no answer, and stepped inside. It was a big bedroom, high ceilinged and with a refreshing breeze stirring the nets at the big sash window on the other side of the room.

The bed was big too, so that the woman in it looked almost like a child lying there.

Annie stepped over to the bed. Mira's eyes were open, but she looked bad. Her hair was slicked flat to her bony head, as if she'd been sweating heavily; her wrists and hands were still swathed in bandages. Her skin was an unhealthy yellow colour and her cheekbones stuck out like knives.

Annie looked at Mira and felt pity pierce her heart. She remembered all that Mira had told her about what she'd been through. The cruelty. The perversions. The rubber thing Redmond had held over her nose and mouth during sex. *Autoerotic asphyxia* – partial suffocation or partial strangulation to heighten sensation during sex. She thought of Gareth, hanging in the flat. Thought of Redmond reaching for her own throat when he'd become enraged. Mira had told her that she had only to smell rubber now to throw up with fear.

'Annie,' said Mira weakly.

'Hi.' Annie went and sat on the bed beside Mira. 'How are you?'

'How do I *look*?' asked Mira with a glint of humour.

'Like death warmed over,' said Annie.

'Yeah, you got that right.'

'Feel rough, huh?'

'Dog rough.'

'It'll pass,' said Annie. 'Stay with it.'

But even as she said that, she wondered just how deeply Mira had become wrapped up in the world of the professional junkie. She wondered if there was any hope of her pulling out of it for good. So many people sank back into the abyss. She hoped that wasn't what lay in wait for Mira.

'Not much option but to do that,' said Mira.

'Mira, I need your help.'

'What with?'

'Aretha. You remember Aretha. You know the soup kitchen at St Aubride's church hall you told me about?'

'I know it.'

'Did you ever see Aretha there?'

Mira thought about it. 'No,' she said after a pause.

'No?'

'Wait. No, I did. Just once. Talking to that little squirt who ran it, little chap with poppy eyes and a fat face.'

Cyrus. So that explained Aretha's tattoo. Cyrus paid the girls to have it done, then killed them. Somehow he hadn't got to Aretha – someone else had. What about the tall red-haired woman?

What about Redmond's involvement? Then, to her annoyance, the door opened and the white-coated nurse was back again.

'She's very tired,' she said pointedly to Annie. 'She had a bad night. She needs to rest.'

Annie nodded and stood up. The woman was right. Mira looked as though she was having a hard time fighting the drugs off, and she probably did need all the rest she could get, poor bitch.

'I'll come back and see you soon,' she promised. 'When you're feeling a bit brighter. Anything you want me to bring you?'

'Yes,' said Mira with a grimace. 'A new life. I'm sick to death of this old one. All I do is throw up and sweat and shiver.'

'That will pass,' said the nurse reassuringly. 'Given time.'

'Yeah, right,' said Mira, and slowly closed her eyes.

46

She phoned Ruthie to be sure that Layla and her were okay. 'We're fine,' said Ruthie, and put Layla on to enthuse about the kittens. Annie listened to her excited little voice and smiled and thanked God for her. Soon, maybe, she'd have her baby back with her. She really hoped so. For now, it was more important to keep Layla safe, even if she did miss her like crazy.

'I love you, baby,' she said as she rang off, feeling the prickle of tears in her eyes.

'Love you too, Mummy,' said Layla.

Then Annie phoned her cousin Kath. 'I've got minders coming out of my arse here,' moaned Kath. 'What you got kickin' off this time?'

She soothed Kath's worries and was just off out the door when Ellie phoned. 'Any news about Chris?'

Annie felt so sorry for Ellie – she'd always

carried a massive torch for Chris. 'No – no news at all,' she said.

'He's going down for this, ain't he?' She could hear the tears in Ellie's voice.

Annie had to be truthful. It would be cruel to get the poor mare's hopes up. 'He could be,' she said. 'Ellie, you've got to be prepared for that.'

At which point Ellie started to sob. Annie soothed her as best she could, but she felt in her heart that there'd be no good ending to this particular nightmare. Feeling depressed, she locked up and went out, got into the back of the Jag. Tony started the engine.

'Where to?' he asked.

'Let's have a check around the venues. Make sure everything's running smooth.'

They did the grand tour of the arcades, snooker halls, pubs and clubs. Everyone greeted Annie Carter respectfully but there was an edge to their greetings. She thought of Gary's warning and knew that the rumours were spreading. Knew she was walking a thin line. But then, hadn't she always done that? They were nosing through the traffic up the King's Road when a black cab veered in front of them.

'*Jesus!*' said Tony loudly, hitting the brakes.

Annie was jolted forward.

'Bloody *idiot!*' Tony was leaning on the horn.

Annie looked around, startled, starting to feel a

twinge of anxiety. There was another cab right up their arse. Another edged alongside and suddenly, just like that, they were boxed off. The driver of the cab alongside the Jag jumped out and came round the car as Tony reached over to the glove compartment.

'Tone!' shouted Annie. It was all happening so damned *fast*.

The man flung open Tony's door just as Tony was turning back with a pistol in his hand. Tony was a fraction of a second too slow. The man coshed him hard behind the ear and he crumpled. The man grabbed the pistol and heaved Tony over into the passenger seat.

So *fast*.

Then another one threw open the back door and jumped in beside Annie. She shrank back. The one up front – in the fucking *driving* seat now – tossed the pistol to the one in the back. The one in the back was grinning, and wearing a deaf aid.

It was Deaf Derek. The treacherous *bastard*.

'Hiya Mrs Carter,' he said, and rammed the pistol's cold butt up hard against her throat.

The cab blocking them pulled away. The man beside Tony's slumped body eased the Jag forward again, into the flow of traffic. The cab that had stopped alongside the Jag was still there, blocking that lane. Horns were honking, people were shouting, but the traffic flow soon picked up and then that was all far behind them.

The driver glanced back over his shoulder with a malicious grin. Annie saw that he had a finger missing from his right hand, which was clenched on the leather-covered steering wheel. Her heart froze in her chest.

Charlie Foster, the number one Delaney boy. Charlie, who had big scores to settle with her. Now, he was going to get his chance.

'Comfortable back there, Mrs Carter?' he sneered.

He didn't wait for her answer. The Jag sped toward Battersea. Tony was slumped unconscious in the front. No help there. No help anywhere.

Deaf Derek kept the gun pressed to her throat as the car roared along.

She'd rattled some cages all right. And now they were going to make her pay.

47

They shoved her inside a shed in the Delaneys'
breaker's yard. Just her. God knew what they'd
done with Tony. They slammed the door shut on
her and she heard them bolt it from outside.
Leaving her in the semi-dark, terrified of what
might come next. Annie stood there and told herself
to keep calm, to keep thinking – but all the time,
panic was exploding in her brain and she was
thinking: *They're going to kill me.*

She'd done the unthinkable – she'd crossed
Redmond Delaney over something that mattered
greatly to him. It mattered so much to the twisted
git that he was obviously even prepared to risk
Constantine's wrath – and if he was prepared to
go that far, she knew she was toast. Unless
somehow she could get out? Escape? But there
was a guard with an Alsatian on the gate. The
guard looked handy and the Alsatian looked as

if it would rip her guts out if she set foot in the yard.

It was still daylight, though, and chinks of light were now becoming visible to her, permeating the gloom inside the shed. She was able to look around and actually *see* things. There were piles of rope on the floor, and a mounded heap of grubby tarpaulin sheets. It smelled stale in there.

If I could find something to use, she thought. *Maybe a hammer?*

But she couldn't see any tools, only the ropes and tarps. She went over to the nearest pile of tarps, hoping there was something useful underneath them. She lifted the top tarp and fell back with a cry of horror.

She'd found Pete Delacourt, the tattooed man.

He was there, his tattooed face frozen in a hideous death mask, his staring eyes as blank and milky as a cod's on a slab. The scent of decay rose from the body and she quickly dropped the tarp back over the corpse, gagging and backing up against the shed wall.

Oh Christ, she thought in fear and disgust.

And now there was a noise and the door was opening. She'd had no time to get anything to defend herself with, no time at all. She turned to the door. Charlie Foster was stepping inside, smirking at her as he closed the door behind him.

She'd run out of chances, and now Charlie was about to get *his* chance for revenge.

Annie stepped back, but the wall of the shed was right behind her. She had nowhere to run. If she could reach the door, maybe she could get out – but she'd have to go through Charlie first. And that wouldn't be easy.

'Hi, Mrs Carter,' he said, sneering at her panicked expression, edging closer.

Annie said nothing.

'Aw now, that's not polite. You ought to be nice to me, you know. Maybe we could cut a deal and I could get you out of this mess. But only if you're *nice* to me.'

Ha! What total bullshit. Annie stared at him with loathing. Charlie would *never* cross Redmond. He was too scared of that unpredictable Irish temper. Too scared of waking up *dead* one fine day.

'I've given you gifts, after all,' said Charlie silkily, coming closer. 'The flowers, did you like the flowers?'

'You bastard,' she said. The dead flowers. It had been *him.*

'Oh, what's up? You didn't like them? And the cat. Now did you like the cat?'

So *he'd* done that.

'You're one sick sorry son of a bitch,' said Annie,

feeling behind her for something – anything – to use. She'd brain him without a qualm, given the slightest chance.

His smile dropped and his pale blue eyes wore a fake look of hurt. 'Now that's not nice. And you could be nice to me, Mrs Carter, you know you could if you tried. Like you're nice to that fucking *Yank* Barolli.'

Annie stiffened.

'Oh yeah, I saw you go in his house. I've been keeping tabs on you,' Charlie went on, edging closer and closer. 'I saw you there on his desk. In your undies.'

'You sneaky little arsehole,' said Annie flatly.

So he'd been snooping around after her, the creep. Now she was *glad* she had once had him done over. They should have finished the slimy little fucker off: letting him carry on breathing had been their only mistake.

'It's all over for you, Mrs Carter,' said Charlie. 'You think Steve Taylor and Gary Tooley and the rest of the Carter boys are going to take you boffing Barolli's brains out? They won't. You're finished. Hell,' he laughed, 'you're finished *anyway*. Redmond's gonna see to that – but not before *I'm* finished with *you*.'

He lunged forward very fast and caught her. Annie struggled away from him, disgusted and furious, while he tried to get his mouth on hers.

She tried to get her knee up, but he was clever: he had his lower body turned aside, she only connected with his thigh.

'You dirty little shit,' she gasped, grunting with the effort of trying to wrench free of him.

'Now just hold still . . .' His hand, the one with the missing finger, the one *she* had had her boys cut off, was on her jaw, trying to hold her head still while she strained away from him.

Oh fuck, she thought in desperation.

He was stronger than she'd thought. She could feel her own strength draining away. She didn't have a gun, or she'd have shot him dead in an instant. She didn't even have the kiyoga. She'd been taken completely unawares and that was sloppy, careless; she knew it. She had nothing, and she was getting weaker by the second.

He was going to rape her. And *then* he was going to follow out orders and kill her. A scream escaped her before his mouth, his filthy repulsive mouth, fastened on hers. It felt cold and slimy. She started to retch. Suddenly, light flooded into the shed.

'Charlie!' The voice cracked like a whip.

Charlie dropped her like a well-trained dog called to heel. He turned. Annie sagged back against the wall, breathing hard, and blinking against the light she saw Redmond Delaney standing there, outlined in the open doorway.

* * *

'Get out,' said Redmond.

Breathing heavily, Charlie gave her one last sneering glance, and went.

And then, to Annie's horror, Redmond came inside and shut the door behind him.

'Mrs Carter,' he said softly into the semi-darkness. 'What a talent you have for poking your nose in where it's not wanted. And you know – it's really got to stop.'

Annie gulped. Seriously shaken from her tussle with Charlie, nevertheless she could clearly see that there was much greater danger here. Redmond was less predictable than his henchman, and ten times more deadly.

'I'll stop when *you* stop,' she said with bravado. She was panting, close to exhaustion.

He gave a low laugh at that. She saw him moving closer and braced herself for whatever was coming. But he didn't lash out. Instead, very, very gently, he reached out and stroked her face. She flinched.

'Such a pity,' he said.

And she knew what he meant then. She knew she was going to die here.

'You'd be wasted on Charlie,' he said in that soft, soothing Irish brogue. 'He's got no refinement, no imagination. Unlike me.'

He came in even closer. Now, straining back against the wall of the shed, she could feel his breath on her face. She'd come within a whisker of violence

463

from Redmond before, but now there was no one here to restrain him. No witnesses. Nothing.

Oh God help me, she thought.

'Try and relax, Mrs Carter,' he said in that same low, charming voice. 'Relax and you'll begin to enjoy it.'

And suddenly there was something over her nose and her mouth. She choked, struggling for air. She couldn't breathe, she was drowning in the stink of rubber; it was nauseating, she couldn't *breathe*.

She raised her hands and clawed at his, holding the thing over her face. She could feel the blood pounding in her head, could feel consciousness starting to waver.

This is what he did to Mira, she thought in a crazed whirl of terror. *This is what excites him.*

She struggled, kicked out, but he was stronger than Charlie, stronger than she would ever have believed; she couldn't fight him. She felt blackness starting to envelop her. He was killing her. He'd threatened it, and now he was carrying out his threat. She could dimly see his face, handsome, deadly, focused entirely on her. He was *smiling*.

'Redmond,' said a female voice. Maybe she imagined it, she could hardly stand now, she was sinking, falling . . .

But there was light flaring into the darkness now. She could see light.

'*Redmond!*' The voice was sharper. 'Come on. Stop. Enough of your games.'

Suddenly, her face was free. Annie whooped in a huge gasp of precious air. Her head was spinning, and for a minute she could see nothing. But then her vision cleared and she saw Orla standing there at the door. Redmond had stepped away. He was holding a small square of rubber in one hand.

'*Bastard*,' she choked out.

Orla stood there, very erect, very cool, staring at the pair of them. Charlie, sneering, appeared at her shoulder. Redmond might have spoiled *his* fun, but he'd made damned sure that Orla had ruined his, too.

'Come on,' said Orla. 'Bring her over to the office.'

Much to Annie's surprise and relief, Redmond didn't object. Charlie grabbed her arm, and with Redmond walking ahead with Orla, he bundled her over and inside the static.

48

Once inside the static, away from any possible prying eyes, Redmond and Orla went to the desk and stood there, staring at her. Annie was swaying on her feet like a drunk. She clutched at the wall, held herself steady. Charlie was right by her, grinning.

Vipers, just as Max had always told her.

Orla was in a neat black suit, beautifully cut, perfectly fitted. She leaned back against the desk and watched Annie like she was an insect impaled on a pin. Redmond was standing there, one arm casually resting on the filing cabinet beside the desk, his face impassive – as if he hadn't just tried to smother her at all. As if everything was normal. Which, to him, it probably was.

Annie knew she was going down. But she wasn't going down without a fight, and she *wasn't* going down before she had let this sick pair know precisely what she thought of them.

Her thoughts went briefly to Tony. They'd dragged her out of the Jag and into the compound, but she didn't know what they'd done with him. He might be just unconscious, he might be tied up, fuck it all, he might be *dead*. That blow to the head could have damaged his brain, caused haemorrhaging. She didn't know. And right this instant, she couldn't even give it much thought.

She had to try and stay alive for as long as she could. She didn't hold out much hope in that direction. Tony might recover and come to her rescue. Or he might not. Either way, she was going to say her piece.

She was very aware of Charlie standing close by, leaning against the closed door, listening in. Anticipating another chance to damage her. She knew he could hardly wait.

'I know all about what happened with you and Mira,' said Annie, looking at Redmond. Her mouth was dry. She had to swallow several times to get the words out.

Redmond was quiet for a beat. Then he said: 'I doubt that.'

'Oh but I do. She told me, you sadistic bastard.'

'Sticks and stones, Mrs Carter.'

'If I had a stick I'd beat you to fucking death with it. Put you out of your misery like a dog, you bastard.'

'Ah, but you haven't, have you? No sticks, no

guns, not even that strange little flick-out Eastern thing you carry around with you. Nothing. You're out of your depth, Mrs Carter.'

Orla was staring at Annie.

'What, cat got your tongue, Orla?' Annie demanded shakily. 'Nothing to say?'

She couldn't let them see how terrified she was, even though she felt literally sick with fear.

Orla shook her head. 'How's the club going?' she asked with a sneering smile. 'No problems, I hope? No one trying to sabotage all your good efforts? No one been cutting pipes in the cellar or anything like that?'

Well, that explained that. 'You bitch,' said Annie, consumed with cold fury.

'And I thought we were such good friends too! Why couldn't you just carry on playing business-woman of the year – that's what you're best at, after all, fiddling around with your new club and making it all pretty, ready for the punters – and leave the rest of it alone?' she asked. 'Why did you have to get involved?'

'Because there's such a thing as loyalty,' said Annie. She felt stronger now, and angrier too. 'There's such a thing as standing up for your friends and fighting their corner. And you know, the very fact that I *had* to fight Chris Brown's corner when you were so reluctant to do it – that should have made me see the light much sooner.'

Redmond half smiled and put his hands in his trouser pockets. He looked perfectly relaxed, very much in control.

'And what light would that be, Mrs Carter?' he asked her.

'I should have seen that you were involved right from the start,' said Annie. 'Fuck it, you were even there the morning after Aretha got killed; you were right there at the hotel. The cops told me that the one who's committed the crime, the one who's *killed*, often feels an uncontrollable urge to revisit the scene.'

'I didn't know that,' said Redmond.

'And, there you were, meeting Constantine, at that hotel the very next day. And you suggested that hotel.'

'Well done, Mrs Carter,' said Redmond with a faint smile. 'How clever you are. And at the same time, how stupid to be telling me this if I *had* committed a crime at the hotel.'

Annie kept her face blank, even though she could feel the sweat running down her body, even though her heart was thudding sickeningly hard in her chest. She was going to have this out with these bastards, even if it killed her – and it probably would. 'Stupid? I don't think so. Don't make a sodding bit of difference now anyway, does it? You're going to get rid of me anyway, ain't that the plan?'

They were both silent, staring at her.

Annie nodded slowly, her eyes glued to their faces.

'Yeah, that's the plan,' she said. 'Because I've confided in Dolly, and Dolly's a Delaney woman. She's told you what I've told her, and now I'm fucked. Ain't that right? We may as well be straight with one another now.'

'I didn't kill Aretha Brown, Mrs Carter,' said Redmond flatly.

'No?' Annie's eyes were fixed on Redmond's face. He shook his head. Annie's eyes slid over to Orla.

Orla let out a laugh. 'What, you think *I* . . . ?'

Annie thought of all that Sir William had told her. A tall, red-haired woman running up behind Aretha . . .' I don't know,' said Annie. 'Why don't you tell me, you cold-blooded bitch?'

That stung. Annie could see it in Orla's face. But she soon recovered and stared at Annie with the gleeful calculation of a cat with a trapped mouse.

Redmond shot his twin a glance. 'You don't have to say a thing,' he said.

'Why not?' Orla shrugged. 'The fact is, we're very close, Redmond and I. We've had to stand together over the years; we've had no one else to depend on.'

'I know that,' said Annie. She knew all about

their background. She knew they'd been abused as children, knew that the abused sometimes become abusers in their turn. 'I think *unnaturally* close would cover it better.'

'Unnatural?' Orla shook her head. 'We're a single unit, Mrs Carter. We work together.'

'And play together?' quipped Annie.

Orla's eyes clouded, concealing a faint flicker of rage. She folded her arms across her body.

'What exactly are you implying? That my twin and I have some sort of unhealthy intimate thing going on?'

'Well, don't you?' Annie demanded. Her voice was growing stronger now. Her anger was sustaining her, overriding her fear. 'You set up the escort appointment with Dolly; you phoned it in. You pimped for Redmond, what else would you do for him, I wonder? Or did you know that he'd do these things anyway? Did you hate the fact that he needed these kinky sexual encounters, but did you think – he'll do them *anyway*; I hate it but this way I can control it. He'd asked for Aretha several times, he liked the rough stuff. Ain't that right, Redmond?' demanded Annie.

He looked at her with icy loathing and didn't answer.

'Yeah,' said Annie. 'That's right, ain't it?' She turned back to Orla. 'And you didn't like that: the fact that he had a particular liking for these sessions with Aretha. And now I'm thinking you hated the thought of him with *any* woman, so much so that you just snapped and killed her.'

'Say nothing,' said Redmond to Orla, his eyes fixed menacingly on Annie.

'Why shouldn't I?' Orla looked unfazed by Annie's accusation. 'I didn't kill that *whore*. I wanted to. I really did. No, I don't like the fact that Redmond has these needs. But I accept it – even though it causes trouble, even though it becomes a nuisance at times.' She glanced at Redmond. 'That costly *blonde* whore you became so obsessed with for a while, for instance. I really think—'

'What you *think* about it,' snapped Redmond, 'isn't relevant. That's my business – not yours.'

Orla's face reddened at the unexpected rebuke.

So *there is trouble in their sick paradise*, thought Annie. *Orla really is jealous of his women. I almost feel sorry for the twisted bastards.*

'You're talking about Mira?' Annie's eyes were moving between them both. Orla blinked at the mention of Mira, and Redmond seemed to freeze to the spot. 'That was something more serious, wasn't it? More long term. Quite pleasurable for you, Redmond, but a fucking disaster for her. You introduced her to drugs. You taught her some nasty little habits and you bloody near killed her. She told me about how you liked to half throttle her during sex, and about that little square of rubber you use to get your jollies. If Orla hadn't interrupted us when she did, you'd have done me with it too. You're one sick fuck, Redmond, you know that?'

A swift flush of hot colour swept up over his pale cheeks. He didn't look in the least ashamed: he looked *furious*.

'That's why you sent Charlie and the boys round to Dolly Farrell's place to get Mira back. You didn't want her blabbing your disgusting little secrets all over the place, did you? And she belonged to you. She was your own personal high-class whore to do with as you would. But the drugs and the abuse and the abortion all took their toll on her, and I guess she started to annoy you once you'd knocked all the spirit out of her and ruined her looks, and so the games got sicker and then she began to think, fuck it, he's going to kill me if I don't get out of here. And she was right.'

Redmond was breathing hard. He looked as though he was going to kill her with his bare hands, right now. Annie knew he'd enjoy it, too.

Annie thought of the horror she found under that tarpaulin in the shed across the yard. 'So she ran and ended up at Pete Delacourt's tattoo parlour. He put her on to his brother Rizzo, who kept her drug habit fed and who put her on the streets earning. Funnily enough, you know what? Pete went missing.'

They were silent, staring at her. Their faces said it all.

Annie swallowed. Her mouth was dry as dust. She had to get all this out now, had to let them know they were sussed.

'And Gareth, what about Gareth? The cops are in two minds. He *could* have committed suicide, but I don't think he did. I think he blocked you when you picked up Mira's trail and traced her to his flat, and you lost your temper and strung him up, ain't that right?'

Maybe I'm dead meat, thought Annie with a shudder. *But I'm going down with all guns blazing.*

'Orla – it was *you* who killed Aretha. There was a witness. She left the hotel fit and well. Then a tall red-haired woman was seen hurrying up behind her outside the hotel that night. It was you.'

Orla unfolded her arms and leaned back against the desk again. She shook her head.

'Oh come *on*,' said Annie. 'What's the use of denying it now?'

'You're right. Whatever gets said here today won't go any further. So if I'd done it, what the hell – I'd admit to it. But I didn't.'

Fuck it, thought Annie savagely. She couldn't

be wrong on this. Orla *had* to be lying. But why would she bother?

'I'm not lying,' said Orla, straight-faced, as if she'd read her thoughts.

'I don't believe a bloody word that comes out your mouths.'

'We really don't care what you think, Mrs Carter, and it really doesn't matter any more because you are in no position to argue, as I see it. However, for what it's worth, neither of us murdered Aretha Brown.'

Then who the hell did? A tall red-haired woman. Annie looked at Orla. Orla was about five feet six inches tall. A tall red-haired woman.

How tall exactly was the woman who'd chased after Aretha, though? That was something she should have questioned William about more closely. Something she wasn't going to get a chance to do . . . and she thought of Teresa Walker, who'd had red hair too. Shit, Teresa's *mother* was tall. Teresa's mother had red hair . . .

It was all too late. She'd never know now.

'This is all getting a little tedious,' said Redmond. 'We have work to do, and we have to get on with it.'

'Wait,' said Annie.

'Wait for what?' Redmond gave a terse half-smile. His eyes flickered past her, behind her.

Annie started to turn. She saw Charlie coming up fast, too fast.

The cosh caught her right behind the ear. Pain crashed through her brain. And then – blackness.

49

Consciousness returned to Annie in fits and starts. Her head hurt; there was a sore spot behind her right ear. She opened her eyes to semi-darkness and a dim, familiar interior.

She was in the car. *Her* car. Charlie'd hit her *hard*. Her mind was spinning. *Her* car, that was right. Had to get a grip, start thinking straight. The black Mark X Jaguar. Her beautiful car.

She was lying across the back seat, which smelled of leather and cologne; familiar smells, comforting smells. But she didn't feel comforted. Alarm bells were ringing in her addled brain; her guts were screwed up with unfocused anxiety.

Tony.

Where the fuck was Tony?

He was usually up there behind the wheel – big, suited shoulders, bald head, gold crucifixes glinting in his ears. Weaving through the London traffic with his usual casual grace and asking where she wanted to go now, then saying, 'Sure Boss, okay.' But he wasn't there. She was in the car alone.

Her heart stalled. She was beginning to remember what had happened. They'd coshed Tony as well as herself.

How long have I been out of it? she wondered, sitting up stiffly, wincing as her head started to thump sickeningly in protest at even the slightest movement.

It was all coming back to her. The Delaneys. She'd been talking to them. And Charlie . . . oh Jesus, the shed. Pete Delacourt's corpse under the tarp. Charlie in the shed and then, worse, far worse, Redmond. She was up shit creek, and she knew it. On Delaney turf, on Delaney streets. She had no chance.

Charlie had knocked her out cold. She remembered that now. The sudden pain, the swift descent into blackness. Tony was fuck-knew-where. Now they were going to take the wheel and drive her off in her own damned car to some remote place, where they would blow her brains out, what little brains she *had*, because who but a fool would push their luck so far as to cross Redmond Delaney the way she had?

She thought of Layla, her little girl, her little star. She knew she had to get the fuck out of here, because she was all that Layla had; she couldn't afford to get herself wasted. She was reaching for the door when the noise started – a high mechanical whine, deafening in its intensity. She clutched at the seat. Her heart kicked against her chest in alarm.

What the fuck . . . ?

Suddenly the car lurched to the right, flinging her back against the right-hand door. She watched with horror as the left-hand door started to buckle inward. There was a ferocious shriek of tortured metal, louder than a thousand banshees at full moon. With a sound like a gunshot, the glass of the door shattered, showering her with fragments. She ducked down, covering her head momentarily with an upraised arm, then staring in terror as the left-hand door just kept coming at her, buckling inward, metal tearing, ripping, screaming.

And then the door behind her was coming in too. The noise was mind-numbing, beyond pain, beyond anything she had ever experienced before. The second window imploded, and again she was smothered in pieces of glass, felt her cheeks sting with the impact of it, felt warm blood start to ooze from cuts on her face.

'*Jesus!*' she screamed, knowing exactly where she was now, and knowing what was going to happen to her.

She was in the car crusher in the Delaney's breaker's yard.

Then the roof crashed in upon her, folding inward not like metal but like soft cardboard. The car lifted with a violent heave and she fell sideways, ending up on the floor, nearly gibbering with fear. She was going to die, she knew that now.

Just make it fast, she thought desperately. *Please make it fast.*

She was curled up into a ball, eyes clamped shut, waiting for the car to become her coffin. In anguish she thought again of Layla, felt a hot spasm of guilt and grief because Layla was going to be devastated all over again. Bad enough to lose her father. Now she was going to lose her mother too. And there was not a bloody thing Annie could do about it.

The noise was awful, mind-numbing. It seemed to reverberate all around her head, killing sensible thought, destroying reason. She was screaming, crying, she knew she was, but she couldn't hear her own animal sounds of terror, she could only think, *I'm going to die, I'm going to die.*

How long would it take?

Would she feel her limbs being pulverized, would she feel her legs, her arms, being twisted and snapped like twigs beneath the huge crusher's relentless pressure? Would her pelvis disintegrate, would her ribs crack, pushed inward to pierce her lungs, her heart? Yes, all of that. She had all that to come. All that inhuman pain.

Help me, she thought in a paroxysm of fear.

Everything was moving around her, drawing inward. She felt the front seats encroaching on her small space, felt them push inward, inward, so that the space became smaller still, and now her foot was trapped beneath Tony's seat, she couldn't move it, couldn't get it out and it was getting tighter and tighter, just the merest pain now, but it was clamped tight in there as if in a vice, she couldn't get free.

Then, suddenly, the machine stopped. Suddenly, she heard herself screaming. She was screaming like a soul trapped in a fiery hell. But the machine had *stopped*.

But it's going to start again, she thought in hysterical fear. *Any second now. They're playing with me, that's all.*

Suddenly she couldn't get her breath to scream. She gulped down air, sobbing weakly, gripped by a gut-churning panic. It was going to start again. She knew it. She could hear the metal tomb the car had become still popping and wheezing all around her. She opened her eyes and saw that she was jammed into the tiniest of spaces, the roof crammed up against the top of the front seats, the floor impacted beneath her, the car's sides encasing her with mere inches to spare.

She drew in a shuddering breath and yelled: 'Help! For God's sake someone help me!'

And then she heard voices, coming closer.

Oh shit, they were coming to gloat. Coming to see her lose it before they started the damned thing up again and finished her off.

Annie bit her lip and stifled more screams. *Fuck* them. She wouldn't give them the satisfaction. For long moments she listened to her own unsteady breathing and her galloping heartbeat, and kept as quiet as she possibly could.

'Mrs Carter?' said a male voice nearby. 'Can you hear me?'

Redmond.

But no. It wasn't an Irish voice. It was . . . she thought she knew, but her brain was so skewed with fright that she couldn't think straight.

'Mrs Carter,' repeated the voice. 'Can you hear me?'

Now her frozen brain started to fire up again. Now she thought, yes, I know it. Don't I?

She thought she was probably in shock. She had to think about it, very carefully. Trying to think of *anything* above the almost overwhelming fear of that thing starting up again was difficult, almost impossible. But she was thinking, trawling her brain, and now it came up with a name.

'Hunter?' she gasped out.

'Mrs Carter?' He'd heard her.

Annie said nothing. No, it was going to start up again. She knew it. She was going to die.

'Mrs Carter, can you see me?'

Annie turned her head just a little, and looked upward, towards the shattered left-hand side window. She couldn't see a face. What she *could* see was a hand. There was a gold wedding band on it. And there was a faint flickering blue light.

Police car, she thought.

She'd never been glad to see the Bill before, but *shit* was she glad to see them now.

'A hand,' she said hoarsely. 'I can see a hand.'

'Can you reach it? Grab hold?' he asked. He sounded very calm.

Shuddering, Annie unravelled her aching limbs just a little.

Straining through a gap of just inches, she stretched her hand towards his.

But in doing that, she became aware of how firmly her legs were held, how securely her ankle was clamped into the dead body of the car.

So securely that her foot was numb.

She felt a scream building at the back of her throat, felt a claustrophobic spasm grab her and gnaw at her guts.

'I can't move,' she burst out.

'It's all right,' he said, still very calm. 'You're going to be fine. Can you reach my hand? Try to reach my hand.'

Annie strained harder. With an enormous effort she reached out and managed to touch the hand. It fastened firmly on to her fingers. The hand was warm. Hers were icy with shock. Jesus, she was so glad he was there.

'That's good.' His voice was soothing, like he was trying to talk a jumper down from a tall building.

She wanted to ask him if they'd got the Delaney twins, but she knew better than anyone else that it wouldn't be the Bill who dealt out justice, not around here – it would be herself. She'd make those bastards suffer for this.

'Can you squeeze my hand?' he asked.

She tried to move closer to the hand that had wrapped itself securely around hers. She couldn't. 'My foot,' she said, and now her teeth were chattering. *Yeah, that's shock*, she thought detachedly. 'I can't move my foot,' she told him.

'We'll need cutting gear,' he said to someone else, and there were more voices, radio messages being sent. To Annie he said: 'Try to relax, Mrs Carter. Help's on the way. Just hold on now, and try to stay calm.'

Stay calm. So easy to say.

'How did you know where to find me?' she asked unsteadily.

'I didn't. We had a lead on the disappearance of Peter Delacourt, and we ended up here. Call it fate that we got to you in time.'

484

Fate.

It was pure fate that she hadn't died. And it was fate that decreed she was going to hunt down those Delaney bastards and finish the job.

50

The Delaneys were over so far as Hunter was concerned. He'd got so much evidence against them that the whole firm would be going down for years.

'We've closed all the ports and airports,' he told her later in the day, when she had been checked out at the hospital and Tony had been found groggy but unscathed in one of the breaker's yard other outbuildings.

They had both been given a clean bill of health, and told they ought to stay in overnight. Both had refused, despite the fact that they had sore heads, Annie's ankle was bruised, and her face bore several scratches from all the flying glass.

'We'll get them,' Hunter assured her. 'They'll be behind bars soon.'

Annie didn't believe it. It was too easy to slip in and out of the country, if you really wanted to and had the means to do it. For now, anyway, their rule was over. Deaf Derek, the treacherous bastard, had fled. The cops had nearly caught Charlie Foster, but only *nearly*. He'd given them the slip. Fuck it: they'd all got away with it.

She felt robbed. Behind bars was too good for those bastards, anyway. They'd tried to kill her, they'd nearly taken Layla's mother from her; banging them up would almost be like letting them off. All right, her contacts could get to them even on the inside, but she wanted *revenge*. She wanted to see them suffer, right in front of her eyes. She wanted it *done*.

Still shaken by her ordeal, she was grateful to the cops who dropped her back at the club, and drove Tony back to his flat. They were lucky to be alive. She knew that. Death had been *this* close. She sat in the flat, her newly refurbished club beneath her, and thought: *I could be dead right now*. She thought of opening night on Saturday, a big celebration, and she might never have seen it thanks to those fucking Delaneys. They had to be caught. Had to be put down, like the crazed animals they were.

She looked around the small sitting room of her flat, at the mounds of beautiful red roses Constantine had sent her. Suddenly the scent of them was suffocating. They could have been decorating her *grave*, if things had gone as Redmond and Orla had planned.

Anger stung her at the thought of that. Of what they could have inflicted on her, and Tony, and Layla. Of what Redmond had inflicted on Mira. She thought of Orla's denial over Aretha. Oh, she so *wanted* it to be Orla who she could pin that on. It would fit, it would be truly neat, she wanted that so much it hurt. But Orla's words had rung true. That was the awkward thing, the damning thing. She felt strongly that Orla had been telling the truth.

Fuck it.

So Chris was still in the frame for his wife's murder. Nothing had changed. Val Delacourt and Teresa Walker were down to that twisted little git Cyrus. Gareth Fuller and Pete Delacourt were down to Redmond. But still Aretha could not rest easy because *still* they didn't have a clue who had killed her.

A tall red haired woman, Sir William had said.

The phone rang. Annie snatched it up.

'When are we going to do dinner and talk?' said Constantine.

She sat down on the couch with a thump.

Dinner!

'There's something I need to talk to you about,' he said.

'There's something I want to talk to you about, too,' she said.

'Tomorrow night? Eight? I'll send the car.'

488

'It can't wait until tomorrow night,' she said shakily, and told him all about what had happened at the Delaneys' yard.

He was silent, taking it all in. Redmond Delaney had gone against her and in doing that he had gone against Constantine too. 'So what are you going to do now?' he asked her.

She felt peeved at him. He'd said nothing. She had expected outrage, a fierce surge of protectiveness towards her. What she *hadn't* expected was that he should be so fucking calm about it all.

'What, like you care? Ain't you even mad that you wouldn't have gone on getting your sex on tap, if I'd got done?' she demanded, feeling so irritated at his lack of response that she could have screamed.

'*What*?'

'And while we're on the subject, it would be really fucking convenient for you, wouldn't it? Me in the penthouse in Manhattan, all neatly tucked away. No family rucks over *that*, I suppose. Course you'd have to keep me on the Pill – Christ, what *would* they think if you had a kid off me?' She dragged a hand through her hair. 'Look, I'll catch you later,' she said, and hung up the phone.

Then she went to the sideboard and rummaged in the drawer, ignoring the phone when it rang again. It would be him. And, right now, she was too damned angry, too hyped up by all that had happened to her to speak to him. She found Sir William's business card and waited for the phone to stop ringing. Then she dialled the number on it.

He picked up at once. 'Hello?'

'How tall was the red-haired woman, did your man say? Aretha was a six-footer.' *And Orla Delaney's only five foot six.*

'Is that you, Mrs Carter? Well . . . he said she was at least as tall as the woman she was clearly following. Perhaps taller.'

'Over six feet tall? That's big for a woman.'

'Nevertheless, that's what he said. He particularly noticed the woman's height, because it was unusual, just as your friend's height was unusual.'

Orla really didn't do it.

Annie thought of Teresa Walker's mother. Tall. Gaunt. Red-haired. Sitting there stroking her Bible, a mad gleam in her eyes. Aretha was connected to Teresa and they shared a mutual love of money. Yeah. At last. She *had* it.

'Thanks, Sir William, that's all I wanted to know.'

'A pleasure, my dear. If I can be of any further assistance . . .'

He hung up. She dialled through to the police station, but Hunter was out.

Annie stalked around the apartment, thinking. She had escaped death thanks only to Hunter's sharp thinking, to his nose for trouble. She couldn't just sit here, watch some telly, eat a meal, behave normally. She had to do something.

She looked at the roses. She picked out a bunch of twenty, wrapped them in yesterday's newspaper. Picked up her keys and her bag, and left the flat, left the club. Out in the street, she hailed a cab and told the driver where she wanted to go.

The house at Harrow was quiet, as usual. But this time there was no heavy on the door, and that surprised her. She knocked, and the white-coated nurse opened it.

'Ah,' she said, as Annie pushed past her.

'Yeah, me again,' said Annie, already trotting up the stairs.

'I have to talk to you,' said the woman, following Annie up.

'Look, I don't want to hear about bad nights and bad days and all that shit. I've had a pretty bad day, too. I've had a pretty fucking bad *year*, actually, don't give me earache, I don't . . .'

Annie had flung open the door at the top of the stairs and now she stood frozen in the doorway, looking at the empty bed. She turned and stared at the nurse as she reached the top of the stairs.

'What the . . . ?' started Annie.

'That's why I wanted to talk to you,' said the woman.

'Where the hell is she? Has she run off again?

Jesus, you people are supposed to be watching her!'

Then a worse thought occurred. Had Redmond somehow managed to track Mira to this address? Had he found Mira? Had he taken her away?

'We have been watching her, I assure you.' There was a glint of something other than hostility in the woman's eyes now. 'Look, I'm sorry. She didn't make it.'

'Didn't . . .' Annie echoed faintly. She turned and looked at the empty bed again. She shook her head. 'No . . .'

'I'm sorry,' said the nurse, and there was compassion in her eyes. 'I don't think she wanted to go on. She . . . she must have been hoarding up sleeping pills, stashing them away . . .'

'You *what*?'

'She . . . she overdosed. We lost her during the night.'

Annie looked down at the red roses clutched in her arms. She looked at the empty bed. At the nurse.

'No,' she said again.

Mira, she thought. *For God's sake, couldn't you have just held on? You came through so much, why did you have to give up now?*

'I'm sorry,' the nurse said again, her eyes avoiding Annie's.

Annie took a breath. She looked down at the roses again; roses for life, for love. Neither of which

Mira was going to know about, not any more. She held them out to the nurse with a gesture of barely suppressed fury.

'Here. You have them.'

'Oh, I don't . . .'

'*Take* them.' Annie slapped the flowers into the nurse's arms.

She took one last look at the empty bed, swallowed hard past a sudden choking lump in her throat, then went past the nurse and back down the stairs.

'Thank you,' the nurse's voice drifted after her, but she was already down in the hall, going out of the front door and down the path to the road, her heart like a block of ice in her chest, her head full of hatred.

She didn't blame that stupid nurse for this. *Redmond* had killed Mira, as surely as if he had throttled her during one of his loathsome sex games, as surely as if he had put a gun to her head and pulled the trigger. And he'd got away. He'd *got away.*

51

At eleven the next morning, Tony drove Annie over to Soho in a borrowed Rover.

'This is dog rough,' he complained the minute she got in. 'I hate this fucking car, pardon my French, Boss. The Jag had *class*. Look at this cheap trim, and what colour do they call the exterior, what is that, *beige* or something? Beige with a black roof, that looks like a frigging abortion. They call this a "compact executive" car. Well it don't look very executive to *me*.'

'It'll do for now,' said Annie. It was obvious that Tony was feeling no after-effects from his experiences with the Delaneys, and that was good. 'We'll get another car, a better one.'

That seemed to placate him. Annie explained what they were doing today. They pulled up outside the tattoo parlour. Annie thought of Pete Delacourt, the tattooed freak, another victim of

Redmond's obsessive pursuit of Mira Cooper. She had relived time and again that moment when she'd found him dead in the Delaney yard.

They walked around the side until they reached the back entrance to the Alley Cat club. They went in, went to the dressing room they knew he'd be in. Tony opened the closed door, and they walked in on Bobby Jo, all glammed up in long red wig and sparkly blue dress, getting busy with a blonde club hostess wearing nothing but a frilly skirt, stockings and high-heeled shoes.

'What the fucking hell?' demanded Bobby Jo, while the girl let out a screech and covered her oversized naked breasts with her hands.

'Sorry to interrupt your knee-trembler, Bobby Jo, but I want a word,' said Annie. She turned her attention to the girl. 'Out,' she said.

The blonde shot past Annie and Tony like a bullet. Tony closed the door after her, leaving them with one enraged drag queen, a visibly wilting hard-on pressing up against the front of his sequinned frock.

'You've got a fucking *nerve*, coming in here again,' Bobby Jo started in, looming over Annie.

Tall and red-haired. But not a woman at all.

'Tone,' said Annie, and stepped back.

Tony hit Bobby Jo square on the jaw. Bobby Jo shot back against his dressing table, scattering blusher and foundation. He jumped up again, though, and came at Tony with an inexpert swing. Tony blocked the blow easily and delivered a better one to Bobby Jo's nose. Then he followed through with another to the stomach.

Bobby Jo doubled over, blood cascading down his blue dress. Tony brought his knee up and it crunched into the centre of Bobby Jo's face. Bobby Jo staggered back, floundered against the dressing table, sweeping off more bits and pieces of the trade – his brushes, a pair of falsies, a tub of face powder that plumed up all around them like a dust storm in a desert.

Tony went back in.

'No!' burbled Bobby Jo past a mouthful of blood. He shrank back against the table, one of his false eyelashes hanging off, blood all over his face and down his dress.

Tony smacked him again.

Annie watched impassively. She felt sick inside, but the bastard *deserved* this. This, and more.

When Bobby Jo was on his knees, she nodded to Tony.

Tony drew back.

Annie stepped forward and stood in front of Bobby Jo.

'Now,' she said. 'Tell me why you killed Aretha Brown.'

'I didn't, I don't know what—'

Annie stepped aside and Tony moved back in,

twisting Bobby Jo's arms up behind his back until he shrieked.

'I didn't, I didn't . . .' he was babbling, his face a mask of blood and make-up, his red wig askew.

'You want my friend here to take you apart bit by bit?' she asked. 'Because believe me, he will. Until you start telling the truth.'

'But I didn't, I didn't do nothing . . .' he sobbed.

Tony wrenched harder.

Bobby Jo screamed.

'No! Don't! All right, I'll tell you! I'll tell you!'

Tony held him there. Any more lies, he'd get more.

Annie pulled up a chair and stared at the grotesque, ruined face without pity. After all, what pity had *he* shown?

'Tell me,' she said.

'It . . . it was that cow Teresa. I was fucking her, you know I was,' he was babbling.

'Yeah, I know. Move on.'

'I've got a . . . a thing going, a long-term thing, with Selma Callow who owns a share of the club. She's a jealous woman. Wants to keep me all to herself.'

Fat chance of that, by the look of things, thought Annie.

'So?'

'Teresa walked in on us once in here,' said Bobby Jo, tears and blood running in rivers down his face. 'She was such a little chancer. I told you about her, passing round fucking business cards inside the club, pushing her luck.' He paused, coughed, spluttered. 'But I was turking her sometimes so I overlooked the problem . . .'

She looked at him with distaste. 'And?'

'She was friends with this Aretha Brown. Said they met at church or some damned mad thing. Teresa in a church! Crazy. But that's what she said, and it was *her* idea, this Brown woman, to blackmail me.'

Aretha and her love of money, thought Annie.

'Go on,' she told him.

'I can't, I can't . . .' He was panting, doubled over. Tony gave him a tweak. Bobby Jo yelled and straightened up. 'All right! I thought they'd drop it after a couple of payouts . . . but they didn't. They just kept coming back for more. I didn't know what the fuck to do: if Selma found out I was dead in the water. Out of the best job I've ever had; out of the flat she bought me. I'd lose my car. She said if I ever cheated on her she'd see me dead, and I believed her. You don't know what she's like. She's an obsessive bitch, she's fucking scary. I was frantic. And then . . . Teresa was killed. I tell you, that was my lucky bloody day.'

'Keep going,' said Annie when he slumped again.

'Think I'm going to be sick . . .' he panted,

turning his hideous painted face aside and spitting out teeth and blood on to the carpet.

'Keep going,' she said again.

'*Jesus . . .*'

'*Keep going.*'

'Teresa was killed like the other one.'

'Val Delacourt.'

'That one, yeah. So Teresa was gone, and that was good news. I relaxed. Thought it was all over. Then that Aretha Brown came calling, saying it was *not* over, that she was going to keep taking payments from me, and she upped them, upped them a *lot*. I was desperate then, I didn't know what to do . . .'

Oh fuck it, Aretha, was the damned money that important, really? Important enough to die for?

Bobby Jo hunched over, and with a convulsive movement was sick. The stench of vomit filled the little room. Gasping, he straightened again. Annie watched him steadily, her stomach knotted up with revulsion.

'Then I . . . oh shit . . . I worked out a plan. The Delacourt woman and Teresa had been garrotted, it was in all the papers, and I thought if I made it look the same, then I could get rid of the Brown bitch the same way and . . .' Bobby Jo paused, gasping down a breath, '. . . and the police would think it was the same man who'd done all three. They'd never suspect. I'd be home and dry.'

And Chris would have rotted in prison.

Annie stood up, weary and disgusted.

'Now you're going to tell all that to the Bill,' she said. 'And you're going to serve time.'

Bobby Jo was shaking his head, his bloody mouth twisted into a ravaged smile. 'No! You got this out of me with your pet ape beating lumps off me: that won't stand up.'

Annie drew in close to the wreck in front of her, her face set with rage. She grabbed the wig and threw it aside. Grabbed the skullcap and his own hair through it. Wrenched his head back.

'Now you listen to me, you arsehole,' she spat. 'You're telling the police what you just told us. This ain't negotiable. You die – *now* – or you confess to what you done. Tell them you fell down the stairs or a jealous husband beat you up, some crap like that. Then you keep your head down, you do your time. Inside or outside, my boys can reach you. Inside or outside, you step out of line just once and I'm telling you – you're *fucked*.'

She let him go, breathing hard. She stepped past him to the dressing table and snatched up the phone. She dialled. When it was answered, she said, 'DI Hunter please,' and gave Tony the nod.

He let go of Bobby Jo. She put the phone into Bobby Jo's shaking hand and stood over him while he confessed to the murder of Aretha Brown.

* * *

When she got back to the club, the phone was ringing. She picked up. It was Constantine.

'Okay, what?' she demanded.

'What do you mean, okay, what? Where do you get off, talking to me like that?'

'Fuck you,' she said, and hung up.

The phone rang again. She snatched it up. 'I *said* I had an apartment in Manhattan, that's all,' he said. 'What, did you think I was propositioning you, making some sort of indecent suggestion?'

No, I thought you were tucking me away out of sight of your family. As if I was something shameful, something sordid, to be hidden away.

She couldn't say that. She was too *proud* to say that.

'I wasn't doing that,' he said.

'No? Your family hate me.'

'I don't care.'

'Well *I* do. Only Alberto's nice to me, and I'm starting to wonder why, when all the others detest me and don't bother to hide it.'

'They'll come around. Give it time.'

'Ha!' Annie put the phone down. It rang again. She snatched it up. 'I don't want to talk about this,' she said.

'You silly bitch, I'm asking you to marry me,' said Constantine.

Annie sat down suddenly.

'You still there?' he asked.

501

'Yeah, I'm still here. And that's a hell of a way to make a proposal, calling me a silly bitch.'

There was a pause on the other end. 'And now an answer would be good,' Constantine said softly.

'I'll think about it,' said Annie, and put the phone down in a state of shock.

52

Finally opening night at the club had arrived. The club – *her* club – was throwing open its doors at last. There were limos all up and down the street, offloading a glittering array of celebs, and the general public were out in their masses, rubbernecking to see who they could catch a glimpse of.

The press were there, flashbulbs popping.

Annie was centre stage in a long black halter-neck dress, her dark hair swept up in a chignon, diamonds twinkling at her ears and throat as they caught the light of the strobes, the music pounding out a happy beat, champagne flowing freely. The place was buzzing. *She'd done it. Annie Carter had created a place to be seen in.*

'Well, you made it,' said Constantine at her side. His heavies were there, about six feet away. Close enough to watch; not close enough to be intrusive. *Her* heavies were there too; they were out in force. Squat Steve and lanky Gary were to be seen everywhere in their DJs and bow ties, moving among the crowds, checking invites and making sure everyone behaved themselves. Tony was a few feet away, keeping an eye on Annie.

'I never thought I would,' Annie admitted to him, having to lean in close to him to make herself heard over Thunderclap Newman's *Something In The Air*.

Annie looked around, flushed with pleasure and success. The bar was heaving, the kitchen doors were swinging crazily from all the back-and-forth of the waiters and waitresses ferrying food and drinks out. The go-go dancers were gyrating wildly on their gilded platforms. The dance floor was a writhing sea of bodies.

Half of England's victorious 1966 World Cup squad were in. She spotted Geoff Hurst and Jackie Charlton. And film stars too: Donald Sinden was in; she was *sure* that fabulous-looking man over there was Dirk Bogarde; and wasn't that the beautiful Bond girl who had been painted gold . . . ?

'Yeah, that's her. Shirley Eaton,' said Constantine.

'Friend of yours?'

'Friend of a friend. Sean's coming by later.'

'Sean *Connery?*'

He'd drafted in a truckload of famous faces and young aspiring stunners to give the place some fizz tonight.

Constantine clinked his champagne flute against hers and smiled. 'To *Annie's.*'

Annie's heart did a back-flip when he smiled liked that. Yeah, there were gorgeous people here, glossy and polished and elegant, but none of the men measured up to Constantine Barolli. She saw many of the women giving him interested looks and thought: *Hands off, ladies – he's mine.*

'Thought any more about my offer?' he asked, his eyes holding hers.

'Yeah. I have.'

'And?' He was gazing at her intently.

Slowly, she nodded. 'Yeah, okay. I'll marry you.'

Constantine grabbed her and twirled her around. Annie laughed and clung to him.

'You sure?' he said against her mouth when he settled her back on to the floor. 'Not still hung up on Max?'

Annie shook her head. She'd loved Max and would cherish his memory forever – he was the father of her daughter. But he was gone. And now she was in love, absolutely and completely, with Constantine Barolli.

'Yeah. Very sure,' she said, and reached up and kissed him. Then she drew back. 'You're sure too?'

'Oh yeah.' He pulled her in closer and his answering kiss made her go limp. 'Now relax and have fun. Enjoy the night: you've earned it. That's an order.'

'I'm not good at taking orders,' she said against his mouth. 'And I'm still hopping bloody mad that Redmond Delaney got away.'

She had the word out. He and that twisted bitch sister of his *had* to be found.

'Yeah, I noticed,' he said, and kissed her more deeply. 'But come on. Let it go.'

Annie drew back and stared into his blue, mesmerizing eyes. 'I love you,' she said, stifling a pang of irritation.

How could he be so damned *casual* about it? She wanted to be mad at him, but she couldn't. He was right, anyway. She had to enjoy this night; she'd worked hard enough to bring it about, after all.

'Hey, Annie!' It was Ellie, pushing through the crowds, all glammed up and carrying Layla in her party dress.

Layla looked a picture. Her dress was turquoise, all frills and flounces. She'd been trying it on for days. Her dark hair was tied up in bunches with matching ribbons. She had new shoes. Annie felt overwhelming pride and love when she looked at Layla. She'd invited Ruthie tonight, of course she had, but Ruthie had declined. Ruthie wasn't a party person – she never had been – and Annie respected that.

'Hey, who's this little beauty?' said Constantine, handing Annie his glass and sweeping Layla up into his arms. Layla laughed excitedly; from the first minute she had set eyes on Constantine, she had decided she loved him.

Animals and kids, thought Annie. *They know instinctively who they can trust.*

'I'm Layla,' said the little girl, taking him literally.

'I remember you,' he told her.

'I remember you too! I got new shoes, look.'

Constantine admired the shoes. 'And a new dress too, uh?'

Layla nodded.

'You look beautiful, honey,' he told her. 'You wanna dance?'

Constantine carried her on to the busy dance floor and swayed around to the beat with her, Annie and Ellie watching from the sidelines. Layla was laughing fit to bust a gut. Constantine was smiling and chatting to her.

'He's *gorgeous*,' said Ellie in Annie's ear.

Yep, he certainly is, thought Annie. She looked at Ellie. 'You look pretty good yourself, Ellie.'

Ellie blushed and smoothed her hands down over the long red mock-velvet dress she was wearing. The shade flattered her dark colouring to perfection. Ellie in her workaday overalls looked a mess, but this dress was the business. In this she was sumptuously curvy, and it nipped in and out in all the right places, the plunging neckline displaying her milky-white shoulders and ample cleavage, the cunning cut displaying to perfection a surprisingly small waist.

'Do you think they'll let Chris out soon?' she asked Annie anxiously.

Annie nodded. 'They're just going through the formalities. They've got the real culprits, Chris'll be out in no time.'

'Thank God,' said Ellie, and waved to someone in the crowd and was off again.

Annie stood there and sipped champagne, her eyes scanning the crowds. They met up with another pair of eyes, calm dark ones, *also* scanning the crowds. She went over.

'You came!' she said in surprise, then shot him a teasing glance. 'Looking for villains, DI Hunter?'

'Yes, Mrs Carter,' he said, still looking like the Grim Reaper with his long, handsome, sober face and immaculate suit, totally out of step with the party atmosphere in here. He was holding a glass of champagne as though it might explode on him. His eyes still skimmed over the throng, passing over Steve Taylor and Gary Tooley, over Tony, over several heads of neighbouring 'firms', and finally resting on Constantine. 'Finding a few, too.'

'Don't you ever go off duty?' asked Annie.

'Don't *you*?' His lips twitched.

'Hey, was that a smile? Or just wind?'

'The manager of the Alley Cat gave me a full

confession to the murder of your friend Aretha Brown.'

Annie kept her face carefully blank. 'Yeah? That's good news,' she said.

'Isn't it? Although when he came into the station he appeared to be in a bad way. He said he fell down a flight of stairs.'

'That can hurt,' said Annie.

'Yes it can. It looked more as if he'd been beaten, but he insisted he hadn't.' He looked at her. 'Nothing to say, Mrs Carter?'

'*Should* I have?'

He sighed and gave up. 'I've spoken to your friend's aunt.'

'Louella? How'd she take it?'

'With shock. She was convinced Chris Brown was guilty.'

'I nearly thought that myself, at times.'

'We've released him.'

'Now *that's* good news,' said Annie, happily clinking her champagne flute against his. 'Let's drink to it.'

He sipped the fine champagne as if it was arsenic. Annie smiled. Never thought she'd like a cop, but she'd taken to this one. She couldn't forget the way he'd held on to her hand when she'd been stuck in that bloody car crusher, either. Here was a handsome man with staying power, a man who might look like he was sucking on lemons, but who had *endurance*. She appreciated that. In another time, another place, she could have gone for him.

'Help yourself to food, drink, anything,' she said, then she hesitated, looked down at his left hand. *Still* wearing that wedding ring. 'You talked to her? Your ex-wife? Since the divorce?'

He shook his head.

'Maybe you should. Maybe things would be different now.'

'Maybe. Maybe not.'

Annie nodded slowly and smiled. 'Well . . . I gotta mingle.'

And Annie was off again, shaking hands, smiling, schmoozing the celebs. Suddenly she found herself face to face with Dolly Farrell.

'Oh!' said Dolly.

Dolly was in flowing pink lace to complement her blonde bubble-perm. She looked terrific. But when she saw Annie standing in front of her, her eyes grew wary. 'Hi,' she said cautiously.

'Hiya, Doll,' said Annie.

'I had the invite but I wasn't sure I'd still be welcome. Well, after . . . after all that business with the Delaneys, and Mira . . . I wasn't sure.'

'Look, Doll,' said Annie seriously, 'you were in a corner. You couldn't go against the Delaneys, and I understand that. Forget it. Water under the bridge. Okay?'

Dolly looked more relaxed. 'I've been hearing word on the streets that the Carter boys are moving into Limehouse and Battersea. There's been violence, but not much.'

Annie nodded. The Delaney boys were leaderless and rootless without Redmond and Orla. And she had wasted no time in grabbing the moment. She had told Steve and Gary to start the push, take over. There had been small pockets of resistance, but nothing significant. There was no way the Delaneys were ever going to run that manor again. Now it would be part of the Carter empire, a lucrative extension of their security business.

The Delaneys – finally – were yesterday's news. But still, they'd walked away. Police block or no police block, they'd legged it. It gnawed at her that they were still alive and well, when they had caused such mayhem.

'You'll be paying your wedge to the Carter boys soon,' she said.

'Well, I for one won't be sorry,' said Dolly with a sigh. 'They scared us all shitless, that family. Weird lot. But what could you do? Talk about money with menaces.'

'Let's go upstairs, Doll. I need to talk to you, and we can't do it down here.'

Up in the office it was quieter. Annie sat down behind the desk and indicated that Dolly should

511

sit too. Dolly sat down and looked at her, puzzled. 'Well, what's this about?' she asked.

Annie got straight to the point. 'It's about you running this place, Doll. I want to put you in here, as manager.'

Dolly's jaw dropped.

'And in a year or so's time, if it runs at a good profit, you'll be opening the other two Carter clubs for me in the same style.'

Now Dolly's lower jaw *really* hit the floor. 'You're *kidding?*'

'Do I look like I'm kidding? I'm serious, Doll.'

'But . . . for f . . . *You* run this place.'

'I won't be running it, Doll,' said Annie, smiling at Dolly's shock. 'I'll be owning it, that's all. It was something I wanted to do, something I wanted to achieve. Now it's done and my situation's changed. Now I need a manager, a bloody good one, and the first – and the best – person that comes to mind is you.'

'But I've never done anything like this!' protested Dolly.

'It's a business, Doll. You've been running a bloody business for years. Just scale up a bit.'

'A *bit?*'

'Of course if you're not interested, I can soon find someone who is,' sighed Annie.

'Who the fuck said I'm not interested?' Dolly burst out. Then her face closed down. 'What about wages?'

Annie named the figure she'd been turning over in her mind for days.

'Jesus,' said Dolly.

'You're supposed to say that's not enough,' suggested Annie.

'All right. It's not enough.'

'Tough shit. That's the deal. Accommodation's included, the flat's furnished.'

'But where will you . . . ?'

'Car too. And driver.'

Annie had a brief, enjoyable vision of Tony driving Dolly around, Dolly being a big noise in the club scene, Dolly shouting happily at the staff, running the show, throwing her weight about, greeting the punters.

Scale up, that was all she had to do.

Dolly was staring at her, dumbstruck. 'I can't believe this. What about the parlour?'

'Put in a manager, Doll. Easy-peasy.'

'Yeah, but *who*? Who could I trust to run the place right?'

'Ellie.'

'Holy shit!' said Dolly, and started to laugh.

Later she had one of the boys send Tony up to the office. Annie told him all about her plans, and Tony sat there looking like he'd lost a pound and found a penny.

'So I'm out of a job,' he said.

'Have you been listening to me? You got a job. You drive Dolly instead of me, that's all.'

'I'm not sure I'd *want* to be driving her,' he said.

'Hey, it's a job,' said Annie.

'Dunno.' He folded his arms over his barrel of a chest.

'Well, it'd be a damned shame if you didn't take it, because *someone* is going to have to drive Dolly around. She don't drive and she needs transport on tap, plus a minder, and that should be you.'

'Huh,' said Tony, still looking put out.

Annie rolled her eyes. 'And *someone* is going to have to get their arse down to the Jaguar show-room this week and pick out a brand-new motor, because I'm not sure I can *take* any more earache off you about that fucking Rover.'

'New, uh?' asked Tony grudgingly.

'Brand new. Any colour so long as it's black.'

Annie saw Steve and Gary up in the office next. They sat there and looked at her expectantly, coolly.

'Gary,' said Annie, looked at the lanky, hard-faced blond. 'You once said to me that you and Steve could take over the manor.'

'Think you'll find I actually *threatened* you with it,' he said.

'That's right, you did. Didn't want to take orders off the Yanks, ain't that right?'

'What's this all about?' asked Steve, sitting there

like a block of stone, his dark eyes flat as they stared at her.

'It's about you and Gary,' said Annie. 'Running the Carter manor. Running Bow.'

'And Limehouse and Battersea,' said Gary.

'Yeah, how's that going?'

'Going good.'

'It's no job for a woman, this game,' said Steve. 'Too dirty.'

Annie kept quiet about that. Knew she could do it, had *proved* she could do it, and didn't need to prove it any more.

'We got Derek,' said Gary.

Annie looked at him. 'And?'

'He's sorted.'

Annie nodded. She didn't want to know what they'd done with Deaf Derek; it was enough to know that the problem had been attended to.

'What about Charlie Foster?' she asked with a faint shiver of revulsion. To think the horrible little creep had damn near *raped* her . . .

Gary looked at her with his cold blue eyes. Vicious, that was Gary, and his eyes told the whole story. He glanced down at his watch, back at her face. 'No sweat. Being attended to . . . oh, just about . . . *now*.'

Across town in Bow there was another breaker's yard, owned by a friend of a friend of the Carters.

As the roaring semi-hush of the city night settled around it, things came to life in there. Suddenly there was activity. Machines working, men moving.

Charlie Foster was sitting in the driver's seat of his elderly Ford. His hands were taped to the wheel. His body was tied in to the seat. *No way out.* If he tried, if he really stretched, he could reach the glove compartment with his foot, but not the passenger-seat window, and that was what he wanted to do, kick out the glass.

And then what? And then . . . nothing. He slumped over the wheel, sweat running in rivulets down his face. He gave a roar of rage and terror and pulled wildly against the tape on the steering wheel once again. Slumped again.

No good. No fucking good at all.

He heard the machinery start to roar, and then the grab hit the top of the car like a ton weight.

'Bastards!' he yelled, spittle flying, and the grab's talons broke the window beside his head, and the passenger side window caved in too, and the whole car lurched.

Then he was in the air. He turned his head and he could see them down in the yard, Carter boys. Watching. Waiting. *Bastards.*

53

On Sunday, Annie had Tony drive her in the despised borrowed Rover over to the church.

'Picked out a beauty,' Tony told her excitedly about the new Jag he had ordered. 'Black. Tan leather trim, walnut dashboard, she's terrific.'

It tickled Annie to think of Dolly being driven around town by Tony. They'd either rip each other's heads off or get on like wildfire, she wasn't sure which.

Tony pulled into the churchyard and parked up. Annie got out, clutching a large assorted bouquet of fresh pink flowers and fern. It was windy today, but bright. Soon summer would give way to autumn. Tony followed, six paces back, as she walked across the rough-mown grass to Aretha's grave.

Someone was there already.

A large figure, crouched beside it.

There was a patchwork of yellowish turf laid out on the grave. Soon the grass would bed in, start to grow. Soon there would be a fine big headstone. Annie would see to that if Chris was okay with it, and if Louella wasn't too proud to allow it. For now, Aretha's grave was unmarked.

'Chris?' she said gently, touching his shoulder.

The big man looked up. Tears were rolling down his face. He wiped at them, looked at her. He stood up. Looked past her to Tony and nodded. Tony nodded in return.

'Wanted to come and see her,' he said.

'We'll go,' said Annie, placing her flowers beside his own offering on the grave. 'We'll come back later.'

'No, I . . .' Chris swallowed and ran a hand over his huge bald head. 'I wanted to thank you, for all you did. She can rest easy now.'

'She was one of the best friends I ever had,' said Annie. 'I'll never forget her.'

Suddenly Chris broke down. '*Why* did this have to happen to her?' he sobbed.

'I don't know, sweetheart, I really don't,' said Annie, feeling tears starting in her own eyes.

'I'd like to kill that freak with my own bare hands,' he muttered.

Annie nodded. Bobby Jo was banged up now; he was going to have a hard road to walk. No Krug or willing hostesses where *he* was going, that was

518

for sure. That couldn't give Chris much comfort, but it must give him some.

'I'll come back later,' said Annie, and this time he let her walk away.

When she glanced back he was on his knees again, hunched over his wife's grave.

The hot August sun was twinkling through the trees, throwing shadows and dancing shapes.

Annie blinked. There was Aretha, in hot pants, feather boa and Afghan coat, leaning over Chris.

Aretha looked up and her eyes met Annie's. *It's okay, girlfriend. I'm just fine.* Annie blinked again. Aretha was gone.

Shit, now I'm seeing things, thought Annie. But she felt oddly comforted.

'Come on, Tone, let's go,' she said, and they started back to the car.

Ellie was walking toward them, clutching a bouquet of yellow roses and wearing a neat emerald-green skirt suit.

She looked good. There was a new spring in her step, a new aura about her. Things had changed. She wasn't a brass any more, catering to the chubby chasers. She wasn't Dolly's cleaner. She wasn't Kath's cleaner, either – and that had always been a bit of a lost cause, anyway; Annie loved Kath, she was family, but even she was prepared to admit that Kath would probably always be a bit of a sloppy mare. Ellie was going to be madam of the

Limehouse parlour now, and she wouldn't have to kowtow to the Delaneys any more. Already, it was starting to give her confidence.

'Hi, Ellie.'

Ellie smiled faintly. 'Thought I'd come and put these on the grave.' Ellie looked ahead, saw Chris crouching down. 'Oh.' Her face clouded. 'I'd better come back another time.'

Annie glanced over at Chris, then back at Ellie.

'No, don't,' she said. 'Go and see him. I think he could do with some company.'

Ellie shook her head, uncertain. 'I wouldn't know what to say.'

'Say what you feel,' said Annie.

Ellie looked at Chris. She straightened her shoulders, clutched more tightly at the bouquet. 'Okay,' she said, and started walking towards him.

Annie stood there and watched her go. Then she turned away, got into the car with Tony.

She glanced back at Aretha's graveside. Ellie was there, touching a tentative hand to Chris's shoulder. He looked up at her. Ellie was talking to him. *Maybe*, thought Annie. *Just maybe . . .*

Tony started the engine and swung the Rover out through the church gates. Aretha's Aunt Louella was just coming through them.

'Stop the car, Tone,' said Annie, and she got out and stood in front of the woman, blocking her path.

'Hi, Louella,' she said. 'Um . . . Chris is at the graveside. I don't know if you want to talk to him . . . ?'

'What, an' say sorry?' Louella sighed. 'I thought he done it. I *believed* he done it.'

'Well, now you know he didn't. The police have got the one who did. And Chris is out. All charges dropped.'

'*You* believed in him,' said Louella.

'I knew him better than you.'

'That's a fact.' Louella said, standing there looking at the ground. Then she bit her lip and looked up at Annie's face. 'You know, I wasted a lot of time being angry with my baby girl, but now I wish . . . I wish I'd just accepted her, *whatever* she was, whatever she did, and been happy for her so long as she was happy.'

'It's not too late to accept Chris. *He* made her happy.'

Louella looked at Annie's face. 'No, it's not. You're right. Maybe I will. Some day.'

But not yet, thought Annie. The pain of grief was still too raw for Louella to reach out and say sorry.

'I'm going away soon,' said Annie.

'Oh yeah? Well . . . you have a safe journey.'

Louella gazed at her keenly, almost in puzzlement. Annie knew she'd blotted her copybook more or less for good with Louella. She didn't expect a fond farewell or any of that crap. But there was a tiny hint of a smile playing around the woman's lips.

'You know,' said Louella at last, 'that policeman told me how you helped to straighten this whole thing out. He said how you put yourself at risk to make sure the evil people who hurt my girl – and those others – were made to face up to their sins. So maybe you're not *all* bad, after all.'

Which wasn't too shabby, coming from Louella. *Not all bad, after all*, thought Annie. Not exactly praise, but it would do.

Annie got back in the car. Louella stomped on up the gravel drive to the church door, bypassing the grave, Chris and Ellie for now. Later, she might come to it. Annie really hoped she did.

Time heals all wounds, she thought. Tony restarted the engine and pulled away. She didn't look back again.

Epilogue

Constantine Barolli's private Gulfstream 111 jet was sitting on the tarmac at Heathrow Airport, the engines running, ready for takeoff.

Annie Carter fiddled with her seatbelt, leaned over and checked that Layla's was secure. Constantine's minder was up the front of the cabin, out of earshot but close enough. Annie smiled across at Constantine.

'You a nervous flyer?' he asked, putting aside the newspaper and looking at her. Blue, blue eyes. He had to be the sexiest, most gorgeous man on the planet.

'No,' she said. 'But it's a big change for me, all this.'

'You'll love New York.'

'I love *you*.'

'That's a start.' He leaned over and lightly kissed her lips.

'Urgh,' said Layla.

'Can't beat kids for puncturing that romantic moment,' he said with a grin.

'Are we doing the right thing?' Annie asked, and her eyes were serious now as they looked into his.

Constantine nodded slowly, his eyes holding hers. 'The only possible thing,' he assured her. 'I tried doing without you, remember? It drove me nuts.'

The plane started to move, taxiing along the runway.

Constantine sat back, perfectly relaxed. He closed his eyes.

'And it's too late for second thoughts *now*, Mrs Carter,' he pointed out. 'We're going.'

'Shit,' muttered Annie.

'Shit, shit, shit,' sang Layla.

'Don't *say* that.'

The throb of the engines was deafening now, growing in pitch to a roar. Suddenly the plane shot forward, zipping along the runway.

'Wheee!' shouted Layla.

Annie held her hand. Constantine grabbed Annie's. All at once they were up in the air, Annie's stomach dropping like a stone as they soared up into the blue sky, London falling away beneath them.

'New York, here we come,' said Constantine, opening his eyes and looking out of the window as the city shrank in size.

Annie looked at him. Mobster. Mafia. Dangerous. Alluring.

Oh Jesus, I'm really out of my depth here, she thought. It was frightening. But exciting, too. And so what if his family hated her? Annie Carter had never yet backed away from a challenge.

'There's something here you might want to see,' said Constantine, passing her the paper. 'Page four, bottom right.'

Annie took the paper. She opened it, found the right place, and sat there staring in disbelief. The headline shouted: THREE PEOPLE MISSING AFTER PLANE CRASH. She caught her breath. For a moment the words danced meaninglessly in front of her eyes. Then she gathered herself and read the story. *Three people are missing believed dead, among them London entrepreneur Redmond Delaney and his sister, Orla, after air-traffic controllers at Cardiff Airport lost contact with a light aircraft shortly after an unauthorized takeoff. It was believed the Cessna may have been heading for Dublin, but never arrived. Accident investigators believe it crashed into the Irish Sea. Despite extensive searches, no survivors or wreckage has been found.*

Feeling limp with shock, Annie looked at Constantine. 'Three people. Redmond, Orla and the pilot. *Did* it crash into the Irish Sea? I mean, did you . . . ?'

Constantine held her gaze steadily. 'You really want the details?' He glanced at Layla. 'I told you. Anyone who goes against you goes against me. It's done now. It's finished.'

She thought back to how mad she had been at him, how *furious* in fact, thinking he was so calm, so controlled, that he didn't care about all that had been done to her. But he had. He did. He'd sorted the Delaneys, once and for all.

She gave him back the paper. 'No. No, I don't want to know the details.' Her voice shook a little.

The Delaneys were history at last. Annie looked out of the window, watched Windsor Castle fading like a fairy tale beneath the billowing clouds. Her London life was history too.

'Tell me again about the penthouse,' she said.

'It's big,' said Constantine.

'How big?'

'Huge. Lots of floor space, a roof garden, you'll love it. Big floor-to-ceiling windows that look right out over Central Park, and there's . . .'

She lay back in the seat and listened to the sound of his voice as he told her all about it, the dream of their life together unfolding with every word. Nothing left to do now except *live* it. And shit, she was going to do that.

'I want a big wedding. The works,' she said.

'You got it,' said Constantine.

'First an engagement ring. A disgustingly big, vulgar diamond engagement ring.'

'We'll do Tiffany's. First thing.' He paused. 'Maybe it's time you took that ring off now?'

His eyes were on Max's ring, the slab of bright lapis lazuli set in gold. She was still wearing it on the thumb of her left hand.

'Yeah,' said Annie softly. 'Maybe it is.'

She took it off then, slowly, almost reverently, and slipped it into her handbag.

'Feels strange,' she said, looking at her bare hands. 'Not wearing it.'

'This disgustingly big, vulgar diamond – how big are we talking here?'

'*Enormous.*' Annie brightened and flashed him a grin. Electricity sparked between them. *Oh, she loved him so much* . . . 'And set in platinum.'

The dream was unfolding: she could see it all now. Layla would be flower girl. Dolly would be matron of honour. Oh, and the *dress*. This was going to be fun.

This was going to be *bliss*.

She couldn't wait.

Annie Carter had finally got it all.

A word from Jessie Keane

Picture this. It's early January 2008, it's mid-afternoon and it's dark and cold outside. Actually, it's cold *inside* too, there's no central heating in here so I sit under a quilt, toying with the idea of playing a DVD and contemplating my future. Frankly, it doesn't look too rosy. I've just got another rejection slip to add to the pile. These rejection slips - varying from coldly polite to a brusquely scribbled *not interested* – have finally convinced me that I am never going to be a writer.

So I make a decision, then and there. I am going to give up writing and retrain as something else. Having made the decision, I feel better. Not good (hey, writers are born, not made, and the urge to write is so strong it's damned near overwhelming) but better. I can relax and watch my DVD. I turn it on. It's The Krays, starring the Kemp brothers. The Krays are rampaging across London's East End in the swinging sixties like twin Caligulas on bad acid. My jaw drops as the film progresses. And ... something else happens. I start wondering what it would be like if a woman were to be there, mixing it with the big boys. I leave the comfort of my quilt (*Wow! Cold!*) and I grab a pen and paper. And just like that, Annie Bailey is born.

She's in love with Max Carter, who is due to marry her sister Ruthie. All her life Annie has had Ruthie's cast-offs, and finally she snaps — and makes a decision that is going to set her on a very different path in life from the one she had supposed she would walk.

Annie Bailey is tough, intelligent, beautiful — everything any woman would want to be. As I started to write her (she sort of poured out of me, like water out of a bomb-struck dam) I knew that Annie was going to fill more than a single book. In between the mad spurts of writing, I delved into research on the sixties and the big organised gangs who ran the various 'manors' around London. These were deeply scary people, but was Annie scared? Well, sometimes. But never for long, because Annie had a destiny to perform. She was Annie Bailey, then she would become Annie Carter, and from there, well, that would be telling. All you need to know right now is that she takes up a whole trilogy (*Dirty game, Black Widow* and *Scarlet Women*) and one day — who knows? — she may reappear to fill up another book with her escapades. In the meantime there are other heroines queuing up to tell their stories – Lily King for one – and these girls have a style and a passion that's all their own.

Now what about me? I've done a lot of writing since that January day under the quilt, that's for sure, but way back before I even dreamed I could be a professional writer I was just the youngest in a big family. My Dad was a surveyor with an edge of brilliance. My Mum was from gipsy roots and used to drive around in a goat-cart (yes, really!) when she was little. Once we were rich (although I didn't know it then, and it was all thanks to my Dad's ingenuity) and then suddenly – pretty shockingly, really – we were poor (thanks to greedy people who exploited his kindness). I have to tell you, rich is better. But the great thing about life is, even painful events pass, and if you make bad choices, hopefully you learn from them.

For a while back there when the stuff *really* started hitting the fan, it's true to say that I lost my way. Bunked off school (I'm qualified for precisely nothing: kids take note – you *have* to study), worried my Mum, dated bad boys (my first proper boyfriend was a car thief, and not even a good one – he got caught) and even badder men.

But things settled. The fog cleared. And all the hard, horrible stuff – bankruptcies, betrayals, burials of loved ones, crap jobs and living on the edge of desperation – well, they linger, who can deny that? But eventually that stuff starts to hurt a little less. It's trite but true – that which does not kill you really *does* make you strong. Everything passes, and that's a comfort.

Now, since that day under the quilt I write a lot. A *lot*. But that's no hardship, because I love it and I feel that's what I was always meant to do. In the immortal words of Ranulph Fiennes as he scaled the mountain, all I've got to do is 'plod on'. Which is actually what I'm best at.

Jessie Keane